A Dangeours Performance

Other Books by Stephenia H. McGee

Ironwood Plantation

The Whistle Walk

Heir of Hope

Missing Mercy

**Ironwood Series Set*

*Get the entire series at a discounted price

The Accidental Spy Series

*Previously published as The Liberator Series

An Accidental Spy

A Dangerous Performance

A Daring Pursuit

**Accidental Spy Series Set*

*Get the entire series at a discounted price

Stand Alone Titles

In His Eyes

Eternity Between Us

Time Travel

Her Place in Time

(Stand alone, but ties to Rosswood from The Accidental Spy Series)

The Hope of Christmas Past

(Stand alone, but ties to Belmont from In His Eyes)

Novellas

The Heart of Home

The Hope of Christmas Past

www.StepheniaMcGee.com

Sign up for my newsletter to be the first to see new cover reveals and be notified of release dates

New newsletter subscribers receive a free book!

Get yours here

bookhip.com/QCZVKZ

A Dangerous Performance

THE ACCIDENTAL SPY

SERIES

Book Two

Stephenia H. McGee

An updated and revised rewrite of the previously published title:
Losing Lincoln

Cover Photography: Period Stock, LLC

Cover Model: Katie Beth Simmons
Cover Design: Carpe Librum Book Design

Library Cataloging Data
McGee, Stephenia H. (Stephenia H. McGee) 1983–
A Dangerous Performance; The Accidental Spy Series Book Two/ Stephenia H. McGee
356p. 5.5 in. × 8.5 in. (13.97 cm × 21.59 cm)
By The Vine Press digital eBook edition | By The Vine Press Trade paperback edition | Mississippi: By The Vine Press, 2020
Summary: A Southern Belle caught in the crossfires of America's first presidential assassination.
Identifiers: ePCN: Library of Congress 2020933994 |
ISBN-13: 978-1-63564-049-6 (trade) | 978-1-63564-047-2 (ebk.)
1. Historical Christian 2. Clean Romance 3. Presidential Assassination 4. Action and Adventure 5. Southern Fiction 6. Overcoming Racism 7. Spies and Espionage

For Jadon and Levi,
My two little monkeys.

One

"Always bear in mind that your own resolution to succeed is more important than any other."
Abraham Lincoln

Elmira, New York
March 14, 1865

To the victor belonged the spoils, but to the defeated, humiliation and despair. Annabelle shivered against the northern wind and pulled her wrap tighter. Beside her, Matthew repeatedly clenched and released his fists as if they were itching to land a blow. Not that she could blame him. What kind of people did such things?

She studied the backs of those waiting in line in front of them. From all appearances, they seemed normal enough. Nothing about their heavy winter outerwear or their idle chatter marked them as heartless. But what else could they be?

When had the suffering of one's fellow man become a means of entertainment?

Annabelle shivered again, and this time not from the biting cold and drizzling rain. The man in front of them took another step forward, moving the line and bringing their little group to the bottom of the wooden staircase leading to the observation platform above.

"This here ain't right." Peggy plopped her hands on her hips, earning more than one raised eyebrow.

Annabelle shot her a warning glance. They didn't need to draw attention. Matthew's piercing gaze—which would have cowed a more timid soul—only made Peggy scowl.

"What?" Peggy lowered her voice. "We're all thinking it."

Matthew stepped closer to Annabelle. "Perhaps your maid should wait for you over there with the others."

Annabelle glanced behind her at the groups of colored folks gathered around hitched carriages and chatting among themselves. "Why don't you wait for us, Peggy?" Peggy opened her mouth to protest, but Annabelle didn't give her the opportunity. She leaned close to Peggy's ear. "Keep your ears open. See what they know."

Peggy hesitated. Ever since the three of them had been on the road, Peggy had clung to Annabelle like a wet shawl. Finally, she grumbled something and stalked toward the carriages.

The man ahead of them paid his fee and walked up the stairs as a well-dressed couple descended. Annabelle studied the woman's fine furs. Did the wealthy people in this town have nothing better to entertain themselves?

"That'll be ten cents, sir, for you and the lady." The young man held out his hand expectantly.

The muscles in Matthew's jaw tightened and Annabelle slipped her hand into the crook of his arm, giving it a small squeeze. His jaw barely unclenched enough for him to speak. "I was told it cost three cents to visit the observation tower."

The youth shrugged. "Sorry, sir. It's a nickel apiece now.

Includes binoculars, though, so don't worry, you'll get your money's worth."

Annabelle could practically feel the anger seeping out of Matthew. "Oh, that's good, isn't it? We'll be able to get a closer look…." She trailed off, hoping Matthew caught her meaning.

He thrust his hand in his pocket and shoved a dime into the boy's open palm. Unfazed by Matthew's glower, the boy nodded toward the steps. "Got refreshments for purchase, too, case you want to linger."

Disgust bubbled in her stomach. Annabelle drew Matthew up the stairs before the boy found himself at the wrong end of Matthew's ever-growing fury. At the top, they stepped onto a wide platform raised as high into the air as the top floor of Rosswood. It was like standing on a balcony, except this one was disconnected from a building.

The entire structure was a bit unsettling, being so high in the air with nothing beneath her other than some planks and a few poles. Annabelle tried not to think of the open void below and took a place near several other visitors, careful not to touch the railing. The flimsy thing didn't look as though it would hold her weight.

Out of the corner of her eye, Annabelle watched Matthew snatch a pair of binoculars from a spindly man. Matthew stalked to her side, the veins in his neck bulging with fury. Without a word, he put the looking contraption to his face.

"Excuse me, miss?" The spindly man dangled another pair of the lenses from a short loop of rope. "You forgot to get yours." When Annabelle hesitated, he wriggled his bushy gray brows. "You'll get to see their punishment much better with these."

Annabelle swallowed her disgust and grabbed the binoculars. He flashed a yellowed grin and continued down the platform to the next waiting group of onlookers. She turned the contraption over in her hand. She'd never used a pair before.

Matthew pressed the glasses to his face and scanned the area below. "I don't see him."

Annabelle put the smaller set of lenses up to her eyes. Immediately, everything in front of her appeared larger, revealing the scene with sickening detail.

Below the platform, a swollen river snaked between the town proper and the massive walls of Elmira prison. Tents lined both sides of the muddy banks. Scattered between the rows of sagging structures, small clusters of men huddled among piles of debris and refuse. With their pitiful clothing hanging loosely on gaunt bodies, they looked like little more than walking bones.

"Why are they out there in tents?" she mumbled to herself. "I thought all the prisoners were kept inside the walls."

"Too many of them now." A middle-aged lady to her left pointed below. "Word is they have nigh on ten thousand in there. Too many for the barracks to hold for sure. They stacked them in there until the walls nearly burst."

How would they find George among so many? Most of them didn't have jackets, and some wore clothing so shredded and ragged that it was little more than strips of cloth flapping in the wind. How could the guards not give them proper protection from the elements?

Annabelle tried to cool the anger churning inside her, lest it seep into her words. She lowered the binoculars. "Ten thousand seems like far too many."

The woman lifted her shoulders. "They're letting some of

them out, at least. It's a right shame. Traitors or not, no boy should be forced to live like that." The sadness in her voice made Annabelle lean closer, close enough to smell the rosy scent of the lady's soap.

"Letting them out?"

The woman nodded. "But only the ones that sign the allegiance papers, of course."

Annabelle's pulse quickened. Could it be that simple? All George had to do was sign his allegiance to the Union and he would be free to go? Matthew shifted his weight next to her. Was he listening to their conversation?

"I'd think men would be flooding out of there if that's all they need to do."

Matthew grunted. So, he was listening.

The woman solemnly watched the prison walls. "You'd think so, wouldn't you? But it's only one or two every few days."

Annabelle studied her refined profile. "How often do you come here?"

The woman stuffed her hands back into her muff. "I best be off. Good day to you, miss."

Annabelle watched her hurry down the steps. "That was rather odd."

Matthew grunted. Resigned, Annabelle lifted her binoculars again and scanned the tents below. On the breeze, the stench of human waste drifted up to assault her nostrils. She swept her focus up from the tents and onto the tall stone wall peppered with men in blue holding rifles. What of the men inside those walls? Did they fare better than the poor souls at the river?

Rows of squat buildings huddled inside the wall, with scores of men crammed against the sides of them in an effort to escape the wind. Anger burned in her gut. Who was responsible for this place? Annabelle scanned faces until her shoulders cramped and her eyes burned.

Behind them, a man cleared his throat. "Excuse me? It's, uh…getting dark, sir."

Matthew tensed beside her but didn't lower his looking glasses. Annabelle turned to the man, who appeared rather uncomfortable. Good. Someone who peddled misery deserved no less. Though she figured it was more Matthew's imposing presence than the wretches below that had him shifting his weight from one shiny boot to the other.

He extended his hand. "Miss?"

Annabelle tried to force a tense smile but didn't achieve more than a slight raise of her lip as she handed her pair over. Matthew didn't move from his position.

After a few more moments the man reached out as if to touch Matthew's shoulder. Annabelle shook her head, and he let his fingers drop. He might be a weasel, but she couldn't let him unleash Matthew's wrath. Otherwise they would probably never be allowed on the platform again or, worse, would be detained by Elmira lawmen.

The weasel man hesitated only a moment longer and then garnered a pinch of courage. He straightened his shoulders and spoke with more confidence. "I'll have to ask you to hand over the binoculars now, sir. The platform is closing for the evening. You may return tomorrow."

Matthew lowered the glasses and turned his heavy gaze on the spindly little man. They matched stares and Annabelle held her breath. Finally, Matthew reluctantly handed over the lenses. The man scurried away, clearly relieved. Annabelle slipped her hand into Matthew's arm, gently turning him toward the staircase.

Dusk settled, and Annabelle suddenly felt guilty about the warm bed and hot meal she would soon enjoy while George sat out there somewhere, freezing. She gave Matthew's arm a squeeze. He blamed himself for his brother's capture, and Annabelle knew Matthew well enough by now to know that he would hold himself responsible for whatever condition they found George in.

Oh, please, let us find him soon.

Peggy waited for them at the bottom of the steps and fell in behind Annabelle and Matthew. They made their way across the dusty street and away from the abominable observatory deck toward the crowded inn just a few streets away.

Matthew had managed to get them a private room. While Annabelle was glad not to be put into a room she'd have to share with other unmarried females, Peggy had been quite upset about the arrangement. Matthew had adamantly refused to leave Annabelle and Peggy in the room alone, declaring the three of them could share the room just as easily as they had shared a campfire.

Despite Peggy's protests, pleading, and prods at his sense of honor and propriety, Matthew had calmly insisted. Not only were his limited funds from David O'Malley running low, but Matthew had determined the women would be safer in a room with him. By the end of it, he'd somehow managed to gently bring Peggy over to his side. He'd treated Peggy with respect and, because of that, he'd gained a deeper level of fondness from Annabelle.

Fondness. That's what she'd call the stirring in her heart.

Inside the inn, warmth and the yeasty scent of bread washed over Annabelle's senses and stirred her hunger. They passed the crowded tables of people already taking their evening meals.

But rather than choosing a table, Matthew stomped up the stairs. Annabelle followed him, Peggy close on her heels. He burst into the room like a bull, the vein in his neck bulging in fury.

"Blasted, dirty Yanks!"

"Shhhh!" Peggy waved a hand at him, unfazed by his seething anger. "You want to let the whole building know you ain't one of them?"

He cast her an annoyed look but clamped his mouth shut. Peggy shook her head and went to start a fire in the hearth.

Matthew paced like a caged bear. "Who pays a fee to watch men suffer and die? What a demented lot."

Peggy struck a match and held it to the kindling until a flame leapt to life. "What you gonna do about it?"

Matthew stopped his pacing and studied her. "What would you have me do, woman? Burn the vile platform down?" He paused, as if considering it. "Would serve them right if the whole town went up."

Annabelle gasped. "Surely you can't mean that."

He drew a long breath and rolled his shoulders. When his eyes turned to her, his features softened. "Forgive me. You shouldn't have to witness my temper. If you'll excuse me, I think I'll go for a walk."

She reached for him as he passed her. "Please, don't do anything rash."

He slipped out from under her touch and stalked out the door.

"That man's wound tighter than a coiled spring," Peggy said, tossing a log onto the fire and prodding it with the poker.

Annabelle plopped onto the bed, which sagged under her weight, and fingered the quilt. "Can you blame him? You didn't see them, Peggy." She shivered. "All those poor men. It's a wonder they've survived such conditions. How could the government allow something so deplorable?"

"You know war ain't nothing pretty. What you expect to see?"

"I don't know. Not that."

"Seems to me Captain Daniels got plenty of schemes in his head. He'll think of something." Peggy laid the poker beside the hearth and extended her hands toward the fire.

"Perhaps," Annabelle mused, "but I've discovered a simple solution. I'll call on someone in prison affairs first thing in the morning."

"That so?" Peggy left the fire and busied herself spreading out sleeping mats, positioning herself between Matthew's pallet and Annabelle's bed.

She'd suggest they rotate use of the bed, but knowing that both Peggy and Matthew would adamantly refuse, Annabelle didn't bother. "A woman on the platform said they release prisoners who sign allegiance papers."

Peggy scratched her headscarf. "Hmm. Seems to me like they'd get lots of papers signed if that's all it takes for freedom."

Something in the way she said it made Annabelle's heart ache. They called Lincoln *the Liberator*. Maybe if his emancipation papers were signed by the states, then Peggy's people would be free as well. Annabelle gave Peggy a sad smile, which she returned. "I thought so, too. It's entirely too easy. There must be more to it than we know. That's why I need to speak to someone at the prison."

"And you think they'll give you whatever information you want?"

Annabelle shrugged. "Worked last time." Going into the Commissary General's office and asking for help enabled her to find George's location in the first place. She didn't see why doing the same wouldn't help them now.

Peggy smoothed the blankets again and sat on her pallet. "Miss Belle, we need to talk about your plans."

She shifted uncomfortably. "The plan is to get George out of that horrible place."

Peggy rolled her eyes. So much for avoiding the subject of her odd betrothal, which, technically, the groom wasn't even aware of.

"All right, then." Peggy splayed her fingers. "Say you find him, get him outta prison, and ride off free as a summer chicken."

Annabelle crinkled her forehead. What made a summer chicken free? All of Peggy's chickens were kept in a coop. Then they went in the frying pot.

"Then what?" Peggy snorted. "Have you even thought about what's going to happen then? When you have *two* Daniels men to deal with?"

Annabelle scrunched her nose. She *had* thought about it. Every night it kept her awake, and it wiggled into her thoughts at random moments throughout the day. The problem was that no matter how much she thought on it, she still hadn't figured out what to do. "I suppose once we see George freed or escaped, we could go home."

"Escaped? Lawd, child, you—" Peggy shook her head and pointed her finger at Annabelle. "No you don't. We'll talk 'bout that later." She fisted her hands on her hips. "So you think you, me, and them two men is gonna go back to Rosswood?"

Annabelle nodded.

"Hmm." Peggy crossed her arms. "We do still have Andrew to deal with, and your mean ole grandfather, if he's still alive." Annabelle nodded again, unsure where Peggy was going with this. "Yes, ma'am. Even after all this here gallivantin' you've done, we ain't found no solution to the problem that started this here mess."

Annabelle balked. "Gallivanting? Really, Peggy?"

She waved a hand. "What? It's a word I learned from Captain Daniels."

"I'd hardly call what we've been through *gallivanting*. More like running for our lives!"

Peggy shrugged. "I reckon. But we did save the president, and I got high hopes for that man. He's gonna set my people free."

Annabelle grinned. "And if we can do *that*, well then, we can surely save George and Rosswood. Once we have George, then maybe the rest will work itself out."

Peggy's smile faded. "How you gonna tell him about the betrothal?"

Annabelle rose and lit the lantern. She set it down on the small table beside the bed, sending shadows dancing across the quilt. "I was hoping I wouldn't have to."

Peggy lifted her brows. "You decided to tell him the truth?"

Annabelle cut her eyes at Peggy, knowing exactly which *he* she meant. "I've told you, there's nothing to tell."

"Humph. Then what're you talking about?"

Annabelle pressed her fingers into her rumpled skirt. "I'm going to let Matthew and George discuss it. I won't be the one telling George anything." She held up her hand. "And before you say it, there's nothing I need to tell Matthew either. I'll simply let the two of them talk before I go running my mouth."

"Ha! And let them men decide your fate? Since when have you been all right with that?"

Annabelle crossed her arms. "George doesn't know about any of this, and I *don't* want to be the one to tell him."

Peggy's eyes softened and she came to sit by Annabelle on the bed. "You're afraid he's not gonna want you?"

Was she? Or was she more afraid that he *would*… and that Matthew would let him? "I…." She took a deep breath to keep tears from burning her eyes. It was bad enough her heart strained toward one brother who didn't want her. But if George didn't want to marry her so she could regain Rosswood, what would she do? "I fear he won't like the deal Captain Daniels made." She pushed her fingers into her hairline. "Then what? Andrew's probably already seized Rosswood. I'll need an alliance with a strong family in order to get it back."

"There's still hope your Uncle Michael will be able to help."

"Maybe. But it's been so long. Do you truly think he's still alive?"

"Ain't no reason to think otherwise." She patted Annabelle's knee. "You want to know what I think?"

As if her answer mattered. Peggy would tell her anyway.

"I think we still need to get to your momma's family. We're already in New York. Let's see if blood can help you, child. Don't put all your faith in these Daniels men."

Annabelle nodded slowly. Peggy was right. Why leave her fate up to hoping someone would want to marry her? "I don't have any reason to think they'll help, but you're right. We should try."

Peggy wrapped her in a squeeze. "Good girl." They sat there a moment, then Peggy grinned. "And besides, that boy needs to court you proper. It ain't good he thinks he ain't got to woo you."

Annabelle gave Peggy a playful push. "Come now, who *wouldn't* want to court a homely girl with a rundown plantation she can't save? I'm sure I'd be first on George's list of desirable ladies."

Peggy sobered. "Miss Belle, it ain't right you do that. Just because your grandfather was pathetic enough that he needed to put you down in order to make himself feel more important don't mean you should believe him. You're not a plain girl, and you got plenty to offer. Don't go selling yourself short."

Annabelle swallowed the lump in her throat and pulled Peggy into a quick hug. "I was just teasing."

Peggy gave her a squeeze. "Well, I ain't. No more talk like that."

Annabelle stood. "I'm starving. I don't suppose Captain Daniels will return for supper, so why don't we see if we can get us some plates to bring up here? I'd rather we ate alone instead of with the crowd."

A sad expression washed over Peggy's face. "Don't give up hope yet, girl," she said, not allowing Annabelle to shift the subject. "I still think the captain cares too much to see you go to anyone else. Brother or not."

Annabelle's heart flipped in her chest, but she forced her

features to remain smooth. "Don't be silly. This is simply a matter of convenience."

"Sure it is." Peggy patted her hand and then stepped out the door, leaving Annabelle alone with an ache in her chest she could not ignore.

Two

"Good news at last. Mrs. S has arrived at our house from Richmond. She brought dispatches from that city for the Confederate agents in Canada."
John H. Surratt

Elmira Prison
March 15, 1865

George Daniels rose from his makeshift bunk constructed of two discarded crates and pulled his Yankee overcoat over what remained of his ragged Confederate uniform. He hardly noticed his tent mates' groans or the debilitating cold anymore. So what had roused him from his fitful sleep?

Light poked tentative fingers into the darkness, separating men from shadows. Roll call would come soon. He wove his way through the tent he shared with seven others, stepping over their huddled forms to make his way to the flap.

Outside, blessed silence cloaked the prison yard. The only movement came from the guard on duty as he swung his weapon in George's direction. *Daft man.* Did he really think George was stupid enough to try to run?

Some *had* escaped, though. The prisoners talked often

enough about the three—or was it four?—who had dug a tunnel under the wall and actually managed to get free. But that had been months ago, when the prison was still new. Maybe the Yanks didn't watch it as well then as they did now. Or maybe the story was just a lie the men told themselves in order to find a measure of hope among the misery. As he passed along the muddy bank, his gaze drifted to the observation deck across the river.

As though guards trailing the prisoners' every move wasn't enough, the citizens of Elmira had apparently volunteered to watch the prison as well. All hours of the day they could be seen up there, spying on the despondent captives below. Some said the platform was purely for entertainment, but he couldn't fathom how observing men at their worst could be a diversion. Surely they could find better things to do with their time. So George held to the idea that the Elmira citizens took turns keeping watch to be sure no stray Rebel contaminated their fair city.

George trudged to the trees at the end of the rows of tents and did his business by the edge of Ford's pond, which had been designated as their latrine. Disgusting. Did the Yanks have no concept of sanitation? At least they'd finally dug trenches. Some of the fellows who'd been here longer than George said that before the trenches so many men were sick from the waste that they died too fast for the burial crews to keep up.

Not that they were keeping up now.

George trudged back down the tent row. At the opposite end of camp, a lone sapling had become George's way of holding onto sanity. His friend Bill had said it would be better not to torture himself with knowing how many days he'd been here, but George disagreed. He couldn't get trapped in an endless cycle of hopeless days, clinging to a pitiful existence without end.

If he had a blade, his morning ritual wouldn't be so difficult. He'd had a sharp stick once, but they'd long since used it for firewood. Now all he possessed was his ragged thumbnail.

He ran his fingers over the smooth trunk, the middle area devoid of bark because the men in his tent had bloodied their fingers stripping the tree's coverings. Someone had told them they could eat the inner bark.

It gained them little more than the comfort of chewing.

Nonetheless, the spot made a good place for George to keep his records. He put his nail into the soft inner wood and pressed, working it back and forth until he made an indention in the tree.

George ran his finger over each of the little indentions standing like tiny soldiers. The Yankees had loaded scores of captured Confederates on a train bound for New York. The days ran together in the cramped confines of those rail cars, and he still wasn't quite sure how long he'd been forced to endure the smells of men locked inside without the mercy of having anywhere to do their business.

However bad he'd thought the train, at least it was warm.

When he rubbed the last mark in the bottom row, George traced his finger back to the beginning and counted all the marks on his tree. Then he wished he hadn't.

Thirty-one! Despair clawed at him. Only a month? He'd already lost so much weight that he'd had to scavenge some twine to keep his pants up. How much longer could he make it on one meal a day? If boiled water with a few beans floating in it and a chunk of stale bread could even be called a meal.

How much longer before scurvy set in? By his estimation, it took men around here about a week—two if he was especially strong-willed—to die once sickness hit. Trying not to let his mood turn too sour, George gave one last look at his marks and turned to trudge back to his tent. Bill had been right.

Knowing only made it worse.

The morning bugle sounded, drawing men out into the daylight. No one slept past bugle if he was healthy enough to rise. They had only a few moments to see to personal business after morning call before they fell into the line, and no one wanted to be caught missing when the corporal took the count.

George nodded to some of the prisoners as he passed, but most ignored him. Several held up their hands to protect their eyes against the bright light as they scurried this way and that. George turned his face to the sky, having been too consumed with his thoughts to notice. Clear and blue, the sky offered cheer they could not feel and a promise of warmth it would not deliver.

Nonetheless, he'd choose the blue over the drab gray. His gaze roamed over the gaunt faces of the men still clad in bits of ragged Confederate uniforms as they took their places in line. Their vacant expressions, tinged with a faint ray of hope, drew his own gaze back heavenward.

How long had it been since a day dawned without a heavy layer of clouds? Long enough that any scraps of wood they'd tried to gather and burn for warmth were too soaked to even take a spark. They'd quit trying three days ago. Perhaps if they were lucky, the sun would be bright enough today to dry out some tinder so they could warm their feet by the flames tonight.

The hope of a warm fire soothed some of George's festering despair. He tried to keep his focus on blue skies and warm feet as he waited at attention for the corporal to pass by and finish counting.

His first week at Elmira they'd called out each man in line by name. Now, they didn't bother. The Yanks had two counts. The living, and the dead.

After they were dismissed, George fell into step beside Bill as they made their daily walk to the wall.

"Wonder how many more'll need boxes today," Bill said, pulling his patched gray cap low on his head. His shaggy beard swayed in the wind and bobbed with his jaw.

"I don't know," George said. "Hopefully not as many as yesterday."

Bill snorted. "You say that every day, and every day there's more than the day before."

"Then why do you always ask?"

Bill lifted his scrawny shoulders. "Just making conversation. We should make a game out of it, you know. See who can guess the right number."

George gave him a sour look. "That's disturbing."

They approached the guards at the gate and were gestured through to the inner section of the prison.

"Why?" Bill stepped through the iron gates and onto the primary road leading through the center of the prison. "Man needs a little entertainment around here."

George eyed the poor souls crammed inside as he turned to the left to follow the wall. They might not have as much protection from the wind inside their tents along the river, but the men in here appeared sicker. And that was worse.

George's gaze lingered on the listless faces of the men lining the inside of the wall. Some of the dirty faces of the Hopeless turned pleading eyes on him, but most had given up entirely. If a man was conscious, they added him to the line running from the hospital building all the way down to the gate. If he was lucky, a doctor would check him on his way to the hospital barracks—a place reserved for only the worst among them.

George suppressed a shiver. He didn't want to be one of the Hopeless on the wall. Too sick to make it to shelter on their own, but not quite sick enough to be taken inside. They were lining up for the reaper, they were.

"So, what do you say?" Bill prodded, jabbing him in the ribs and breaking into his thoughts. "Let's make a wager out of it. Whichever man gets the closest to the right number wins."

George frowned. "Wins what?"

Bill stroked his beard and stepped over the legs of a man slumped against the wall. "Well now, let's see. I've got three apples."

They turned past the hospital building and under the guns of the men on the corner tower. "You do not," George mocked. "You're spinning tales."

Bill grinned. "Says you. I snuck them out of the sack and hid them in my pants. I've eaten two already, but I've got three left."

George stopped and stared at Bill, dropping his voice to a whisper. "You *stole* from the guards' rations?"

Bill's eyes sparked with a mad gleam. "How else do you think I've lasted this long?"

George's stomach growled at the thought. Eating something other than bean water was enough to tempt a man to set aside his convictions. "Fine. If I win, I get your apples."

Bill started walking again. "Nope. One. I ain't giving them all up for some foolish game. They's right hard to come by, you know."

George cast an incredulous glance at Bill, but he didn't point out that the foolish game had been his idea. "Fine. One."

"And if I win, I get that fancy coat of yours." His gaze flared with jealousy.

George couldn't really blame him. The guards had brought in crates of supplies about a week into his stay at Elmira Prison. George had fought off two weaker men to get this coat. Shame over how he'd turned on his own countrymen still plagued him, but this blue wool was the only thing keeping him from freezing at night.

He hadn't received a blanket when he arrived, since they'd been out of those. The first few nights he'd been too cold to sleep, and on the fifth night three of his toes had started to turn black. So when the guards gathered the river's-edge prisoners and tossed out the contents of two crates, men who'd tried to maintain a sense of Confederate camaraderie had been reduced to nothing more than a pack of dogs fighting over a bone. The guards seemed to find that a more entertaining method of distributing supplies than handing them out.

George still wasn't sure how he'd managed such a find, and he couldn't help but think that the Union coat had mistakenly been put in with the stacks of threadbare blankets and used civilian jackets. For a week he'd expected one of the guards to take it from him, but they never did. Some of the men still sneered at him and called him "Yank" or "Guard," but George didn't care. No more of his toes had turned black with frostbite.

"You going to take the bet or not? You done thought on it

long enough," Bill said, slapping George on the back.

George shook his head. "Sorry. I won't risk this overcoat for an apple."

"Where's the thrill of the risk if the stakes aren't high?" Bill prodded.

They stepped into the rear corner of the prison used as the lumber area and picked up their saws from the pile. The guard motioned them away with the muzzle of his rifle. George had volunteered for sawing detail because the men sawing got an extra chunk of bread if they cut their quota of planks. It was the only way the guards were able to keep the prisoners on coffin duty alive long enough to build the boxes they would eventually find themselves buried in. A man used up too much energy sawing not to need another few bites. And at least the work kept his muscles moving. They didn't get as cold that way.

They took their place by the stone wall. The sun had risen enough to shine on their little corner and chased some of the bitter chill from the wind. "So," Bill said as he made his mark on the first plank and started sawing. "I guess twenty today."

George ignored him and examined the edge of his saw. Would the guard let him sharpen it?

"What's your guess?"

George sighed. The man wouldn't leave him alone until he answered. "I don't know. It's not right to make guesses on how many men died and are going to need these poorly constructed coffins."

"Ain't poorly constructed," Bill said with a snort. "I know my way around a saw."

George lowered the tool. Why bother asking if he could sharpen the saw? They would just tell him to get back to work and stop looking for excuses to be idle. He positioned the blade on the edge of the plank and let the teeth sink into the wood. Bill mumbled something and George turned to look at him. "What?"

"Are you going to make your guess or not?"

The familiar scent of sawdust was a pleasant distraction from the stench that always lingered around the prison. "I'm not betting my coat," he said loudly enough for Bill to hear over the sound of his saw. "And you won't goad me into it by insulting my pride, my honor, or my manhood, so don't try."

Bill grinned, tilting his hat back. "Good for you. Fellow needs to stick to his guns." He laughed and leaned back over his plank. "Naw, we won't wager. Just guess."

Knowing the man wouldn't let it go until he did, George sighed. "Ten."

Bill grinned and renewed his sawing. "No wonder you didn't want to wager your coat. Done made fifteen yesterday, and I know for sure it's going to be even more poor souls heading out to the holes today."

George set his jaw. At least he wasn't digging the holes. Grave duty was worse than saw detail. "I still say ten."

"Suit yourself."

Bill might find it foolish, but George had to hope each day could be better than the last. Otherwise, despair would consume him. He clenched his teeth and focused on the glide of the saw into the rough-hewn planks, praying that he wouldn't soon find himself on the finished end of one of his boxes.

Three

"There was no time to be lost, and if the South ever hoped to succeed, it was with the belief that we would faithfully carry out the plans she brought with her."
John H. Surratt

Annoyance buzzed in Matthew's veins. He sat with Annabelle at a table at the inn and waited for their breakfast. He pulled three Union coins from his pocket. How was he going to keep their room here and take care of the women if he ran out of money? He needed to get George out and return to Westerly, and soon.

He drummed his fingers on the table and absentmindedly watched the inn's serving girl walk away as he tried to sort out his plans. He'd spent half the night wandering the town trying to figure out every possible way to get past the guards. A few ideas seemed plausible, but he kept getting stuck. Even if he got into the prison, how would he find George and get back out? He couldn't risk getting caught and finding himself a captive as well. Who would be left to take care of Annabelle?

He glanced over at her and found her staring at him, face flushed. She lifted her chin and turned her gaze away. Matthew frowned.

What? Had he missed something? He glanced at Peggy, who stood behind her mistress with her back against the wall. She gave a small shake of her head and then turned her gaze to the serving girl who scuttled toward their table with plates of food.

She plopped Annabelle's plate down in front of her without a word, then smiled sweetly at Matthew. "Here you go, love. Got you an extra two eggs, I did." She winked at him. "Big fellow like you needs a hearty breakfast."

Matthew nodded in thanks. She lingered a moment, but when he said nothing, she lightly brushed her fingers across his sleeve. "If you need anything more, you just call for Betty. I can give you anything you're looking for."

She swished off with an exaggerated sway of her hips. What had she meant by that? The fire in Annabelle's cheeks told him he wasn't the only one who'd caught the undercurrent of the server's words. This was no place for a lady, but what choice did he have?

Annabelle pushed her eggs around on her plate, her shoulders stiff. A different thought occurred to him, and a small smile tugged at the corner of his mouth. He sat back in his chair. Could Annabelle be jealous of the attention the server had shown him? He crossed his arms and waited, but she wouldn't look at him. "Well?"

She looked up sharply. "Well what?"

Matthew lifted his brows. "Oh, I don't know," he drawled. "You look like you have something you want to say. Why don't you go ahead and let it loose before your ears pop off?"

Annabelle gasped, and Peggy let out a sound that seemed half snort, half contained laugh. Annabelle narrowed her eyes. "I have nothing to say."

"My mistake then." He picked up his fork and began shoveling browned potatoes into his mouth. He'd nearly finished off the eggs before she could no longer stand it.

"I don't see why you encourage such behaviors. It's hardly proper."

He tilted his head. "What behaviors?"

She glared at him. "One would think you like such illicit attention, Captain Daniels."

They were back to *Captain Daniels* again? Either she was truly angry at him, or her jealousy was worse than he'd thought. He shrugged. "Not many women are as beautiful as you, so they have to try harder. It doesn't mean anything."

He wouldn't have thought it possible, but her face reddened further.

"Yet you still encourage it." She dabbed her pink lips with her napkin. "Just like with that dressmaker," she mumbled.

Dressmaker? When had they been to a dressmaker? Matthew thought back until he remembered the curvy brunette who'd let out some seams in the ready-made shirts and trousers O'Malley had purchased for him when they'd first started for Washington. He hadn't given any attentions to that girl, had he?

Matthew chose to say nothing on the matter. He couldn't remember enough about his time with the woman to rebuff Annabelle's accusation, so it was probably safer to keep quiet. But after they'd both nearly finished their meals and she hadn't said another word to him, Matthew began to think this was less of a flirtatious game and more something that truly bothered her. He cleared his throat. "I didn't mean to upset you."

She folded her napkin and placed it on the table beside her

plate. The other travelers had already finished, and the dining room was beginning to clear. "Why should I care if you play with the attentions of random women?"

Her jab stung. He studied the determined glint in her eye. "I have no control over how people talk to me. I did nothing to encourage that young woman's attention, nor do I have any intentions to return it." He looked at her earnestly until the tension melted from her shoulders.

"I suppose you are right." She sighed. "You can't help that they throw themselves at you."

He pressed his lips into a line to keep the corners from turning up. *Throwing themselves* at him? How had he ever thought this innocent young woman might be a camp follower? She apparently had no idea what women would do in order to tempt a man. And he loved her all the more for it.

His thoughts came tumbling to a halt. He could no longer deny it. At least, not to himself. He loved her.

Her clear blue eyes filled with a guarded hope and it churned his gut. Surely his brother would understand if—

Matthew lurched to his feet. *George!* They needed to be thinking about George. How could she have distracted him to the point he'd nearly forgotten why they were here?

Annabelle startled and rose with him. "What's wrong?"

He tossed the coins on the table. "We should get going. I want to get up on that platform before the crowds start." Disgust rose like bile in his throat and curled his lip.

Annabelle blinked at him. "Oh, yes, of course." The hope in her eyes vanished, replaced by the cool formality Matthew had grown to dread.

Drat. Did she think the look of contempt was for her? Annabelle started toward the door. Peggy, ever the mother hen, trailed behind, shaking her scarf-wrapped head at Matthew's foolishness. Not that he could blame her. Peggy had seen his feelings for Annabelle days ago, and it seemed her patience with him was wearing thin.

Matthew hurried to get in front of Annabelle so he could hold the door open for them, and the three stepped out into a clear morning.

"I was thinking," Annabelle said, tugging the ribbon on her bonnet tight. "We should go to the prison this morning instead of to the platform."

"What for?" He held out his arm and, surprisingly, she took it. Together they stepped onto the muddy street.

"That woman on the platform yesterday said that some of the prisoners were being released if they signed loyalty papers."

A thin hope. George would never betray his country.

"If nothing else, inquiring at the prison office seems better than hoping we see him from the viewing deck." Her voice tightened. "At least then we'll know for sure he is here."

Matthew tried to ignore the doubt threading her words. He couldn't bear to think George wasn't just inside those walls. He'd come through too much these last weeks to give up hope now. "I understand your point, but I don't know if it'll be a good idea."

Something caught the corner of his eye and he cut his gaze over the top of Annabelle's head and to the building on his right. A figure ducked behind the wall before he could get a good look. He tightened his grip on Annabelle and quickened his pace.

"Why not?" she asked, bobbing along to keep up with him.

"You can't just sashay into a prison and ask if George is there. It'll raise too many questions." He guided her around a puddle.

Annabelle bristled. "That's *precisely* how I found him in the first place."

She had him there.

"You know, people often prove helpful if you'll only ask them."

He slowed his pace and glanced down at her, lowering his voice as he leaned closer. "If you go in there asking questions about him, it'll bring him to their attention. Then it might be that much harder for me to break him out."

She pulled her lower lip through her teeth. "That woman said they were letting men go if they signed the papers. That has to be easier than breaking him out." She watched him closely, and seeing that he could not deny her logic, she continued. "What could be simpler? I'll pose as a poor Union girl whose brother defied the family and chose the wrong side of the war. Then I'll ask if he can be offered the papers and be returned to his family."

Matthew frowned. She did make a good point. "Perhaps it's not a bad idea."

A gloating smile flowered on her lips. "Of course it's not."

"But you won't be the one going in there." He straightened and quickened his pace again, trying to nod at the loathsome people of Elmira as if they were decent folk. The way most hurried out of his path hinted he might be failing at the attempt at civility.

Annabelle came to a halt, her hand slipping free of his arm. "What? Why not?"

Matthew paused and looked back at her, cocking his head. "Too dangerous."

She huffed. "As opposed to what? Fleeing Confederate soldiers across the South?" She narrowed her gaze, and he nearly recoiled from the anger erupting on her features. "Or perhaps you think that talking to a man at a desk is more perilous than trying to stop an abduction?"

Matthew snatched her elbow and drew her up close to him. She was getting looks from people as they passed. "Keep your voice down."

She squared her shoulders and kept walking, pulling herself free from his grasp. "I'll have you know, Captain Daniels…." He inwardly groaned. "That I'm perfectly capable of handling myself."

"Of course," he said with a sneer. "You would have done just fine in detainment with my unit on your own. I apologize for getting in your way."

She glanced up at him sharply, then the anger tightening her features dissolved into melancholy. "Is this how it's always going to be?"

Unable to answer her, he said nothing more and the moment passed. They made their way down the street in uncomfortable silence. Behind him, Matthew heard an obvious sigh. He'd nearly forgotten that Peggy, Annabelle's ever-present shadow, trailed behind them. She met his glance with a flat stare.

He gave her a smirk, which she returned with a frown. What did Peggy think of Annabelle going into the prison? He probably wouldn't face the brunt of Annabelle's displeasure if he had her trusted maid on his side. He slowed his gait and fell into place next to Peggy. "And what do you think about the matter?"

Peggy looked at him as though he were an idiot, her brown eyes flashing from shock to amusement before finally settling into discomfort. "Captain Daniels, this here ain't proper. You walkin' beside me like this."

He shrugged. "As I recall, *proper* went down with the boat some time ago. Now, I know you have an opinion, so you might as well just be out with it or I'll simply walk right here beside you until you do."

Peggy glared at him and snapped her jaw tightly closed. It was to be a war of wills then? "How about I take your arm so you don't slip while you're thinking it over?"

Peggy gasped and tried to quicken her pace to escape him, but found she could not outpace his longer stride. Annabelle looked at them over her shoulder, but she snatched her head back around before he could determine the true nature of her expression, though he thought her eyes had held amusement. He looked back down at Peggy, who hugged both arms tightly around her middle.

"Well, if you're askin'...."

"I am."

Peggy sighed, resigned to his victory. "I don't want her in no danger."

"Exactly, so—"

Peggy cut him off. "I ain't finished."

Matthew startled. She was getting bolder. He hardly remembered the quiet maid who had first joined them.

"We all know you sure enough can't go in there," she continued, "and it wouldn't do no good for me to try, so I reckon if this fool plan is goin' to work, she'll have to be the one to do it."

Matthew's brows gathered. "I don't see why I cannot pose as a Union brother same as she can pose as a Union sister."

Peggy stared at him like he sat in the corner with a dunce hat. "I'm guessin' it probably has something to do with you being a wanted man."

He balked. "I am not."

She shuffled down the street, her eyes pinned to her shoes. "You could be. Probably is. We don't know if the rest of them's been caught or what. They coulda told the law you was part of it. You gonna take that chance?"

In front of him, Annabelle bobbed her head. Matthew groaned. "Fine. Then she can try. But don't expect them to do anything," he grumbled, frustrated that his plan to bring Peggy to his side had misfired.

"You let her help you try to get your brother like she is right determined to do. Then in return, you take her to her family."

The pleading in Peggy's face melted his lingering annoyance. She was right. He couldn't keep dragging Annabelle through his messes. He gave a nod, and Peggy smiled.

"I'm gonna need your word on that, Captain."

"You have it."

She seemed satisfied, and he stepped back into place next to Annabelle, wondering which of them had won the battle of wills after all. Annabelle offered him a triumphant smile as they came to a stop by the viewing platform.

"You go on up and keep looking," she said. "I'll go to the gate and see what I can find out. I'll meet you back here as soon as I can."

He shoved his hands into his pockets to keep from reaching up and brushing his fingers along her cheek. "Please be careful."

She promised she would and scurried toward the gate. Peggy gave him a grateful look, begrudging respect on her features.

Matthew tossed a coin to the boy on the platform steps and clomped up the stairs, taking a pair of binoculars from the attendant as he passed. He placed the lenses to his face and scanned the swollen riverbanks below. *Deplorable. Dirty Yanks and their rotten—*

"Excuse me, sir?"

Matthew growled. "What?"

The boy of about twelve flinched. "Would you like a tea cake, sir?"

"I think my appetite is rather spoiled by the sight of men starving and wallowing in their own sickness and filth. I hardly think such conditions are suitable for taking refreshment, wouldn't you say?"

The boy cringed and shied away. Matthew glanced at the shocked expressions on the surrounding onlookers. Let them stare. What did he care? Matthew's nostrils flared and one couple hurried away from him. He took their place at the rail and lifted the lenses to his face. By the fifth time he'd scanned the riverbanks with no sign of any wretch who resembled George, his shoulders slumped.

He tilted his head to the clear sky above and closed his eyes. He hadn't prayed since he'd asked God to help him shoot down men across the lines and to stay alive as he killed them. Now, all he wanted was a man saved. Would God honor that prayer? It seemed better than the others he had whispered in desperation.

Please, God. I could sure use a miracle.

He stood in silence for a moment and then, feeling nothing, turned his focus back on the tents and renewed his search.

Four

"Saw Booth today and introduced him to Mrs. S. After a few minutes conversation with her, John came to me with his eyes dancing with an unusual and almost unnatural brilliancy."
John H. Surratt

The constant sound of sawing and the warmth of the sun on his back almost lured George into forgetting the pain in his stomach and the ache in his arms. Maybe if he simply concentrated on the task in front of him, he wouldn't have to think about the men huddled in tents with their blackened toes and sunken eyes.

"Prisoner Daniels!" A guard's voice carried over the wood yard, drawing attention.

Bill straightened himself and propped his saw on his shoulder. He let out a low whistle. "What'd you do?"

George eyed the corporal warily. "Nothing." Unless they'd started punishing men for marking trees.

Bill arched his brows and returned to work before the corporal could get close enough to accuse him of slacking.

George lifted his hand. "Here, sir."

He waited for the beefy brute the men called Corporal Carnage—on account of his taste for blood—to make his way across the wood yard.

The corporal scowled at the papers in his hand. "Where do you hail from, prisoner?"

George laid down his saw and scratched his dry scalp, nails catching on scabs. "My family holds lands west of Tupelo, Mississippi."

The corporal gave a curt nod. "You're coming with me." Dread settled in George's empty gut like a sandbag, and he stood rooted to the ground. The corporal narrowed his eyes. "You hear?"

Regaining himself, George stepped forward.

The corporal jabbed him in the back, and he stumbled. "Get your feet under you, Rebel scum!"

George had barely righted himself when a second jab sent pain through his side. He grunted and hurried through the wood yard. He didn't know where they were going, but he was smart enough to know better than to ask. George just kept walking forward until the corporal slapped the rifle barrel against his right arm. "Turn left, maggot."

What was this about? He'd always kept his head down and gone mostly unnoticed—simply tried to survive long enough for this cursed war to be done.

If he ever saw Westerly again, he'd be content never to leave. He and Matthew could run it together and never again have to set eyes on these blasted Yanks.

If he's still alive.

Matthew *had* to be alive. He had to be, or George's sacrifice meant nothing. He'd seen them pull Matthew from the clearing, and just before he lost sight of him, Matthew had been standing at the edge of the woods. He'd been favoring a leg, but he'd been alive.

Please, let him still be alive.

The corporal marched George around the wall of the Hopeless and up to the main road. Then a jab in the spine told him to continue forward. They came to a stop in front of the guards' barracks, and George's shriveled stomach turned. He dared a look over his shoulder at the corporal and received another jab for it. George grunted, but he refused to cry out despite the pain that coursed through his back.

"Inside," the corporal barked.

George drew a deep breath and put his hand on the cold iron of the heavy doorknob set into a thick wooden door. Before he could earn another stab of the rifle, he yanked on the handle and pulled open the door to a small, dim chamber.

He hesitated only an instant, then stepped inside. The toe sticking through his left boot touched stone floors for the first time since…sometime last summer. He studied the way the stones all fit together, matched to create a pattern.

Hard metal jammed into his spine, and he bit his tongue to hold back a yelp. "Here, Major Patterson," the corporal said. "This is the one you're looking for."

George tried to shake away the fog that seemed to linger in his mind more and more often. The small room contained nothing more than one large desk and the overweight man who sat behind it.

The officer glanced up from his papers and waved the corporal away. The brute gave George one more jab for good measure before turning and striding out the door. It closed behind him with an ominous thud.

Patterson returned to his paperwork, obviously not in any hurry to address George. He made a point not to shuffle his feet and waited with his hands clasped behind his back. He wouldn't give the man any reason to be irritated with him.

George looked across the major's balding head to the door behind him, wondering if it led to the guards' quarters. Did they have mattresses? He'd never take such a luxury for granted again.

The major sifted through his papers until he finally banged the stack on the desk, straightened them, and set them aside. He leveled thoughtful brown eyes on George. "George Daniels?"

George shifted his weight. "Yes, sir?"

"Do you know why you're here?"

"No, sir."

The major tapped his finger on his desk. "Elmira was supposed to hold five thousand. Do you know how many are here instead?"

What kind of game was this man playing? George shoved his hands into his coat pockets. "Many more, I would guess."

Major Patterson grunted. "Twice as many. We don't have room for those and still they send me more!"

The major regarded him for a while, long enough for George to break a sweat. Finally, as if making up his mind about something, he nodded. "I've been granted permission to allow a few men an opportunity that all would covet."

George swallowed, but his mouth felt too dry.

The man leaned back in his chair. "My men say you never cause trouble and work harder than most."

George let out a whoosh of air. So he wasn't here for some

sort of punishment. Did they give prisoners rewards for good behavior? Before he let his mind travel to food, he forced himself to focus on the rest of the major's words.

"Now, that alone won't do a man much good, but coupled with a few certain other factors, well, it just might help you out."

George's brows pulled together. The man was being decidedly vague.

The major picked up one of the papers on his desk and scanned it. "I'm told you're a major landholder in Mississippi. Is that correct?"

Since his father's and brothers' deaths, George had become head of Westerly Plantation. But what did that matter to Patterson? "Yes, sir."

Patterson rubbed his chin. "A rather large holding, correct?"

What did it matter how much land he had? "Westerly holds more than seven thousand acres. Or did, before the war. I cannot say what's left now."

Patterson leaned back in his chair. "I'm offering you an opportunity to leave this prison as a free man."

George shook his head to clear the fog. He must have misheard. "Sir?"

The major smirked, obviously finding George's stupor amusing. "War's nearly over. We'll take Richmond within the week."

Relief, rather than defiance, stirred. And he wouldn't feel guilty for it. If the war was ending, then perhaps his time in this purgatory was as well.

"Since the Union will need to be restored, men with assets will be rewarded for their willingness to help with such endeavors. Tell me, what would you do if the war ended today and you were free to go?"

George leveled his gaze on the man and answered honestly. "I'd try to rebuild my life. Take a wife, make a living for my family, and finish my days in peace. I've seen enough blood for one lifetime."

The major nodded. "Wise answer. I believe it, too. I'm good at telling when a man's lying." He lifted a stack of papers. "These are loyalty papers. If you denounce your treason and swear your loyalty to the Union, promise to abide by United States Government laws, and not seek to use your position or wealth to stir up further Rebel treason…." He looked at George expectantly.

George swallowed hard and nodded. He wouldn't be stirring anything more than his morning coffee if he could help it.

The major appeared satisfied. "Then the Union Army is prepared to offer you your freedom in exchange for your reestablishing working crops and partnering with the government as it seeks to mend the nation."

George hesitated. What exactly did that mean? The government would control what he did with his lands and who he traded his cotton and tobacco to?

The major tapped the papers again. "Choose wisely. I'd say your very life depends on it."

George tightened his jaw. Better to provide cotton to the Union than to die in prison. "Where do I sign?"

The major pointed to the bottom of the page. In swift order, George scrawled his name and told himself that this would be his family's best option. The major had just finished replacing the cork on the inkwell when the door banged open behind George.

A bearded guard poked his head inside. "Major? Got a lady out here that wants to see you."

"Lady?" The major scoffed. "Since when are women allowed in?" The major pushed away from his desk. "That will be all, Daniels. I'll see that this is processed, and someone will send for you once it's approved."

George's heart sank. He'd hoped he'd get to leave before the ink dried. "Thank you, sir."

He followed the major out the door. The gloomy light felt like a punch to the gut as he stepped outside. Where had the sun gone? Half a day and already they were back to gathering clouds? His hope for dry firewood snuffed out. He dropped his eyes from the heavens with disgust.

At the bottom of the steps stood a lovely young woman with golden hair and flashing eyes. She held herself with a regal air, despite the fact that two Union officers held each of her elbows. George frowned. What was a woman doing in here?

He paused on the bottom step and studied her face. She must have felt his gaze, because her eyes swung from the portly major and landed on him. She gasped, her features growing pale.

George frowned. Hadn't she seen worse than him? Surely she'd had to step over one or two Hopeless before making it to the guards' barracks. Suddenly her image was replaced by a sour face with bushy red eyebrows.

Corporal Carnage's nose was only inches from his own. "Back to work!"

George ducked his head, hurrying away before the corporal could find another reason to jab at him or before the major could renege on his offer. After a few steps without a jab in the back, he dared to glance over his shoulder. The lady had straightened herself and boldly addressed the major. The corporal caught his eye and took a step forward. George turned his head and quickened his pace.

His Union coat flapped in the wind, reminding him he'd just become a traitor.

But better a living traitor than a dead prisoner.

Five

"What could he have learned from her?"
John H. Surratt

The soldiers' eyes nipped at her, looking for signs of weakness and taking her measure. Annabelle ignored them and watched the prisoner scurry away. Could he be George? He was tall, though not as tall as Matthew, and his sunken features could carry a family resemblance.

Or perhaps she was letting her desperation to find him make her manifest his features on a stranger.

Annabelle dismissed the retreating prisoner and settled her focus on the red-faced major in front of her. She longed to snatch her elbows away from the soldiers holding her, but she dared not. She certainly didn't want to end up in detainment again and give poor Matthew two people to rescue.

"This lady insisted on seeing you, Major Patterson," the soldier on her left said, jiggling her arm for effect.

Annabelle straightened her spine and offered the balding man her best smile. He narrowed his eyes at her but spoke to his soldiers. "And I'm sure you told her that visitors were not allowed?"

The one to her right shifted his weight, and she dared a look at his profile. The set of his brows suggested he was strongly displeased with his situation. "We did, sir. But she wouldn't leave."

"You see I—"

The major held up his hand to silence her. "One moment, miss, while I try to understand why my men have disobeyed my orders."

"I'm sorry, sir. But she wouldn't go, and her presence was…." He glanced at Annabelle and she shot him a sugared smile. He cleared his throat. "She was distracting the guards and causing prisoners to gather at the gate."

The major lifted his brows. "Miss, if you wish to donate, you may do so with Mrs. Green. She's head of the women who take pity on the dogs here." He turned away.

"Wait!" Annabelle stepped forward. The guards tightened their grip on her arms. She sighed, hanging her head. "I only wanted to see if my fool brother was here. I've come so far and we've been so worried." She added a hitch in her throat, which came rather easily, and looked up to bat her lashes at him. Major Patterson regarded her with lowered lids. "Please, sir. I only wish to know if he still lives. I promise I won't cause you further trouble."

The major grumbled something she didn't understand and nodded to the soldiers, who promptly released her elbows. She heaved a sigh of relief and straightened her mantle against the probing wind.

"Your brother joined the Rebels?"

Annabelle nodded. "It's been so hard on us all. I learned from the Commissary General's office in Washington that he may be here."

The major tugged at his long mustache, and she tried to let all her pent-up fears and worries from the last weeks show in her eyes. It must have worked because, looking resigned, he huffed. "Oh, very well. I'll check the records for you, miss. But you are never to return. Understood?"

"Oh, yes, sir. Thank you, sir."

"What's your brother's name?"

"George Daniels."

The major's face instantly hardened. "I think you should come inside. I have some questions for you."

Annabelle glanced at the confused faces of the soldiers at her side and tried to keep her panic in check. The last time an officer had questions for her, she'd found herself tossed into a tent with her feet bound. She clasped her hands in front of her to try to keep them from shaking. "Oh, that's all right. We can talk out here. I don't want to take up too much of your time."

"I insist." He gestured to the soldiers. "Return to your posts."

The soldiers saluted and then hurried off, leaving Annabelle with the major's heavy frown. He opened the door to the stout stone building and motioned for Annabelle to enter. She swallowed the gathering lump in her throat and stepped past him into the dim room.

Annabelle stood as near to the exit as she could. The heavy door closed with a thud that made her jump. Thankfully, the major didn't seem to notice as he made his way around the desk and sat down behind it. He regarded her thoughtfully for a moment, then leaned back in his chair.

"So, Miss Daniels, I take it."

Annabelle hesitated, then nodded.

"Tell me about your brother."

Annabelle fidgeted with the blue fabric of her only good dress and gave him the same story she'd given to the young Union soldier in Washington. "My brother decided to join the Confederates. He split up the family and caused my mother a great deal of worry. Ever since we heard he was taken captive we've been trying to locate him."

"And you believe he's here?"

Her nervous fingers gathered her skirts until her hemline rose two inches off the floor. She quickly dropped the fabric and clasped her hands at her waist. "Yes, sir."

He picked up some papers on his desk and looked them over. "Do you know what unit he was in or where he was taken prisoner?"

Feeling hopeful, Annabelle bobbed her head, bouncing the curls hanging down by her ear. "He was in one of Forrest's regiments in Mississippi. We believe he was captured near a town called Lorman."

The major stroked his mustache again. "I might have some-one who came from there. Don't recall his name, but I don't think it could be the same man."

"Oh?"

He watched her closely. "This man claims to be a plantation holder from Mississippi, not a man with his family in the North."

Her pulse quickened. That could be George!

"And where did you say your family was from?"

Annabelle thought quickly. "My family's from New York, just a day's ride north of here, in Watkins Glen." Not exactly a lie. However, she suspected that by this point, one more lie wouldn't truly make much difference.

"Hmm. Interesting. You don't suppose your brother would have claimed to be a landholder from the South, do you?"

Oh, heavens. What if that *was* George she'd seen? Oh, this tangle of falsehood might well trap her this time. She hadn't dreamed they would know so much about him! She chewed her lip. "Honestly, I wouldn't know, sir."

He thought a moment. "I'll tell you what. Let me look into the matter and see if I can figure this out."

Annabelle nodded slowly, apprehension settling in her chest like a weight. "I…appreciate that, sir."

"Where might I send you a message?"

She studied his face. She'd seen enough people regard her with suspicion these past weeks to recognize it now. She smiled sweetly. "I can return to the gate in the morning and one of your men can pass along your findings."

He regarded her flatly. "Fine."

She turned to hurry out.

"One moment, miss."

Annabelle paused, her heart thudding frantically. His heavy footsteps sounded behind her, and he reached past her to open the door. "A lady cannot go through the prison unescorted."

She let out her breath in a whoosh. "Oh, yes, of course." She waved a hand. "How silly of me."

The major took her elbow and she tried not to cringe. They made their way down the long dirt road through the center of the prison. Men lined the wall and crowded the open areas, everyone in deplorable condition. Her stomach churned, and she lifted a hand to her face to mask the smell.

They had to get George out of here.

As they neared the gate, Annabelle came to a stop. "I heard men would be released if they signed papers of allegiance. Is that true?"

The man tugged on the hem of his blue jacket, his gaze traveling over the men on the wall instead of looking at her. She saw only frustration in his eyes and not the slightest sign of compassion. She almost thought he wasn't going to answer when his cold gaze fell on her again. "And where did you hear that?"

Annabelle gestured across the river. "A lady at the observation tower told me."

The major wrinkled his face in disgust. "Those fools and their tower. What do they think we are? The local theatre?"

Annabelle gave a small shrug. Perhaps he had some humanity after all.

"A few prisoners meeting certain requirements are going to be released. The war's nearly finished, you know," he said, gesturing for her to pass through the gate.

So everyone always said. "Yes, sir," she replied, remaining where she stood. "I certainly hope it is. Do you think perhaps my brother might be one of those considered?"

His features tightened again, and she regretted asking.

"I said I'd look into it." He grasped her elbow again, practically pulling her through the gate and past the sentries on duty. "Here we are," he barked, dropping her arm. "I don't expect you to cause my men trouble again."

She opened her mouth to respond, but he didn't give her the chance.

"Your presence will not be tolerated again. Do you understand?"

Annabelle ground her teeth. She wasn't a child. "Yes, sir. I understand. I don't wish to cause trouble. Only to see my brother again."

"And," he said, pointing his finger in her face, "you will not position yourself at the gate and cause a distraction for my men or my prisoners again."

She inwardly groaned, but she kept a gentle expression on her face. "Of course not, sir. I'll only wait for as long as needed to receive your message in the morning."

His face reddened, and Annabelle forced herself to hold his gaze.

"Of course," he said through lips that didn't seem as if they wanted to part enough to let words free. "I'll have a message ready for you tomorrow afternoon at three. You can promptly receive it and then quickly be on your way."

"Thank you for your kindness."

He spun on his heel, leaving her standing just outside the prison gate among the curious stares of a score of men in blue. A fine mist began to fall and cling to her clothing. She hurried away from the guards, keeping her head down and her focus on her stained slippers as they peeked out from under the hem of her skirt. Had Momma been alive, she would have chided Annabelle for such an unladylike gait. But at the moment, distance from the stench of the prison and the lingering eyes of too many men was simply more important than a lady's graceful walk.

Peggy gained her side as she passed by the bottom of the observation tower. "Did you find anything?"

Annabelle gave a slight shake of her head and gestured for

Peggy to follow. The older woman frowned, but she dutifully obeyed. Annabelle made her way to the shade trees where the colored servants had been yesterday afternoon.

Peggy let her draw several long breaths of cold New York air before she divulged her story. Peggy listened with interest, her features clouding at several points.

"Something don't seem quite right about that."

"Exactly." She twisted her fingers. "Unless he knew I was lying."

"Then why didn't he just say something?"

Annabelle tilted her head and watched a bird settle on a swaying branch overhead, free from the pains of war and the woes that came from delivering too many lies. When she looked back down at Peggy, the woman's face held a mixture of worry and sadness.

"I don't know. Perhaps the man I saw leaving the building was actually George. If it was, he probably wondered why I didn't recognize my own brother."

"Seems unlikely."

Annabelle couldn't deny that fact. "True, but he *did* look like a shorter, starved version of Matthew. I do think it's possible." She twisted her skirts. "Oh, I should have just been honest instead."

"And tell them you're a Mississippi lady wanting to get her beau out?" Peggy shook her head. "Don't think that would have been much better."

Matthew strode toward them with a determined gait, the wind pulling at his hair. He wouldn't be pleased that she hadn't come straight to the platform as promised. She steeled herself and nodded in his direction. Peggy turned to look at him and clamped her lips. The look on her face mirrored Annabelle's own apprehension.

Worry lines creased the strong planes of his face. "What did you find?"

"I think he might be in there," she said, trying to sound hopeful. "I may have even seen him."

Relief flooded Matthew's features and she wished that was all she had to tell. Matthew stepped close and grasped both of her shoulders, his body only a hand's breadth from hers. She had to tilt her head back to see the hope radiating from his face.

A few days' worth of whiskers dusted his jawline and she resisted the urge to reach up and sweep away a lock of hair that had escaped the twist of leather at the back of his neck. Unfashionable, as most men wore their hair short, but Annabelle loved the Revolutionary look of him. She looked up from his lips and into his eyes. His pupils dilated, and she was close enough now to feel his breath on her face.

Peggy made a noise in her throat, breaking the moment and reminding her that she stood inappropriately with a man in public. How was it he made her forget all else? Would a marriage of convenience always leave her heart longing for what it felt now?

Peggy made a louder noise. Heat seared her cheeks and she stepped back out of Matthew's grasp. He blinked like he had been as swept away as she. Suddenly his eyes cleared, and he stabbed her with a penetrating gaze that was not nearly as warm as the one she'd bathed in only seconds earlier. She suppressed a shiver.

"How would you know if you saw him? You've never seen my brother before."

"The man I saw was around a hand's length or two shorter than you, not as wide in the shoulders, and light of hair and eyes. I do believe there was some resemblance, though I could be mistaken."

Matthew's eyes grew wide. "It *could* be him! Did you speak to him?"

The excitement in his voice clawed at her heart. She shook her head. "No, he was told to leave."

"But he's alive!"

She twisted her hands together. "Perhaps. I truly do hope it was him."

The joy on Matthew's face faded. "What are you not telling me?"

Annabelle dropped her gaze to Matthew's boots. After a few seconds, his finger came up under her chin and gently lifted her head. "Annabelle?"

She blinked back the moisture gathering in her eyes. "I… Well, I think my story made the Union major at the prison suspicious."

She told him the details, cringing as his features darkened. When she finished, the muscles in his jaw worked as he clenched his teeth.

"I… I do hope I didn't cause any problems."

When Matthew finally spoke, his voice was hard. "Why are women so deceitful?"

She bristled. "Do you actually think the truth would have been better?"

Matthew's nostrils flared. "I told you you'd make his circumstances worse."

She stiffened. "How? Just because they thought I was lying

doesn't mean they will make things worse on him. How can anything be worse than being in that awful prison?" As soon as the words left her lips, she wished she could call them back. Matthew's face went from pained to seething in the span of a second. She swallowed hard. "I was only trying to help."

Matthew drew in a long breath, and some of the tightness drained from his shoulders, though it hadn't left his voice. "From now on, I'll handle these things."

Annabelle tried to remember that Matthew's nerves were understandably taut. She tried to offer an encouraging smile and smother her own frustrations. "I did ask about the release option. The major said he would look into it and have someone give me an answer tomorrow afternoon."

She'd hoped her words would ease his frown, but, instead, it only deepened. Without a word, he stalked back toward the observation tower, the falling rain obscuring his form as he disappeared from sight.

Six

"Booth told me that he had gotten together in Washington all who were necessary for the purpose intended."
John H. Surratt

Elmira Prison
March 16, 1865
3:00 a.m.

Cold rain ran underneath the collar of George's Union coat and slithered down his back like a slippery snake. For hours it'd been falling so heavily that he could barely see in front of him. Now the rain eased up just enough that he could make out the dull silver of his saw in the darkness. The wind hit hard against his face and muffled the words the guards shouted over them, but he'd long since given up trying to understand what they said.

George bit his saw into another small log, operating mostly by touch. His hands shook, making the cuts rough and uneven, but that didn't matter.

Just had to make the rafts.

He finished cutting through the soaked sapling and let the

two unusable ends drop to the ground with a muffled splash. George looked around for the man who had been taking the finished cuts, but didn't see him anywhere. Since this was his last available log, he'd take it down to the flats himself. The more he kept moving, the better.

George sloshed through the mud, his feet soaked from the water seeping in through the soles of his shoes. He hated the flats. It was bad enough they camped on the northern side of Foster's Pond—the disgusting river backwash they used as a latrine—but it was even worse that the Yanks had put the smallpox patients on the southern side of Foster's. Any fool could see the flats were prone to flood.

The banks had been high for some time now, and this latest storm proved their limit. The stench of the festering pond as it overflowed into the flats had already caused him to heave up what little his stomach contained. George tried to ignore the smell that even the torrents of water from heaven could not wash away. His muscles ached, but he kept moving toward the groups of scrambling men along the edge of the flats.

"You! Bring that over here!"

A blurry figure waved to him. Dutifully, George pivoted and trudged in that direction.

A guard shouted something obscene at him, but George ignored it as just another bit of filth he wouldn't let sour his gut. He dropped the log with a splash of nasty water. The guard cursed again.

"Pick it up and lash it to the others, you dumb Rebel!"

George obeyed, tying frayed bits of rope as tight as he could. Heaven help the poor souls who wouldn't make it onto one of these pitiful rafts. Drowning was a right hard way to go.

George held on to the little raft to keep it from floating away and forced his fumbling fingers to tie off the ends of the rope.

Water lapped at his ankles and got deeper over by the banks. By the time he and the men on the northern side of the pond had been roused, some of the men in the flats had water in their beds.

George wondered where exactly they planned to float the sick off to. A strange thought prodded his brain. If the sick were to float far enough down the river, undetected in the chaos, they might possibly be able to get away before—

"Get that thing over here!" someone shouted, breaking into his thoughts and reminding him that if these men were well enough to attempt escape, they wouldn't be in the flats in the first place. George heaved a lungful of damp air and willed his depleted body to push the raft forward.

By the time he neared the doctors, the dark water circled his waist. He shivered uncontrollably, and something told him that if he didn't get dry soon, he wouldn't live long enough to find out if they would release him.

He reached a haggard-looking doctor, the man's tight features barely visible through the sheets of rain and thick darkness that his outstretched lamp couldn't disperse. "Here! Help me get them on!"

Bless the man for caring about the smallpox-ridden Confederates under his care. At least some of these Yankees seemed to have a soul. George put his hands under the arms of a pockmarked man and struggled to lift him up. The doctor plunged his arms into the churning water and managed to fish out the man's feet. They soon had him and one other coughing, panting man onto the raft.

"Get them moving!" The doctor yelled before turning away to the next makeshift raft.

George looked at the pitiful souls on the lashed logs and saw no option other than to move forward. He leaned against the raft and slowly put one foot in front of the other. He'd gone only a few steps when his right foot sank so far into the mud that he plunged chest-deep into the icy water. Teeth clattering, George struggled until his foot came free, but his shoe remained buried in the muck.

Time lost its meaning as he pushed the men across the pond and into the flow of the Chemung River. George was fairly certain one of the men was already dead, given the way his head lolled and one arm trailed along in the water, but George kept pushing anyway. Tendrils of water clung to his clothing and tried to pull him down to his death. Struggling against their strength, George finally made it to the far bank, where welcoming arms reached out to pull the men from the raft.

"Good work, guard. Get another load!"

George blinked up at the man in confusion. They thought him a guard? He stood there in the water, a voice somewhere in the back of his murky mind telling him he was losing his capacity for clear thinking. The man who'd shouted the order was already farther down the river pulling more bodies from watery graves.

His teeth chattered so hard that he must have bitten his tongue, because the coppery taste of blood filled his mouth and jarred his senses. Perhaps he should just sit a moment. Yes, just a moment. Then he would return for more of his brothers in gray. George pushed toward the bank with the last of his strength, clawing into the mud and finally succeeding in dragging himself onto the bank. He flipped over on his back and drew in rapid breaths of frigid air.

Just a moment. Only a moment to rest.

Then he curled into a tight ball and surrendered to the comforting call of the darkness.

Matthew bolted upright. Was it the pounding rain on the roof that had roused him, or something else? He rubbed the tight muscles on the back of his neck and rose to stoke the fire. The women slept soundly, neither aware of his movements.

A growing sense of unease rubbed his already frayed nerves. Something had startled him awake, but he saw nothing to cause alarm. No predatory noises punctured the dark. He stepped over to the bed and looked down at Annabelle's sleeping form. She looked peaceful with her hand curled under her chin and her long hair splayed over the pillow. Something in Matthew stirred, and he reached out to brush a wisp of hair from her face. She moved slightly, and Matthew stepped back, tamping down the feeling. This was entirely too intimate. He shouldn't be so near without her permission.

He crossed the cold plank floor and prodded the fire again, though it danced merrily already. The flickering flames sent shadows dancing across the room and drew his eyes back to the warm glow cast across Annabelle's smooth cheeks. What would it be like to see her that way each morning? To awake with her in his bed, her hair spread over his chest?

Matthew turned away and struggled to douse the fire rising

within him. He shouldn't think such things. Thunder rumbled and a flash of lightning lit the room, and for an instant it was nearly as bright as day. Annabelle made a soft sound and rolled over, turning her back to him.

You should go now.

The thought pushed so vividly into his mind that Matthew froze. The small hairs on the back of his neck rose and Matthew rubbed at them, his sense of unease growing.

He silently chided himself for conjuring imagined threats and placed the poker back by the fire. He should get back to sleep. He was dreaming even in his waking hours. He should at least let his body rest while his mind spun fables.

You should go before the miracle expires.

Matthew ground his teeth. He was losing his senses! He shook his head as though the movement could dislodge the remnants of this ridiculous dream. Where were these strange thoughts coming from?

Suddenly the hot blood in his veins ran cold. He remembered that moment on the platform. The desperate prayer flung to the heavens. He'd asked for a miracle to get George out.

George!

A volley of thoughts fired through Matthew's mind. That river had already been swollen from melted snows. With rains like this, the men in tents along the banks were likely in danger. They would be scrambling to get away from the rising waters. All those men running about in the dark.

Matthew pulled on his boots and flung on his coat without another thought. In a matter of seconds, he was out the door and down the stairs. He plunged out into the darkness, pulling his cap snugly on his head. The heavy cloud cover blotted out the celestial light, and he could barely see the muddy road in front of him. Pulling his collar tight, Matthew hurried down the slick road and toward the looming structure of the observation tower. By the time he reached it, he was nearly soaked through and already shivering.

He heard the shouts before he saw the men. Dots of light bobbed like giant, disoriented fireflies, their scant glow barely enough to carve out small circles in the darkness. The inadequate light offered just enough for him to make out the figures dashing around along the riverbanks. Matthew crept between the timbers holding up the observation deck. When nobody noticed him, he eased forward and came to stand along the edge of the river without being stopped by a single guard.

Matthew looked at the figures pulling limp men from bits of broken wood. He frowned. What were they doing? They appeared to be floating men across the pond from the southern banks. He'd spent enough time looking at the prison from the tower to know the layout of the facilities. Matthew guessed the rains had caused them to evacuate the sick from the lower flatland on the southern side of the murky overflow pond.

He scanned the banks of the river where men huddled in groups or helped pull others to this side. From what he could tell, the black waters had claimed all of the low lands. But where was George? Was it possible he was here among these at the river?

No one questioned him, so Matthew strode down to the banks as though he belonged there and started poking at the forms lying in the cold mud. He made his way down the river's edge, squinting at faces and turning cursing men over to see their features in the meager light.

The shivers became almost violent by the time he reached the end of the line, and his teeth clacked together. Where was George? He turned his face toward the misting rain, the cold in his body forgotten as searing heat throbbed in his chest.

Some miracle! Where are You now?

Nothing happened. Cursing himself for his foolishness, Matthew shook the water from his face. Why had he allowed himself to think that God would see him? That his prayer would be heard above the clamor of so many others that were more worthy than his own? Despair clawed at him like a creature rising from the depths. *Failure!* Once again he'd proven himself a disappointment in anything that mattered. And once again someone else paid the cost for his foolishness.

Matthew sank to his knees. The clouds splintered and silvery moonlight filtered through the sparkling water droplets drifting in the air.

What was that?

Farther down the bank, away from the rest of the men, a single lump of darkness separated itself from the shadows. Matthew shook his head. His desperation claimed the lump could be a man. The form was more likely a log, or a pile of mud or…his feet moved toward the object even as his mind told him the effort was futile.

Matthew set his jaw and hurried over to the form. *A man!* A curled, huddled and half-covered-in-mud man, but a man all the same. He reached out and touched the sodden woolen overcoat with trembling fingers, shaking the form. Try as he might to suppress it, hope reared. He would not give up.

The figure groaned. Matthew turned him over and squinted down at the face below. His heart hammered. It couldn't be.

No, he saw only what he desperately wanted to!

"George?" The name slipped through his trembling lips, barely heard on the cold night air and nearly lost on the foggy breath that spilled from him.

The man groaned again, and the teetering hope surged once more. His pulse pounding furiously in his ears, Matthew shook the man again. "George! George, is it you?"

The man coughed and rolled away from Matthew and then sat up. Matthew crouched in the mud, the edges of the river lapping against the leg of his trousers. He grasped the man's shoulders and leaned close to his face.

"Matthew?" the voice croaked.

Relief and joy surged through him and he pulled his brother into a tight embrace, barely able to believe it. "I've found you!"

George touched Matthew's face, confusion evident in his rapidly blinking eyes. "Why are you here?"

Matthew leapt to his feet. "I've come to get you out!"

He tugged George to his feet and started pulling him farther down the bank, away from the men shouting and pulling the sick from the river. George planted his feet in the mud. "No, we can't run."

Matthew wanted to slap him. "Have you gone mad, man? This is your chance to get out!"

George shook his head. "I signed the papers."

"Papers?" Matthew glanced behind George. Two men seemed to be looking their way. Panic surged and he grabbed George by the collar of his heavy coat. "Are you wearing a Union jacket?"

He couldn't be sure against the heavy cloak of night, but he thought he saw George grin. "Didn't lose it in a bet either. And one of those fool guards thought I was one of them when I brought up the raft...." His words dissolved into a cackle.

George was delirious. Matthew had to get him out of here. Now. A thought struck him and he started pulling George's coat off. The shorter man growled, and tried to dance out of Matthew's reach. "No! You won't take it from me!"

Matthew caught the fist George swung at him. "Brother! Let me save your life!"

George stopped moving. "Matthew? Is that you?"

"Yes, and we don't have much time." Matthew tugged him away from the bank and to the cover of a small stand of trees just off the water's edge. He had to hurry. The others along the bank had seen them and would be upon them at any moment. He tugged George's coat off and traded it with his own. George mumbled something, but then his head rolled back and he slumped. Matthew caught him just before he hit the ground.

The bobbing light of a lantern appeared just before the gruff voice of the man carrying it. "Who goes in there?"

"It's me, you cur!" Matthew shouted without thinking. Would they buy his ruse?

"What?" The man lifted the covered lantern higher, but Matthew remained just out of the light's reach.

Matthew pulled George's limp form forward, careful to keep his chin ducked and most of his face to the shadows. "Found this one trying to crawl out here to the trees. I got him though."

The man leveled a rifle and scowled. Matthew forced himself to remain still and prayed they couldn't see him well enough to know he wasn't a guard. Finally the man shrugged and lowered his weapon. "Fine. Bring him out here with the others. I'm ready to be out of this mess."

Matthew's shoulders slumped and he had to reposition his grip on his stumbling brother, whose head had dropped back against his arm. He got George situated and started walking toward the Union guard. As he'd hoped, the Yank turned his back and led the way out of the line of trees. Matthew followed, slowly pulling George along until the distance between them and the prison guard grew and the darkness nearly obscured the man's form.

Then Matthew turned, hefted George across his shoulders, and ran as fast as he could in the opposite direction.

Seven

"They could be ready at a minute's notice."
John H. Surratt

Surratt Boarding House
Washington. D.C.
March 16, 1865

David O'Malley brushed the curtains back from his second-floor window and watched Washington awaken from its slumber. He tugged on his jacket as the filthy Yankees below began their day oblivious to just how close they had come to losing the war.

Nine days. It had been nine days since they had failed, and with each passing day David grew ever more frustrated. Booth had gone back to his normal life as though nothing had ever transpired. John Surratt had assured him that they were still working and that news from Canada was soon forthcoming. They would be making a new plan anytime now.

David laced up his boots and checked his reflection in the mirror on the bureau. He rubbed at the stubble on his chin, then decided he could go another day without a shave. Tucking his hat under his arm, he made his way through the narrow boarding house and toward the front door. As he passed by the parlor, Mrs. Surratt hurried out after him.

"Mr. O'Malley, will you be joining us for breakfast?"

David pulled on his hat. The stately woman's fine black gown fit her form nicely. For a woman of her age, she kept her appearance neat, and he could tell that in her younger years she'd probably been something to look at. Though not as lovely as Liza, of course. No woman had ever lived—or ever would—who would be as beautiful as his wife. An unbidden image of her charred face sprang into his mind and his teeth clenched.

"No, ma'am," he said through his tight jaw.

She frowned. "You haven't joined us for four days now."

Not since she'd started taking other people into the boarding house and seemed to have forgotten they were trying to complete a mission. Why did she expect him to sit with Yankee fools and act as if nothing had ever happened? "And I shall not today or any other day."

He reached for the knob and left her frowning after him. He traipsed down the short flight of stairs and onto the street, not bothering to nod at anyone who passed. He forced himself to remember his role.

He should try to be more accommodating. She allowed him to stay without payment while they awaited news from Canada. He bit down hard on his lip and felt the familiar sting and taste of blood awakening his senses. Why was he allowing his acting skills to slip? It would profit him nothing. He'd long since learned that women, especially ones upward in years, were easily charmed and maneuvered. He mustn't let the failures of the group affect how skillfully he dragged them forward. And forward they would go. He would see to that.

David could not allow his annoyance to undo all the work he had put into this plan. He'd spent far too long positioning himself with the key players to let it be ruined now. Booth had said they must watch and wait. But it had now been long enough that they could rest easy. The lawmen weren't after them. Nearly every end was tied up.

He stepped into the American Telegraph Company office and waited for an elderly woman ahead of him in line to finish her business before taking his turn at the window.

"Name, please," the portly man on the other side of the counter asked without looking up.

David forced his voice to be pleasant. "O'Malley." Every morning he came here at the same hour, and every morning this dullard asked the same question.

The man looked up and leveled muddy brown eyes on him. "Oh, yes. Let me see…." He shuffled things around on the counter, finally picking a paper from the stack. "Ah. Here it is."

O'Malley plucked the paper from the man's pudgy fingers and scanned the words.

D-

Have been following the lost sheep. He still hasn't wandered into the fox den. Don't think he is going to cause trouble. Waiting on further instructions.

-H

David shoved the paper into his pocket and fished out a coin, pushing it across the counter to the clerk.

He picked it up, squinted at it and then tucked it away in his jacket. "Ready to send a response?"

No, he merely wanted to give away good coin for nothing.

David plastered a smile on his face. "Yes, sir. I would like to send a response."

The portly man nodded and picked up his pen and a slip of paper. "This is returning to Elmira, correct?" he said as he dipped the pen into the ink.

David withheld a groan. "Yes, of course. That *is* where it came from."

The man seemed annoyed but said no more.

"Please send this response. H – Continue to track our lost sheep. His location is not coincidence. Once he finds the others of his flock, he may begin to bleat. No news here. Report back if the mutton is in the butcher's shop. –D"

The man scribbled out the words and David waited as he tapped out a series of long and short clicks on his telegraph machine. When he finished, he nodded at David. "The message has been sent down the wire. You can check back tomorrow for a response."

David stepped back into the cold northern wind. He'd sent Harry to track Matthew Daniels the day the traitor had thought he'd given David the slip. Harry had orders not to kill him until he reported where Daniels had run off to with the girl. As he'd suspected, it wasn't to the South.

The traitors had gone farther north, giving themselves up for the Yankee spies they were. He didn't know when the wench had turned Daniels, but the pup had followed at her heels. Two days ago he'd finally received word from Harry that they had stopped in Elmira, New York. Since there was a prison there, David assumed Daniels was still after his brother.

But then what? He stepped around a patch of melting snow and made his way farther down the street and toward the

National Hotel. As the days passed and Daniels still didn't try to unveil his little group, David had begun to wonder just what the man was about. Perhaps he'd been honest. He wanted his brother and nothing more.

A shame. Holding the brother out as bait was the only way he'd gotten Daniels to trail along. They didn't need him now. He'd proven that he wasn't nearly the man David had hoped. He'd tucked tail and run as soon as they'd met their first bit of adversity. Now Daniels was just a lost sheep they would have to put down. He'd wait a day or so more to see if Daniels succeeded in getting his brother. Then he would give the order for Harry to dispose of all of them. He should have done it by now, but his curiosity got the better of him. He'd made a bet with himself that Daniels's desperation would drive him to find his brother at any cost. He was near enough to seeing himself proven right that he let reason slip just long enough to enjoy the satisfaction. Besides, might as well get both Daniels brothers together. A shame, really, since George had nothing to do with any of it, but it simply couldn't be helped.

David opened the door to the National Hotel. His leather shoes clicked across the polished floor as he crossed the grand entry and ambled up to the ornate receiving desk.

"I'd like to call upon Mr. Booth, please."

The man behind the counter regarded him with distaste. "Mr. Booth is not seeing anyone today. He left instructions not to be disturbed while he studies his lines."

"Will you let him know Mr. O'Malley called upon him?"

The man's lip curled slightly. "Of course, sir. I will let him know you have come by, *again*."

David tugged on his collar and pinned the pretentious little man with a cool glare. "See that you do. It would seem he is not receiving my messages."

The clerk sneered. "Oh, he is receiving them, sir. But he rarely responds to the attentions of admirers. Have a good day."

Heat climbed up his neck. *An admirer! Of all the foolish….* He straightened his jacket and kept his face passive. "Good day." He would not waste his breath explaining to this uppity worm that he was not some sniveling admirer of a mid-rate actor. How could he be, since he himself could have been a bigger name than Booth?

He sighed and made his way back out of the hotel. He had given up a great many things for the Cause. Playing this part of the silent conductor was just another feat he would master. What did it matter if they didn't know his true worth? He sought results, not fame. Not like Booth. On the contrary, his heart was true to the South. True to the Cause. He was better than those weasels seeking nothing more than their own glory. Oh, but soon enough his name would make the headlines of every paper South and North. He would accept the accolades, of course, but justice rather than glory drove him.

He only had to bide his time just a bit longer. Let Booth hide and practice his lines for that ridiculous *American Cousin* play. He could not ignore David forever. He would either convince Booth to get him in the White House or he would find someone else who could. He wouldn't tolerate Booth's yellow belly much longer.

Eight

"Booth had a long conversation with Mother today, at the end of which he said that 'if anything were to be done, it should not be delayed, otherwise it would be too late.'"

John H. Surratt

Elmira Inn
Elmira, New York
March 16, 1865

The door flew open and banged against the wall. Annabelle bolted upright from underneath the covers. The fire in the hearth of their small room at the Elmira Inn cast enough light to reveal a hulking bear crowding the doorway. A shriek lodged in her throat and she scrambled back away from the edge of the bed, her pounding heart dashing all remnants of sleep.

The thing filled the entire doorframe. Its unnaturally wide shoulders turned to the side to enter the room. Massive paws thumped hard against the plank floor as though its own enormous bulk proved too much to carry.

The scream she could not loose found its way out of Peggy's mouth instead. An instant later her friend brandished a fire poker and waved it at the bear.

"Hush, woman! Before you wake the entire building and see us arrested!"

Annabelle clutched at the throat of her nightdress. The familiar voice skittered through her scattered thoughts and brought her mind into focus.

Matthew stumbled into the room with the body of another man slung over his shoulders. Water fell from them in steady drops, causing a cascade of unnatural rain all over the worn rug. Peggy found her wits before Annabelle did and dropped the fire poker. She rushed to Matthew as he jutted his shoulder and brought the limp man sliding down his side. Peggy helped steady him as Matthew repositioned his arms under the other man's weight. Once secured, Matthew tugged him toward the fireplace.

Matthew thrust his chin toward the open hallway. "Peggy, the door."

As Peggy scrambled to close the room off from any onlookers, Annabelle recovered from her shock and leapt from the bed, hustling to Matthew's side. "What in heaven's name happened?"

She helped Matthew lower the limp body to the floor in front of the fire.

"We have to get him warm. Now!"

Right. They had a patient. Questions could wait.

Annabelle squared her shoulders and tried to project more confidence than she felt. "We must get him out of these wet clothes and get him dry."

Her nimble fingers quickly loosened the buttons of his sodden coat. Matthew pulled the garment free. Peggy tossed the remainder of their logs on the fire, coaxing it into a roaring flame. The flickering light illuminated the pale, blue-tinged face of the man in front of her. Her heart clenched.

She pulled back the fabric at his neck and placed her fingers to find a pulse. His skin felt like slick snow under her touch, but life beat within him. Slowly. She risked a glance up at Matthew. His features reflected her own fears.

In short order, they had the man stripped of his coat, single boot, and frayed socks. The thin shirt covering his bony chest nearly pulled apart in her fingers as she tugged it over his head. The man's matted hair clung to his scalp, and the eyes nestled in sunken sockets remained closed. Matthew clutched the man's thin shoulders and began to shake him.

"Wake!"

When he didn't respond, Matthew shook the unconscious man harder. His head lolled back, revealing translucent-looking flesh under his chin.

Annabelle clutched Matthew's arm. "Stop it!"

Matthew didn't seem to hear her. He leaned close to the body and then let out a low moan, pulling the man forward against him. "He's dead! He's dead, and I have failed!"

Annabelle put her hand on Matthew's shoulder. He mumbled words she couldn't decipher, though the agony in them was clear. She closed her eyes to pray.

Suddenly, the man gave a small cough and Matthew jerked his head up, thrusting the limp man away far enough to peer at his face.

Annabelle tugged on Matthew's sleeve. "Get up!"

He stared at her dumbly.

Annabelle clenched her fingers. "We must get him dry and

warm."

As if her words broke a spell, Matthew immediately lurched into action. She left him to remove the man's pantaloons as she stepped over to the bed, wrenching the quilt free. Keeping her eyes downcast, she thrust the blanket at Matthew. In a moment, he and Peggy had the man tightly wrapped inside.

Annabelle dropped to her knees beside them and vigorously rubbed the man's arms. "We need to get his blood flowing again."

Matthew and Peggy complied, and soon the poor fellow shook with their efforts. Annabelle watched his face and prayed that their actions would be enough. Beads of sweat popped up along her hairline from the roaring flames and the quick work of her hands.

"It's not working!"

Annabelle shifted her weight so that Matthew could see around her. "Some of the color's returning to his face."

Matthew seemed satisfied with this and returned to his efforts, rubbing the man's legs while Peggy massaged his feet. Finally, the man moaned and moved his head. Breathing a sigh of relief, Annabelle sat back on her heels and studied her patient.

She'd seen him before. "George?"

Matthew nodded, his gaze locked on the rise and fall of his brother's chest.

"How?"

He cut his wild gaze over to her, as if seeing her for the first time since he'd stumbled in. "A miracle."

Suddenly remembering that she wore nothing more than her thin shift, Annabelle drew her arms over her chest. The movement caught Matthew's eye. Surprise dawned on his features, followed by the bob of his Adam's apple. He averted his eyes in the same moment she started to scramble away.

Peggy either noticed the exchange or had also just realized Annabelle's state of undress. She snatched her pallet quilt from the floor and draped it around Annabelle's shoulders in one fluid movement.

Matthew gently placed George's head on a wad of bedding.

Scrunching her bare toes back beneath her quilt, Annabelle waited for Matthew to look up at her. "What're we going to do with an escaped prisoner?"

Matthew rubbed his temples. "I'd like to say we let him recover for a few days, but that's not an option. I'll get a wagon and we can be out of Elmira by noon."

Annabelle pulled the quilt tighter around her shoulders even though she wasn't cold. "We'll go to my mother's family."

She doubted they'd be received, but what choice did they have?

George's wasted frame and gaunt features barely showed any resemblance to the brother who stood watch over him. She closed her eyes and dropped her chin. *Oh, Lord. What a miracle You have woven. Only You could have brought these things together.*

When she opened her eyes, she found Matthew studying her. She offered a tired smile he didn't return. "Tell me about this miracle."

Rather than lighting with excitement as she expected, his face hardened. "Another time. We have much to do."

Annabelle opened her mouth to retort that until the dawn arrived they'd nothing more to do than wait and allow George to warm, but Peggy gripped her elbow. Warm brown eyes spoke words her lips didn't need to. Annabelle stifled a sigh. Peggy was right. Let the poor man have a few moments.

Besides, they needed to get him dry before he took a chill. "We need to get you out of these wet clothes, lest you catch your death while trying to save your brother."

Matthew's expression darkened and she wondered if he would gladly make the exchange. Alarmed, she secured her blanket with one hand and reached out with the other to unhook Matthew's top button.

Peggy yelped. "Oh, no, Miss Belle! You'll do no such thing!"

Annabelle dropped her hand, blinking at Peggy in surprise. She had another patient to tend and they best hurry before he followed his brother's fate. Why would Peggy object to such a thing now, when they'd just finished the very same treatment on the other?

Peggy placed both hands on her hips, taking a stance that Annabelle knew all too well. "That man is right capable of taking off his own clothing. He don't need no young lady to help."

Annabelle's cheeks flushed. "Of course. I'll turn my head while you ready yourself, Captain."

Matthew chuckled.

Peggy scoffed. "There's been too much going on that ain't proper."

Annabelle looked over her shoulder to remind Peggy they were merely caring for a patient. Instead, her gaze landed on Matthew just as he pulled his shirt over his head and revealed the hardened muscles underneath.

She saw only a flash of skin before Peggy's face filled her vision and her fingers dug into Annabelle's arm. "Out with you!"

Annabelle gaped at her. "You're going to put me out wearing a blanket?"

Peggy's brows furrowed. "Better you stand in an empty hall than in here."

Without waiting for a reply, Peggy tugged her across the room and out into the much cooler air of the unheated hall. She caught just a little of Matthew's chuckle before the door clicked into place.

"Really, Peggy, that was rather unnecessary." Peggy huffed and crossed her arms over her blouse. "When did you get dressed?"

"Whilst you was makin' moon eyes at the Captain."

Annabelle balked. "I was doing no such thing!"

Peggy lifted one eyebrow.

"What?"

"Nothing, child. You just go right on denying you're smitten with that fellow."

"Peggy!"

What a ridiculous time to be having such a foolish argument. Annabelle pulled her blanket tighter, choosing to ignore Peggy's silly exaggerations.

Instead, she focused on what might lie ahead. From what she could tell from the map the innkeeper had shown her upon their arrival, her grandparents' home was no more than a good day's ride farther north. If they left early and kept the horses at a quick pace, they could get there before nightfall. But, with the time lost in securing a wagon and the slower pace George would likely require, it could take longer. Would George survive a night outside if they couldn't get there today?

Or if her grandparents turned her away?

They waited in silence for so long that Annabelle began to fear that any one of the four doors down the darkened hallway would open. She didn't need anyone finding her wrapped in a blanket.

Finally, the door swung open and Matthew appeared, dressed in his Confederate gray uniform pants and a spare undershirt. She hadn't seen him wear the gray in weeks. His damp hair fell across the top of his collar.

He ushered them inside.

"It's almost dawn. I'm going to the livery for a wagon." Matthew stepped into the hall. "Keep him warm and be ready to go as soon as I return." He cast one last look at his brother and pulled the door closed behind him.

She kneeled by George and pressed her hand to his cool forehead. He shivered now, and Annabelle hoped that marked an improvement in his condition. It at least seemed better than him lying limp. She hated that they would soon remove him from the fire and into the cold New York air. She tugged the quilt from her shoulders and draped it across him, tucking the ends beneath his body.

"Come now, child. Let's get you dressed." Annabelle complied, reaching down to lift her hem. Peggy gasped. "No! You ain't doing that right in front of a man!"

Annabelle looked at her flatly. "He's asleep. Might not even be conscious."

"Makes no difference." Peggy scooped up a damp quilt Matthew had obviously used to dry himself and ushered Annabelle toward the far corner of the room.

Annabelle eyed the bundle of shivering blankets on the floor before stepping behind the quilt Peggy held up to provide her a makeshift changing screen. She sighed as she pulled her worn garment over her head. "You know full well that man's in no condition to look at me."

Peggy merely snorted at the comment and gave a small shake to the curtain to hurry Annabelle along. Knowing it would make little difference what logical arguments she gave, she popped her head out from behind the blanket to meet Peggy's glare. "May I use the rag?"

Peggy's features scrunched as though she were annoyed with herself for not thinking of it first. Then she scowled as she realized she didn't have enough hands to both hold the blanket and fetch the rag.

Peggy tossed the quilt onto Annabelle's tousled hair.

Annabelle released a small squeak and clutched the blanket to her, feeling a bit foolish standing there with a quilt slung over her head and her bare feet sticking out from the bottom.

"The water's right cold, Miss Belle. Sorry for that."

"It's plenty warm in here."

Peggy handed Annabelle the damp rag, then repositioned the curtain. Annabelle made quick work of wiping down and then pulled on her single petticoat before she reached for the frayed pink skirt hanging over the footboard.

A sudden memory, brought on by the skirt's shortened hem, flashed through her mind. She'd had to rip it free to use as a ribbon to secure her hair after escaping from Matthew that day in the woods—a time that felt like months, rather than mere weeks, ago. The bottom of her petticoat had been sacrificed to cool the fevered brow of Lieutenant Monroe, now gone from this world.

"I think you should wear the gown instead," Peggy said, breaking into her thoughts.

Annabelle peeked around the curtain. "Why?"

"You're going to your momma's homeplace."

Annabelle chewed her bottom lip. "I just hate to travel in my only good dress."

"You're gonna be in a wagon this time."

True. "Drop that quilt and help me tie my strings."

Peggy spread the quilt out to dry on a clear spot on the floor before tying Annabelle's stays and helping her pull on the blue gown's fitted bodice.

Peggy secured the loops over the buttons on the back. "There now. You look more like a proper lady."

In a few moments, her tangled locks were combed and secured, and she and Peggy gathered their belongings and stuffed them into Father's carpetbag.

By the time the sun painted the sky with light, they were ready.

Matthew returned soon after with a wagon and a few provisions he'd used the last of his money to secure. Annabelle refused to dwell on what would happen if her Northern kin turned them away. They didn't have enough supplies to take them anywhere else.

They stepped out of the room to allow Matthew to dress George.

Annabelle pulled back the curtain on the window at the end of the hall. The day had dawned clear and bright, the merry glow of the sun in stark contrast to the clouds hanging over her thoughts. She searched the citizens below, studying each one who crossed into her vision. Did any of them hurry to the law with news of a prison break?

How had Matthew gotten him out? And alone in the middle of the night, no less?

Footsteps sounded on the stairs, and the rounded form of the innkeeper's wife came into view. The woman's gaze slid over Peggy and landed on Annabelle. Annabelle's pulse quickened, and she chided herself. This woman had no way of knowing they shielded an escaped prisoner only a few feet away.

The woman smiled cheerfully. "Morning, miss. My husband says you'll be resuming your journey today."

Annabelle nodded. Matthew must have already spoken to the innkeeper as well.

The woman tucked a strand of gray hair under her white cap. "I'm going to gather the linens. Got others needing the room."

Annabelle moved quickly to block her path. "Oh, not just yet. My…um…Mr. Daniels is still changing."

The woman's eyes tightened with the sting of disapproval, and Annabelle desperately wanted to explain that their sharing a room was not inappropriate.

"Very well." The woman sniffed and her gaze roamed down Annabelle like she was something distasteful.

Peggy spoke up, surprising them both. "Sure has been kind of her cousin to help Miss Smith here reach her kin, seein' as she done lost both of her parents now."

The woman blinked at Peggy, though Annabelle didn't know if she was caught off guard by Peggy's words or the mere fact that she'd spoken. Peggy never spoke to white people she didn't know unless they addressed her directly.

"Oh. Yes, well," she said, eyeing Annabelle again. "How

kind of your *cousin.* I'm sorry for your loss, miss."

She hurried back down the stairs, leaving the two of them in the hall. Annabelle crossed her arms. "You know she didn't believe you, don't you?"

Peggy shrugged.

"I thank you for your intent, but you needn't lie."

Peggy placed her hands on her hips. "I didn't like the way she was lookin' at you."

"Neither did I, but what difference does it make? We're leaving."

As if on cue, Matthew swung the door open. "I've gotten him as dry as possible. He even opened his eyes for a moment." He looked at Annabelle hopefully. "That's a good sign, isn't it?"

Annabelle put more confidence into her smile than she felt. Fevered men opened their eyes and still didn't see what was in front of them. It didn't mean much, if anything at all. "Of course it does."

Matthew didn't look convinced. "I've left the wagon out back. We just need to get him down without notice."

Annabelle didn't see how that was possible in the busy morning hours. "Perhaps we should take the bags down first, leave Peggy with them in the wagon, and then I can help you get him down with as little notice as possible."

Matthew dipped his chin in compliance, but Annabelle could tell from his expression that he did not truly believe they would go entirely unnoticed. He and Peggy hurried away with the bags while she stood guard at the door, though her patient never once stirred.

Matthew returned a few moments later. Annabelle watched as he scooped his brother up like a child and cradled him in his arms. George's head fell back across Matthew's sleeve, and his bare feet protruded from the bottom of the blankets. Matthew looked as though he were carrying a dead body in those quilts, and he would most certainly raise suspicion. She hurried ahead of them, glancing down the staircase. Seeing no one, she nodded for him to follow her down.

As they descended, the din of the dining room increased. Voices mingled with the clink of silverware scraping on plates and people laughing as they ate their eggs and pork. The smell of cured meat filled Annabelle's senses, and she had to push aside her hunger.

The patrons filling the busy dining room took their meal oblivious that two wanted spies—one a conspirator against the Union president and the other an escaped Confederate prisoner—were in their midst. Her gaze landed on the bold serving girl who had batted her eyes at Matthew. She watched the woman sway across the room, narrowing her eyes at the way the young woman flaunted herself at the men, even the ones with women and children right at the table with them.

Matthew made a sound in his throat, jarring her back to her senses. The receiving desk was blessedly empty. She motioned to Matthew and hurried that way, feeling him close on her heels. They passed the receiving desk and stepped up to the door leading into the kitchen. Annabelle held out her hand to keep it from swinging out on them and motioned for Matthew to go past her toward the door in the rear.

Matthew stepped around her and as Annabelle glanced back toward the receiving desk, she saw a young boy standing there looking at them curiously. She turned full to him, hoping her form would hide some of Matthew's movements as he tried to both secure his hold on George and unlatch the door without her aid.

She smiled sweetly at the boy, and he waved in return. The door unlatched behind her and a cool breeze tickled the back of her neck. She raised her hand and wiggled her fingers at the boy, breathing a sigh of relief as he darted back toward the dining area.

Annabelle turned and hurried out into the bright sunlight, pulling the door closed behind her. Matthew gingerly placed George in the back of a wagon that appeared it might fall apart if they hit a bump in the road.

Once Matthew had George secured, he helped Peggy and then Annabelle step up into the small space, each woman taking a place on opposite sides of George.

She barely had time to adjust her skirts around her outstretched ankles before the reins snapped and Matthew sent the wagon forward with a jerk. Annabelle grasped the wood slat at her side and steadied herself.

The wagon swayed and tugged at the spare horse tied to the rear with a length of rope. George didn't stir. His skin looked so sallow that Annabelle feared he would not make it. They turned onto the main road. The people they passed kept to the wooden sidewalks, and in a matter of moments, they would leave Elmira behind.

But how far could they go before someone discovered George was missing?

Nine

"He declared his intentions of going to New York at once to perfect matters."
John H. Surratt

At this rate, they'd never make it. Annabelle laid a comforting arm on George's shoulder. The poor man groaned each time they hit a bump in the road. Peggy gave Annabelle an encouraging smile and then settled against the back of Matthew's driving bench and closed her eyes. How could Peggy rest with all this jostling?

Clean sunshine with a few wisps of fresh white clouds dotted a pristine sky. It was cold still, the kind of cold that would have already fled Rosswood by now. But the crisp air didn't settle bone deep, and warmer weather rode in behind yesterday's storm. Poor George needed any amount of warmth he could get.

Bare trees and dead grass flowed along both sides of the road, but as soon as spring kissed the North, this land would burst into beauty. Annabelle swayed in the wagon, enjoying the simple blessing of admiring passing landscape that had not been marred by war.

The people of New York had sent scores of their men to the South and had surely seen heavy losses, but at least no one had scorched their fields or set their homes ablaze. Annabelle pushed the bitter thought aside. She shouldn't begrudge the people for having their lands left alone. At least somewhere in this divided country the women and children left behind didn't bed down each night in fear.

For the moment they were safe, George was found, and the earth was clean and fresh. A small smile tugged at her lips, and her heart whispered a prayer of thanks for such great blessings. She tilted her face to the sun for a moment and closed her eyes.

The wagon lurched and she glanced down at George. He stared up at her with clear eyes.

"You're awake!"

Matthew suddenly drew up on the reins, bringing them to a quick halt. He twisted around in the driver's seat, pulling his knees up underneath him.

George's amber eyes widened, and a grin split his face, making him appear truly alive for the first time. "Matthew?"

"Yes, brother!" Matthew's voice hitched, and Annabelle's heart swelled. "I found you!"

George squirmed, wrenching one of his arms free of the tightly wrapped quilts and thrust it toward Matthew. The men grasped one another by the forearms, and though no words were spoken, Annabelle suspected none were needed.

As the moment passed, George glanced at the two women flanking him. "Care to tell me why I'm packed tight in blankets and riding in the back of a wagon?"

Matthew let out a hearty laugh. "You tried to find your death in an icy river, but I denied you the opportunity."

George's brow wrinkled. "I remember moving men on the rafts during the flood, but nothing more. Where did you come from?"

Matthew spat over the side of the wagon. "I've been in Elmira for a couple of days looking for you from that loathsome platform. The flood gave me a chance to steal you away."

George struggled to sit up. Annabelle placed a staying hand on his shoulder, giving a slight shake of her head. George settled flat on his back and stared at the face of his brother hanging over him. "Tell me this is one of your jests."

Matthew's features turned thunderous. "Why would I jest with your life?"

George drew a long breath, coughing a little as it exited his lungs, then gave a small shake of his head. "Your loyalty and courage knows no bounds, but you acted rashly."

Matthew scowled. "If I left you on that bank, they'd be burying you this very moment."

George blanched. "Perhaps you're right. I don't know if they really would have given me the papers, anyway."

Matthew tensed. "What papers?"

"The allegiance papers I signed. They were in process to release me."

Matthew glanced at Annabelle, his expression slightly incredulous, as if he had never really believed such papers existed. "You signed loyalty to the *North*?"

Instead of anger, sympathy dawned in George's eyes. "I was offered my life, my freedom, and a chance to return to Westerly and run it in peace. So, yes, I did what I thought needed to be done." His voice took on more strength as he spoke, and determination entered his steady gaze.

Matthew's chuckle surprised her, but apparently not his brother. "Always the responsible one, you are. You'd give your own hide to the tanner if you thought it *needed to be done.*"

George grinned. "One of us has to be responsible, you know. Else we'd probably both have been worm food long ago."

Matthew tilted his head in Annabelle's direction. "George, forgive my lack of manners. May I introduce Miss Annabelle Ross of Rosswood Plantation."

"A pleasure, Miss Ross. I do hope you'll forgive my current condition. It's hardly an acceptable way to greet a lady."

Annabelle almost laughed. Why would he apologize for a condition he most surely could not help? The embarrassment tightening the lines around his mouth gave her pause. She offered a reassuring smile. "I'm pleased to meet you, Mr. Daniels. Don't worry. You'll very soon be robust with health once more."

Tension dropped from him like a discarded coat. "Thank you, miss."

She patted his shoulder, discreetly tucking the quilt tightly around him to seal in the warmth. "And this is Peggy."

Peggy sat with her eyes downcast. George simply nodded.

Matthew cleared his throat. "We best keep moving. If I keep at a good pace, we might make it there by dark."

Apprehension squirmed in her gut, but Annabelle managed to keep it from her face. Matthew turned back in his seat and popped the reins, bringing the two horses into a brisk walk. The rope tightened and tugged at the gelding in the rear, pulling his head up from his vain search of the roadbed for a bit of grass to eat. The scraggly gelding had been Peggy's mount, and the two seemed about as fond of one another as two old hens trying to share a nest. He nipped at her and she swatted at him. Both the horse and Peggy seemed glad to be free of one another for the time being.

They swayed into motion again, and Annabelle could feel George's eyes on her face. She looked down at him and smiled. With his wild beard and gaunt cheeks, he hardly looked anything like Matthew, save his piercing eyes.

"I saw you at the major's door, didn't I?"

She nodded.

"Why were you there? They never allow women inside."

Annabelle lifted her shoulders. "I insisted."

George opened his mouth to speak but Matthew's voice came first. "It's a long tale, brother. One I'll recount in front of a hot fire after we've filled our bellies. For now, you need rest."

George looked at Annabelle and then glanced to the sky, shaking his head. Annabelle covered her mouth to smother a laugh. She already liked George. The thought unsettled her.

Better to follow Matthew's lead and put off such things for now. Telling too much of how she'd discovered his location would lead to a multitude of questions she did not want to face here on the road.

The next time she glanced down at George, he slept.

The afternoon passed quickly, and the miles remaining between Annabelle and her mother's family shortened. When they pulled into a small town where Matthew stopped to water the horses, the sun touched the tops of the trees.

Matthew dismounted the wagon and took the horses by the leads. He led them to a watering trough near the hitching posts in front of the postal station. Annabelle stretched her arms over her head, and watched the people on the street.

That's when she saw him.

Annabelle gasped. She struggled forward and put a knee into George, who groaned under her weight. She looked down at him and shifted, her gaze immediately returning to where she had seen the man on the road, but he was gone. Annabelle narrowed her eyes, scanning the faces of the few people entering storefronts, but none of them looked familiar.

Matthew grasped her arm from over the side of the wagon. "What's wrong?"

Annabelle swallowed the lump gathering in her throat. Surely she had just imagined it. Why would *he* be all the way up here? Any answer she could think of was not a pleasing one, and she did not want to cause Matthew any undo worry. "Nothing. I just…thought I saw something."

His features tightened. "Saw what?"

She removed her arm from his grasp, trying to brush away his concern. "I merely saw a man who resembled someone I know, that's all."

Instead of easing his tension, her words only seemed to stoke it. Matthew scanned the town, his face hard.

"It is nothing, Matthew," she said low. "Let's not worry your brother over my silly imagination."

Matthew glanced at George, then narrowed his eyes. "If you *do* see someone you know," he said, his tone thick with meaning, "tell me immediately."

She nodded, giving him a smile she hoped conveyed unconcern. Matthew didn't look any more convinced by it than she felt, so she let it slide from her lips.

"You women stretch your legs and see to any personal

business quickly," Matthew ordered. "I'll ask directions to the Smith house."

Annabelle scrambled down from the wagon, her muscles protesting. From the one visit she'd made as a child, she remembered the Smith lands were nestled along the banks of a grand lake just outside Watkins Glen.

Peggy and Annabelle went to see to their personal needs quickly. Annabelle's movements proved shaky and her eyes constantly probed any shadow untouched by the late afternoon light. As much as she wished otherwise, Annabelle knew she hadn't imagined anything.

Harry was following them.

Ten

"Booth left today for New York."
John H. Surratt

By the time they reached the road to the Smith house, the sun had already fallen below the trees and the shadows had lengthened. The pleasant cool of the day began to dissipate, soon to be replaced by the deep chill of night. Annabelle shivered, hoping they wouldn't spend the night outside.

"This the right place?" Matthew asked over his shoulder.

Annabelle twisted around to see her Northern kin's home. Vague memories strained to reach the surface of her jumbled thoughts. She'd only seen it once as a child, but she was fairly certain this was the massive house she remembered. "I believe so."

Matthew let out a low whistle. "Looks like your Yankee kin do well."

Far larger than her home at Rosswood, the great stone house boasted three floors and dozens of windows.

"Lawd, look at this here place," Peggy said as they drew near.

Where Rosswood greeted guests with large columns and

wide porches, the Smith house seemed to say that guests were not welcome to come and sit a spell. Despite its enormous size, the front of the mansion had only a small portico with a handful of skinny columns embracing the front door, with room only for a person or two to spend hot summer nights catching the breeze. The space served little more than an area for a caller to escape the rain. A low stone wall wrapped a protective arm around the front of the house.

"Bet that place has dozens of rooms," Peggy whispered. Annabelle shrugged. Perhaps. She couldn't remember.

The house itself was made of blocks much larger than the bricks they produced at Rosswood. Four of their bricks could have made one of these cut stones. Annabelle preferred the bricks made from the warm red Mississippi clay to the sad gray stones that blended into the gathering dusk.

Smoke drifted lazily from some of the chimneys. Warm lamplight bathed two of the four lower windows on the front of the house, and numerous worked iron lampposts flickered along the drive. Obviously someone resided within, but no one exited the house or came around from the side to offer to take the horses to stable—or even to inquire about their presence this late in the day. Matthew looked at Annabelle with questions in his eyes she couldn't answer.

"Perhaps we should knock on the door."

Matthew jumped down from the driver's seat and tied the horses to a hitching post by a small gate in the low stone wall. Annabelle scrambled down and tried to shake some of the wrinkles out of her skirt.

"Stay here with George and make sure he behaves," she whispered to Peggy. George huffed, having heard her. He must have awakened when she got down from the wagon.

"You go on, Miss Belle. I got him," Peggy said.

Matthew extended his arm and together they climbed the steps leading to the covered area at the front door.

Matthew knocked soundly on the door, then stepped back as far as the shallow stoop would allow. Annabelle pulled her hand from the crook of his arm and straightened her dress. Thank goodness she hadn't shown up here in her tattered skirt and blouse.

They waited for several moments, but no one came to the door. Matthew looked at Annabelle in confusion.

"Perhaps they didn't hear."

Matthew stepped back up to the door and pounded loudly. Annabelle cringed and hoped the occupants would not take the rattling of their front door as an offense. After a few moments, however, they finally heard a lock sliding from place and the heavy wooden door opened slightly, revealing the face of a young woman near Annabelle's age.

She had skin the smooth color of copper. Her ebony hair was pulled tightly away from her face, but even the severity of her hairstyle did not detract from her seemingly effortless beauty.

The woman eyed Annabelle and Matthew suspiciously with deep brown eyes. "Yes?"

Matthew took a step forward and the woman recoiled. Annabelle placed a hand on Matthew's arm and he stepped back, giving Annabelle room to come forward. The woman seemed to relax a bit, but did not further widen the opening. She eyed Annabelle through the cracked door.

"I'm Annabelle Ross. My mother's family resides here, and

we have come to seek lodging with kin. We have a man traveling with us who's in great need of a warm room and a place to recover from—"

A woman's voice barked out from behind the door. "No sick are welcome here!"

Annabelle startled. "He's not sick," she said to the unseen voice. "He's merely suffering from the lingering cold caused by falling into a winter river. Well, that, and a severe lack of nourishment."

There was a pause, and the young woman at the door glanced at whoever had spoken behind her. After a moment, she stepped back from the door. It swung wide and the doorway filled with the rigid figure of an elderly woman. With a stiff spine, angled features, and a stern cast to her face, she looked the very image of the crone her father had warned Annabelle about. Annabelle swallowed hard, trying to find the moisture that had disappeared from her mouth.

The moment the woman's steely gaze landed on Annabelle, her eyes widened in surprise. "Katherine!"

Annabelle hadn't heard her mother's name spoken aloud in quite some time, and the sound of it even now warmed a forgotten place in her heart. She shook her head sadly. "I'm her daughter, Annabelle."

The old woman stared at her long enough that Annabelle grew uncomfortable. Then she shook her head, sending gray curls bouncing. "You look ever so much like your mother when she was young."

Annabelle dipped her chin at the compliment. "Thank you, Grandmother."

The woman's lips turned up slightly. "And what brings my

only grandchild this far to see me? Has your father finally loosened the reins enough to let you slip from his sight?"

Father had always said her grandparents chose not to have anything to do with their family, but her grandmother seemed to imply the opposite. "My father died in battle several months ago."

Her stern features softened, if only slightly. "I'm sorry to hear it, child." She looked at Matthew. "Your husband, I take it?"

"No, he, um, is…" She stumbled for the right words, thankful when Matthew stepped forward and bowed to save her the embarrassment of answering.

"I'm Matthew Daniels. My brother is betrothed to Miss Ross, and is the chilled man in great need of a warm bed."

Annabelle inwardly groaned. She should have answered herself.

Her grandmother pointed a long finger at Matthew. "I'll not have sick men in my home, regardless of their spoken ties to my family. I'll have to see him for myself to be sure he isn't eaten up with fever."

Matthew gestured behind them. "Certainly, ma'am. He's in the wagon."

Eudora pulled her evening wrapper tightly around her thin frame and stepped out into the cold. She walked with purpose, and Matthew and Annabelle trailed her down the front walkway and over to the side of the wagon.

She was a small woman, several inches shorter than Annabelle, and she had to lift herself up on her toes to look over the side of the wagon at George.

"What is your name, boy?"

George shifted in his blankets, trying to get up. He finally managed to get himself untangled and sat upright to regard the woman narrowing her eyes at him. The purple tint in the sky gave a deep glow to the final moments of the day. Thankfully, the hue made George's face appear a bit less pale.

"George Daniels, ma'am," he said, unfazed by her scrutiny. "Please forgive my condition and my inability to greet you properly."

Eudora sniffed and turned her attention to Annabelle. "He seems coherent, at least, and his eyes are clear. Scrawny thing, though. You'd have fared better with the stout one."

Poor George looked confused.

Annabelle fumbled for an answer, but she turned back to George. "I'm Eudora Smith. Mr. Daniels, please tell me what ails you." She pointed a finger at him. "And don't try to deceive me, young man."

He gave a curt nod. "I was a Confederate soldier, taken prisoner by the Union Army back in early February." Eudora stiffened and Annabelle inwardly groaned. Why couldn't he have left that part out? "Prison conditions were poor, and I lost a lot of weight during my time there, but I don't suffer from any sickness."

"And how did you end up here?"

George looked at Matthew before answering. "A great storm came, and the river flooded. There were too many prisoners for everyone to be inside the walls, and I was one of the groups camped along the riverbanks on the north side of the pond."

Eudora gave an unladylike snort. "Elmira. They filled that disgusting place beyond its capacity." She turned up her nose.

"During that flood, I helped move the pox patients from the flatlands across the water. I was able to save some, but I became chilled too deeply from the cold." He dropped his chin as though sorely ashamed. "I only meant to rest for a few moments, but my brother found me there sometime later, too cold to think properly. I would have died if he hadn't saved me."

Eudora lifted haughty eyebrows. "You've touched men with the pox."

George met her challenging gaze. "So they wouldn't drown." He said it as if daring her to shun him.

Annabelle guessed she likely would. She'd made her fear of sickness evident, and little was worse than the pox. It could wipe out whole families. She'd even heard that it had taken entire towns. Exaggerations, likely, but frightful nonetheless.

Instead of asking more about the pox, Eudora focused on the other thing that would surely condemn them. "You're an escaped prisoner, looking to hide behind my walls and label me a traitor."

Matthew stiffened at Annabelle's side, but thankfully kept his comments to himself. Annabelle stared at her grandmother's profile. She'd never met a woman quite so blunt. Eudora seemed far removed from Annabelle's soft-spoken mother.

"No, not entirely," George answered.

"You only half-escaped, then?"

George remained passive. "I left without permission, though I was in no condition to ask it. However, on the day prior, I'd already met with Union officials and signed an oath of allegiance to the North. My papers were in processing, and they would have soon released me."

Eudora's stiff shoulders relaxed, but her words were still clipped when she turned and fired them at Annabelle. "You've stolen this man from prison prior to his proper release—a man who has touched the pox, no less—and have brought him, another man, and apparently your slave here to me to beg resources?"

Annabelle refused to cringe. Father had been right. The Smiths were a harsh, unfeeling people with little care for others. She straightened herself. "Yes, Grandmother. That's mostly the truth of it."

The older woman stared at her for a moment, and then smirked. "You're an honest lot, even if you are fools. That counts for something. Come, bring yourselves inside. I tire of standing here jawing in the cold."

The breath left her in a rush. "Thank you."

Eudora looked at Matthew. "The stable is behind the house. You can stall your horses there."

"Thank you, ma'am."

The woman simply nodded and turned on her heels, leaving them to gather their things and Matthew to heft a protesting George into his arms.

"You put me down this instant, little brother, or you'll see my fist!"

Matthew chuckled. "Even at full strength, you never could land a blow to drop me. It'd be like a woman's kiss now."

George growled. "You've already unmanned me enough by leaving me wrapped in blankets like a suckling babe!"

Matthew sobered and placed George on his feet. "Without a dry overcoat, and only one boot, we thought it better to keep you beneath any warmth we could give."

"And my trousers?" George said in a harsh whisper.

Matthew shrugged. "Mine wouldn't stay around your waist, so I left them off. Didn't figure you'd need them until you awoke."

George's face reddened. Annabelle glanced at Peggy. Peggy lifted her brows, and the two of them hefted the traveling bags and started for the door while the men argued.

Behind her, George groaned. "Fine. I'll accept that. But I will *not* accept being toted like a babe into the house when my own legs will carry me."

A few seconds later their footsteps sounded behind her. At the front stoop, the young woman who'd first opened the door now held it wide, allowing Annabelle and Peggy entrance. She kept her eyes on the floor as they passed. Annabelle placed Father's bag on the floor and waited as Peggy deposited her load just inside the wide entryway. Overhead, a chandelier dangling with crystals caught the light and sent sparkling dots dancing all over the walls. Annabelle had seen this trick of light with her mother's diamond, but had never seen it happen on such a large scale before.

Matthew came to the door first, but paused. He gestured for George to enter ahead of him. George stepped into the house with a shuffling gait, his legs hindered by the blanket wrapped around him. Annabelle scowled at his socked feet. Pride or no, walking like that was tempting the death they were trying to stave off.

Once the others were inside, Matthew dropped his pack roll and hurried out to get the horses stalled before the last of the light faded. If the young woman at the door was surprised at the man wrapped in bedclothes, she gave no indication.

Eudora, however, scowled. “Foolish man! You’ll catch your death walking on those stones without shoes.”

George looked at the floor. “Yes, ma’am.”

He endured Eudora’s scrutiny for several moments. Had the woman already changed her mind? Or perhaps she planned to contact local lawmen. Annabelle tried to suppress such thoughts, but failed.

Matthew tapped on the front door. The pretty young woman immediately swung it open to let him inside. He must have simply unhitched the horses and stalled them, leaving them for further care until tomorrow. For once, Matthew didn’t spend time checking the horses’ legs and brushing them down.

Eudora clapped her hands as soon as Matthew stepped through the door. “Now that you’re all inside,” she said as the young woman slid a firm bolt into place on the door, “we can see you settled. Lilly Rose, show the men the guest quarters so they can get the scrawny one properly dressed. I need to speak with my granddaughter.”

The young woman Eudora called Lilly lifted her hem to climb the wide staircase at the rear of the entry. Matthew scooped up everything but Father’s bag, which contained Annabelle’s and Peggy’s personal things, and the men followed along behind her.

When they reached the top of the stairs, Eudora turned and let her gaze fall on Peggy. “I don’t accept slaves in my house.”

Annabelle bristled. She was tired of Peggy being treated so poorly. When the slaves of Rosswood had run, Peggy proved her love once again and had stayed at Annabelle’s side. She didn’t know what would have become of her without Peggy’s gentle guidance and steady strength. She didn’t care if Eudora was the only help available, she would no longer tolerate ill treatment of Peggy.

"I will not have her cast out." Annabelle straightened her spine and ignored Peggy's quick intake of breath. "She deserves to be treated with the respect due any human formed from God's own breath."

Eudora looked positively shocked.

Peggy opened her mouth to protest. Annabelle held up a hand. "No, Peggy. This has happened enough. Each place we go, they sneer at you, disregard you, and tell you to go to the kitchen. I've had enough, and I'll stand for it no more." She turned flashing eyes back on her grandmother, too fired with frustration to care about the consequences of her words. "If you put Peggy out, I will go with her."

To Annabelle's utter amazement, her grandmother's face split into a wide grin. "Well, look here, a little abolitionist of my own, right up from the bowels of the South. Imagine that."

Peggy's jaw hung limp, and it was several seconds before she regained enough composure to snap it closed.

Annabelle was dumbfounded. "What?"

Eudora's features softened. "When I said I would not have a *slave* in my house, I didn't mean that I wanted you to put the woman out. I don't tolerate one human owning another under my own roof. All people get treated the same here." She smirked. "Whether they like it or not."

"Oh," Annabelle squeaked out. "I'm sorry."

Eudora laughed, a genuine sound that came from deep in her chest. "Don't be, child. I'm beyond pleased to see you feel as I do." She turned to Peggy. "Do you wish to stay with Annabelle, or have a room of your own?"

Peggy blinked at the other woman, then shrugged. "I'm happy as long as I'm close to her."

"Very well. Let's get you two into your rooms to get unpacked and then I'll have Lilly find you all something to eat."

Without another word, she turned to go up the stairs, leaving Annabelle and Peggy to follow along behind her in awed silence.

Eleven

"We agreed on a first rate cipher to send by telegraph,
so that we might know what each other was doing,
without letting anyone else into the secret."
John H. Surratt

George readjusted the blankets that kept tumbling down around him like a woman's dress. How could ladies walk with so much fabric entangling their legs? He clenched his teeth, caught somewhere between humiliation over his condition and pure joy that both he and his brother had lived long enough to find themselves reunited.

Though he certainly had a mountain of questions for his little brother, including why they were deep in Union territory and why Matthew had apparently deserted the Confederacy. He didn't want to believe that his brother had run, but he could find little other explanation for Matthew's plain clothes and unfettered travel.

They slowly ascended the staircase, and he fought off his annoyance with Matthew's constant gaze by flashing him a grin. Despite the cursed weakness in his limbs, he felt more alive at this moment than he had in weeks.

Lilly paused at the landing to retrieve a lantern. When she touched flame to wick, light glowed warmly around them, revealing that the hallway that extended in both directions ran a great length and likely opened onto several rooms.

She turned toward the hall on the right, and the hem of her dress slid across the carpeting as she stepped away. He hurried to be the first one behind her, digging his toes into the softness. The thick, ornate rug squished under his socks, giving his calloused feet more cushion than he'd felt in a long time. Better still, the wide carpeting was a welcome reprieve from the cold stone floors below. He would never admit it to Matthew, but his frozen toes almost made him regret his insistence to walk on his own.

Lilly held up the light, and George let his eyes drift up from the hem of her deep, almost golden yellow gown to the large black bow tied neatly around her trim waist. What would her hair look like if she allowed it to fall from its pins? He drew up short. What was he doing?

She dressed too finely for a maid. George found it odd that this lady took orders from the old woman like a servant. But then, the elderly woman had a tongue like a dagger, and everyone likely jumped at her command. Lilly paused to hang the lantern on a hook midway down the hall, then swished away again without even turning to look at them.

George and Matthew followed her down the hallway until Lilly stopped to open the last door at the end and retrieved another lantern from just within. She produced a match from a hidden pocket of her gathered skirt and turned up the wick, bathing her face in warm light. Her skin had a deep glow to it, so different from the ivory skin of the ladies George was used to.

She inclined her head toward the room, and George had to pull his gaze up from the long curve of her slender neck. When he met her eyes, the pull of her delicate brows put her displeasure on display. Had he offended her?

Lilly gestured toward the room. "One of you gentlemen can take this room, and the other one take the room directly across the hall. I'll come get you when we have something warmed for you to eat." She leveled her focus on Matthew. "I trust you can tend the hearth in both rooms?" At his nod, she continued. "They've not been used in quite some time, but there should be wood enough at least for tonight."

"Yes, miss. Thank you." Matthew said.

Without sparing either of them another glance, she placed the lamp on a small table just inside the door and slipped from the room. George watched her go, the gentle sway of her movements nearly hypnotic. He glanced back at Matthew and found him scowling. "What?"

"You shouldn't look at her that way."

George gaped at him. "Since when is my brother offended by admiring beauty? I wasn't looking at her in any way indecent." Though even as he said it, he could feel heat crawling up his neck.

Matthew pushed his bulk past George. "So you say." He scoffed. "I'll get your fire going while you get out of that dress."

George balked. As Matthew stomped past him, George let the blanket fall from his shoulders as he swung a half-hearted punch at Matthew's arm. The younger man laughed and sidestepped before George's blow could find meat, and George stumbled off balance. Matthew's fingers clamped down on his shoulder and righted him before he could fall. He looked up into Matthew's eyes and relished the humor he saw there, any frustration he had felt at Matthew's comments melting away.

But Matthew's humor suddenly dissipated, replaced by the serious glare he'd seen too often since they had joined the war. Matthew stared down at him, a good five inches taller than George, even though George was the elder. He gave George's shoulder a tight squeeze. "You're nothing but skin stretched over bone."

George shrugged and moved out of Matthew's grasp. He closed the door before someone came down the hall and found him standing around in his drawers. "It's nothing a few good meals won't fix." He forced more levity into his tone than he really felt. Prison had been hard, in more ways than just the gnawing hunger, but he wouldn't add to his brother's worry.

Matthew responded with a sad smile and plodded across the room to the hearth. In a few moments he had a fire blazing. George pushed aside his weariness in the same manner he had learned to push away his hunger and stretched his hands toward the growing flames. George suppressed a shiver.

"Right nice place here," George said, turning away from the flames and untying Matthew's pack. He fished around until he found his threadbare pants. He hated to put on rags in the company of such fine folks, but he had little option. At least the rain had cleansed most of the smell.

He pulled on his trousers and took in the tall four-poster bed, complete with curtains that could be used to surround the mattress and keep in the warmth—or foil summer insects seeking to feast on the flesh. He ran his fingers over the soft material of the blankets covering what he guessed would be a feather mattress and swallowed down his guilt. His brothers in arms would be spending another night in freezing temperatures sleeping on the hard, damp ground and hoping they didn't wake up to blackened toes.

"I couldn't get them all out," Matthew said at his back, as if reading George's very thoughts.

George nodded and stepped past Matthew to warm himself by the crackling fire again. Even the sounds of popping wood and the faint scent of smoke was a luxury he'd nearly forgotten. "I'm amazed you found me."

Matthew took a place next to him, both keeping their backs to the fire. "That's something we can thank Miss Ross for. She discovered which prison they'd taken you to."

"Would this be the daughter of Elliot Ross, the man our father wanted to partner with in brick-making?"

"It is."

George turned his head to look at his brother's profile, which seemed oddly tense. "And why is she with you?"

Matthew remained silent a moment before appearing resigned. "Her grandfather tried to force her to marry her uncle." George's eyes widened at the atrocity, but before he could make comment, Matthew continued. "An uncle by marriage only, and not by blood. Andrew, I believe. But even still, this *grandfather* by marriage sought the union only to be sure his son would take over the plantation and rob Miss Ross—or her father's blood brother, if she did not marry—of their family lands."

"I see. A difficult situation for her, I'm sure." *Though not an uncommon one.* "Even so, this still doesn't explain her traveling with you, or why you and I are here with her Yankee kin. I find all of this rather strange, and more than a little confusing."

Matthew chuckled, but it seemed more rueful than amused. "I fear it'll only become more so as the tale unfolds."

George waited. Matthew would speak when he was ready.

Matthew prodded at flames that didn't need tending before finally gathering his thoughts. "Her grandfather struck her, so I took her under my protection and removed her from Rosswood."

George nodded. He would have done the same. "But how did you even discover such a thing? Were you on furlough?" He felt like a miner trying to extract information like ore from a vein.

"Not exactly." Matthew rubbed the back of his neck.

"What aren't you telling me?"

Matthew sighed, then a flood of slippery words tumbled from his mouth. "I was on perimeter duty when this girl showed up with a bad countersign and then got taken in. O'Malley had promised me he had a way I could get you back, and he thought the girl was a member of their secret group. I had to get her out. Then we were on the run, because Lieutenant Colonel Hood thought she was a spy and they would have strung me up for releasing her. But, then she got away from me. I thought she was Miss Smith, you see, but the shopkeeper said she was Miss Ross, and I had to find out. So when I went to Rosswood and heard the old man strike her, I decided I had to take her with me to Washington so that—"

George held up his hand, bringing Matthew to a halt. "Wait. Miss Ross, who you thought was Miss Smith, came to the perimeter while you were on duty there?"

"Yes, because I got shot in the calf and couldn't do much else."

"And then she was taken in as a spy?" George ran his hand through his hair, wondering if he would ever get this web untangled. He turned and placed his hands toward the flame, relishing the warmth that radiated from the hearth. He tried to get his mind to concentrate on his brother's highly confusing words.

"Yes, because she had some kind of coded message."

George cocked his head. "So she truly *was* a spy?"

Matthew's jaw muscles clenched in that way they always did when his brother became vexed. "No!" He drew a long breath. "I'm sorry."

George simply shrugged.

"She was given the note by a soldier who'd been under her care before he died. We suspect he was the real spy. She only delivered it because she was hoping to use the army to get a message to her blood uncle. She didn't have any idea what she carried. The spy used her."

George tried to digest the tale, though it sounded more like a fable. "What did you say made you decide to release a suspected spy from custody?"

"O'Malley," Matthew spat the man's name like a curse. "He had all these *contacts,* and he said that they would be able to help me find you and get you back."

George nodded. "As you said." Though he still couldn't picture O'Malley as anything more than a common soldier.

"They thought they could leverage the Union to reopen the prisoner exchange."

The tale became more outlandish the longer Matthew spoke. He eyed his brother. "Are you speaking true, or is this one of your jests where you'll make me a fool in the end?"

When they were young, his brother had always exaggerated his tales with the ladies or had come up with wild stories to gain everyone's ear. George had often been the only one to believe him. It had taken years to realize the boy only sought the attention he was often denied.

Matthew shook his head vigorously, and his eyes begged George to believe him. "I swear it on my life."

Seeing the earnestness on his face, George nodded. "What kind of plan could they possibly have that would carry such weight?"

"They were going to abduct Lincoln, and hold him ransom in Richmond."

The words lingered in the room for a moment. George searched his brother's eyes for signs of the coming laughter at his gullibility. He found only sincerity there, and that disturbed him greater still. "Surely you cannot be serious."

"I once thought the same, but it's true. There is a group of them. I don't know how many, but they have a long reach. They do, indeed, have contacts deep into the Union and had plotted out a detailed plan. That's why I went to Washington. O'Malley promised me that if I helped him take Lincoln, he would make sure you were the first prisoner released with the ransom."

George clapped his hand on Matthew's shoulder and gave it a squeeze. "You risked much for me."

"You and I are all that remains of our family, and it's my fault you were taken. I would have done anything in my power to keep you alive."

George turned to stare at the flames, tearing his gaze away from the mixture of guilt and determination in his brother's eyes. "Don't blame yourself. It was my choice. The Yanks were too thick, and we wouldn't have escaped. Better one of us remained than our name die out with our spilled blood."

They were silent a few moments and George processed the things Matthew had said, suddenly realizing something important. "But the plan surely failed. Otherwise the war would have shifted, and I would've heard the news. I don't think even a Confederate prison would be secluded from something as monumental as a presidential abduction."

"It did fail. But only because of Annabelle." Matthew barked a laugh.

"What?"

"The entire thing was unraveled by one tiny woman. She found a way to warn Lincoln's driver, and the carriage that appeared on the route we guarded turned out to be empty."

George let out a low whistle.

"That's why we are all here and I didn't come looking for you alone. I knew if O'Malley found out what she'd done, she'd be in grave danger. He's…not as stable as I once thought. I had to get her to safety. Even before I could come for you." The guilt in Matthew's voice once again pulled at him, and he patted his brother's arm in a futile attempt at comfort.

"That's why we left Washington," Matthew continued. "I was going to deliver her here, to her only living kin other than her blood uncle she can't find. But, before we had even made it from the edges of the city, she said she'd gone to the war offices in Washington and discovered you were being held at Elmira." Matthew's tone turned near wistful, and George didn't miss the tenderness lacing his voice as he spoke of Miss Ross.

"My, brother, you do have a tale, indeed. So here we stand—a deserter and an escaped prisoner—at the mercy of a sly young woman and her family of Yankees."

The chuckle he expected from Matthew didn't come. Instead, his brother shoved his hands into his pockets and turned to stare into the flames. "This family of Yanks could soon enough be tied to our own."

So Matthew did care for the Ross girl! He'd guessed as much, though his brother usually only chased kisses and good times. The fact that he hinted at marriage was a good thing. He reached out and punched Matthew's shoulder, giving him a wink. "Does it now?"

Matthew kept his eyes on the flames, ignoring the comment. "Do you remember how Elliot Ross had declared that Rosswood would go to his daughter and her husband upon Miss Ross's wedding?"

George nodded. "Ah, yes." It had been just prior to the war, and Father was looking to position himself to take over the Ross lands and the wealth of bricks they produced.

"I told Annabelle that you'd marry her and save her plantation from being stolen," Matthew blurted.

George could only stare at him for several moments before his tongue found its ability to form words again. "I beg your pardon?"

Matthew stiffened his spine. "It was done in the heat of the moment, when I was trying to find a way to get her away from that sniveling excuse for a man who was her only available male relative."

"So you promised *me*?" George frowned. "Wait." He clicked his tongue. Matthew paled, and George stuck a finger in his wide chest. "*You* were the one who was supposed to marry that girl and take over the brick-making!"

Matthew rubbed the place where George had poked him, looking sheepish rather than angry. "You'll be master of Westerly when the war is over, and you'll need a wife."

A pang shot through George's heart, and his hand unconsciously lifted to rub at it. Charlotte had been a good woman, and her gentle spirit and kind touch would have made her the perfect lady for a plantation. His father had arranged the match, and while the fondness that flowered between them was not like the burning passion he'd once hoped to find, it was a warm comfort that was pleasant to them both. Charlotte grew with child only a few months after their wedding, but the babe came too early. He'd been away on business when it happened. The doctor said it was complications with the babe that cost both his son and his wife their lives, though no one ever told him any details.

Not that it mattered. His family had been stolen from him in little less than a year, and the ache it left in return had never fully left him, not even six years later. He pulled himself from his thoughts and found Matthew watching him intently. "And what did Miss Ross have to say on the matter?"

"When I reminded her that her father had arranged for her to court a Daniels brother and decide for herself if it would be a match, she agreed."

"But not to marriage?"

Matthew rubbed the back of his neck. "We've been speaking of it as a betrothal and she has not objected to the term."

"My little brother *betrothed* me without my input? Audacious, Matthew, even for you."

The muscles in his jaw tightened again, and when Matthew spoke it was through clenched teeth. "It was the most logical move I could see at the time. Of course, if you object, it can easily be dissolved."

The young woman's predicament must be dire if she'd been willing to go to such lengths. "I'll consider it, though I'd like to discuss this with the young lady before anything proceeds further."

Matthew nodded, as if he expected such a response.

"I wonder, though," George continued, "why not pledge yourself? She's nearer your age, and you *are* the one Father planned to match."

Matthew turned away from him, stepping over to the door. "I have nothing to offer her." He pulled the door open to leave, but stopped short.

"Oh!"

George moved to look around Matthew. Lilly stood in the hall, her hand still raised to knock. She glanced between the two of them and then her features smoothed as she dropped her hand. "Mrs. Smith has asked you to come downstairs." She turned away without waiting for their reply and glided off.

Matthew looked to George, signaling that their conversation was over. George gave a slight nod and followed Matthew out into the hall, content to let the matter rest until his weary mind had time to sift through all the information. They followed Lilly down the stairs and turned left at the entryway, passing through a lavishly furnished parlor and into a dining room. Lilly pulled the pocket doors closed behind them, sealing the warmth within the occupied space.

The scent of food washed over him as soon as George stepped into the room. His shriveled stomach let out a robust growl in response.

"Come, have a seat and fill that belly before it eats you instead."

Eudora Smith sat at the head of the polished table, primly dressed in a black velvet dinner gown.

"We cannot thank you enough for your hospitality, ma'am."

She lifted her hand and waved his words away, gesturing that he take a seat. George looked to the others already seated on both sides of Mrs. Smith, surprised to see the very uncomfortable-looking colored woman sitting across from her mistress at the table.

George shrugged to himself, in no mood to worry with radical abolitionist whims. He chose the seat next to Miss Ross, who smiled at him warmly. "It's nice to see you up and moving about, Mr. Daniels. You look much improved."

"Ha!"

Every eye turned to look at Mrs. Smith. A flush of pink colored Miss Ross's cheeks.

"Forgive my candor, Mr. Daniels," Mrs. Smith said, "but you look like a wretch."

Despite himself, George grinned. "Indeed I do, ma'am. I beg your forgiveness."

Ignoring him, she looked to Lilly, who had sat down at the table between the slave woman and Matthew, directly across from George. "Lilly Rose, where did you put my husband's things?"

"They're still packed in the trunk in his room."

"In the morning, please take them to Mr. Daniels."

She dipped her chin in acknowledgment. "As you wish."

George waited patiently for the exchange to end, but the grumbling in his stomach proved he was far more interested in completing the meal than finding clothing.

Eudora clicked her tongue. "And shoes. It's a right shame to have a man at the table with nothing on his feet but a pair of holey socks."

George could only nod. There was nothing more she could say that would make his embarrassment worse.

"Lilly will see to that as well."

The younger woman made no argument.

Mrs. Smith gestured to the plates of food covering the table. "This is far from a proper dinner, but the help have all gone home for the night. We warmed what we had left. Just serve yourselves."

They passed around bowls of boiled potatoes and cabbage and then a plate stacked high with sliced ham. George was salivating before the polished silver fork even touched his lips. He chewed rigorously, trying his best to maintain some of his manners but letting too many slip as he devoured the meat. The flavors of the salted pork exploded on his tongue, flooding his mouth with pleasure.

"My late husband was quite fat, so his clothes will hang off of you, but you can cinch them up until we can get you something better."

George looked up to see Mrs. Smith watching him. He nodded his consent and shoveled potatoes into his mouth, their delicate flesh bursting easily between his teeth. How nice to actually have something to chew! He felt another pang of guilt knowing his friends would be drinking boiled bean water while he feasted like a king.

"I'm sorry to learn of Grandfather's passing," Miss Ross said at his side, thankfully turning the attention away from George.

"Thank you, dear. It's been two years now."

"I didn't know," Miss Ross said, shifting in her seat.

"How could you? It's not as though we've spoken since you were, what, six years old?" The bite in her tone made even George wince, and he felt sorry for the young woman at his side.

To George's surprise, Miss Ross kept her tone even. "I think that's correct."

The old woman sighed and sat back in her seat. George stabbed the last piece of boiled cabbage on his plate. Her keen eyes missed nothing and she pointed a long fingernail at him as soon as he placed the cabbage in his mouth. "Help yourself to another plate, boy. It'll take more than that to put some meat back on you."

George complied and gathered another helping. They finished the meal awkwardly, with Mrs. Smith breaking the silence only when she thought of a command to give Lilly or a question to pin on Miss Ross. For the most part, George could only focus on the food, but he got enough of the conversation to know that Miss Ross was not one easily cowed by a prickled tongue. *A good quality*, George thought, smiling to himself.

George sat back in his chair, his shriveled stomach stuffed until it felt nigh on bursting.

Mrs. Smith clapped her hands. "Off to bed with you all. I haven't had this much excitement in some time, and it's well past when I usually retire."

They all hurried from their seats, each expressing thanks for her hospitality. She brushed away every compliment on the food and ushered them out.

"Lilly," Mrs. Smith said, turning back after she had hurried the men through the door. "You can do that in the morning."

"No, ma'am. I'd rather I did it now," the soft voice said.

The other two women offered their assistance and Mrs. Smith pulled the doors closed on the sounds of them clearing the table. Then she gestured for the men to follow her upstairs. The woman moved with the ease of one half her age.

"Good night, gentlemen." Mrs. Smith paused at the top of the staircase to light a lamp.

The one Lilly had left hanging in the hall glowed warmly, beckoning George to come and find the soft comfort of his bed.

The brothers bid their hostess goodnight and Matthew walked George to his room. He stoked his fire, though the room was pleasantly warm enough already.

"Go to your bed, Matthew." George patted his brother's shoulder. "The fire is fine."

Matthew eyed him, but then nodded. "I want to be sure you don't catch your death of chill. It would be quite a waste after all I've been through to get you back."

George chuckled. "A thick quilt and a fire in the hearth are more warmth than I've known all winter."

Matthew wiped his hands on his breeches, stalling.

"I'll still be here in the morning." George laughed. "Go, find your rest. Heaven knows I need mine."

Matthew pulled George into a tight embrace. "I'll see you in the morning."

George patted his wide back and then Matthew stepped out of the room, leaving George alone with the dancing shadows. He removed his shirt, but not his trousers, and slipped under the soft blankets. He'd barely had time to relish the lushness of the mattress when his heavy lids drooped and he fell into a dreamless sleep.

Twelve

"All seems likely to go on well."
John H. Surratt

The next morning Matthew waited in the hallway as soon as the first strokes of daylight painted the sky. With nothing to do until the others emerged from their rooms, he took a moment to study the first Yankee house he'd ever entered.

The grand homes in the South always offered wide upper halls lined with furniture where the family would gather, and on blistering days they would open the doors at each end to catch the breeze. When guests would stay the night, the seating area offered them a place to wait on one another before descending to the formal areas for breakfast.

The Yankee mansion was, in many ways, the opposite. Here the halls were narrow, and save a few delicate tables topped with vases that he assumed would be overflowing with blooms come spring, there wasn't a stick of furniture to be found.

Matthew stood at the top of the stairs, uncertain. It wouldn't have been strange for him to take a seat in the hall and wait for the women in his traveling company to emerge from their rooms, had such a place been available to him.

Standing around outside Annabelle's door didn't seem proper.

Finally, he tromped down the stairs and onto the sparkling clean marble floors in the foyer. Surely Mrs. Smith had servants. She didn't seem the type to scrub these floors herself.

As if to confirm his suspicions, a colored woman bustled out of the parlor to his right and came to an abrupt stop when her eyes landed on Matthew.

"Oh!" Her hands fiddled behind her, tying a white apron around her ample middle. "I wasn't expecting the company up so soon."

"Sue, what are you—" Lilly's sentence halted as soon as she rounded the corner. "Good morning, sir."

He could see why George might admire her. Pretty, with a warm glow to her skin tone in a shade he'd never seen before. Not the striking beauty that Annabelle was, of course, but lovely in her own way. "Good morning."

"We thought you all would be tired from your travels and wouldn't rise before the dawn." Her brown eyes spoke displeasure even if her tone remained conciliatory. Before he could offer an apology, she turned her attention to the older woman at her side. "Sue, would you please see if the kettle is ready?"

The other woman nodded and scurried off. Matthew watched Lilly closely. She dressed in an expensive, well-made gown and gave orders to the help. But she also took orders from Mrs. Smith and had cleaned up after their meal last night.

"Coffee or tea, Mr. Daniels?" Lilly asked, her flat stare indicating she did not appreciate his study of her.

Matthew dropped his gaze to the cut stones on the floor. "Coffee."

"Would you prefer to wait in the parlor or the study?"

The parlor they passed through last night contained nothing but narrow furniture and a large piano. "Study, please."

"This way."

They entered a large room on the front corner of the house. The windows here stood taller than Matthew. Lilly tugged heavy curtains aside, securing them back with braided ropes finished with tasseled ends, revealing a pleasant view of the lake shimmering with the warm glow of the new day.

The wall separating the study from the foyer held bookshelves from the marble floor to the coffered ceiling. Perhaps attempting to read while he waited would distract his thoughts and keep him from mulling over the conversations he feared having.

Lilly secured the cord on the fourth window and then offered Matthew a curt nod. "Someone will be in to build the fire, and your coffee will be ready soon."

"Thank you."

She hurried from the room. He stepped over to the massive fireplace on the other wall. The intricately carved marble surround featured a pheasant hunt.

A boy of about fourteen years entered the study with an armload of wood. He gave Matthew a grin. "Morning, mister."

"Good morning."

The boy scurried to the hearth and stacked the wood.

"What's your name?"

The youth plucked a match from the canister on the hearth and struck it. "Pete."

"Are you a member of the Smith family?"

"What? Me?" He looked up at Matthew, grinning. "No, sir. My family's been working here since before I was born, though."

He had a slight accent that Matthew couldn't place. Not that he'd listened to many Yanks talk. He'd usually been left out of most of his father's business in the North. But he'd guess that this boy's family had likely come through the seaport in New York City from somewhere in Europe.

"So you live nearby?"

The boy lifted his thin eyebrows. Probably didn't usually get so many questions from Mrs. Smith's guests. "Yes, sir. Like most folks who work for the fine families."

"How many work here?"

Pete shrugged slim shoulders. "Used to be more of us before the Mister died." He made quick work of coaxing a flame to life, then rubbed his hands across the sturdy material of his pants. "Those your horses in the barn?"

Matthew clenched his hands. He should have already been out to the stable. He'd done nothing more than place them in stalls last evening, and they needed to be brushed down and checked for lameness. "Yes, and I should get to them."

"Thought so," Pete said. "My papa's done got them fed. I'll get 'em brushed down for you real nice."

Matthew paused. "Thank you, Pete."

"No thanks needed, mister. If the Missus knew I didn't take good care of any horse in her stable, she'd make me work extra to get my dime."

"Best be off to it then." Matthew grinned. "I don't want to cost a man his pay."

The boy puffed out his chest and then hurried to the door. "Nice day to you, mister," he said over his shoulder.

"To you as well," Matthew replied, but the boy was already gone.

He scanned the leather-bound spines on the bookshelf. Before he could select one, the slight tinkling of china preceded a young woman with fair hair and a warm smile. She set a silver serving tray on a low table near a leather chair by the far window.

"Here we are, sir. Brought the cream and sugar, too, since we didn't know how you take it." She spoke with the same accent as the boy, only much stronger.

"Just sugar, please." He took a seat in the leather armchair.

"Nice to see someone sit here again." She poured his coffee. "We haven't had a man here since we lost Herr Smith." She flashed green eyes at him. "You being the first guests Frau Smith's let in the house and all."

Matthew shifted uncomfortably.

She giggled. "Apologies, sir. Sometimes I still use the German terms. Means mister and missus, as you would say."

He accepted the steaming liquid from her and scooped in a hearty spoonful of sugar. Who knew when he'd get another chance for that much sweetness?

"My name's Anka." She smiled brightly, revealing a line of perfectly straight teeth from under rose-colored lips.

"Matthew Daniels."

The silver spoon clinked against the side of his cup as he stirred.

Anka stepped back and folded her hands. "I'll just leave the tray, in case your other companions come down before the breakfast is done."

"Thank you, Anka."

She dipped a small curtsy and turned to go. Before she made it to the doorway, Annabelle appeared. She glanced between Matthew and the taller woman.

Matthew rose. "Miss Ross, Anka has brought coffee. Would you care to join me?"

Annabelle offered Anka a polite smile. "Yes, thank you."

Anka dipped into another curtsy. "If you need anything, Fraulein, just send for me."

The woman slipped from the room, leaving him in awkward silence with Annabelle.

"She's German," he blurted.

So much for easing the tension. Annabelle's cool eyes roamed over the room, either avoiding him or entranced by the décor.

"Did you sleep well?" He picked up the tray and moved it over to a table by a couch so they could sit together.

Annabelle took a seat at one end of the upholstered divan and arranged her skirts before answering. "Well enough, I suppose. I haven't slept in a bed that soft in some time."

Matthew wiped slick palms down his trousers. "I'm sorry for what I've put you through."

She looked up at him sharply.

He ran a hand through his hair. "I've dragged you through battle-torn lands, made you sleep outdoors—in the winter, no less—and have countless times put you in danger. Now that we've found George, it's time I hold up my end of our arrangement and see to it that you're properly cared for."

Annabelle caught and held his gaze. "I'm fine, Matthew."

"No thanks to me." Tension coiled around his heart, threatening to flay him. "I let my blind determination and my pride put you at risk, jeopardizing everything from your reputation to your life. I hope that one day, when you're safe in a nice home with children clinging to your skirts, you'll be able to forgive me."

Annabelle shook her head and warmth flooded her icy eyes. "My own choice to show up at your camp led to trouble. And I also made the choice to get involved in O'Malley's scheme. If not for you, I'd have no hope of saving Rosswood." Her lips turned into a rueful smile. "And you kept me from being tried by the Confederate Army as a spy."

His chest tightened. Annabelle deserved better than what she'd found at his side. She deserved the kind of life war had stolen from her. He wouldn't let his own passions steal anything more. He sealed away the longing raging in his heart and forced a smile. "I have good news for the future."

She cocked her head.

"George is pleased with the arrangement. We'll leave as soon as he regains his strength." He held her gaze, hoping she could read the sincerity in his eyes. "I promise to get the two of you safely to Westerly."

Annabelle paled, but Matthew dared not hope she no longer wished to keep the arrangement with George. He'd determined to let her make her own choices, and he would not let any of his feelings muddy that choice for her.

Or perhaps, somehow, she'd forgive him for not immediately declaring he wanted the arrangement for himself, and she would see through his guise. She'd see that he'd only offered George because he thought his brother would be able to give her the home she deserved, even if she lost Rosswood.

More than that, he yearned for her to choose him instead. Not for what he could offer, but simply for him. He waited, his heart pounding rapidly.

When her pink lips finally parted, her tone held sorrow. "We agreed that I would consider courtship, not me moving to Westerly."

"Westerly is safest."

"And who will save Rosswood? Andrew has probably already claimed it by now!"

Matthew's shoulders tensed. Another of his failures. If he'd not spent weeks hauling her across the states, then she might not have lost control of her family lands. But how would he have saved George if he'd stayed at Rosswood to defeat the other man? Frustration boiled within him, and his words came out clipped. "He has no claim. George will see it regained once you're married."

Annabelle paled further, her beautiful blue eyes wide and marred with hurt. "That's it then?"

Matthew watched her closely. "Is what it?"

The color returned to her face, the pain in her eyes replaced by flashing anger. "You've found your brother and successfully handed me off, so you are free to go."

"Annabelle." He groaned.

She shot to her feet. "Spare me your apologies, Captain Daniels. I was never more than a responsibility you were eager to shed."

She turned her face from him, but not before he caught the glimmer of tears in her eyes. He rose and tried to grasp her arm, but she stepped out of his reach. The study door swung open before she could leave.

George stood in the doorway in an ill-fitting black suit, his face clouded with frustration. Frustration turned to confusion as his gaze landed on Annabelle. "Here you are, Miss Ross. I wanted to ask if you would join me after breakfast. It seems there are things we need to discuss."

Annabelle cast a cold glance over her shoulder at Matthew. Every spark of pain in her eyes, every beautifully angry line on her face cut deeply at his resolve not to cross the room, haul her into his arms, and kiss her until she knew she held his heart.

Instead, his feet remained rooted to the floor.

She straightened herself, effectively dismissing him, and turned her focus on George. "Yes, of course, Mr. Daniels."

Matthew swallowed words that longed to escape his lips and pressed them into a hard line. Annabelle cast him one final glance before she ducked out of the room and left George staring after her.

He crossed the room to Matthew, polished shoes clicking on the floor. "I'm most grateful for something decent to wear, mind you, but I had to use a strip of leather to keep these trousers around my waist. Not even one of Mr. Smith's belts fit. Without these braces,"—he gave the suspenders a pop—"I bet they would still end up around my ankles."

Matthew stared at him.

"Not even a chuckle, huh?" George cocked an eyebrow. "Everything all right?"

Matthew simply nodded, not trusting himself to words.

George looked at him doubtfully, but kept his peace. "Mind if I get some of that coffee?"

Matthew shrugged and cast another look at the door before

sitting down on the couch once more.

George filled a floral-print cup with steaming coffee, cream, and a heaping spoon of sugar, then sat back to stir it. Leaving the spoon in the cup, he tasted a sip and closed his eyes, smiling. "Oh, how I've missed good coffee."

Despite his mood, Matthew let a small smile turn up one corner of his mouth.

"Thank you, brother," George took another sip, his expression turning pensive.

"I didn't make the coffee."

"No. Thank you for coming for me."

Matthew nodded, the emotion in George's tone saying more than words. He gripped George's forearm. "Always."

They sat in silence for a few moments, and then Lilly appeared at the door. "Breakfast is ready, gentlemen." Without waiting for their response, she bustled away again.

George cocked his head toward the space Lilly vacated. "Interesting one, that lady."

"How's that?"

"Not entirely sure…yet," George put his hands on his knees and pushed up off the divan. "And a beauty like none I've ever seen," he added under his breath.

Matthew grunted. "And what are your thoughts on Miss Ross?"

George tugged on the hem of his oversized jacket. "About that. Are you sure this is the best course of action?"

"Are you changing your mind?"

"When did I say I agreed?"

Unease skittered over his skin, pricking him with needles of useless hope. "Just last night, when we first discussed it."

George lowered his brows in thought. "Did I? Forgive me, but I was so tired and hungry, I don't remember all the details of your wild tale."

"Miss Ross has gone to great lengths to help you." He unclenched his fists and flexed his fingers. "Her family's lands depend on her finding a husband to help her retrieve her home."

"You're the one who had the arrangement, not me," George said, as if Matthew needed reminding.

"That's only because you were already planning a wedding of your own. Besides, you're master of Westerly now. You'll need someone to help you run it, and you'll find no woman finer than Annabelle."

George narrowed his eyes, his gaze so intense that Matthew had to resist the urge to squirm. "Are you trying to convince me, or yourself?"

Matthew set his teeth, refusing to look away from the challenge.

Finally, George shook his head. "We best get to breakfast. The others are likely waiting on us."

Matthew followed his brother toward a meal he knew his stomach contained too many knots to receive.

George caught Matthew's arm before he stepped into the dining room. "This discussion on Miss Ross isn't finished."

Insides in turmoil, Matthew's words came out strained. "Speak with Miss Ross first, and then you and I will talk."

Satisfied, George clapped him on the shoulder. "Then let's go eat!"

Thirteen

"They are all ready to cooperate at the proper moment,
so that the plan cannot fail this time."
John H. Surratt

After breakfast Annabelle found herself alone in the parlor with George Daniels. Her grandmother had waved off George's request, insisting Annabelle didn't need a chaperone. Annabelle had tried not to be bothered by the comment. Perhaps they did things differently in New York.

She arranged her skirts and watched George as he sat in a chair across from her. Courting couples usually shared a couch. She tried to dismiss the oddity, telling herself it didn't mean anything. Besides, why should it bother her?

He seemed as uncomfortable as she felt, and he tugged at the collar of his shirt. Beard trimmed, he no longer appeared unkempt. He'd smoothed his hair back away from his face, but a few strands fell across his forehead. Two meals removed from prison and already he looked improved. Still deathly gaunt, but his eyes were bright and alert, and she glimpsed the gentleman he'd been.

He cleared his throat, startling Annabelle out of her scrutiny.

She dropped her gaze.

"I'd like to know more about you, Miss Ross, if you don't mind."

How did one answer a question like that? "There's little to tell." She fiddled with her skirt like a nervous ninny with her first beau. "I grew up on my father's plantation in the same fashion as any other young lady. When the war came, my father joined the Cause, leaving me to the care of his second wife's father. Our house served as a hospital for both North and South, thus surviving most of the destruction. When this war is finished, I hope to see it someday returned to normal."

George considered her words. "If they're letting Southern men go on loyalty papers, then I would guess the end is quite near."

Annabelle sighed. "Forgive me for saying so, for I know war has cost you much, but I hope the South will surrender and let it be finished. I don't see how they still hope to win. Supplies are scarce and the armies are wearing thin. We have suffered enough for a cause that cannot be accomplished, and we should now turn our energies to rebuilding our lives."

George stroked his beard. "Most women don't have such staunch opinions."

His tone held neither reprimand nor judgment, merely curiosity.

Annabelle folded her hands in her lap. "Perhaps they might not have, once. Much has changed. There might be more women now with a mind for things outside of child-rearing than you might think." Even as she said it, she knew the words nipped too hard. Her father would have been appalled.

To her surprise, George chuckled. "I must say I agree with

you. The South cannot win. That's why I signed the papers. There's no hope for us now. The best we can do is try to pick up the pieces and begin anew."

Annabelle blew out a breath. "Yes."

"My brother tells me your lands are in jeopardy," George said, turning the subject to the matter at hand.

If neither of the Daniels men wanted her, would she be able to keep Rosswood? Her throat constricted. Marriage meant saving her home. A business transaction, and nothing more. "My father planned to bestow Rosswood to my husband when I wed. But he died in the war. My stepmother's father is determined to wed me to his own son and control the plantation."

But was a house worth a life without love? It certainly wouldn't justify marriage to Andrew. Could she just leave it all behind? Why continue to fight a losing battle?

Eudora might let her live here, if she asked. The Smith home seemed entirely untouched by the war. She could start over.

No. She couldn't give up. It would forever haunt her if she didn't at least try her best to salvage her father's legacy. If she ran and hid, she would always bear the stain of guilt.

"I see," George said. "And this was not an agreeable match?"

Did men never think of love? Matthew's face as he'd once again rejected her and pushed her toward his brother surfaced. No, love meant less to them than the advantages marriage brought.

Annabelle leveled a cold gaze on the elder Daniels brother, trying to speak in terms a man would understand. "Andrew is not a good man. Not only do I suspect he wouldn't treat a wife gently, he's lazy and far too fond of drink. Rosswood needs a man who can run it properly, not see its assets squandered. Restoring the business will most certainly require more work than Andrew would be willing to give. The match was born out of greed and not the good of the plantation."

George's forehead creased in thought. She'd presented an argument based on a man's logic rather than a woman's emotion. Ironically, Grandfather would have been pleased. He'd been right. Her woman's feelings were of little use. If she'd pleaded wanting to marry for love, he would have looked at her with that patronizing expression she so hated.

"Which brings us to the arrangement my brother mentioned."

Annabelle ran her tongue over parched lips. "It does."

"Miss Ross." George tugged on the collar of a crisp white shirt several sizes too large. "You seem to be a rather pretty young woman with a level head. I cannot understand why a lady such as yourself would have any trouble finding a suitable husband who wouldn't mismanage her father's holdings."

Heat flamed in her cheeks. "Time is of great importance, and there are few men left in the South who aren't away with the army or dead in the ground." The bitterness in her words shocked her. But she wouldn't apologize for the truth.

George splayed his fingers over his knees. "I'm deeply grateful for your part in helping me be reunited with my brother." His eyes bore into hers. "I give you my word. Matthew and I will do whatever's needed to be sure you're not left destitute."

Relief and apprehension fought over her heart like two dogs with a bone. "So…you agree to the arrangement?"

"Something tells me that you needn't worry over it."

A vague answer bereft of any commitment. Tension unwound from the corded muscles in her neck. They'd help her, and that was all she needed. "I cannot express the depth of my gratitude."

George leaned forward and rested his elbows on his knees, closing the distance between them. "You never needed me nor this arrangement at all. Matthew's affection for you means he'd find his grave before he let you come to harm."

Annabelle tried to laugh, but it sounded forced even to her own ears. "Your brother is an honorable man and brought me under his protection when I needed it. He's kept his word to see me safe. But don't mistake his obligation for affection."

Amusement skittered over his serious features, and he reminded her of her father when he thought she'd overreacted. "I wouldn't be too certain of that."

It hurt badly enough that despite Matthew's rejection, her heart still strained toward him. She'd tried time and again to stomp the pitiful hope that he would change his mind and that the interest in his eyes would prove to be more than simple attraction. Peggy had forced him to admit he cared for her, but as the time passed without him ever saying more, she knew that Matthew did not look at her as a potential wife. Now she had to reveal his rejection to George?

She squared her shoulders. "Your brother has made it quite clear, on several occasions, that he has no interest in me."

Once the Daniels men ousted Andrew from her land, she and Peggy would be fine on their own. Her resolve hardened as she met George's steady gaze. "He doesn't want to court me, and he doesn't wish to be shackled to me. He's quite ready to be free of me as soon as possible." Annabelle rose, pieces of her crumbling heart cooling into hardened iron. "I'm very sorry he's put you in this situation. I don't expect either of you to be forced to marry me."

He rose with her, but she held up her hand and turned toward the door, making it clear she didn't wish for him to follow. "If you'll excuse me, I really must get back to Peggy."

George opened his mouth to respond, but the look on her face must have changed his mind. He offered a small bow. "As you wish. We can always discuss these things at another time."

Irritation seethed in her, but she kept her face passive. *Dense man!* Not trusting herself with words, Annabelle simply inclined her head and strode out the door.

Before she'd even had a chance to breathe freely, her grandmother appeared on the stairs.

"Ah! There you are, child."

Annabelle struggled to keep her features smooth. "Yes, ma'am?" How could Eudora know that calling her "child" clawed at her wounds? Did *no one* see her as a woman?

"The girls are ready to wash your things." Her gaze traveled down Annabelle's dress and she narrowed her eyes. "Why are you in the same gown as yesterday?"

Apparently Eudora hadn't taken note of her attire at breakfast. "Because it's the only gown I have."

Unaffected by the bite in her tone, Eudora lifted her brows. "I thought your father did well enough for himself that his only daughter shouldn't be reduced to rags."

Rags! This beautiful dress, made by her dearest friend's own hand? Good thing she'd listened to Peggy and not worn the tattered skirt! Her fingers traveled down the fabric. Her heart sank. The edges of the lace down the front of her skirt had started to pull free, and the fabric had become frayed in several places. Heat traveled up her neck and settled in her cheeks.

Eudora looked infuriatingly smug.

Annabelle gathered as much dignity as she could muster. "I'm sure it's easy for you to have forgotten this country is at war, seeing as how your lands are untouched, but in Mississippi our homes were raided, our things stolen, and our men lost. Even if we had time to make new gowns between trying not to starve and keeping wounded men alive, there wouldn't have been fabric enough anyway."

Instead of the sharp retort she expected, her grandmother's eyes softened. "I'm sorry, dear."

Annabelle hung her head, her anger flowing out of her in a gush. "It seems I've become a brash woman with a harsh tongue. Just the opposite of what I promised my mother I would be."

Eudora reached out and awkwardly patted Annabelle's shoulder. "Don't fret. There's nothing wrong with a woman speaking her mind."

Annabelle crossed her arms. The men in Eudora's life must have been very different from the men in her own. "Momma always said a lady carries more influence with a soft touch and a well-placed phrase than she does with harsh looks and rash words."

Eudora laughed. The full-belly sound washed over Annabelle like a balmy breeze, so genuine and infectious that, despite herself, Annabelle couldn't help but smile. "What?"

"Is *that* what my Katherine told you?" Eudora dabbed at her eyes, still chuckling. "I must have told her that a hundred times. Usually after she'd let her tongue run away with her, making a scene with one of her fits. I guess she finally got the hang of it in her later years."

Annabelle's mother had always been calm and gentle. Nothing ever riled her, and Annabelle couldn't think of a single time Momma had raised her voice. She couldn't picture her mother ever pitching a fit. She could only stare at Eudora, incredulous.

"Don't believe me?"

Annabelle looked down at the floor. "I never once saw her act as you've described. She was the perfect picture of a lady, and I've tried so hard to be like her."

Suddenly Eudora crushed Annabelle against her chest. "Oh, you're so much more like her than you know." She gave her back a pat and then held her out at arm's length. "And not just because you look like her. You have the same spark in your eyes and the same strength. You try to channel it better than she did, though. Katherine could be a very selfish girl. But that was our fault, I think. We never denied her anything, and she became demanding."

Flurries erupted in her stomach. "But she made me promise that I'd always put others before myself. That I'd strive always to be fair and honest, and to treat other people with respect, no matter their station. She told me to seek the Lord and be a woman of gentle spirit." Tears burned. She let them escape and slide down her cheeks.

Eudora pulled her close again, whispering in her ear. "I should have come to you after she died. I shouldn't have been so set in my foolish pride. My girl learned to be a lady of more class down there than she would have ever been here." Her grip tightened. "I sorely misjudged your father. Oh, sweet girl, I'm so sorry."

Annabelle clung tight as her grandmother stroked her hair. When the tears quieted, she pulled back and wiped her eyes with her sleeve. "I failed her. I haven't been able to keep that promise."

"Come now, you're the very image of a lady." Eudora grinned. "Just one in dire need of a new dress."

A laugh hitched in Annabelle's throat. "If you only knew how many lies I've told lately or how quickly I've lost my temper or how I've driven people away, I don't think you'd still believe that."

"Ha! If you did what you must to survive and still managed to keep your honor intact, then I say you've more than fulfilled your promise to your mother. My eyes might be old, girl, but even I see that the people under your care have been well tended. To a one, they look at you with affection and respect. Don't dismiss such loyalty so lightly."

A weight seemed to slide from her, and Annabelle straightened, drying the remaining moisture from her face. Her grandmother didn't seem to be one who spoke such words thoughtlessly, or one who offered false compliments. That a lady of such presence would think those things about her filled Annabelle with pride. She lifted her chin and received a nod of approval from Eudora.

"Now," Eudora said, taking her arm and leading her up the staircase, "let's see what we can find for you to wear."

Annabelle laughed and allowed herself to be led away, deciding she could learn a great deal from her elder.

Fourteen

"The very boldness of the movement will strike terror in those around and prevent anyone from coming to the rescue."
John H. Surratt

A man knew which battles to avoid. And upset women on the other side of the door was one of them. George had planned on stepping out of the parlor, but Mrs. Smith's voice and Miss Ross's sobbing had him trapped.

George contemplated the richly furnished space while he waited. How quickly life could change. One day he was starving and almost dead on his feet as he worked, and the next he was contemplating the best place to spend his leisure.

He might be able to pass through the dining room and find another way back to his room. He opened the pocket door and poked his head inside to find a curvy blonde woman dusting the china hutch. Lilly sat in a chair at the dining table polishing silver. Both looked up at him.

"I'm sorry to bother you."

Lilly rose from her seat. "What can I do for you, Mr. Daniels?"

George stepped into the room and pulled the door closed behind him. "I only wondered if I could pass through this way, and perhaps find a different route to my room."

The other woman cast George a curious look and addressed Lilly before she could respond to George. "Going on to the next chore, Fraulein."

"Make sure you tell Sue not to use so much spice in the meat pies this time. It don't sit well with Mrs. Smith." The other woman bobbed her head. "Oh," Lilly said as the blonde one turned to go. "And please don't let Frankie have too many sweet rolls. You know how they make him."

The blonde woman giggled. "Yes, Fraulein." She went out the rear set of pocket doors opposite from where George waited.

Lilly leveled her warm brown eyes on George. His chest tightened. He smiled, but she didn't return it. She laced her fingers in front of her gown, looking uncomfortable.

Fool! He looked like a boy swallowed by his daddy's clothes, not a man giving a charming look to a lady. The sudden thought caught him off guard. How many years had it been since he'd thought of charming a woman? Sure, he'd admired beauty a time or two, but had kept his distance otherwise.

He dropped his gaze, clearing his throat. "I, uh, just wanted to see if there was another way out of the sitting room."

"You can't go up the main stairs?" Confusion pulled at her brows, and she tilted her head, putting the curve of her neck on display.

His pulse quickened, and he had to divert his eyes again. He'd never seen a woman more beautiful. Most women shaded their skin from the sun's light, but this one must have let it caress every inch of her, turning pale tones to golden warmth.

She narrowed her eyes expectantly. He'd let his thoughts wander. "Mrs. Smith and Miss Ross are…talking in the entryway. It seemed to be a private matter, so I don't wish to disturb them."

Her frown dissipated. "Come, then. I'll take you around." Her smooth brow puckered again. "You'll have to take the servants' staircase."

"That's fine."

With a swish of silky blue fabric, Lilly led him out the rear door and through a narrow room filled with serving platters, plates, and cups of every shape and kind. They continued past the servants' pantry and around to a much smaller staircase than the grand one in the entry. Lilly gestured toward it. "This will take you to the upper hall."

She turned to go, and words tumbled out of George's mouth in an effort to keep her company a moment longer. "Are you a part of the Smith family?"

She looked at him like he was daft. "Of course not."

George shoved his hands into the pockets of his oversized trousers. "I meant no offense."

"I work here." She took two steps before hesitating and looked over her shoulder. "If you need anything, there's a bell in your room."

He brightened. "If it's not too much to ask, perhaps I could get a bath today?"

"Of course." She slipped away before George could say more.

He shook his head. He acted like a smitten youth. What had come over him? Probably sheer joy over being alive, warm, and fed had him acting like a boy.

He topped the stairs and knocked on Matthew's door, but received no answer. He must be out tending the horses. Some time alone in front of his fire to kick up his feet and open the paper was just exactly what he needed.

At least until he could think up some way to spend more time with Lilly.

Annabelle frowned as Eudora pulled a gown out of the armoire and thrust it toward her. "This should fit you well enough, dear. Try it on."

Biting her lip, Annabelle gave a small shake of her head and stepped back. "Thank you, but I cannot."

Eudora scoffed. "And why not?"

She glanced around the large room, its ceiling-height window flanked by rose-colored velvet drapes and its marble floors warmed by a massive floral-print rug. She'd thought her guest room was elaborate. This was a room meant for a princess. The former fineness of Rosswood felt nearly humble by comparison.

The gowns that Eudora pulled from the armoire were made of expensive silks and taffeta and her fingers itched to touch them. But she wouldn't take what didn't belong to her. "I'll not take Miss Lilly's things."

Eudora laughed. "These are ones she's never worn, or didn't like."

Annabelle stood stiffly by the dressing table—Lilly's personal hair combs and perfume bottles lined neatly across the top—and shook her head again. "I don't feel right taking her things without her permission."

Her grandmother simply smiled. "If it makes you feel better, I'll call for her."

Annabelle blanched. She wasn't sure about the nature of her grandmother's relationship with Lilly, but the woman must be a ward of some sort. She would likely do whatever Eudora asked, whether she truly wanted to or not.

Eudora stepped over to a long golden rope dangling by the door and tugged it three times. "We'll have the seamstress come and get your measurements, but for the time being, I'm certain Lilly won't mind loaning you some of her dresses." She fingered the fine embroidery of a Zouave jacket. "I always liked this one. It's the height of fashion, but Lilly's never worn it. She prefers plainer day dresses, no matter how hard I try."

Annabelle thought about the shimmering golden-yellow dress Lilly had worn last night and the blue silk she'd seen Lilly in at breakfast and wondered if Eudora understood what *plain* meant. Eudora dressed in black, as was appropriate for a widow, but her gowns were elaborate cuts, decorated with velvet trims and ribbons. Her current dress was silk, detailed with golden embroidery around the collar and cuffs.

The door opened and the young blonde woman who'd served Matthew coffee stepped inside. "You sent for someone, Frau Smith?"

"Yes, Anka. Do you know where Lilly is?"

The young woman bobbed her curls. "She was polishing the silver last I saw her, Frau."

"Go fetch her for me, if you please."

Anka dipped into a small curtsy and then hurried to do

Eudora's bidding. Annabelle tried to keep the confusion from her face, but the woman's keen eyes missed little.

"Wondering why Lilly is polishing silver?"

Annabelle twisted her hands in front of her. "Well, yes. I mean, I'm confused about her place here."

The elder woman gazed out the window at the manicured lawn below. "Lilly came here with the Underground Railroad."

Annabelle had heard tales of secret lines of abolitionist homes granting safety for slaves escaping the South, but she'd never believed they were actually true.

"The sickness came while I was still looking for placements for that last group. We were an end-point. It was my job to find paying positions for as many as I could, or get safe passage to another waypoint if I could not."

Moments passed. Eudora continued to stare out the window. "It took all of them," she finally said softly. "That awful fever took four women, including Lilly's mother, seven children, and two men."

Annabelle's heart clenched. A familiar pain wracked Eudora's tone. Pain brought on by being unable to save those under her care. "That's terrible. I'm sorry to hear it."

Eudora's eyes held a faraway look. "Then it came for my Franklin," she said, her voice distant. "It's my fault he's gone."

Annabelle's heart wrenched and she crossed the lush carpet to place a hand on her grandmother's shoulder. "Oh, Grandmother. You cannot help that sickness struck."

The older woman turned glistening eyes on her. "Oh, I know that, I do. But if I hadn't brought them in the house—"

"If you hadn't accepted people into your home, then how many others wouldn't have found a new life?"

Eudora gave a sad smile and patted Annabelle's arm. "You're a sweet girl." She drew her shoulders back and her regal air returned. "Now, where was I? Oh, yes. Lilly and I were the only ones who didn't take the sickness. Well, except for the German bunch, but I made sure to keep them out of the house while the worst of it raged. Lilly helped me care for them all, even though she was nearly bursting with child. No matter how harshly I tried to send her away, she was always there, her hands in the middle of it all." Annabelle smiled at the admiration in Eudora's voice, but her tone soon turned sad again. "When it was done, and the last one buried, I asked Lilly to stay with me."

Annabelle nodded, having a new respect for the quiet young woman.

"She and the boy have been here ever since."

"Lilly has a son?" How hard must it have been to tend the sick while that close to childbirth?

"I do," a female voice said from behind.

Annabelle's cheeks colored.

Lilly must have noticed, because she offered a comforting smile. "I don't mind Mrs. Smith sharin'—"

"Shar*ing*," Eudora interrupted.

"Shar*ing*," Lilly corrected, unfazed, "how I came to work here. She's been very good to me and little Franklin." She smiled at Annabelle's confused expression, answering the question even as it sprang to her lips. "Frankie stays in the kitchen with Sue most of the day. It's warm in there, and she lets him play with dough and his tin soldiers on the floor. Keeps him from breaking any of the fine things here in the house."

Eudora snorted. "I've told you he's fine in the house." She looked at Annabelle. "He usually eats with us, but he was already in bed last night when you arrived. Lilly took him straight to the kitchen first thing this morning."

"I didn't want him disturbing your company." Lilly shot Eudora a look that seemed to challenge her to protest.

Eudora smirked. "I didn't call you up here for that. Do you mind if Annabelle borrows some of your dresses until I can have some proper ones made?"

"'Course. Take any you fancy."

"The term is *of course*, though *certainly* would have been the better choice."

Lilly kept her gaze on Annabelle. "Your grandmother has insisted I learn to speak a lady's English."

"If we wish to find you a proper husband, you can't go around sounding like a milkmaid."

Lilly gave Eudora a flat look. "And as I've told you, I'm happy to work here. You've given a good life to Frankie and me, and I don't need no man."

Annabelle clasped her hands behind her back, her gaze darting between the two women. They suddenly seemed to remember she was in the room, and Eudora waved her hand. "A discussion for another time. I'll leave you girls to your dresses."

She swept out of the room and left the two young women staring after her. Lilly let out a good-natured sigh. "She means well. She's not really as overbearing as she seems."

Away from the others, Lilly seemed more relaxed. Annabelle couldn't help but like her. "You don't have to give me your dresses. Truly, I'm fine with what I have."

Lilly rolled her eyes and grabbed Annabelle's wrist, pulling her to the overflowing armoire. "Don't be silly. I have more dresses than I could ever wear. Mrs. Smith is always getting me new ones, even though there's too many already stuffed in here." She glanced at Annabelle. "Good thing you're here. She can dote on you instead."

"Oh, no, I'll be going home soon."

Lilly looked at her curiously. "You better pick out a couple of these anyway, or neither one of us will get a moment of peace. Believe me, she won't let you go around in a dress that shows any wear."

"As I've discovered." She pointed at the wardrobe. "Pick out the ones you don't like or you're ready to hand down. I promise to return them as soon as we leave."

Lilly gave a tinkling laugh. "Oh, Miss Ross, if you think Mrs. Smith is going to let you leave here with nothing but the gown you came with, you don't know her at all!"

Annabelle drew her lip between her teeth.

"I'm very sorry." The smooth mask of formality slipped back over Lilly's face. "I spoke out of place."

Annabelle reached for her hand. It'd been so long since she'd had a young woman to talk to. "Please, call me Annabelle. And you don't need to apologize." She dropped Lilly's hand and twisted her fingers. "You're right. I don't know my grandmother very well, but I'd like that to change."

Lilly's eyes brightened. "That would mean a great deal to her."

"And to me."

Lilly turned back to the array of brightly colored fabrics in the closet. She selected a deep burgundy and held it up against Annabelle. Then she shook her head. "You're too pale for this one. It makes you look like you've got skin the warm color of snow."

Back home, women tried to keep their skin as light as possible. It was a mark of beauty. She tilted her head. "Where are you from, if you don't mind my asking?"

Lilly put away the dark dress and pulled a pale green one out instead. She held it up to Annabelle. "Oh, yes. Much better." She went over to the bed and tossed the gown across the floral quilt. She stuck her head back in the armoire. "New Orleans, before we made the run."

Why had the lady traveled with slaves? Perhaps she'd had a beloved Peggy of her own.

Lilly pulled out two other dresses and held them up to Annabelle, selecting one and putting back the other. "Now, where did I put that one with all that stitching?"

"The Zouave?"

Lilly pulled her head out of the armoire. "I can't keep up with all the stuff in those fashion periodicals Mrs. Smith is always pointing at."

"It's on the bed under the others. Grandmother pulled it out."

"Must have missed it." Lilly sifted through the pile of dresses. "This'll look wonderful on you. The style doesn't suit me."

"I appreciate your generosity."

"It's nothing." She tugged taffeta and silk over the hanging rod. "Let's see what else…."

"No, thank you. These are plenty."

Lilly studied her a moment, then nodded. "Try them on. You can always get more later. I need to be gettin' back to work anyway."

Annabelle hated to see the carefree time end, but understood the other woman had responsibilities. She gathered the dresses in her arms and followed Lilly out the door.

"If you need anything, I can have Anka pick it up from town. She goes with her papa to town when we need women things." She offered a conspirator's grin. "Unless you want to let Mrs. Smith take you shopping in New York City."

Annabelle laughed. "I'll let you know if I need anything else. Thank you."

Lilly smiled and headed toward the servants' stairs at the end of the hall, and Annabelle clutched her new treasures to her chest. It took a great deal of effort to keep a steady pace and not dash to her room to try them on.

Fifteen

"No news yet received from Booth. I do not understand this. What can he be doing?"
John H. Surratt

Smith house
Watkins Glen, New York
March 30, 1865

Matthew entered the stables, the familiar smells of horse and leather a comfort. He shook off the morning chill and fingered the wool overcoat over his arm. Would he really need it? The day would likely warm considerably, though the early mornings still brought a northern winter's bite.

The past two weeks he'd enjoyed seeing the light return to George's eyes and health return to his features. They'd enjoyed a most welcome time of rest and recovery, but they hadn't set foot out of the house except to take afternoon tea in the gardens since they'd first arrived. Being cooped up indoors for so long made Matthew restless.

"Need something, mister?" Pete asked as Matthew closed the barn doors behind him.

Matthew smiled at the youth who carried the firewood and

tended his horses. "I thought I might go for a ride before the midday meal, if that's all right."

The boy laughed, slapping his polishing rag across his leg. "What are you asking me for? It's your horse!"

A voice came from a side room. "Pete! Don't you be talking to the elders like that!"

The boy's eyes widened. "Sorry, Papa!" He cast Matthew an apologetic look just as an older, bulkier version of the boy stepped from the side room. The man stood a few inches shorter than Matthew, but the shoulders under his suspenders were equally as wide. The boy's father wiped his hands on a dirty cloth, his thick forearms extending from underneath rolled-up sleeves.

"I make apology for the boy, mister," the man said. "Sometimes he forgets the manners for his betters."

Matthew shook his head. "No harm done. He seems like a fine youth."

Pride swelled the burly man's chest. "He came so many of the years after Anka, we thought his ma would never have the son."

"Anka is your daughter." The entire family must work for the Smith house.

"My eldest. Came with us from the homeland. But the boy, he was born here, in the new land."

The man seemed rather proud of that fact, and Matthew smiled.

He grinned in return, then seemed to remember his manners. "Oh! Your pardon. My name's Günter."

Matthew grasped the extended hand and gave it a firm squeeze. "Matthew."

A few moments later, Pete appeared with one of the mares, saddled and ready to go. "Thank you, Pete." Matthew took the reins.

"Sure thing, mister." He hurried to return to his saddle polishing.

The boy's father shook his head and looked back at Matthew. "When you are done with the ride, my boy will put the horse up again for you."

Matthew nodded his thanks and took the horse into the morning sun. His breath turned to mist in the air. He looked down at the blue coat on his arm, loathing the thought of dressing as a Yank. But his brother's Union frock would be warmer than his own gray shell jacket, and both warmer still than the civilian coat he'd thus far endured.

He fingered the blue wool. Besides, he was already a deserter; wearing blue couldn't make him any more of a traitor. Matthew pulled on the coat, surprised that it fit quite well, and swung up into the saddle.

He laid the reins across the mare's neck and turned her to the left. They set out at a slow walk, going around the side of the large stable and toward the long narrow lake behind the house. A flash of movement caught his eye.

A shadow ducked around the back of the barn before Matthew could get a good look at it. His pulse quickened. He dug his heels into the horse's flanks, startling the animal forward. Matthew rounded the edge of the barn just as a man dashed across the lawn.

The animal darted forward, her powerful legs quickly outpacing the runner. The man glanced over his shoulder, fear written all over his familiar face.

Harry!

Harry nearly dove into the cover of the trees at the edge of the lawn. He stumbled in the underbrush but quickly regained his feet. Matthew's horse plunged into the trees, her hooves crunching leaves and fallen sticks. Harry ran desperately through the tangle of vines and tree limbs, but he was no match for the horse's stride. In a matter of moments, Matthew overtook him.

Matthew launched himself from the saddle and slammed into the man's back, bringing him to the ground. The horse snorted and pranced as the two men rolled across the damp leaves. Harry struggled to free himself from his grasp. Matthew flipped the scoundrel on his back and pinned Harry's shoulders beneath his knees. "What are you doing here?"

Harry snarled at him. "Can't you get off me so we can talk like men?"

Matthew grunted and shifted his weight off of Harry's chest. But before he could gain his feet, the smaller man bounded upright and dashed off through the trees.

Fool! Matthew chased the surprisingly spry man deeper into the woods. He leapt over upturned roots and slipped between trees. Matthew lowered his head, ignoring branches that slapped him in the face and tore at his clothes.

He got close enough to Harry to grab him. His fingers barely brushed the back of the man's coat, however, when Harry gave a yelp and launched himself forward with a new burst of speed. Matthew growled and pumped his legs harder, the old wound in his calf protesting his efforts. Ignoring the ache, Matthew made a giant leap over a large stump that Harry had to run around.

That slight advantage brought Harry within his reach. Matthew caught the man by his collar and yanked him backward. Harry dropped to a shaded patch of snow and cursed. Matthew centered his knees across the man's chest again and pressed hard until he stopped struggling.

Breathing hard, he jerked Harry to his feet. Harry staggered, his eyes wide. Matthew slammed Harry against the nearest tree, hard enough that the air left Harry's chest in a whoosh.

Harry gasped, struggling for a moment to regain his breath. He fixed a cold glare on Matthew. Matthew pressed his forearm into Harry's sternum, securing his body to the tree. "Why are you here?"

"Been following you, traitor." Harry spat. "Been waiting weeks for you to come out of hiding."

Matthew's nostrils flared. "Why?"

Harry sneered. "Ain't telling you nothing. You ain't my captain no more, *traitor*, and I don't have to do what you say."

Matthew leaned the bulk of his weight forward, increasing the pressure at Harry's throat. The man's eyes widened but he said no more. Matthew slipped his free hand up to Harry's neck, clamping his fingers on the soft spot just underneath the jaw. Panic washed over Harry's face when Matthew squeezed. After a moment, he began to thrash.

Matthew held him until his bulging eyes became dazed and his struggle weakened, then pulled back. "I won't ask you nicely again. Why are you following me?"

Harry gasped as air flowed back into his throat, and Matthew let him cough a few times. Harry dropped his head back on the tree behind him and closed his eyes. "O'Malley made me do it! He said you was going to turn us in."

Matthew narrowed his gaze. "Surely by now you can see I

don't intend to do that."

Harry glared at Matthew. "Says the man wearing a Union coat. I always knew you would turn on us."

Matthew snarled. "I'll wear whatever best keeps out the cold. Not that I have to explain myself to you." He shoved hard and then pushed Harry away with disgust. The man dropped to the ground. "I left Washington to save my brother on my own, since none of you kept your word. I haven't betrayed anything I swore to do."

Harry's bravado dissipated as gained his feet. "He shouldn't have strung you along like that, telling you he meant to help when he never planned on findin' your brother."

Matthew had always suspected as much, but hearing O'Malley's deception spoken out loud brought another snarl to his lips and his hands into tight fists. Harry backed away, holding up his hands to shield his face. Matthew took a step back. "I'm not going to tell the law about what we did. Do you think I'm foolish enough to condemn my own neck to a noose?"

Harry shook his head. "O'Malley said I had to follow you anyway and report back once you found your brother."

"Then what?"

Terror flicked in Harry's eyes. Harry took another step. Leaves and bits of snow crunched beneath his shoes.

Matthew closed the distance in a single stride and caught Harry by the collar. "Then what?"

The blood drained from Harry's face. "He told me to kill you, but I swear I wasn't going to do it! I ain't no murderer!"

Matthew thrust him away. "O'Malley wants me dead?" O'Malley's obsessions drove the man to madness. Once David

O'Malley had something in mind, he wouldn't stop. Soon enough he'd send someone better than Harry. What dangers would that bring to George and Annabelle?

"Yeah," Harry answered. "He thinks you're a loose thread that has to be cut. But I say if you know how to keep your mouth shut even after Lincoln's gone, I don't know why he can't leave you be."

Matthew startled. "He's still planning on taking him?"

Harry sneered. "That's the plan from Canada, but O'Malley wants the problem permanently solved."

"It's assassination now?"

Harry cursed. "I done said too much." He stepped away. "How about you just get back on that horse and be on your way and I'll be on mine. We won't ever see each other again."

"And let O'Malley send another after me? I think not." Matthew shot forward and grabbed hold of Harry before he could run. "You need to come with me."

Harry swung a fist and caught Matthew by the nose, bringing instant moisture to his eyes. Matthew blinked it away and pulled back his balled fist, landing a punch to the smaller man's face. His nose shattered.

Harry went limp and fell to the ground.

Matthew wiped the water from his eyes. Harry didn't move. Matthew wiped the blood from his face with his sleeve, then bent to turn Harry over.

Harry's bloody nose sat at a crooked angle. Better he put it back in place while the man wouldn't feel it. He clamped the nose between his fingers and tugged. It made a sucking noise, like when a baked chicken leg popped from the thigh. Matthew surveyed his work. Straight enough. He wiped as much of the blood free as he could and pinched the nostrils closed, making sure Harry's mouth was open so he could breathe.

Harry groaned, but didn't wake. Satisfied he'd given the man more mercy than he deserved, he hoisted Harry over his shoulder and trudged off in search of his horse. Thankfully, he found the animal nibbling at vines nearby.

The horse sidestepped as he neared, but Matthew grabbed the dangling reins before she could prance out of his reach. He draped the unconscious man over the saddle and stroked the mare's nose to calm her. Matthew took a deep breath and tugged on the reins, leading the horse out of the woods.

He trudged out of the forest and across the lawn, his mind working through the repercussions of Harry's tale. O'Malley would have to be stopped, but he didn't want Annabelle catching wind of it.

He'd have to come up with a believable story.

Sixteen

"I am afraid he will yet suspect something, and then, by some blundering remark, upset the whole thing."
John H. Surratt

Smoked meat pies and hearty vegetables surrounded Matthew with a delicious aroma that did little to help his appetite. He smiled to himself as George shoveled in another bite, the look of satisfaction on his face evident as he chewed vigorously. A week or so more of these hearty meals, and his brother would truly be on his way to returning to his old self.

Matthew tugged on his collar. Did no one else suffer this stifling heat? The crackle of wood in the hearth reminded him of the young boy who earned his wage by chopping and toting it inside. Did the boy ever go to the potato shed out back? What about the cook? How often would she venture out that way for supplies? He tugged again, a bead of sweat running down his spine.

"Matthew?"

He looked up sharply. "Yes, Mrs. Smith?"

She arched a thin brow at him. "You didn't hear my question?"

Matthew glanced across the table at Annabelle, but her smooth expression and cool eyes offered no assistance. He jerked his head to the side. "Forgive me, ma'am."

Eudora dabbed the side of her mouth with her linen napkin and placed it back on the table. "Too lost in your thoughts, were you? Pray tell, what has you so preoccupied?"

An erratic pulse ricocheted through his veins. Could he keep any indication of distress out of her prying gaze? Mrs. Smith, however, appeared more amused than suspicious. She flashed a suggestive glance at Annabelle.

George's gaze traveled Matthew's face like a swarm of ants on a discarded scrap of bread.

Matthew cocked his head, feigning confusion, and turned the subject. "I was thinking about the state of affairs of the country. I've been out of touch."

Mrs. Smith smirked. "Hasn't Anka been bringing you the paper?"

His grip tightened on his fork. "I haven't been reading. I'll have to catch up."

She lowered her lids, but not before Matthew caught the humor in her gaze. Annabelle sat primly across from him. And next to George. Sudden irrational jealousy spiked in his gut and soured his stomach.

Annabelle stared at her plate and uncomfortably pushed a carrot across the painted china. He flicked his attention to George. His brother unabashedly stared across the table at Lilly. How dare George look at another woman like that when one so desirable sat right by his side, ignored?

Matthew's grip tightened harder on his fork, and he glanced at Lilly from the corner of his eye. She hadn't said anything the entire meal, just as she'd kept quiet all of the other times they'd gathered around this table for an awkward meal. She seemed every bit as uncomfortable as Matthew with the unconventional line of souls sitting in a horseshoe around the table—a slave, a servant, a deserter, a wealthy widow, a displaced lady, and an escaped prisoner of war. If he hadn't been in such a foul mood, Matthew might have thought the group amusing.

He glared at George until his brother caught his eye. The slight narrowing of his eyes, the tightness of his mouth, and the steel in his gaze proved all George needed to catch Matthew's meaning. Instead of showing the proper embarrassment for ogling, George only lifted the side of his lips and hitched one shoulder before putting another heaping spoonful of potatoes into his mouth.

Matthew's simmering frustration boiled. Flames churned in his chest and sizzled up his neck. Annabelle must have noticed. She tilted her head and studied him before her gaze darted around the table in search of what had caused his ire. Lest she discover the truth, Matthew forced his breathing to slow and offered a tight smile.

Annabelle frowned. Then, as if remembering her disdain for him, she gave a small sniff and lifted her chin, pointedly turning her gaze away from him. Matthew followed her eyes and once again was confronted with the old woman's infuriating amusement.

Matthew placed his napkin by his plate of uneaten food and rose from the table. "I'm not feeling well. If y'all will excuse me, I think I'll retire for the evening."

Their stares bored into his back as he strode from the room. He willed his pounding heart to slow, but nothing short of a walk out in the freezing air would douse the fire burning within him.

Matthew pulled the doors closed behind him with a thud. Annabelle jumped when he slammed the front door. She avoided the questioning faces of the other women at the table and stabbed a piece of carrot with her fork.

Probably best to find a safe topic to distract from Matthew's display of temper. "Lilly, I was hoping Frankie would be able to join us tonight."

Lilly looked up from her plate and darted a glance at Eudora, her face a mixture of surprise and displeasure.

Had she said something offensive? The rules were all different here.

Eudora's lips curled into a sly smile. "I've told her to let him eat here with us, but she can be awfully stubborn." Her amused tone belied the nip in her words.

"And I told *her* it would be better that he did not disturb the guests."

Eudora snorted, but Lilly ignored her. Annabelle drew her lip between her teeth.

"That boy should be able to eat with his mother." Eudora pointed a finger at Lilly. "It's not good for him to be raised by others."

George stiffened, and his gaze openly locked onto Lilly's usually serene face now flushed with annoyance. George laid down his fork, clearly disturbed. Annabelle frowned. Did he not know Lilly had a son?

What difference would that make to him anyway?

Lilly flicked her gaze at George. The slightest flash of fear sprang into her eyes before Lilly donned her mask of indifference. "As I've said on many occasions, I'd be happy to take my meals in the kitchen. As a servant should. Then this wouldn't be an issue."

Eudora's amusement disintegrated. The lines around her mouth tightened, but not in anger. Hurt washed over her hazel eyes.

"And as *I* have said, you're more family than hireling. I wish you'd realize both you and Frankie deserve a place at my table. Whether we're joined by guests or not."

Lilly's features fell, and she shifted in her seat. Annabelle's heart went out to her. She knew something of the fragile balance of not quite understanding one's place.

"I'd like to meet Frankie," George interrupted.

Lilly looked up at him sharply, her mask of serenity lost. "Why?" Then, as if remembering herself, she eased the hard lines from her forehead with obvious concentration. She drew a long, steadying breath, and then spoke to George like a child. "He's not ready. He has too much energy to remain quiet and still."

George leaned back in his chair and laughed. The rich, hearty sound seemed too robust for the emaciated man. Lilly blanched, the warm color of her face fading to almost the shade of Annabelle's own.

George slapped his knee. "A boy is *supposed* to be full of energy! Only little girls will sit prim and proper at a table, all done up in fancy clothes. A boy is supposed to be struggling with itching collars and forced stillness!" He chuckled. "You should have seen us four boys at the table as little ones."

Lilly looked stunned, but Eudora barked a laugh to rival George's. "Frankie needs a man in his life to say such things. You put too many expectations onto a boy of two."

Annabelle pressed her fingers into the wadded napkin in her lap, her meal forgotten. Something passed between Lilly and George, but Annabelle couldn't quite name it. She looked to her grandmother, who also seemed to notice the exchange.

Eudora clapped her hands suddenly, making everyone jump. "Let's have our dessert. Lilly, why don't you go to the kitchen and fetch our pie. And let the little one come and eat it with us."

Lilly rose from her place and slipped out of the room without argument, her former fire forgotten. Peggy, whom Annabelle had all but forgotten during the awkward meal, now sat alone on her side of the table. Annabelle parted her lips to speak on the weather or some other mundane topic that could not possibly add to the discomfort already thick in the room. Peggy gave an almost imperceptible shake of her head.

Fine.

Without being asked, Peggy rose and picked up her plate and removed the scraped-clean china from in front of George. She took Annabelle's hardly touched meat pie and stacked her plate on top of the others. She reached for Eudora's setting, then hesitated.

The retort Annabelle expected never came. Instead, Eudora smiled sweetly and allowed Peggy to scoop up her plate and then scamper away, escaping the tension in the room. A shame Annabelle couldn't join her.

As soon as the door closed behind Peggy, Eudora pinned

Annabelle with a look that made her squirm. "Mr. Daniels," she said, eyes still locked on Annabelle, "who approved your request for my granddaughter's hand since her father is no longer alive?"

Annabelle could not withhold her gasp. "Grandmother, I—"

Eudora silenced Annabelle with a cutting look.

If George was rattled by the imprudence, he didn't let it show. "Annabelle and I are not betrothed."

Resigned to yet another scraping of her wounds, Annabelle lowered her gaze and studied the grain of the wood on the table.

"Then why did your brother say otherwise when you came to my door? And didn't you court her in my parlor?"

Annabelle almost couldn't hear over the pounding blood in her ears that was very quickly evolving into a headache.

George answered in that easy and unaffected way she'd come to expect from him. "My brother sought to secure such an arrangement, but Miss Ross and I spoke on the matter and decided the match unnecessary."

Surprise widened Eudora's eyes. Annabelle wished she could melt out of her chair and seep into the thickly woven rug underfoot.

"Unnecessary?"

Her kin should hear of her failures from her own lips. "I sought a union to secure Rosswood's future."

Eudora studied Annabelle, but her expression remained entirely unreadable. Annabelle refused to wither under the older woman's gaze and kept her chin high.

"You've been at that plantation by yourself all this time?" The horror in her grandmother's voice caused warring emotions of annoyance and tenderness in Annabelle's chest. She would be perfectly capable of caring for her home herself, but appreciated Eudora's concern. As soon as the prideful thought rose up, she pushed it aside as foolishness. A lone woman so far from town would never truly be safe, not even once the war ended. Despair tried to rear again, but she pointedly pictured herself crushing it, and the feeling passed.

"My grandfather by marriage tends Rosswood in my uncle's stead, until either Uncle Michael returns or I am wed. Grandfather sought to remedy this issue by pledging me to wed his own son, but that match is most…unfitting."

The lines around Eudora's mouth tightened. "Those details are something I wish to discuss with you at another time." Annabelle nodded. "But that matter aside." She waved her hand. "If you've decided Mr. Daniels is not a match, and neither is…." She hesitated only a moment, but Annabelle caught the way her nostrils flared. "This other man, then how do you plan on securing your holdings on your own?"

"I'll figure something out."

"I assured Miss Ross that marriage is unnecessary for her to receive aid from my brother and me," George said. "We'll make sure her land is returned to her."

Eudora laced her fingers on the table. "That's noble of you, boy, but you're a fool if you think she can live there on her own."

"Grandmother!" That was bold, even for Eudora, and crossed into rudeness. She shot Eudora a snide look. "*You* live here without a man."

She regretted the words as soon as they left her lips. The pained look that crossed her grandmother's face pricked her.

Eudora stroked the base of her throat. "Oh, child." She

shook her head. "I'm an old widow living in lands blessedly untouched by scavengers and raiders. I have a rather burly stableman who lives but a stone's throw from my rear entry. These are hardly the same circumstances."

At that moment, Peggy bustled in with a pumpkin pie. Lilly followed on her heels with a toddler perched on her hip. The boy reached under a mop of dark curls to tug on his ear, his brown eyes trying to see everything at once. His gaze quickly fell on George, and he wriggled in his mother's grasp.

George grinned. "Look what a fine young fellow we have here!"

Lilly's face remained passive, but the boy squirmed in her arms until she finally sighed and released him. The moment his tiny shoes touched the floor, he scurried up to George's side. George ruffled his hair. "We've got some pie here. Do you want some?"

Annabelle smiled as the little one's face lit up, and without a word he climbed right into George's lap.

Lilly gasped. "No, Frankie! He don't want—"

George laughed. "Nonsense! He's perfectly fine right here. We're going to share a big old slice, aren't we, Frankie?"

Frankie giggled, reaching his chubby fingers toward the table. Lilly looked perplexed and cast a helpless glance at Eudora. Eudora, however, looked rather smug.

Peggy cut and served each of them a slice, even cutting one for herself and placing it on the table. When she finished and returned to her seat, Eudora lifted her fork and stabbed a tiny bite. The others quickly followed suit. Save Lilly, who focused on her son sitting happily in George's lap.

After three bites of her pie, Annabelle asked to be excused

from the table. Eudora gave permission with a pitying look that Annabelle loathed. As she rose, Peggy did the same, and the two shut the pocket doors on Frankie's giggles and George's hearty laugh. They crossed through the parlor without a word. Peggy started up the staircase.

Annabelle placed a hand on the rail, but then hesitated at the bottom. "I think I'll take a quick trip out back before we retire."

"All right. But let's be quick about it." Peggy mumbled under her breath, "Don't know why you can't just use the chamber pot."

Annabelle avoided the chamber pot as often as possible. She didn't like emptying it and didn't want anyone else to have to, either. "You go on to your room. I'll be fine."

Peggy parted her lips to protest, but then seemed to change her mind. "Be quick. I'll go ahead and get some coals into the bed warmer and heat your sheets."

"Thank you. That sounds delightful." She hurried out the rear door, careful to pull it tight behind her. The sun had dipped low during their supper, and she'd need to hurry if she wanted to get back to the house before full dark. She lifted the wide hoops Eudora had insisted she wear to the evening meal and stepped quickly across the lawn. The cold New York air poked through her thick velvet gown.

She reached the privy, but just as her fingers touched the handle, she heard a muffled thump. She paused, listening. The noise came again, this time followed by a grunt. Curious, she walked around to the back of the privy. Another building stood off to the side of the yard opposite the stable, several paces removed from the other structures near the main house. Likely a smokehouse or vegetable cellar.

What if someone needed help?

Armed with the thought, Annabelle hurried forward. As she neared, the scuffling sounds fell silent. She pressed her ear to the rough wooden door. Caution warned that she should go back to the house and get one of the men to come inspect what caused the stir, lest it be something dangerous.

Then she remembered her grandmother's words and George's placating looks, and Annabelle straightened her spine. She wasn't so dependent on men that she must run to them at every turn! Without another hesitation, she wrenched open the door.

Annabelle gasped.

There in the gloomy light, surrounded by stacks of potatoes and shelves lined with canned vegetables, stood Harry. The man who'd been one of the conspirators determined to abduct Lincoln had his arms stretched high over his head, secured by a rope looped over a support beam in the roof. Harry's nose had swollen to twice the normal size, and both of his eyes were darkened with bruised and puffy skin. When Harry saw her, he began to thrash.

Annabelle stepped into the damp room to calm him. Then she noticed the gags stuffed into his mouth.

Her caution forgotten, she rushed to the struggling man. Fear widened his eyes as much as the bruising would allow. As recognition dawned, his thrashing ceased.

Annabelle regarded him evenly. "I'm going to remove your gag. Don't make me regret it."

He bobbed his head frantically, and she reached around behind his head to undo the strip of bloody cloth. He'd lost his liquid on himself, but she tried not to let her disgust show. When the knot finally came free, Annabelle quickly dropped the rag to the ground and stepped back, breathing through her mouth.

Harry spat out another wad of cloth that had been shoved into his mouth.

"Who did this to you?" Annabelle kept a safe distance and watched for any indication that he could spring from his bonds.

Of course, if he could release himself, he'd have done so by now.

Harry spat a thick, red wad of mucus. He eyed her with nearly as much suspicion as she watched him. "Your lover's the one that done it, you twit."

The day's light continued to recede. As the shadows grew so did her unease. She ignored his comment. "Why are you here?"

He glared at her, unwilling to answer. She lifted her shoulders. "I'll leave you, then." She spun around and stepped through the door.

The door almost latched before his plea finally came. "Please! Wait!"

She swung the door wide again, letting as much light in as possible.

"I was just following Daniels. Was supposed to see if he got his brother out."

Annabelle narrowed her eyes. Why would Matthew tie him up? Especially if Harry only wanted to see if they found George? And for that matter, why follow them in secret? Whatever his intentions, they weren't innocent. "You think me a fool?"

"It's true!"

She placed her hand on her hip and did her best to imitate

Eudora's superior tone. "Perhaps. But probably only a piece and not the whole truth. I'll know your purpose on my family lands, sir, or that mangled nose won't be the last of your woes."

Harry gaped at her, then lowered his head. "O'Malley sent me to be sure Daniels didn't let his mouth leak. We thought once he got his brother out, he might talk."

"Matthew was as much a part of that mess as any of you. Doing so would only see him captured as well. Surely you don't think he's that dimwitted?"

Harry's eyes narrowed with defiance. Momma had always said a lady turned a man with a sweet word and not a snarl, so she plastered a sugared smile on her lips. She stepped closer. "I'm sure you meant no harm. You were only sending information, after all."

Surprise washed over his face for only an instant before he shielded his features again. She thought she'd failed, but then he nodded. "That's right. That brute had no call for attacking me like he did."

Annabelle clicked her tongue. "No, of course not. And I'll be sure to speak with him about his actions."

Something growled behind her. Annabelle whirled toward the exit. Matthew filled the doorway and blocked out the rest of her light. She squinted, but couldn't make out his features. She needn't have anyway, since the tension in his shoulders and the way his fists clenched at his sides told her all she needed to know.

Refusing to be intimidated, she pulled herself to her full height and straightened her shoulders. "Would you care to explain why you've strung up a man in my grandmother's potato shed?"

He took a heavy step forward, and she regretted speaking to him like an unruly child. Still, she wouldn't back down. Not even when his hand gripped her elbow and he started to tug her away from Harry. "You and I will discuss this outside."

Annabelle allowed herself to be hauled out of the shed and into the purple glow of the day's last light. She wrenched her arm free from his grasp as soon as they were a few steps away. Tension practically rolled off him, and neither of them spoke. Annabelle wrapped her arms around herself and tilted her head back to see Matthew's face. Instead of the rage she expected, he simply appeared exhausted.

He scrubbed a hand down his face. "I found him following us, with orders from O'Malley to have me killed."

Annabelle drew a sharp breath and cast a look at the shed. Harry didn't seem to be the type, but then, what did she know about such things?

"I had to restrain him. At least until I could decide what to do." Matthew massaged the muscles on the back of his neck, and Annabelle's annoyance began to wane.

She rubbed her throbbing temple, trying to hold a headache at bay. "Were you going to tell anyone about this?"

"I didn't think the dinner table was an appropriate place to announce I'd stowed a would-be murderer in the shed."

Annabelle bit back a sharp retort and tried to keep her mother's advice at hand. "What do you propose to do with him?"

Matthew snarled. "I'd like to haul him back to Washington, take him to the law, and tell them the entire story. Let them get to O'Malley and the others before they do anything reckless."

Annabelle chewed her lip. A reasonable plan, even if a dangerous one. "And what if they arrest you as well?"

Matthew shrugged. "So be it."

The bitterness in his words stabbed at her heart. "Why would you say such a thing?"

He looked at her for a moment, and with the last light of day she saw the pain in his eyes. "I got myself into this mess. Now that you're safe, George is free, and…" He hesitated, and her pulse quickened. He cleared his throat. "Now that you and George have secured the arrangement, it's my responsibility to stop them before they make things worse."

Secured the arrangement? Had George not told his brother what they'd discussed? Annabelle pushed aside the words she longed to speak. She wouldn't tell him she and George didn't plan to wed. Right now, she had a bigger problem. "You said 'before they do anything reckless' and 'before they make things worse.' What are you not telling me?"

He reached out and brushed her cheek with his knuckles. A whisper of a touch, and then it was gone. "You won't let it rest, will you?"

She lifted her brows. "You expect anything else?"

He chuckled softly. "No, I suppose not." He stared at her a moment, the night creatures and his breathing the only sounds in the darkness. He sighed and stepped back away from her, putting a distance between them that was for the best, but hurt all the same. "Harry said they're still trying to carry out their plan."

"They're still trying to abduct him?"

Matthew nodded, a barely noticeable gesture in the faint moonlight. "They've grown more desperate, and I fear O'Malley's obsession. I don't think once they smuggle Lincoln into Richmond that O'Malley will stop there."

Her blood ran cold. "Assassination?" The word squeaked out in a bare whisper. Annabelle's hand flew to her heart in an attempt to calm its rapid beating. "We have to stop them."

"Lincoln must live." His quiet words lingered between them. "If there's to be any hope for us."

Annabelle looked up at him sharply. "I don't understand."

Matthew tilted his chin to the sky, searching as though the twinkling stars could give him the words he sought. "Aside from the fact that no man should be murdered, once the South has lost this cursed war, Lincoln will keep the repercussions in check."

Annabelle watched him closely. At what point had his fervent Confederate loyalty waned?

He cocked his head as if sensing her thoughts. "I still despise the man who brought his army into our lands and destroyed us for simply holding to our way of life."

Harry remained silent, even with his gags undone. Could he hear their words?

She drew a steadying breath, remembering the day she'd seen Lincoln at his second inauguration. "He seems the type that would seek healing and not punishment," she said carefully, watching Matthew as she spoke. "He said *with malice toward none.*"

"I feel the same." He glanced toward the shed. "If those idiots haul Lincoln off to Richmond and have him murdered, the North will rage. Take the man they herald a hero and stain the South with his blood?" Matthew slowly shook his head. "O'Malley will only drive them into a frenzy."

Annabelle swallowed the lump gathering in her throat. "What do we do?"

Matthew scowled. "*We* do nothing. I'm taking Harry back to Washington and finding O'Malley. *You* are staying here, where it's safe."

Hot words flew to her tongue, but she bit them down. Raise a fuss now and he'd only find more ways to ensure she stayed. Better to find another path when he wasn't so riled. She smoothed her skirts and kept her words even. "Of course. I'll stay here and see to George's care. We'll wait for your return."

Matthew seemed surprised for only a second, then gave a curt nod and turned back toward the shed. "Go back inside while I have a little talk with our friend."

Annabelle watched him stalk into the shed.

Then she prayed for forgiveness for the lies she planned to tell.

Seventeen

"He is both powerful and desperate. I felt like being uncivil to him, but thought it might excite suspicion."
John H. Surratt

Washington, D.C.
March 30, 1865

A tap at his door drew David's attention from the maps he'd been studying. He tucked them away in his satchel before opening the door. Mrs. Surratt's eyes darted around his room as they always did. Once again, he pretended not to notice.

He had no doubt she searched his things whenever he left, which was why he kept his most important information on him at all times. He displayed a friendly smile. "Good afternoon, ma'am. I hope the day's been pleasant for you?"

She gave a slight sniff, as if something about his aroma offended her, and then put on a practiced smile herself. "Quite lovely. I enjoyed tea with my son."

David's mask threatened to slip, but he kept it in place. He summoned a look of pleasant surprise and kept his tone casual. "I didn't know John was back in town. Thank you for coming to fetch me. I'd enjoy visiting with him as well."

Mrs. Surratt held up a spindly hand as David made a move to step around her. "He's already gone. He has much business to attend to."

David gave a shrug, maintaining an air of nonchalance. "Of course. Another time, then." He stepped back and waited. He didn't think her the type to flaunt that her son hadn't wanted to see him. But the longer she hesitated with nothing more to say, the more he guessed that might actually be the case.

Finally, the woman reached into the pocket of her skirt and pulled out a folded paper. She extended it toward him. "John regrets not being able to speak with you, but did ask that I pass along this letter."

David let a genuine smile scurry over his mouth. *Finally!* He'd almost begun to fear they were trying to leave him out of the plans. Ridiculous, of course. He bowed to John's mother and plucked the message from her fingers. "Thank you, ma'am."

She stared at him a few seconds longer, but when he said nothing more, the crone finally relented. "I assume you'll join us for the evening meal?"

David shook his head. "No, I have matters to attend to this evening." *Like finding the bottom of a mug of ale and escaping your pitiful attempts at scrutinizing me in secret,* he added to himself. His own cleverness turned up his lips.

"Very well. Good day."

He closed the door and waited until she had time to return downstairs before he unfolded the message she'd undoubtedly already read. No names were given, neither in greeting nor in closure. Good. Then the letter would contain pertinent information and not just mindless prattle.

I regret that you have been left on your own while we have tried to figure out our next course of action. However, your patience has not been unappreciated. We will soon need all available hands for what is to come. Our mutual friend has decided that we can no longer be delayed, and after speaking with her and learning the information she has gleaned from the others, we feel that we must act with the utmost haste.

David paused, then read the words again. The mutual friend was no doubt Booth, but who was *she*? He thought on it a moment and then his blood heated. Of course. John's mother, the crone who seemed to have her long nails into everything they did. Her son still sniveled at her bosom like a babe. He almost crunched the paper between his fists, thinking about the smug look on her face. Booth had met with the *woman*, when he could not even be bothered to speak to *him*? His agitated gaze scurried to the next line.

Our friend has decided to go on to New York, where he has important business.

David paused again, reading the line once more. The blood that had run hot suddenly turned icy. What could Booth be doing in New York? Did he also suspect Daniels? Would he get to him before David had the chance and take the glory of thwarting a traitor for himself? His eyes darted back to the page.

I ask that you remain here in Washington, keeping your ears open and your eyes sharp. All seems likely to go on well, and we have men in place who are ready to cooperate at the proper moment, so that we cannot fail this time.

David paced his small room. Stay here and do nothing while the others planned? His stomach clenched. It had been days, and still no response from Harry. Had Booth captured him in New York? To what end?

His hands began to shake with fury, and he forced himself to calm. It was only his overtaxed mind coming up with such wild stories! They knew his value, and his loyalty to the Cause stood unequaled. John simply didn't have time to waste on idle talk, and he knew that David had the wit to read the meaning that must go unwritten.

While the others scrambled around running errands, David could be trusted to see past men's lies and catch the true meaning of words they tried to speak in code. He alone had the mental fortitude to gather the information the group needed here in Washington. Of course, it made perfect sense. How could he have thought otherwise, even if only for an instant?

I know I have no need to say it, but to ease my own mind, I ask you to remember that even the slightest remark to the wrong person can upset all we have strived to achieve.

David snorted. Of course it didn't need to be said. He knew the consequences of a wagging tongue and a blundering remark. But if it eased John's own fragile mind to put it to paper, he wouldn't begrudge the man the comfort.

I have learned of something I feel will be of great interest to you. I have finally recovered our lost message and was able to use a cipher to decode its meaning. It is of little importance now, as it is months old, but since you were the one who discovered who had stolen it, I thought you would like to know the contents.

A thrill tingled up his spine. He *knew* that harlot had taken their message! Oh, she'd fooled the others, but David had always known.

At the time, he'd only known that a message would soon be delivered and that the plans of those still out of his reach would be detailed within it. The girl bringing the stolen message had actually been a blessing, a sign that David was meant for greatness and that his righteous quest for Liza's justice would be honored. The lost message arrived at *his* camp, even after they'd joined with another regiment and left their own position. How could it be anything other than fate?

He turned his hungry eyes back to the page. This message had launched him from the fringes to the very heart of the battle.

The message read: Descendants of the Cavaliers, the time we have looked to is nigh upon us. The trap is ready to be sprung, and the key players have joined our ranks. It is time for us to step into the light and to take up our given duties. We will make the move before the woodsman takes second oath.

Second oath. They'd planned on taking the lumbering oaf before the second inauguration. If the message hadn't been lost before it found its way into David's life, would they have attempted the heist without him? He couldn't know. But fate had seen to it that he'd be the one to bring the giant Booth had required and thereby transport himself to the forefront of Booth's attention. How the man could have forgotten their time together as actors before the start of the Northern Aggression spoke to Booth's erratic memory, but such things were of no consequence now.

Fate had seen to it that David received his rightfully deserved position of power. And though the harlot had run off and proven herself a Union spy, her schemes had all failed. She'd been forced to return to the North in failure. Now, she and the giant were both out of his way.

He had to let go of his curiosity about whether Daniels's desperation would prove his downfall. Fate had dealt him justly thus far. Daniels's cowardly retreat and the fact that Harry had gone missing were merely distractions to be ignored. Fate simply worked to set him on task again, removing such things from him so he could focus on what was important.

Besides, the harlot and the coward were of little consequence. And Harry, the fool, was just a blunt tool ready to be discarded anyway. He'd likely walked off a bridge or some other thing predestined to a dullard not even bright enough to order his own steps. So David need not worry over the missing dimwit, either. He turned his eyes back to the paper and scanned the final lines.

Report to her if you find anything of note, as I will be checking back with you through her to keep ties unseen.

David breathed a sigh of relief despite himself. What a fool he'd been! Of course Booth and Surratt had kept their distance from him, and likely from one another as well. It made sense they should keep apart to avoid any suspicions that the tyrant's driver might have roused after that day on the road.

New faith in John's wits welled. His use of his mother proved more cunning than it first appeared. Who would think that a lowly boarding woman would be the link between such powerful men? David nodded to himself. Yes, best they keep their team a secret and maintain their distance, at least for now.

He read the lines twice more, and then, breathing easy for the first time in weeks, tucked it away inside his jacket with his other important documents.

Eighteen

"Received a dispatch today from Booth. How well the cipher works! Who could tell that so important a secret was concealed under the simple message?"
John H. Surratt

Watkins Glen, New York
March 31, 1865

The wagon lumbered down the road as the first rays of a new day barely kissed the earth. Annabelle pulled her shawl tightly around her shoulders. No one else had risen to witness Matthew's departure. Harry sat next to him on the driver's bench, his hands and feet bound.

Since she'd discovered Harry in the potato shed, Annabelle's stomach had been in knots. She'd been unable to sleep and had spent most of the night wondering if he'd be discovered.

Or escape.

All night she'd listened for stealthy footsteps in the hall.

When the wagon reached the edge of the drive, Annabelle strained her sight. Would he spare her a look? His frame remained rigid.

As soon as they were out of sight, Annabelle gave a dismissive shake of her head and slipped back through the front door. The curtains were still drawn, and she had to use the banister to find her way up the main staircase in the dim light.

She slipped down the dark hall without bothering to strike the lamp. No one else stirred. Annabelle breathed a sigh of relief and opened the door to her chamber. She slid through, and then closed it gently behind her.

Slumping against the door, Annabelle closed her eyes. What would happen to Matthew once he found the conspirators? Would he keep his word to stop them, or would he be drawn back into their schemes?

He'd left so quickly, she hadn't even had a chance to formulate a plan to help him.

"And just what do you think you're doin'?"

Annabelle yelped and her hand flew to her thudding heart. "Peggy! You nearly scared the life from me. What are you doing in here?"

The older woman stood by the marble hearth, fire poker in her hand. Even with only the glowing embers and the tiny bit of light peeking through the cracks in the curtain, Annabelle knew that Peggy's eyebrows had lifted all the way up to the red scarf wrapped around her head.

"I'm doing what I do every morning. Why're you up and about this early?"

Annabelle pulled her lip through her teeth. A lie sprung to her tongue about coming in from doing her business out in the privy, but she held it back. She'd become far too quick to deceive and she'd hurt Peggy with her lies more than once. "I was watching Matthew leave."

"What do you mean?"

Annabelle crossed the thick blue rug and pulled open the heavy drapes to let in the sunrise. Then she returned to the hearth and stretched out her hands. "He's going back to Washington because those scoundrels are going to try again."

Peggy gripped the poker, her job of stoking the flames forgotten. "They're still going to try to run off with the president?"

Annabelle grabbed a small log from the stack and placed it on top of the charred leftovers from the night before. The embers glowed brightly, and soon small flames licked at the new tinder. "Matthew says they've moved from simple abduction to planning an assassination."

"Murder?" Peggy squeaked.

Annabelle wrapped her arms around herself. "We can't let them. We need to tell someone."

"Oh, Lawd. Not this here mess *again*!" Peggy wagged her head. "I finally got you somewhere safe, with plenty to fill your belly. We ain't doing this again, Miss Belle!"

Annabelle pressed her fingers into the rose day dress she'd borrowed from Lilly. Fear and annoyance played across Peggy's face. "We can't let a man be abducted and possibly murdered."

Peggy shook her head and turned away, busying herself with straightening the bedclothes. Peggy always kept her hands occupied when something vexed her. Annabelle allowed her a few moments to think.

By the time she placed the last fluffed pillow and smoothed the blanket on top, Peggy's composure returned. "You're right. We can't stand by and see a man's life taken. What's the Captain going to do in Washington?"

"He says he's going to try to stop them."

Peggy looked satisfied. "Good. Someone's going to do the telling. You stay right here, where it's safe."

Annabelle twisted her fingers in her skirts and looked down at the floor. "Of course."

Peggy touched her arm. "What is it, Miss Belle?"

"What if…." Annabelle ran a hand down her face. "What if he decides to join them again instead?"

Peggy creased her brow. "What would he do that for? He already got his brother."

"But what if Harry comes up with something? If they really are planning on killing him, he's not safe going back to Washington!"

Peggy grabbed Annabelle's shoulders, giving her a shake. "Harry? Killing?" The whites of her eyes stood out against her face. "You're not talking about the president this time, are you?"

Annabelle told Peggy all about finding Harry in the shed and what Matthew had told her about O'Malley's plans to have Matthew murdered.

Peggy huffed. "No wonder you've been walking around like they's eggs under your feet. And here I thought it was 'cause you was caught between the two brothers."

Annabelle gave an apologetic shrug, and Peggy pointed a finger at her. "You've got to quit with all these secrets. Why you keep stuff from me? Ain't I always been here for you?"

Tears welled in Peggy's eyes and she quickly blinked them away, but not before the sight of them skewered Annabelle's heart. She pulled the woman into a tight embrace, and tears of her own trailed down her cheeks. "I'm so sorry!"

Peggy patted her back. "You're not alone in this world. Why're you trying so hard to act like it?"

Annabelle sniffled and pulled away, wrapping her arms around herself. Peggy let her go, and Annabelle stepped over to the window. A set of bluebirds chased one another through the branches.

"I don't know." She released the hasty knot at the back of her head and ran her fingers through the tangled mess. A shame her emotions weren't as easy to untangle. "I've been trying so hard to be in control. To do whatever I must to prove that I *am* strong. Capable." Her voice hitched. "Worthwhile."

"Oh, my sweet girl." Peggy took Annabelle's cheeks in her hands. "Who you trying to prove that to? You're worth the whole world to me. The Good Lord himself gave all for you. Don't you let the words of foolish men ever make you believe no different."

Annabelle clutched the cloth at her neck. "I was never a stately enough daughter, nor a good enough nurse. Gracious, I wasn't even smart enough to deliver a simple note or get a message out to my uncle without being caught and thought a spy!"

Peggy's deep brown eyes filled with sympathy.

Annabelle's cheeks heated and she pulled off her shawl, flinging it across the room. "I've been nothing but a burden. The *one thing* of any importance I accomplished, saving Lincoln, turns out to be nothing more than a delay in their plans!"

Peggy arched her brows. "But you stopped them. And found Mr. Daniels."

Annabelle ignored her. The dam that had held her churning emotions had cracked, and now everything burst through her defenses like a freed river. "And what do I have to show for everything I tried to do? A lost home. Poverty." She waved her hands. "And nothing but utter rejection from the man I love!"

As soon as the words fled her lips, Annabelle snapped her mouth closed and looked at Peggy with wide eyes.

The older woman crossed her arms. "You 'bout done with that fit, Miss Belle?"

She deflated, dropping her chin to her chest. "Yes."

"Good. Now you look a'here." She waited a moment, but when Annabelle didn't raise her gaze Peggy placed a finger under her chin and forced Annabelle to look into her eyes. "That's enough of that. I know you've got a ripe amount of hurt. Lawd knows what you've been through. But you're looking at this all wrong."

In Peggy's gaze Annabelle found all the love and acceptance she'd been looking for everywhere else. Why had she taken it for granted?

"I reckon I just look at things different," Peggy continued. "See, I watched a young woman survive the loss of both her parents, save the lives of countless soldiers no matter what color they wore, serve and care for her elder and give him the respect he by no means deserved, and even stood up to him when the coward turned to striking a lady. I saw that young woman brave the dangers of traveling and escape false accusations against her. She don't let no man bully her. And after all of that, she even found a way to save the liberator his self."

Tears welled anew and Annabelle wiped the moisture from her eyes. "Oh, Peggy. I do love you so." She patted Peggy's arm. "But don't you see that you only look at me that way because you're like a mother to me? A momma will always see her child in the best light."

Peggy shook her head, sadness in her eyes. "I'm glad you

still think so but that just ain't true. There's many mommas out there that don't see they girls as a treasure. Believe me." Peggy took the hem of her long apron and dabbed at Annabelle's cheeks. "There now," she said with a gentle smile. "Beautiful as ever."

"Just not enough for Matthew."

Peggy swatted at her. "Hush! I watched two stubborn folks dance around the fact that they love each other long enough."

Annabelle was about to protest, but Peggy held up her finger. "Oh, no you don't. No more self-pity." Annabelle gaped at her. Peggy kept talking. "I won't hear another word about that man not wanting you."

Annabelle blinked in surprise.

Peggy brushed her hands together as though dusting off flour after kneading dough. "Now, then. We're done with this foolishness."

Annabelle could only gulp, dumbfounded.

"I tried to go about it easy like, but baby girl, you're in need of some plain talk. You got walls bigger than Elmira 'round your heart, and I can't say I blame you. But you're as stubborn as an ornery mule, and you're letting those walls turn you bitter. I ain't going to stand by and watch it no more. You're going to quit all this lying and deceitfulness, and you're going to start being honest." She pointed a finger at Annabelle. "And you're going to start letting folks help you. You hear me?"

Annabelle's mouth fell agape. When she could find her voice again, it came out in a squeak. "Yes, ma'am."

"No more sneaking around, and no more putting yourself down."

Annabelle wrapped her arms around herself. "Yes, ma'am."

Peggy's eyes softened. "I know you love that Captain. Done seen it for some time."

This time, Annabelle didn't even try to argue. What more could be said?

Peggy tugged on imagined wrinkles in the bedclothes she'd already straightened. "Some things just can't be hid. Didn't need you to finally admit what I already knew to be true. If he's the man the Lawd has for you, then you say your prayers and see what happens."

Annabelle drew her lip through her teeth, any retort she could think of dying on her tongue.

"And Miss Belle?"

There's more? "Yes?"

"I know your heart ain't for the other Mr. Daniels."

Annabelle sighed. Obviously. Why say it?

"So, don't you let foolish pride make you marry him for that house. That was your daddy's land, and I know you loved him, but it's not worth you living out your days in misery to keep it."

Fresh tears stung again, and Peggy swept her up in a tight hug. "I'm sorry I had to be so blunt about it, but it's time you heard these things."

Annabelle clenched Peggy tight. "I…." She drew a steadying breath. "Thank you, Peggy."

Peggy pulled back and patted her shoulder. "Start holding that pretty chin of yours up and take some lessons from that grandma you got. That's a lady who knows how to command respect."

Annabelle couldn't help the laugh that bubbled up inside her. "She *is* something."

"Yes, ma'am. That she sure is." Peggy laughed, and the

tension fell off Annabelle like a mighty weight.

It was time she started making some changes, and the first of those was to start with being honest. She looked at Peggy and drew strength from the quiet dignity that no one had been able to strip from a woman who, at least by the world's standards, stood at the very bottom of society. Despite whatever people had flung at her, Peggy kept her back strong and her heart soft, and there was no one in the world more regal.

Nineteen

"There was no option in the matter, therefore I had to go with Mrs. S on to Richmond. What a condition that city is in! Everything so high that rich men become poor, and those not so well off are starving."
John H. Surratt

As she sat at the table for the noon meal, Annabelle's stomach began to churn. Had it been only a few hours since she'd promised Peggy to be more forthcoming? Though the idea terrified her, it also lessened the burdens on her heart. She'd prayed for forgiveness and found it to be a balm on raw wounds. But now the old doubts already returned. She tried to force them away and keep a tight hold on the peace she'd so recently found.

Peggy and Lilly entered through the rear door with trays heaped with various foods, and little Frankie tottered in on his mother's heels. He went straight to Eudora, who cooed and played with the curls on his head. Annabelle watched the two as Peggy and Lilly placed the food along the center of the wide table.

Frankie had soft, dark curls and his mother's expressive

eyes. Skin a warm, deep olive, Frankie reminded Annabelle of the Spanish gentleman she'd once met. The baby babbled to Eudora, who seemed to understand his words. After a moment, Frankie spotted George. His little face lit up, and he toddled out of Eudora's reach, arms outstretched to George.

George, looking every bit as pleased as the boy, grinned as he scooted his chair back from the table. "Hello there, young man!" He patted his knee. "Come sit with me."

Lilly gave a small cry and nearly dropped her bowl of potatoes on the table. "No, no, baby! You need to leave the gentleman alone." In an instant she rounded the table and scooped Frankie into her arms.

Frankie wailed and began to thrash, but Lilly held firm. Disappointment tugged on George's face. Eudora narrowed keen eyes on George. Her brows furrowed, and then she glanced toward Annabelle. When their eyes met, she quickly looked away.

Lilly bounced Frankie on her hip and stroked his hair. After a moment, his thumb went in his mouth and his cries settled into whimpers.

Eudora smacked her hands together, drawing everyone's attention. "As soon as the other Mr. Daniels joins us, we'll begin our meal."

George picked up his fork and laughed, though it sounded forced. "He best hurry. I'm starved!"

Annabelle smoothed her napkin in her lap and kept her eyes down.

"Did you tell your brother the meal was ready?" Eudora asked George.

"No, ma'am. I haven't seen him all morning. I suspect he

went riding again." He shrugged. "I expected him back by now."

Annabelle gripped the soft linen napkin and studied the twisting ivy pattern dancing along the edge of her plate.

Frankie wailed again, and Lilly sent Eudora a part pleading, part didn't-I-say-so glare. Eudora smiled sweetly at the boy. "Go ahead and let the baby eat, Lilly Rose. There's no reason the little fellow needs to wait."

Lilly placed little piles of vegetables on his plate. They didn't have a child's chair, but someone had fashioned a small seat on a raised platform that Lilly had placed into the chair next to her. She settled Frankie on it, and the boy snatched the morsels up with chubby fingers and stuffed them into his mouth.

With the added height, he could easily reach the table, and with him now quiet, Lilly relaxed. Peggy, ever a mother hen, fussed over him from her place on the other side of his chair.

After she dabbed the boy's mouth with a napkin, which he swatted away, Peggy cleared her throat. Her eyes found Annabelle's, and she lifted her brows. Annabelle bit her lip and looked back down, knowing exactly what Peggy wanted. She had no desire to air out everything here at the table. She'd agreed to tell Eudora, but she didn't have to do it with an audience.

"Miss Belle has something to say."

Annabelle glared at Peggy. So much for privacy.

"What's going on?" Eudora's gaze flicked between Annabelle and George.

Completely wrong track. Heat burned in her chest and moisture popped up along her collarbone. "Matthew left this morning for Washington."

"*What?*" George pressed his palms against the table.

"He had some… urgent business and needed to leave right away."

"Without telling anyone?" Eudora's features tightened, creating crevices on the sides of her mouth.

Annabelle resisted the urge to squirm under Eudora's heavy gaze. "Yes, I'm afraid so."

"That harebrained fool!" George wadded his napkin and tossed it on the table. "This has something to do with those abductors, doesn't it?"

Annabelle gulped. How much did George know?

"Abduction?" Eudora grew rigid. "What in heaven's name are you talking about?"

Peggy showed no remorse for the stir she'd caused and gestured for Annabelle to explain.

She didn't get the opportunity. George leaned forward in his chair. "They were involved with some group that had plans to cart off Lincoln," he said, the tension in his voice nearly palatable. He cut his eyes at Annabelle. "But Miss Ross can better explain."

Annabelle gave him an annoyed glance before pointedly turning away from him to address Eudora. "I intended to speak with you on this matter after the meal." She shot a quick glance at Peggy. "In *private*."

Eudora gave an unladylike snort. "Nonsense. We are all family here." She eyed George. "At least, close enough to count."

Annabelle sighed. "Very well. But at least fix your plates. It's a long story. By the time I finish, the food will be cold."

They passed the bowls around and Annabelle tried to organize her thoughts as she scooped small portions of cabbage, carrots, and stewed beef onto her plate. She shifted through each part of the last weeks of her life and tried to pick out which portions would be best to share and how to put them into the best light.

An unwelcome tightness constricted her chest, and she struggled to breathe. *No!* She wouldn't scuttle around the truth. She'd tell it all, including all her failures and shortcomings. She met each set of eyes around the table, save the baby, and found no judgment, only curiosity. Feeling resolved, she began her story.

"About seven weeks ago, I found a coded message on a dead soldier."

For the next half hour, Annabelle offered her tale, leaving nothing out and laying bare all she'd done. There were times they shook their heads in dismay and other times they stared at her with mouths agape and eyes wide. Much as a doctor let fevered blood out of the body, she hoped the release would bring healing.

When she finally finished, ending with how Matthew had found Harry following them and how she'd discovered him in the potato shed, everything fell silent. They'd forgotten their meals and stared at her.

Frankie wailed, breaking the silence. He flung his arms and knocked over his glass of milk.

Lilly jumped to her feet. She wiped the dripping liquid and tried to keep it from the rug. Peggy moved to help. Frankie's voice elevated to a screech.

George pushed away from the table and had the child in his arms before Eudora could even rise from her chair. He swung the boy up high and tossed him in the air. Frankie's cries immediately turned to giggles, and after two more tosses, he laughed heartily.

George held the boy out to his flustered mother. "I think he's all better."

Frankie reached for his momma. Lilly plucked him from George's arms and squeezed him tight. "I'm going to take him up for a nap."

Lilly tucked Frankie's head under her chin and hurried from the room. George sighed and stepped over to the doors Lilly had left open, pulling them closed. When he turned back around, his familiar, easy smile graced his face.

When he regained his seat and Peggy had wiped up the last drop of milk, Eudora placed her elbows on the table and steepled her fingers. "What does that boy plan on doing once he gets the other man back to Washington?"

Annabelle tucked a loose curl behind her ear. "I wish I knew."

After a moment of thought, Eudora relaxed and gave Annabelle a placating smile. "I'm certain once he goes to the law, all will be made right."

"I fear he may not go to the law," she said carefully. "That's why I planned on following him. I stopped this thing once. I can do so again."

"You'll do nothing of the sort!"

Everyone turned at Peggy's outburst. If it was as easy to read Peggy's dusky skin as it was Annabelle's, she was certain the older woman's cheeks would be bright red. Peggy snapped her jaw shut, but didn't lower her eyes.

"I agree, Peggy." Eudora looked rather amused. "Fortunately, my dear husband had plenty of contacts in Washington." She swung her attention back to Annabelle. "Perhaps you and I could make arrangements to visit, just to ease your mind?"

Annabelle stared at her. "You want to go to Washington with me?"

A smile, threaded with a meaning Annabelle couldn't quite decipher, turned up Eudora's lips. "I don't have any pressing matters here. Besides, I have friends near there I haven't seen in ages."

"We should start travel plans immediately." George stood and straightened his jacket.

Eudora lifted her brows. "And who said you were going?"

"I…he's…what?"

"You, sir, aren't fully recovered." She pinned George with a narrowed gaze. "And you have no business traveling around the state of New York as a wanted man."

Entirely unaffected by the color rising in George's face, Eudora rose and straightened her bodice. "I'll have Lilly pack our things. Anka can send some telegrams ahead for me, and we should be ready to go by morning."

Eudora almost made it to the door before George found his voice. "Wait just a moment. I won't be left behind like some invalid. You cannot stop me from riding to Washington on my own, even if you deny me your company. I'm healthier now than I've been in weeks, and I'll not lounge around while my fool brother places himself into harm. I'm going to Washington, whether you approve or not."

Rather than anger, a slow smile spread across Eudora's face. "I'll just leave Günter in charge of Lilly's and the baby's safety, then. I'm sure his wife won't mind him staying here in the house while we're gone." Her forehead wrinkled in thought. "In fact, I better just move Pete, Anka and the entire family here for a spell. Yes, yes," she said, seemingly to herself. "We might be awhile, and that would be best."

George's eyes widened, and for a second, he hesitated. "Yes, that seems fitting." He gave the slightest bow and then left.

Eudora wrinkled her nose at Peggy, who cleared the table. "You're not a servant in my house."

Peggy offered a genuine smile. "I know. But Lilly needs to tend that little un, and I like to keep busy."

Eudora glanced at Annabelle, but knowing Peggy's stubbornness well, she simply shrugged. Peggy gathered the plates and headed out the rear door toward the kitchen.

"Come along, child," Eudora said. "We have plenty to do if we're going to leave at first light."

Flutters stirred in Annabelle's stomach. They were going back to Washington.

Twenty

"Not only is Richmond to fall, as a fruit of the campaign, but in his dreams General Grant sees General Lee unable to meet him in battle, unable to retreat, unable to subsist, and with nothing to do but surrender. The fatal circle is to be drawn around him at last."
The New-York Times

Frederick, Maryland
April 2, 1865

Annabelle scanned the newspaper she'd purchased at the train station as the carriage jostled along the road. Being enclosed in a fine carriage reminded her of what life had been like before the war. She could close her eyes and lean back against the padded seats, and if she tried hard enough, perhaps she could pretend Father rode across from her.

But pretending helped no one. Once they'd left Eudora's home in New York and taken the train to Maryland, signs of the nation's destruction once again marred the landscape. Trying to imagine all was well only caused more pain when reality bared its fangs.

She glanced up from the bouncing script she still hadn't

managed to read. "Where are we going, Grandmother?"

Eudora covered her mouth with a gloved hand to suppress a yawn. "We'll stay with a friend of mine in Frederick tonight."

Annabelle's brows pulled together. Even with the speed gained by riding the train, Annabelle couldn't help but feel their travel had been unbearably slow. If they hurried, they could make it to Washington, have the law take down the conspirators, and settle the matter before Matthew even had the chance to be seduced by their games.

They really didn't have the time for her to linger with friends. Annabelle opened her mouth to say so, but thought better of it. Without Eudora's aid, she would have been forced to travel alone. Without money for a decent room.

As much as she worried for Matthew's safety, such foolishness would have never been an option. She glanced at Peggy, who rode stiffly at her side. No, sneaking away to Washington without Peggy would have been a betrayal she might never undo.

"All will be well, dear," Eudora said. "You'll give yourself early wrinkles with all those frowns."

Annabelle smoothed her face. "The delay has made me anxious."

"Delay?" Eudora arched a brow.

Strange how she can hike just one like that. She'd tried to practice the trick in the looking glass three nights past, but couldn't get one to rise without the other.

Annabelle clasped her hands in her lap, trying to keep them from fidgeting. "Harry has been following us for weeks. Who knows what they've been doing all this time. They may have already carried out their vile schemes!"

"Ha!" Eudora barked a laugh. "You think if those fools had accomplished that ridiculous plan, you wouldn't be reading about it in that paper?"

Annabelle glanced at the crumpled pages in her lap and sighed. "I suppose you're right."

"Of course I am."

Annabelle glanced at Peggy. She fidgeted with her dress in the same manner Annabelle always did. The dark blue silk looked beautiful on her, and Annabelle had seldom seen Peggy without her head scarf. Eudora had tossed that aside along with Peggy's ragged dress the moment she'd showered Peggy with all the colorful gowns a widow would never wear again. Now Peggy had a trunk just as heavy as Annabelle's. That might be amusing, if things were a bit different.

Peggy had adamantly refused the clothing, but it did her little good. Eudora had her way, and that was that. Annabelle guessed Peggy secretly treasured the fine fabrics, given the way her fingers often caressed them. Peggy noticed Annabelle watching her.

"Do you suppose George fares all right?" Annabelle asked, changing the subject.

Eudora bobbed her head. "The fresh spring air will do him good."

George often seemed tired, and during their stay at Eudora's house, he'd retire as soon as he'd taken his evening meal. She imagined the fresh air *would* do him good. The North had finally begun to warm, and cheery sunlight had always been a lift to her own moods. Besides, she figured George, riding alongside the carriage driver, was probably enjoying his few moments away from female company.

The corners of Annabelle's mouth turned up. "You're once again correct."

"Certainly, my dear." Eudora flashed a smug smile. "You'll find I usually am. Might as well start getting used to it." She winked, and Annabelle could not suppress a laugh.

The carriage slowed, and Annabelle shifted her attention to the window. They'd entered a large town, and the streets were crowded with traffic.

"Should have reached Frederick," Eudora said without glancing outside.

"Already?"

Eudora had made it seem staying the night would be necessary, since they wouldn't make the afternoon train. They had plenty of time to continue farther today.

Eudora waved away Annabelle's annoyance as though it was a summer stable fly. "So we're early. No harm done. Besides, when I sent word to my husband's friends in Washington, I requested they telegraph me here."

Annabelle looked to Peggy for support, but Peggy shrugged. She ground her teeth. Hearing back from her friends that they were delighted Eudora had decided to visit was hardly worth the wasted time.

"Trust me, dear."

Annabelle glanced up quickly.

"Getting there faster and running pell-mell into who knows what won't garner any success. Better to send word ahead and see what we can discover about the state of affairs. Sometimes, it's best to approach with a delicate touch."

Perhaps the woman had a point. Still, she didn't like it.

"And don't look at me like that." Eudora leaned forward

and patted Annabelle's knee.

The carriage rolled to a stop, and in a moment the door swung open and George poked his head inside. She had to admit, he looked rather dapper in a properly fitting suit.

He pushed his bowler hat back. "Driver says we've reached the telegraph station, Mrs. Smith. Want me to run inside and fetch your messages?"

"No, I'll handle it myself. You stay here and look after Annabelle while Peggy and I go inside."

Annabelle tried to cover her grimace. She didn't need tending. She cut her eyes at George, only to find him grinning.

"Me?" Peggy asked. "You need me to fetch something, ma'am?"

Eudora took George's hand and stepped out of the carriage, turning to speak to Peggy as she straightened her skirts. "Of course not. I want you to get used to getting out and doing things as a free woman. You've been one for quite some time, though you don't act like it."

Peggy gaped at her, but Eudora seemed entirely unaware of it.

"Hurry along now, let's get going. Haven't got all day, you know."

Peggy snapped her jaw shut and looked at Annabelle. Annabelle offered an encouraging smile. It would be good for Peggy. The poor woman looked as nervous as a mouse in the kitchen, but she scrambled out of the carriage and followed Eudora anyway.

As soon as they stepped away, George hopped up into the carriage and took Eudora's seat, leaving the door open for propriety's sake.

"Been wanting to talk to you," George said, rubbing at the back of his neck.

Annabelle clamped her hands in her lap, not caring for the resignation in his tone. "Oh?"

George tugged at his collar and looked down at the shiny new boots on his feet. "I've been doing a lot of thinking since we left New York."

Annabelle practiced holding her worry lines at bay and waited for George to continue.

He looked at her thoughtfully for a moment. "I want to be sure we're clear, Miss Ross. I do not *ever* intend to marry you. It's not something that will come about after we have grown accustomed to one another."

Confusion washed over her. Perhaps she hadn't been clear with George. She offered her best smile. "Of course, Mr. Daniels. When we spoke on the matter, I didn't take our conversation to mean that there was simply a delay in the arrangement. I understood it to be a final decision."

He breathed a sigh of relief. That, perhaps, stung a tad, even if his words of rejection had not.

"I'm glad to hear it," he said. "I didn't want things to go on with you thinking it was a possibility sometime in the future."

The muscles in her jaw tightened. "As I said before, I have no schemes for forcing anyone into marriage. All this time, my only intention has been to do whatever was needed to save my father's land."

George nodded solemnly. "I understand. I don't want you to feel the only way to accomplish your goal is through marriage. I know women don't have many options, but as I said when we first spoke on it, I *will* find a way to be sure you're secure."

Annabelle tilted her chin, wondering why they were having this discussion again. "You are truly kind."

George leaned forward, placed his elbows on his knees, and laced his fingers. "It's not merely kindness. I owe you great debt. You took risks to find my location and put yourself in danger on several occasions to help my brother." He stared at her, his genuine gratitude evident.

"I…." She began, unsure what to say.

George held up his hand to stay her. "I wanted you to know my aid comes from gratitude, not obligation. More, I also want you to know that I didn't decline the match because I thought you unsuitable." He hesitated, uncertainty playing across his face.

She kept her face serene and waited, giving him time to gather his words.

Finally, he sat back and regarded her seriously. "I was in an arranged marriage before, and though we enjoyed one another's company, no real love ever blossomed. I do hope you'll forgive my selfishness, but if I ever marry again, I want it to be for affection and not for benefit. I want to know what it's like to spend the remainder of my free days with a woman my heart yearns for."

"I didn't know you were married."

He nodded, pain evident in his eyes. "She died in childbirth, six years back."

Annabelle put her hand to her heart. "I'm sorry for your grief."

A sad smile played at his mouth. "The wounds will never fully heal, but I hope to one day find the type of love that soothes their ache."

Annabelle remembered the way George had looked at little Frankie and Lilly, and suddenly it made sense. Seeing mother and child must have stirred painful memories about the family he'd lost. She met his eyes. "I appreciate your honesty."

He gave a small nod.

"And," she said with a sigh, "you can't know how soothing your words actually are."

George cocked his head, evidently confused.

"You see, I, too, have no desire to be married to a man I don't love. Peggy said that keeping my family lands isn't worth spending the rest of my life in a loveless marriage. In my heart I know she's right, but I fear I may have still been tempted to do so, had you agreed." *Since the one I love will not have me.*

Understanding washed over George's face, and Annabelle felt a weight lift from her as well. "You're a wonderful young lady, Miss Ross."

Annabelle smiled tightly, unsure what to say.

Now that his intentions had been delivered, she expected him to exit, but still he stayed, watching her. "Were you aware that my father's arrangement with your own never actually included me?"

Annabelle almost snorted, but kept her dignity intact. "Of course. My father arranged for me to court the youngest Daniels son, the one nearest my age. I've known that Matthew pushed me off onto you for some time." Try as she might, she couldn't keep the bitterness from her tone.

George's lips drew into a line, thoughtful. Where Matthew tended to be quick with his words, George seemed to consider everything before he spoke. "I think my brother's motives may be different than you think."

She glared at him, and he looked away.

He cleared his throat. "Perhaps it's something the two of you should discuss once we reach Washington." He popped out of the carriage before she could reply.

His boots had no sooner landed in the dust than Eudora appeared, lifting her hand to George. He helped her into the carriage. Then, to Annabelle's surprise, Peggy lifted her own fingers and George assisted her.

Eudora settled in her seat and began giving instructions before George could close the door. "Tell the driver to continue down this street," she said. "And then take a left at the next intersection. Follow that road until it ends. My friend's home will be the one to the right, set up on the hill."

George nodded and closed the door. A moment later the horses stepped into the road. They rode in silence through the town and then pulled down a winding drive, passing large trees and bushes covered in buds.

The carriage came to a stop, and after a moment Annabelle could hear men talking outside. Eudora waited, so Annabelle and Peggy took her cue and remained seated. Presently, the voices outside quieted and the carriage door opened. However, instead of George, an older gentleman with dark skin, a gray beard, and twinkling eyes stood outside.

He beamed. "Mrs. Smith! We're so glad to see you again!"

Eudora took the man's hand as she stepped down. "Oh, Sam! I'm very glad to see you're doing well."

"Been right good here." His eyes twinkled.

"I'm glad to hear it." Eudora patted his arm fondly and then motioned toward the carriage. "I've brought my granddaughter,

Annabelle, and her companion, Peggy."

The two women moved to exit the carriage, taking the man's assistance as they stepped out into the pleasantly warm day. Annabelle shielded her eyes, wishing she hadn't left the bonnet in her trunk. She nodded to the man. "Hello."

He bowed to Annabelle and then looked at Peggy, his eyes lighting. He held out a hand. "My, Mrs. Smith, you sure did bring a lovely lady on this here visit."

Eudora laughed, but Peggy's eyes widened in horror. She put a hand to her throat, ignoring the hand Sam stuck out.

"Come on now, Sam." Eudora swatted a playful hand at his sleeve. "Leave the poor woman be."

Sam's eyes twinkled, but he finally turned away from Peggy. She eyed the man warily. Annabelle giggled, and received the press of Peggy's elbow in her ribs for it. She put her fingers over her mouth as Peggy glared at her.

Eudora pretended not to notice the exchange. When George finished talking to the driver and came around to stand with them, Peggy finally regained her composure. She stood stiffly at Annabelle's side, discomfort radiating off her like heat from the flame.

"Let me take y'all on to the house," Sam said.

The carriage rumbled away, taking with it any hope of them leaving earlier than mid-morning, when Eudora instructed the coachman to return.

Sam gestured toward the house. "She's been expecting you." The tails of his fine jacket flapped behind him as he turned.

The four of them followed along behind him silently. Just off the carriage path, a set of stairs sank into a steep hill and led to the stately house perched on the top. Annabelle lifted her traveling skirts to climb the narrow incline, wondering how difficult such an entry would be to traverse in the rain. Already she feared slipping, and the weather had been calm for days.

When they reached the top of the stairs, Annabelle lifted her eyes from judging her every step to studying the house. Only a single story, the place was nonetheless impressive. Nothing compared to the grandeur of her grandmother's home, but bright and inviting. Where Eudora's house looked like a stern sentry, this home called to mind a squat lady, her arms brimming with flowers.

Annabelle smiled to herself as they stepped up onto a wide porch. In nearly every available space, pots sprouted with plants and lively blooms and gave a warm invitation. As spring progressed, the entire front of the house would likely burst with color.

And, oh, how she welcomed it. She'd never endured a winter so long. Spring waited to nearly the end of March to break the chill hanging over the North. Even when the days warmed, the nights seemed reluctant to let go of their hold on winter. How George had endured those frigid nights spoke to a strength she'd always admire.

Sam pulled open a wide front door, and called inside. "Miss Wesson! She's here!"

Annabelle looked at Peggy and lifted her brows. Peggy gave a small shake of her head, also confused. They'd never seen a doorman shout for the lady before, but perhaps things were done differently in Maryland than they were in Mississippi.

Sam ushered the guests inside. "Come on in, come on in."

Peggy kept her eyes on her wide skirts, pointedly ignoring the way Sam watched her as she passed. Annabelle suppressed a chuckle at the way the older man tried to get Peggy's attention like a smitten boy.

"You made it!" A woman scurried out of the room off to Annabelle's left. She hurried to Eudora and pulled her into a tight embrace. "Eudora Smith, it's been too long!"

Eudora patted her friend's back and the joy on her face made Annabelle regret her previous frustration. A few hours to enjoy a visit wouldn't make that much difference. At least, she hoped not.

The new woman gave Eudora a final squeeze, and pulled away, turning honey-colored eyes on her guests. "And who all have you brought?"

Eudora gestured to Annabelle. "This is my granddaughter." The pride in her voice warmed a place in Annabelle's heart she hadn't realized had been cold.

Annabelle lifted the side of her dress and lowered into a small curtsy. "A pleasure to meet you, ma'am."

The other woman put her fingers to her lips and looked back at Eudora. "Annabelle, isn't it?"

Eudora nodded.

The woman tilted her head and regarded Annabelle with a warm smile. "Isn't she the very image of Katherine?"

"Quite," Eudora agreed.

She stared at Annabelle a moment, then seemed to remember herself when Annabelle began to fidget. "Oh! Forgive me, dear. I'm Bulla Wesson. Your grandparents and I have been friends for…what?" She looked back at Eudora. "Thirty years?"

"Don't you go showing our age!"

Miss Wesson smirked. "Age is nothing but a prize for a life lived."

Eudora shook her head and gestured to the others, trying to keep the proper manners in place. "May I introduce Mr. George Daniels of Westerly, and Annabelle's companion, Peggy of Rosswood."

Peggy showed no surprise at the title bestowed upon her and lifted her heavy silk skirts, dipping into a perfect curtsy. "Ma'am."

George bowed and extended his hand. When Miss Wesson placed her fingers in his, he leaned over and gave the slightest brush of his lips across the back of her hand. "A pleasure, ma'am. We're thankful for your hospitality."

She giggled and then pulled her hand away, a blush coming to her cheeks. "Let's go out to the garden, shall we?" Miss Wesson hurried away without waiting for their reply.

Eudora gestured for them to follow, and they trailed along behind Miss Wesson's swaying pink silk.

Through a rear door they passed out into a lavish garden, meticulously tended and artfully arranged. Miss Wesson plopped down into a cushioned chair and waved her hand at the other chairs placed in a horseshoe shape. They took their seats, hedged in by a flowering bush Annabelle did not recognize. She admired the bright pink blossoms that dangled like bells.

Miss Wesson must have noticed. "These are fetterbushes. Aren't they lovely?" she twittered, seeming much younger than the silver streaks in her hair indicated.

Eudora laughed. "Oh, heavens, don't get her started. Bulla loves those plants too much and will talk you to exhaustion about every bloom out here." Her eyes twinkled as she said it, and her friend wrinkled her nose.

"I'm not that bad." She reached out to caress the soft petals of the nearest bloom.

Eudora opened her mouth to retort, but Miss Wesson waved her away and caught the doorman's attention. "Sam, would you ask Iris Primrose to make us some tea?"

"Yes, mistress," Sam said, turning away.

She clapped her hands. "Oh, and some of those little cakes she makes, too, if it's not too much trouble."

"'Course it ain't, Miss Wesson. I'll be right back with them treats." After a few steps, he disappeared from sight behind the towering plants around them.

"Iris Primrose?" George asked, stroking his beard. "Interesting name."

"Sometimes the girls who come to me want new names," Miss Wesson said with a shrug. "Something to mark their new life, I suppose. I give them the names of the most beautiful things I know."

George's brows gathered.

"Sam seems to be getting on very well," Eudora said to Miss Wesson, tugging her attention away from George.

Miss Wesson became more subdued. "It took some time, but he's finally started to bloom."

Annabelle looked at Peggy, curious, but the other woman kept her eyes downcast. George, too, seemed lost in his own thoughts. Annabelle drew a deep breath of the sweet-scented air, and settled back in her chair as the two friends talked about people she didn't know.

After a few moments, there was a slight lull and George broke into the conversation. "Excuse me, Miss Wesson. I'm rather curious. Have you had your slaves a long time?"

Miss Wesson laughed. "Silly boy. You'll find no slaves at my home." She plucked a flower near her chair and ran it along her cheek. "Something so ugly doesn't belong here."

George tugged at his whiskers. "Forgive my assumption. I just thought that since Maryland is still a slave state…." He let his words trail off.

Annabelle watched Miss Wesson. She'd thought all the northern states were free states. George must be mistaken.

Miss Wesson sighed, tucking the little bloom in her hair. "Unfortunately, that is so. Didn't keep us from being razed by Confederates last year, though." She wrinkled her nose. "Had to replace nearly everything in the house. Not to mention what they did to my poor flowers." She looked sadly over her gardens, though Annabelle couldn't fathom that anything here had ever seen the damages of war.

Miss Wesson brightened again. "But I have it looking almost right again, don't I, Eudora?"

Eudora patted her friend's hand and laughed. "You tend flowers like they were children. It's no wonder you never wed. Poor man would never have had any of your attentions."

Miss Wesson laughed, a sound not unlike the twittering birds overhead. "No man was ever able to capture my heart the way my flowers did."

Eudora chuckled. "Indeed."

Miss Wesson's brows pulled together. "Or was it that no man could accept me for the way I am?" Uncomfortable silence settled on them for a moment, but then Miss Wesson plucked herself from the contemplation and waved her hand. "No matter. Thanks to my father's mill work, I never needed a man anyway." She giggled like a girl, and Annabelle felt an unexpected pang of jealousy.

Her own father's wealth should have rendered her the same freedom. Instead, it had all vanished like a puff of smoke, leaving her with little more than a pile of charred embers to remind her of what should have been. Annabelle picked at her fingernails as the older women twittered on, the rest of the forgotten guests left to their private contemplations.

Twenty-One

"News has reached here that Richmond has fallen. That must be one of Lincoln's lying dispatches! The confederate Capital will not be surrendered."
John H. Surratt

Washington, D.C.
April 4, 1865

The carriage came to a stop and George helped Eudora, Annabelle, and Peggy down. Annabelle looked up at the large building as men unloaded the trunks.

"Ah, it has been many years since I've stayed at the National Hotel." Eudora had mentioned staying outside of the city with friends instead, but when Annabelle had nearly lost her composure over the suggestion, she'd relented.

George offered his arms, and she and Eudora slipped their gloved hands through his elbows. Peggy took her usual place behind Annabelle and followed. An elderly gentleman held open the hotel doors for them, his bright smile charming.

Eudora gave her name to a man in a crisp suit at the main receiving desk, and soon young men came in bearing their trunks. Not for the first time, Annabelle felt as though they'd brought an entire household with them.

After Eudora passed some money across the desk, the man gave her three keys and instructions she waved off. She seemed to know exactly where she was going, and the others followed her away from the man at the desk. Annabelle shot him an apologetic glance, but Eudora's briskness didn't seem to bother him in the least. They crossed the marble floors and climbed a massive staircase, the likes of which made even the one at the Smith house seem diminutive.

When they reached their rooms, George paused as Eudora inserted the key into her door. "When shall we meet to discuss our plans?"

Eudora pushed open the door to her room and cast him an annoyed glance. The men carrying her trunks arrived a second later, and she ushered them through the door. "See to your room, Mr. Daniels." He frowned at that, and she puckered her brow. "I hardly think taking the time to get settled after our journey will change matters."

His features tightened and little lines formed at the sides of his mouth. He stepped around them and stalked toward his own room.

Eudora pressed a key into Annabelle's fingers, then closed her door behind her. Perplexed, Annabelle stood there a moment staring at the door her grandmother had closed in her face.

"Miss?" A male voice startled her back to her senses. Two young men held each side of her trunk. The tall, lanky one jutted his chin down the carpeted hall. "Your room is just next door."

"Of course." After unlocking the door, the two young men hefted her trunk inside. They had no sooner placed hers at the foot of the bed than two more men entered, carrying another filled with the dresses Eudora had given Peggy.

"Right good news, isn't it now?" one of the young men said as he placed Peggy's trunk on the floor. He cast Peggy a curious look.

Peggy held his gaze, her hands clasped at her waist. She did look the contradiction, what with her lady's silk dress and her maid's headscarf. She'd fished it out of her things that morning, ignoring Eudora's protests.

"What news?" Annabelle asked.

He chuckled. "I suppose you haven't yet heard, since you just pulled in, but news is flooding in that Richmond has fallen!"

Annabelle clutched her traveling skirt. "When?"

"Happened yesterday. Rumors swirled last night, but we didn't start getting confirmation until today. Sure enough, the South's capital is under the shadow of Union forces now."

Annabelle swallowed hard. "Thank you, sir."

He smiled. "Certainly, miss. Have a pleasant afternoon." He left the room, pulling the door closed behind him.

She whirled around, skirts flaring. "Did you hear what he said?"

Peggy seemed more interested in the carved furniture and costly rugs. "'Course I did. These ears ain't that old…not yet, anyways."

"Richmond has fallen!"

"Yes, ma'am." Peggy patted Annabelle's arm. "That's what he said." Annabelle blinked at her and Peggy laughed. "What you want me to say, child? I don't know what to do with that news no more than you do." She shrugged. "But best I can tell, it sounds like a good thing. Means war's finally 'bout over."

Annabelle considered the claim. "Yes, I suppose you're right. Let's go over to Grandmother's room. We need to start looking for Matthew."

Peggy caught her arm. "You going to tell him?"

She drew her lip through her teeth, knowing exactly what Peggy meant. "Yes." Peggy's eyes lit up, and Annabelle had to raise her hand to stay Peggy's coming response. "But not until we see this thing finished. Once we know the president is safe, and the end of the war is final, then I'll tell him before we leave for home."

Peggy pursed her lips, but Annabelle gave her a look that said there was no point in arguing.

Finally, Peggy conceded. "All right."

David threw his cravat across the room, wishing the flimsy thing was something that would crash through the walls and give sound to his rage. Richmond fallen!

Lies. They must be lies!

He paced the room. His tiny portion of the house felt like a cage. And that Surratt! Did the man think him a fool?

Booth kept everyone separated. "Laying low" he called it. David called it disloyalty. What were they hiding? David balled his fists. He couldn't wait much longer. Booth gone to New York and Surratt dallying in Canada. Had they lost sight of what needed to be done?

And Richmond lost…

He let out a growl and heaved his writing chair across the

room. It hit the door with a thunderous bang, and one leg cracked. He stood there panting, waiting for someone to come to investigate the sound. But, after many moments without the first footstep on the stairs, David decided they must think it best to ignore him.

His trip to the telegraph office this morning had once again garnered nothing. Not a single line from Harry. He pounded his fist in his hand.

Fool!

Harry had probably gotten lost, or had run off like the other traitors. He should have gone after Daniels himself. Seen to it that the man's brother got out of prison and used Daniels's gratitude to his advantage. Booth said they no longer needed the giant, since he could not be brought to heel, but Booth underestimated David's ability to mold men to his will.

They could have used Daniels's enormous fists to bludgeon the tyrant into a pulp and be finished with this entire thing! He had no doubt he could have gotten Daniels to do it. The man might have once been his captain, but ranks were assigned by wealth, not by merit. Daniels had more wits about him than that dullard Harry, but was still no match for David's superior intellect.

He ground his teeth, and with no other furniture to release his frustrations upon, flung himself down on the bed. He'd wasted too much time waiting as those fools floundered about in their indecision. John Surratt wanted support from the government and from whoever his contacts were in Canada, but David did not see the point. They didn't need approval.

David bounded to his feet, his blood too hot to stay still. *Forget them all.* It was high time he took the matter into his own hands.

Twenty-Two

"There seems to be no doubt now of the fall of Richmond, and it appears that Lincoln has been riding in triumph through the streets of the captured city. He may find such work dangerous! Cowardly triumph! He will yet pay dearly for that triumph! All is not lost!"

John H. Surratt

Washington, D.C.
April 9, 1865

Someone pounded on the door loud enough to make Peggy jump and drop the comb she worked through Annabelle's tangled curls. "Lands! Who needs to be knockin' that hard?" She picked up the comb and placed it on the vanity before going to the door.

Annabelle turned in her seat, half of her hair in pins and the other half tumbling over one shoulder. She pulled her dressing gown up around her throat as Peggy pulled open the door.

"Let me in! Oh, goodness." Eudora pushed past Peggy and into the room.

"Grandmother?" Annabelle leapt to her feet. "What's happened?"

"He's surrendered! He's finally surrendered!"

Annabelle's heart pounded in her chest. She dropped her gown and took Eudora's shoulders. "Who surrendered? You're not making any sense."

Eudora laughed and clutched Annabelle's hands. "Lee has surrendered to Grant! The city is buzzing with the news. Richmond taken and now Lee's surrender." She clapped her hands together loudly. "The war is over!"

She and Peggy stood dumbfounded.

"What?" Eudora asked. "Don't you see this means you don't need to worry any longer? With the war over, they have no reason to abduct Lincoln."

"'Course not!" Peggy agreed.

Both women looked at Annabelle expectantly, but where they felt joy, she felt only the cold hand of dread.

Five days she'd waited for news to come back from the lawmen Eudora contacted. Five days of her grandmother dragging her to every shop in the city, giving her food she didn't taste and clothes she didn't need. Now Eudora thought they didn't need to do anything at all?

"You don't understand." Annabelle rubbed her temples and plopped back down in her chair, suddenly feeling exhausted. "You haven't seen these men. Spent time with them, as I have."

Peggy grunted. "I have."

Annabelle pinned her with a glare. "And what type of men did you see, Peggy? Because I saw dangerous fools who'd stop at nothing to exact revenge for their suffering onto the one they deem responsible. Just what do you think they'll do now that Lincoln crushed their cause?"

Peggy's face went slack. She cut a pained look at Eudora.

"It'll make them more desperate."

Eudora clutched the broach pinned to her lace collar, eyes widening. "I'm terribly sorry, dear."

Blood thudded through her veins, and her chest tightened with a sickening sense of dread. "What for?"

Eudora considered Annabelle for a long moment. "You're such a fluttery little thing, just like your mother. She was always in a tizzy about one thing or another. I learned that if I went along with her, she'd eventually see that she was worked up over nothing at all."

Now her stomach tied in knots. This couldn't be good.

"I… thought this was the same," Eudora continued, her face twisting into a grimace. "You were so worked up over that big fellow, and when he left you, I thought you exaggerated the dangers in order to follow him." Eudora fanned her face, wide eyes apologetic.

"You…you thought I *lied* about the *president* in order to chase a man!" Her breath caught in spurts and starts, and she pinched the bridge of her nose and tried to even out her breathing.

Eudora clasped her hands behind her back. "I believed you thought men with wild fantasies wanted to abduct the president." She lifted her shoulders.

Peggy sputtered. "Ain't no fantasies, ma'am. Miss Belle didn't exaggerate. Those men aren't just making threats. If not for her, Lincoln would've been taken."

Eudora's frown deepened. "But that threat has passed, and Lincoln is under a tight watch. I thought if these men haven't attempted anything else by now, then most likely they would not." She bit her lip. "Surely you must know the president gets all kinds of threats on his life. None of them come to anything."

"How could you possibly know that?" Annabelle flung out her arms.

Eudora straightened, her usual bearing returning. "Don't you swing that sharpened tongue at me, young lady. I have connections with the White House. Now, I'm sorry I didn't take you seriously, but believe me when I tell you these things happen to men in positions of power, and most never come to fruition."

She opened her mouth to protest, but Eudora shook her head.

"If it's as bad as you say, and if it'll ease your mind, I'll let someone know."

The heat in Annabelle's cheeks drained away, leaving a cold sweat in its place. "You haven't already contacted anyone? We've been waiting for days!"

Eudora looked at Peggy but found no support in Peggy's crossed arms or disbelieving features.

She smoothed her skirts. "I thought your claims were exaggerated," she repeated. "I could see in your face that you meant to come to Washington whether I wanted you to or not. I simply took the opportunity to spend a little more time with my granddaughter. I thought once you saw that things here were perfectly fine, you'd calm down and we could have a good time."

Annabelle filled her lungs, held in the air, then let the breath out slowly. Biting at Eudora for her deception would accomplish nothing. "What's done is done. However, now we must move quickly. Even if my claims are unfounded,"—she pointed a finger at Eudora—"which I know they're not, then we must warn someone about O'Malley and Booth's intentions. How will you feel if they succeed, knowing you chose to do nothing?"

Eudora's brows tightened. "Booth? You mean John Wilkes Booth?"

"Yes, as I've *said.*" Had Eudora listened to anything? "He was in on it. I recognized him from the playbills when I saw him on the hill during the last attempt. I told you that already."

"You said there was an actor." Eudora held up a finger. "But not which one. Certainly, though, you must be mistaken."

Annabelle clenched her teeth. "Whether I am or not is irrelevant. You should go to the law, and we need to find someone to warn the president. If you take this seriously, then perhaps the people we warn will also."

Eudora drew her lips into a line and narrowed her eyes. Annabelle held her firm gaze. Finally, Eudora gave a resigned sigh. "I can accomplish both through an old friend."

An unladylike snort burst from Annabelle's throat. "I have no doubt you *can*, it's the *will* that concerns me."

Eudora drew her head back and her countenance bristled like a hen's ruffled feathers. "You have a lot of sass, girl." Annabelle refused to wither under Eudora's stare, and after a moment the older woman chuckled. "I suppose you get that from me."

The matter settled, Eudora took charge and motioned to Peggy. "Let's get this girl presentable. We have work to do."

Peggy gave a nod, and together they took hold of Annabelle's unfinished hair.

About two hours later, Eudora, Annabelle, and George sat at a private table in the rear corner of the eatery in Ebbitt House Hotel near the White House. Annabelle fidgeted with the napkin in her lap. She'd already finished her supper and a piece of cake, and now they were waiting on their after-meal tea.

Annabelle leaned close to Eudora's ear. "Are you sure he's coming?"

Eudora dabbed her lips. "Patience, dear. He'll come. Give the man a chance. I did send for him on rather short notice."

Annabelle clamped her teeth down on her annoyance. If Eudora had kept her word and told him days ago, they wouldn't have had to petition a man on *short notice.* She kept as much of her anger from her face as she could, but doubted she was entirely successful.

Just then, Eudora let out a long breath. "Ah, there he is now."

A tall man approached their table at a steady gait. A full smile flashed between his trimmed beard and styled mustache. George rose and extended his hand while the women remanded seated.

Eudora made the introductions, her regal bearing something Annabelle would expect to see from an English duchess. "May I present my acquaintance and friend of my granddaughter's, Mr. George Daniels."

The new gentleman took George's hand in a firm grasp. "William Crook."

As the gentleman took his seat next to George, Eudora gestured toward Annabelle. "My granddaughter, Miss Annabelle Ross."

Annabelle kept her hands in her lap, unsure if she should extend one or not. She didn't recall ever having been introduced to someone while already seated at a meal. She inclined her head instead. "Good evening, sir. I'm pleased to make your acquaintance."

"The pleasure is mine, I'm sure," he said in the bored tone that accompanied such practiced formalities.

A server returned with an additional setting and then slipped quietly away without a word. Mr. Crook stirred a lump of sugar in his tea and then tapped a finger on the table. "What's this urgent matter you spoke of?"

Eudora tapped a finger on the china teacup. "Always directly to business with you, isn't it, William?" She lifted her tea and took a small sip, then placed her cup back on the saucer without the tiniest clink.

"I'm a lawman, Mrs. Smith, and as you know, I don't have time for dillydallying."

Eudora sighed. "I remember." She waved her hand, and her stern features returned. "Business it is then. My granddaughter claims there will be an attempt on President Lincoln's life."

The gentleman flicked a dismissive gaze at Annabelle. "There are claims on the president daily, miss. We take care of such things. You have no need to worry." He turned back to Eudora. "And it's no cause for any urgency, certainly. A simple correspondence would have sufficed."

Eudora smirked. "I wouldn't dismiss it so easily, Will…Mr. Crook. Perhaps you should hear her story first." She gave Annabelle a small nod of encouragement.

Annabelle leaned across the table as much as she dared without knocking over her cup, so that she could lower her voice. She recounted her tale to the lawman about being in Washington and encountering a group that planned to abduct Lincoln, leaving out the parts about her escape from Confederate detainment and Matthew's role entirely. As Eudora had advised, she made no mention of John Wilkes Booth, lest she be mistaken about the man's identity. She didn't believe that possible, but yielded to the advice nonetheless.

When she finished, Mr. Crook looked at her for a long time, stroking his mustache. "And you're certain that was their intention?"

"Yes, sir. I'm quite certain. I'm sure if you wish to speak with Mr. Thomas Clark, Mr. Lincoln's driver, he'll be able to confirm my story."

He seemed surprised. "I'll do that." He drummed his fingers on the table and then turned to George. "Were you aware of this matter, Mr. Daniels?"

Annabelle's heart thudded, but George appeared perfectly calm. "I've heard the tale, but was not present when the events occurred."

Mr. Crook appeared satisfied. "I'll look into it." He nodded to Annabelle. "But don't worry, miss. We take President Lincoln's security quite seriously. He'll be perfectly safe." He rose from his chair and placed his napkin on the table. "Now, if you'll excuse me, I must go. With Lee's surrender, we have a great deal of important issues to see to."

Without waiting on their returned courtesy of "good evenings," he turned and strode away.

Eudora watched the man go until he was no longer in sight. Sadness hung heavily on her features. Annabelle glanced at George, but he only shrugged. He was right, of course. Whatever Eudora's relationship with the lawman, it was none of their business.

"Now what?" she asked, turning Eudora's attention back to their table.

Eudora smoothed her features. "Now we wait."

"Wait! That's all we've done!"

Annabelle looked sharply at George, surprised to hear her own words coming from his lips. George said little, and when he did, his words were usually composed. Annabelle's astonishment mirrored on her grandmother's face.

"And what else would you have us do?" Eudora steepled her fingers on the tablecloth. "I've contacted one of the most important lawmen in Washington, one with the president's own ear. He'll handle it."

Annabelle straightened her shoulders. "Fine. We'll wait a day."

Eudora nodded, seeming satisfied. She sipped her tea. George left his untouched, his brows wrinkled in thought.

Annabelle folded her hands in her lap. A day. Two, at the most, and then she'd deliver her tale to every lawman in the city, if that is what it took.

Oh, Matthew, she silently pleaded. *Please don't be there with them when the lawmen's noose tightens.*

"Lincoln is again in Washington. Now is our time to act, and avenge the losses we have sustained on those who have caused them."
John H. Surratt

The White House grounds
Washington, D.C.
April 11, 1865

Annabelle adjusted her bonnet and scanned the gathering crowd for any sign of Matthew. He should have arrived in Washington by now, even with the time it took to travel by wagon. She'd waited her allotted two days. She was done waiting. Eudora stood stiffly at her side and watched the White House.

Celebrations had continued throughout Washington for days. Annabelle looked at the jubilant faces and could scarcely believe the war was truly over. The Northern Virginia had surrendered. If Uncle Michael still lived, had he been there when they'd laid down their arms?

It seemed a lifetime, not merely months, since she'd left Rosswood. Would Uncle Michael come to see her when the army dispersed, only to find her gone and the plantation under another's control?

"There he is!" Eudora exclaimed, pointing to the western window on the White House. Others also took notice, and soon the crowd called out for the president to speak.

Annabelle hadn't seen the president since his inauguration speech and now, as then, she stood too far away to tell much about his features. Apparently, if they'd wanted to get a better look, they should have arrived hours ago.

"We meet this evening, not in sorrow, but in gladness of heart!" Lincoln called out, his voice carrying over the crowd even as they lifted their voices in a cheer.

The president waited for their joy to quiet, then began again. Annabelle leaned forward to catch his words, though they drifted over the crowd with ease. He spoke with fervor, much like the first time she'd seen him, and the people held on to his every word.

"The evacuation of Petersburg and Richmond and the surrender of the principal insurgent army give hope of a righteous and speedy peace whose joyous expression cannot be restrained."

The people cheered again with gusto, proving his words true. Eudora gave a hearty yell along with them, and Annabelle couldn't help but smile. As the cries began to fade, Lincoln continued.

"In the midst of this, however, He from whom all blessings flow, must not be forgotten. A call for a national thanksgiving is being prepared and will be duly promulgated."

Indeed, Lord, Annabelle prayed. *We do thank you that this time of horror has come to an end.*

He spoke again on the need for reconstruction and how things would be difficult, since they were not two independent nations, but one that had fractured and must be restored. Annabelle let her mind wander as she scanned the crowd. A head taller than most men, Matthew would have been plain to spot. So, unless he stood behind her, he wasn't here.

"We all agree that the Seceded States, so called, are out of their proper relation with the Union, and that the sole object of the government, civil and military, in regard to those States is to again get them into that proper practical relation. I believe it is not only possible, but, in fact, easier to do this, without deciding, or even considering, whether these States have ever been out of the Union, than with it."

Eudora gave Annabelle's arm a squeeze. "You see, dear? He's a good man and will see that the South won't be punished but healed."

She hoped it would be true. Though her own loyalties had always leaned Northward, she'd secretly feared what would become of her and Peggy should the South lose. She offered Eudora a hopeful smile and leaned close to her ear. "All the more reason to see he remains unharmed."

Something flashed in Eudora's eyes, but Annabelle couldn't pin the emotion behind it. Guilt, perhaps?

Lincoln continued, "Finding themselves safely at home, it would be utterly immaterial whether they had ever been abroad. Let us all join in doing the acts necessary to restoring the proper practical relations between these States and the Union."

Tears gathered in her eyes. The president spoke with such conviction, such enthusiasm, that any doubt of the South's good future and the blessed reign of peace fell away. The president turned to speaking about the government in Louisiana, and something about the affairs of the colored men and the schools.

Her mind drifted instead to thoughts of Uncle Michael, George, Matthew, and Eudora standing at her side as she claimed the rights to Rosswood. If President Lincoln would be giving rights to former slaves, then how could she not have the rights, even as a woman, to own her family lands? Miss Wesson seemed to have no problems in doing so.

The crowd began to shift and people started grumbling. Annabelle pulled herself from her thoughts and looked over to her left, where the jostled people cut annoyed glances at a man pushing his way out of the crowd.

Annabelle's mouth went dry, and she clutched Eudora's arm.

"What is it?"

Annabelle couldn't pull her eyes away from the gentleman as he moved closer to her, his face a mask of pure rage. The styled hair and perfectly tended mustache were exactly the way she had remembered them from that day on the road.

"That's John Wilkes Booth," Eudora exclaimed, following her. "He surely seems riled over something."

The man came closer, and Annabelle froze with fear. Booth walked right up to her and she thought her heart would never beat again. Not even the slightest hint of recognition tempered the storm of anger on his face, and he stepped past her.

Annabelle turned wide eyes on Eudora as those around them turned their attention back to the president's words. "You see? I told you."

Eudora scoffed. "I, too, am standing in this crowd." She gestured to those pressed in around them. "As are hundreds more. It means nothing."

Annabelle opened her mouth to retort, but the crowd shifted again. This time the grumbles grew louder and a few people even flung rude remarks at the man who strutted through the crowd, a huge grin on his face.

If Annabelle's heart had slowed at the sight of Booth, it now froze at the sight of David O'Malley. She yelped and tried to scramble away, but the press of the crowd constricted her.

"Annabelle! What are you doing?"

Annabelle ducked her head, turning her back to O'Malley as he neared. She pressed so close to Eudora that the older woman had to shift her weight to maintain balance. Annabelle's heart remembered its function, and began pounding rapidly. "Is he gone?"

Eudora stiffened. Annabelle tried to swallow, but her mouth had gone dry. She dared a glance over her shoulder, and found O'Malley only a step away. She whipped her head back around, praying he didn't see her.

"He's gone." Eudora wrapped her arm around Annabelle's shoulders. "Are you all right?"

Annabelle straightened and turned back toward the White House, ignoring the looks from the people around her. She and Eudora stood quietly for a moment, and soon the curious looks ceased and the crowd once again ignored them as their attention returned to the president.

She leaned close to Eudora's ear. "That was David O'Malley. And my guess is he was here with Booth."

Eudora gave her a sharp glance, but she relented with a single nod. She gestured with her chin back toward the White House. They stood with the crowd for the remainder of the speech, though Annabelle could not focus on a single word the president said. She shifted her weight from foot to foot, willing him to finish quickly. Finally, Lincoln gave a wave and disappeared back inside the White House.

The crowd dispersed, and Annabelle and Eudora walked silently back toward the eatery where they'd left George. George had been wise to keep away from the crowd. It seemed unlikely, but what if O'Malley had looked at George and guessed his identity? Annabelle shuddered. Something about the look of fevered glee on O'Malley's face left her stricken.

One thing was certain. She couldn't wait any longer. The time had come for her to act on her own.

Matthew urged the horses forward and wished he'd left the wagon behind and ridden into Washington on horseback. The streets were flooded with people, and the sheer number of horses, carriages, and pedestrians clogged the streets so that what should have taken minutes had drawn on for a half hour.

The warm afternoon sun lit the jubilant faces of the swarms of Yankees, still flush with their joy over his country's defeat. Next to him, Harry's jaw remained clenched as he watched the people around them. The man had mellowed during their travels, but Matthew hadn't felt at ease since they'd left the Smith house.

Finally, the crowds began to thin, and most people headed away from them and toward the main part of the city. Whatever was going on, it had drawn a large crowd. So much the better. If the city occupants were going that way, he'd just as soon go the other.

Finally, Matthew spotted what he'd been looking for. *A bit run-down, perhaps,* he thought, *but still better than the cold ground.* And, more importantly, it stood a good measure away from the Surratt boarding house.

"You plan on stayin' here?" Harry spit over the side of the wagon as he judged the crumbling structure.

"Best I can afford," Matthew replied, his voice cold. *And folks here are less likely to ask questions,* he added to himself. He put his hand in his pocket and fingered the few coins remaining within. He hoped it would be enough for a couple of nights and something to warm their bellies. He hadn't felt right taking anything from the Smith storage shed, so he and Harry had survived on the last of his supplies—a few meager provisions left over from when he, Annabelle, and Peggy had left Washington to find George.

After more than a week of hard travel, stopping only when they had to rest the horses or catch a few hours of restless sleep, Matthew regarded anything with four walls as a luxury. His stomach growled at the thought of filling it with something more than a few bites of hardtack.

Harry regarded him thoughtfully. "You mean your lady friend didn't give you none of her wealth for this venture?"

Matthew glared at him, then pointedly turned his attention forward and guided the horses to the edge of the road in front of the building marked as *Hob's Inn.*

Harry grunted, as if pleased that Annabelle would toss Matthew aside. Matthew ground his teeth so hard he felt certain Harry could hear it. If the man took notice, he didn't mention it.

Smartest choice he's made all day.

Matthew pulled the horses to a stop and shifted the reins to one hand, using his other to pull his knife from his hip. He eyed his prisoner. It had been easy to keep Harry in line on the road, where they'd avoided towns and other people, but here in Washington, it wouldn't be so simple.

Harry frowned. "You still think you need that? Done told you I ain't taking part in nobody's plans no more."

So he had. Pleaded, even, for Matthew to let him go free when they reached Washington. Harry had sworn, multiple times, that he would disappear and Matthew would never see him again. Tempting though it had been to be free of the rat, Matthew still needed the leverage.

Matthew nudged Harry off the seat. "Can't have you running off now, can I? Need you to go with me to call on O'Malley."

Harry's eyes widened as he stepped off the wagon. After the third day and Harry giving him no trouble, Matthew had left the man's hands and feet untied. He'd told himself he could catch Harry if he ran. The truth was he'd grown tired of Harry complaining about his chafed wrists.

"I said I'd go with you to the law," Harry hissed, "not to see O'Malley!"

Matthew gathered the horses' reins and tied them over the post. He watched people as they passed. Their eyes quickly slid past him as they hurried on their way. Folks in this section of town didn't seem to be inclined to friendliness.

The buildings along this row sagged, and people kept to themselves as they came and went past them. A few men hung around in doorways, the sort that spent too much time with a bottle and too little time keeping their hands busy.

Matthew's muscles bunched as he grabbed Harry's arm and leaned down to speak in his ear. "You go with me to O'Malley, then after that, I won't bother you again. You'll be a free man."

Harry barked a bitter laugh. "And you think O'Malley will just tell us howdy and send us on our way?"

Matthew growled and pulled Harry away from the horses. He lifted his bag from the back of the wagon with his free hand, keeping a firm grip on Harry's elbow even though the smaller man made no effort to slip free. Harry's words unnerved him more than he wanted to show. "We'll discuss it inside."

Harry spat on the dirt road, but said nothing. Matthew hauled him through a door that protested their entry with rusty hinges and up to a heavy-set woman standing at a rickety desk in the small entry. He flicked a gold coin at her. "Need a room and meals for a week."

She caught it, put it in her mouth, and bit down. Satisfied, she slipped the gold into her apron. "Won't get you a week, not plus meals for two." She eyed Harry, and Matthew clamped his fingers so tightly that Harry winced.

Matthew's patience had long since worn thin. "Fine. How many nights?"

"Three."

He snarled, and she recoiled slightly, her gaze darting back to Harry.

"Four," Matthew barked. "And no questions, or we take our business elsewhere."

She narrowed her eyes, her puffy cheeks red. Matthew feared he'd pushed too hard, but she fished a key out of the drawer under the desk. "Fine. Four. But you get the small room we usually give to the cleaning girl." She shrugged. "She ran off with that stable boy last week and we ain't heard from her since."

Matthew's nostrils flared. "I'm sure you provide stabling for your guests' horses, regardless of the rooms you give them."

She cocked an eyebrow. "Do, but it costs extra."

Matthew pulled another coin from his pocket, loath to part with it. He would never take his family's wealth for granted again. He'd thought he'd learned that lesson camping with the army, but now, knowing that he might not get a meal once his coin ran out, changed a man.

The woman smiled as he reluctantly handed the money over. She added the coin to his other and nodded toward the stairs. "Room's the only one on the third floor. The boy will get your horses unhitched and stalled at the livery stable two streets over. He'll fetch 'em when you need it. Don't serve morning or noon meals, but you'll get dinner at five."

Matthew clenched his fist and stalked away without reply, Harry stumbling along in tow. *Crafty woman.* She'd conned him out of two meals a day. His fault, really, for not asking specifics.

Matthew prodded Harry to take the lead, and they clopped up stairs that groaned under their weight. At the end of the second-floor hall, they found a narrow staircase leading to the attic. Harry drew to a halt and eyed Matthew over his shoulder. "You *sure* your Yankee lover didn't give you none of her spy coin?"

Matthew growled and stuck two stiffened fingers into Harry's back. The man flinched. "Fine, fine," he mumbled. "I'm going."

At the top of the stairs stood a single door. Matthew had to reach around Harry in the narrow staircase to put the key in the lock, their bodies uncomfortably close. Finally, he got the tumblers to click and shoved the door open. Harry stumbled inside and turned slowly, eyeing the humble accommodations. He lifted a brow at Matthew, but kept his peace.

Matthew assessed the room in a single glance—a bed with a lumpy mattress, a threadbare rug, and one tiny oval window. Not even a fireplace. But this far into April, the days had warmed pleasantly. The small room should trap the rising heat of the rooms below enough to keep away the nightly chill. It would do.

Matthew tossed his haversack down by the window. "You take the bed." He tilted his head toward the shoddy thing that likely wouldn't hold his weight, not to mention his height.

Harry seemed surprised for only a second. "Whatever you say. Looks like you're running this here operation."

"It's not an operation."

Harry gave him an if-you-say-so shrug that only further plucked at Matthew's already frayed nerves. "I'll not stand by while O'Malley plots murder." The vein in his neck pulsed.

"That man's responsible for the murder of *thousands* of our own. Not to mention what his soldiers did to our homes and women." Harry flopped down on the bed, stretching his spindly legs out in front of him on the floor. "I won't stick the knife myself, ain't my way." He lifted his palms. "But, if it happens, can't say I'll lose sleep over it."

Matthew clenched his teeth and kicked the bottom of Harry's boot. No sense explaining to this fool that if O'Malley murdered Lincoln, things would get worse for the defeated South. They'd be nothing more than wasted words. "Get up.

We're going to Surratt's."

Harry stared at him flatly, unperturbed that Matthew had kicked him, and appeared to have no intentions of getting up. "Always with the orders. Ever thought of asking a fellow polite like?"

The words startled Matthew more than he would have thought, and he lowered his brow. He was a captain no longer.

"Well?" Harry prompted, wriggling his eyebrows.

Matthew's frustration dissipated a fraction, his amusement at Harry's audacity tempering his ire. Matthew barked a laugh. "Fine. Will you *please* get your sorry behind up so we can go to Surratt's?"

Harry chuckled and made a show of slowly rising to his feet. "Close enough. I reckon there ain't nothing left but to face the piper. But didn't you already send the horses to the stables?"

Matthew pulled the door open and stepped down the first stair immediately outside. He'd hate to need to get up in the middle of the night in any hurry. A man would break his neck tumbling down these steep steps in the dark. He dismissed Harry's concern. "We're going to walk. It's not that far."

And I can keep a hand on you, so you don't get any ideas about leaping out of the wagon or galloping away on one of my horses.

Harry shrugged and followed him to the second floor then he stopped. "Look, we've been on the road together for a week." He shoved his hands into his pockets. "Ain't you figured out by now I'm not going to try to kill you?" His eyes darted down to the knife Matthew had palmed without thought.

Matthew sneered. "Only because you couldn't best me."

Harry stared at him with cold eyes. "Could have shot you a hundred times when you weren't looking. Could have taken that girl, too, if I'd wanted, and been gone before you even knew she wasn't in the privy."

Two steps and the coward's face would bust under his fist again.

Harry held Matthew's gaze and kept talking. He didn't even flinch when Matthew turned those two steps into one. "But I didn't," he said evenly, craning his neck to keep Matthew's gaze. "I'd agreed to see what you were going to do. Have to admit, I was a mite curious myself. But when O'Malley sent word to take you out after you found your brother, if you ever did, I drew my own line. Like I said, I ain't no murderer."

The muscles in Matthew's jaw relaxed and he rubbed the tight muscles in the back of his neck. Unable to deny the truth in the man's words, he relented. "Thank you."

"You messed my nose up right good—I guess that's my due for sneaking around on a man—and now you've already brought me back here, where I was planning on going anyway to collect my belongings before finding my way home."

Where he was…? Matthew inwardly groaned. No wonder the man hadn't tried to run.

"But now that's done." Harry planted his feet. "So let's just go our separate ways."

Matthew drew a long breath through his nostrils and let it out through his mouth slowly. Harry had claimed he wouldn't try to come after Matthew again, and he was safely removed from Annabelle and George.

Matthew studied the still-bruised face. If Harry wanted to attempt anything, he probably would've tried it on the road while Matthew slept. "Come with me to talk to O'Malley, tell him you're done, and then be on your way."

Harry shook his head. "You might not be willing to take me out for not following orders, but O'Malley…." A spark of fear shadowed his gaze and Matthew struggled with indecision. If O'Malley killed Harry for not murdering Matthew, then Matthew would carry the guilt for it.

The other man stood there silently, as if waiting for the judge to deliver his fate.

"You know I can't let you go yet," Matthew finally said. "You go to O'Malley before I get to him, and he'll disappear." He shook his head. "Can't take that chance."

Harry sighed, resigned. "Let's get this done."

Matthew clomped down the stairs and out the front door with Harry on his heels. He half expected the man to bolt once they stepped into the sun, and Matthew realized he probably would have let him. But Harry walked next to Matthew with his hands shoved in his pockets and his head down.

Somehow, that was worse.

It took about half an hour to cross through the town and arrive at the narrow boarding house where they'd first staged their attempt at abducting Lincoln. Matthew scolded himself. Had he really been that foolish? How could he have not seen that such a move would not bring triumph, but rather misery, to his brothers in arms? He'd been too blinded by desperation to heed logic. Now that George was safely hidden in New York, he wouldn't be so easily duped.

Harry paused at the bottom of the steps that led to the front entry of the Surratt house. He cut Matthew one final cold glance and then plodded up the stairs. He waited as Matthew banged on the door. In a moment, it swung open and Mrs. Surratt looked at them in shock.

Taking advantage of her surprise, Matthew pushed Harry forward and Mrs. Surratt had to step back to avoid a collision. By then, Harry was already inside and Mrs. Surratt no longer had a firm grip on the door. Matthew strode in. "I'm calling upon Mr. O'Malley."

Her eyes darted between Matthew and Harry, but Harry kept his gaze on the floor. She straightened herself and smoothed the heavy fabric of her black skirts. "He's not here at the moment. You may leave a message."

"No. I'll wait."

She cast a furtive glance at the stairs. "Certainly. I'll get some tea for the parlor and—"

"No, thank you," Matthew interrupted. He'd stayed at this boarding house, and knew about the rear entry. "I'll just wait right here."

Her brows drew low and Matthew couldn't resist the smug smile that tugged on his lips. Harry shifted his weight and kept throwing glances at the door.

Mrs. Surratt pinned a pleasant smile on her face. "Suit yourself, but I'm sure Mr. Thompson might like a warm cup."

Harry looked up. "Yes. I would."

She had just enough time to start a smug smile of her own when Matthew caught Harry's elbow as he tried to step away. "No, ma'am. He waits with me. My business with O'Malley will require both of us."

Mrs. Surratt's eyes caught fire and she tilted her chin up. "Sir, I may have to ask you to leave if you're going to act uncivil in my home."

Just then the entry door opened, and O'Malley hurried inside, too distracted to notice them. Mrs. Surratt's eyes widened slightly and Matthew grinned.

She caught the look and glared at him. Mrs. Surratt might not take kindly to being outmaneuvered, but Matthew guessed that neither would she make a scene if she lost the game. She crossed her arms and waited without another word.

Matthew's smile of triumph over the busybody faded as soon as O'Malley finally noticed him. Astonishment widened his eyes as he looked at Matthew, then Harry. For only an instant, O'Malley's over-practiced false face vanished, and Matthew saw the rage that burned within him. The sight was brief, but it was enough.

O'Malley slid a smile onto his liar's lips and gave a small bow. "Mr. Daniels! How wonderful to see you."

"Indeed," Matthew said. "I apologize for it being unexpected."

O'Malley gestured toward the parlor. "Shall we retire to the sitting room and catch up?"

Two doors out of the parlor. Hard to guard both. But at least it was farther from the front door and gave Matthew a chance to intercept him if he tried to get away. He gave a single nod. Mrs. Surratt stepped into the parlor, and finding no one, ushered them inside. She pulled the door closed with one final glare at Matthew.

O'Malley went to stand by the cold hearth. He patted his pockets. "It seems I've left my pipe in my room. If you'll excuse me for a moment, I'll run and fetch it."

Matthew stepped in front of the door and crossed his arms. O'Malley sighed, though he looked more resigned than intimidated. That probably shouldn't have infuriated Matthew, but it did. It seemed his temper always bubbled just below the surface lately, and it didn't take much to boil over.

Shrugging, he focused on Harry. He couldn't keep the venom in his voice concealed as easily as he'd hid it from his face. "Ah, my old friend. It's good to see you." His left eye twitched. "Though you're a bit off schedule."

Harry shook his head. "He already knows it all, David. I done told him what you wanted me to do."

O'Malley's lips tightened and color sprang up from around his collar and spread to his cheeks. Still, he kept up the act. "I don't know what you're referring to. Last we spoke you were going north on your own personal affairs."

"But, but… you…" Harry gaped at him and then snapped his mouth shut, realization finally dawning in his eyes. O'Malley would turn his back on anyone to suit his own needs. It was high time Harry learned that truth.

"See, now," Matthew said, his voice even. "Harry and I have come to an understanding. Haven't we?" He looked to Harry, who still stared at O'Malley.

Harry's eyes hardened and he nodded. "Yeah."

O'Malley smirked, gesturing toward Harry's face. "So a busted nose is all it takes for you to turn your back on duty, justice, and those who stood at your side?"

Harry didn't reply.

O'Malley feigned nonchalance that was undermined by the way the muscles in his neck bulged. "Fine. I've no need of cowards, anyway."

Harry balled his fists, but still held his tongue.

After a moment, O'Malley gave a snort of derision and turned back to Matthew. "What have you come here to do?"

"I wanted you to see me alive." He pressed his fist into his hand and several of his knuckles popped. "Next time, any attempts to spy on me or have me put in the ground won't turn out so well for you."

"Hmm." He stroked his chin. "Such bold words. Too bad you turned out to be yellow. We could have used a bull like you." He poked Matthew's chest.

His fist drew back for a punch before he realized it. Matthew lowered his arm slowly. He wouldn't give Mrs. Surratt, who undoubtedly listened in, any cause to send for the law.

O'Malley actually looked disappointed. "So big, yet so weak." He clicked his tongue with derision. "Such a shame."

"This plan of yours is foolhardy, O'Malley. Give it up before you doom us all."

Eyes lit with fanatical fire stabbed into him and Matthew almost drew back from their intensity. It took a bit of determination to hold his ground and look down on O'Malley with cold indifference.

"What else should I expect from a deserter and a coward?" O'Malley sneered. "You don't understand the half of it."

Matthew snarled. "If I remember right, *you* were in my unit and also left in the middle of the night. I'd say that makes the *both* of us deserters."

"That's where you are wrong." O'Malley shook his head slowly. "See, where you were sworn into the army on an oath of loyalty, I only took the part as a means to an end."

He seemed utterly convinced that his words made sense, and Matthew could only stare at him. How had he not seen that O'Malley was completely mad? Had he been too blinded by his own agenda to care? The fact that he and O'Malley had more in common than he cared to admit turned his veins cold. He'd never be able to convince the man to change his mind. It was painfully obvious that this obsession had devoured his capacity for rational thought. Only one option remained.

Matthew would have to stop him, regardless of what he had to do.

"You're right, of course," Matthew said, forcing an even tone. "This was never my mission, and I only used it as a means to get what I wanted."

Something that looked close to respect crossed O'Malley's face, so Matthew kept going. "I never had the fortitude or the cunning wit to see such a feat accomplished."

Harry stared at him with utter confusion, but O'Malley's eagerness practically dripped from his countenance.

"But men like you—those are the ones called to greatness, to glory."

O'Malley beamed, and reached up to slap Matthew on the shoulder. "I knew you'd come to see it. Don't ever let anyone tell you that thick skull of yours can't see the right of things!"

Matthew faked a smile. If O'Malley guessed it wasn't genuine, he gave no indication. Matthew watched him carefully, a plan coming to mind as he mentally evaluated how to deceive O'Malley.

He's delusional. Matthew watched the man puff his chest with a fool's pride. A tiny taste of what he wanted to hear, and O'Malley became like clay. Easy to mold.

"I admit," Matthew said, lacing his tone with just the right amount of contrition. "When I saw Harry here after me, I just…lost my temper." He shrugged. "Happens that way."

"Of course, of course," O'Malley cooed. "Big brute like you is bound to have some fire in him. No harm done."

Harry clenched his jaw and defiance lit his eyes. Matthew gave him a meaningful look, hoping he'd understand the game. Harry's brows only gathered in confusion. Before O'Malley could take notice, Matthew grabbed O'Malley's shoulder and gave it a squeeze, turning him slightly away so that he couldn't as easily see Harry.

"Sure admire a fellow with that kind of courage," Matthew said, laying it on as thick as he dared. "Surely they'll print your name in all the papers and the entire South will shout your name once you carry the lout off!"

O'Malley's eyes glazed. "Oh, and more. I'll go down in history's glory once I run him through!"

There. The truth.

Much as he knew O'Malley was capable of it, and he'd no reason to doubt Harry told the truth, he'd held out hope. Matthew breathed slowly, willing his contempt to stay hidden.

O'Malley suddenly sobered, as if remembering himself. Matthew barked out an imitation laugh before he could grow suspicious. "No doubt."

He patted O'Malley's shoulder and then pretended to sober, as though a thought just occurred to him. "I'm right sorry for getting in your way and nearly making a mess of the whole thing." He puckered his brow. "You were right, you know."

O'Malley cocked his head. "Of course." He paused. "On which account?"

Matthew stroked his chin. "When you told me desperation would be a powerful thing."

"Yes, yes."

Matthew did his best to look repentant. "I got so caught up in finding my brother, so desperate to see him, that I lost sight of the Cause, and what meant the most. I can be an ox, and was too stubborn to see what I did." He hung his head to try to keep O'Malley from seeing the disgust in his eyes.

"Now, now. Don't worry so, my friend." O'Malley soothed, talking to Matthew like a scolded child. "Soon all will be right. Even now, the plans are coming together, and the pieces are being set. We'll have our victory by month's end!"

"Carry on for us all, O'Malley. See the tyrant felled."

O'Malley's eyes danced. "There can still be a part for you, now that you've seen the error of your ways."

Matthew shook his head, looking forlorn. "I can't take the chance that my bumbling might ruin things. How about I just keep an eye on him for you?" He gestured to Harry, who still stood near the corner of the room, hands clenched tightly at his sides.

The smallest hint of understanding dawned in Harry's eyes, and Matthew gave a tiny shake of his head, hoping Harry caught it.

O'Malley opened his mouth, and the anger sparking in his eyes told Matthew he'd protest.

Matthew pounded a fist into his hand and O'Malley's gaze flicked back to him. "Might not be as quick with my wits like you, and get in the way too much to be any good," he said, keeping his eyes on Harry. "I've already proven I can't be of any use in the real plans. But I *am* pretty good at keeping a mouth shut." He pounded his fist again for emphasis.

Harry paled with fear and O'Malley laughed. "Look at him! He's near on wetting himself. I *knew* you'd be useful!" He smacked Matthew on the shoulder. "And look, you've even come back to me, ready to heel and do what's needed to get back in my graces. It's fate, I tell you, and she's on my side."

The words seared Matthew's nerves like the brander's fire and his nostrils flared. He ducked his head in order to obscure the truth.

"That's right," Matthew said. "If you'll forgive my rash temper, I'll be of good use now, you'll see." He took a few long breaths to regain his control before meeting O'Malley's eyes.

The man looked positively feverish with his own pride. "You will of course overlook my sending this dullard to track you. I never expected that he could actually do you any harm. Just wanted to keep connection, you see."

Matthew kept his face blank. "Of course. Who could blame you?"

A few strokes to his pride, and O'Malley already forgot Matthew had threatened him only moments before. How fractured was his mind? "I was so fired up on my desperation that who knows what I might have done? You were right to keep eyes on me. Good thing, too, since coming back here has made me see the error in my ways."

O'Malley clapped his hands like a child who'd been given a sweet. "Delightful. Let's see it then. Give the half-wit his due."

Matthew turned his back toward O'Malley and puffed his chest out, stalking toward Harry. The man's face went completely pale. Matthew took another step and made sure his frame blocked Harry from O'Malley's view.

Then he winked.

Harry's eyes widened. Matthew paused, as if suddenly remembering something. He looked over his shoulder at O'Malley. "I'm not the bright one here, but don't you think if I splatter his face, it'll get blood all over Mrs. Surratt's nice rugs?"

O'Malley looked disappointed, but waved his hand. "Yes, of course. I was just about to say such myself."

Of course you were.

"Let's go out back."

Matthew nodded. "That'll be better." He snatched Harry by the arm and the spindly man yelped. They moved out of the parlor and into the main entry, and Matthew paused again. O'Malley looked over his shoulder. "Well? Come on."

Matthew shifted his weight and glanced up the stairs. "Sure hate to draw the law here to you and this fine house. Maybe I ought to take him down to some side alley. If they catch me, at least I won't have jeopardized anyone important."

O'Malley narrowed his eyes, calculating.

Matthew feared he might have gone too far. "I don't want to hinder anything again. This must happen, and soon, if our cause is to be set right again."

O'Malley considered and Matthew's pulse pounded.

Finally, O'Malley relented. "I see your point." He gave Matthew a placating smile. "Look, with your head clear you're *already* beginning to think smarter!" O'Malley dismissed them with an arrogant wave. "Be gone with you, then. I have business I need to see to."

Matthew tugged Harry toward the door, and he had either enough sense, or maybe just blind fear, to struggle against him. Either way, it made the ruse more believable. Harry was no match for Matthew's strength, however, and Matthew hauled him to the door.

"Daniels!" O'Malley barked.

Matthew swiveled his head. "Yes?"

"See that it's done well, so that even a dullard will remember."

Matthew inclined his head in mock submission. "Yes, sir."

O'Malley beamed. Matthew turned away before he could see the anger burning in his eyes. He snatched Harry's arm and dragged him out the door.

"The Yankee flag is to be raised over the battered walls of Fort Sumter on the anniversary of Anderson's surrender. If Lincoln should go down there, we shall miss our promised game. He must not be lost sight of."
John H. Surratt

Washington, D.C.
April 13, 1865

Matthew rubbed his temple and tried to get the throbbing to lessen. Harry paced in tight circles around their shared room at the inn and his endless steps beat in rhythm with the pounding in Matthew's head.

"I just can't do it." Harry rubbed his hands as he made another pass around their small room.

Matthew sat back on the bed, considering. O'Malley might be flooded with his ego, but he wasn't a fool. Matthew pulled the thong of leather binding his hair tighter and rose to his feet, almost surprised at how long it'd grown these past four years. Harry stopped pacing and craned his head to look up at Matthew.

"You're right. I see no other alternative than to trust you."

Relief, followed by surprise, lit Harry's eyes. Then his eyes narrowed. "You're going to let me go? After you've kept me locked in here for two days?"

"I don't see where I have a choice. I can't keep you with me because O'Malley will know I didn't pummel you. And I can find a way to reason around why I didn't bring your bloody face back for him to see."

Harry looked doubtful, but didn't argue.

"Besides, I don't suppose you'll go to the law any quicker than I will."

Harry nodded. They'd huddled in this rundown lodging, waiting to see if O'Malley would make a move against him. Matthew feared that O'Malley might have suspected something after all and decided it best to keep out of sight for a few days.

But nothing had happened, and both men were getting restless. Matthew decided it was time to make a move of his own, and, truthfully, Harry would be nothing but dead weight. He nodded toward the door. "Get on with you then."

Harry immediately strode for the door, having no belongings other than the clothes on his back.

Just as his hand touched the doorknob, Matthew grabbed his shoulder and spun him around. "If I hear even a whisper that you've tread on my mercy, you'll find yourself sorely regretting it." He squeezed the man's shoulder until Harry winced, then let up only slightly.

Harry's eyes bulged. "I swear it. I want to get as far away from Washington and you fools as I can! Ain't nobody's cause worth swinging from a rope."

Matthew released his grip and Harry darted out the door, not even bothering to shut it behind him. Matthew watched him take the steps two at a time and then disappear from sight. He rubbed his temple again, hoping he had not just made a grave error. When he was certain the scrawny fellow had time to make his escape, he descended the stairs and walked past the front desk.

"Mister?" the portly woman at the desk called.

He paused, barely looking over his shoulder.

"Tonight's your last night," she said. "You either need to pay more, or gather your stuff."

"Thank you." He strode out the door, leaving her sputtering behind him. One final night, then he'd find himself without a place to put his head or a meal to fill his stomach. Not unless he begged to stay with O'Malley. The very thought made his teeth clench.

Matthew hurried down the street and had to resist the urge to nudge loiterers out of his path.

If I haven't used up all my miracles, I could sure use another.

On the other side of town, Matthew approached the boarding house. He put on a dullard's expression, or at least the best he could muster. He knocked, and a moment later Mrs. Surratt pulled open the door.

The smile on her lips dissipated. "Mr. Daniels. How pleasant to see you again." Her words might have been kind, but her tone was as sour as an unripe lemon.

"Good day to you, ma'am. I've come to call on Mr. O'Malley. Is he available?"

She eyed him a moment, but finally conceded. "He's here." She motioned him inside.

He stepped through the door and removed his hat and coat, leaving them on the pegs by the door.

Mrs. Surratt gestured toward the parlor. "I'd offer for you to take your leisure in the parlor while you wait, but it's currently occupied." She arched her brows. "Besides, I know you'll likely refuse the courtesy anyway."

Matthew gave a small bow in lieu of a reply.

She turned on her heel and gestured for him to follow her up the stairs. When they reached the top, she motioned to the second door. "He's in there."

Matthew tugged on the collar of his shirt, then stepped up to the door and gave a single, firm knock. Shuffling sounds came from inside, along with a bit of bumping around. Finally, O'Malley opened the door.

"Daniels!" He flung the door wide. "I'd started to wonder if you'd ever return." He waved his hand for Matthew to enter. "Hurry, let's not waste any more time."

Matthew struggled to contain his surprise at the greeting, and plastered a smile on his face. "Forgive me," he said as O'Malley closed the door behind him. "I had to make sure Harry wouldn't be found, and that my trail wouldn't trace back to you." *Not exactly a lie.*

O'Malley waved his hand, distracted. "Never mind him. We've more to deal with." He started to pace, much the way Harry had done just an hour earlier.

Matthew stifled a groan and put on a submissive look. "Yes, sir. Whatever you say."

O'Malley paused in his pacing and looked hard at Matthew. He stared back at O'Malley blankly. After a moment, O'Malley reached over and slapped Matthew's shoulder. "There's a good lad."

Lad? He'd been this imbecile's captain just three months

ago! He tried to contain himself, but his fist clenched at his side. O'Malley seemed too distracted to notice.

A cascade of words bubbled out of O'Malley, though he didn't exactly seem to be addressing Matthew. "With both of them stalling, it's up to me to accelerate the Cause." He rubbed his hands, increasing the back and forth pace that reminded Matthew of a swinging pendulum. "Yes, yes, of course it would be so. I will not miss fate's hand this time. Oh, no. Not this time." He stopped, swinging his frenzied gaze back to Matthew.

Matthew looked at the floor, pretending not to notice O'Malley's descent into madness.

"Well," O'Malley said, coming to a stop and straightening himself. "There will be time for explaining later. First, we must plan."

Matthew leaned in and tried to put the right amount of eagerness onto his face. O'Malley's eyes gleamed as he plucked papers from his jacket and spread them across his bed. "Now." He tapped a map. "The real work begins. We hold in our power the final hopes of our nation and the coming glory of a new tide."

A bead of sweat rolled down Matthew's neck and down the back of his shirt, but his face held a fanatical smile of anticipation.

Twenty-Five

"Our cause, being almost lost, means something decisive and great must be done."
John Wilkes Booth

"I'm going, and that's that."

Peggy placed both hands on her hips and looked down her nose at Annabelle. "Your grandma told me you're not supposed to leave this room 'til she gets back."

Annabelle strode toward the door. "Then you'll just have to stop me, seeing as you're taking orders from her now."

Peggy's jaw fell slack and it took her a moment to catch Annabelle before she reached for the door. "Miss Belle! You *know* that ain't a good idea. Can't you just wait a bit longer?"

Annabelle whirled around. "No! I will *not* wait any longer!"

Peggy wrung her hands. "I know you're upset. But this ain't the way to go about it."

"Then tell me, Peggy. What is the right way? Because sitting around this fancy hotel and going to shops while *waiting* has not done the first bit of good." She pulled open the door and stepped out, not giving Peggy a chance to come up with anything that might stall her.

Peggy followed her into the hall. "You know that man's dangerous. I can't let you talk to him. No tellin' what'll happen."

Annabelle paused. "I'm not going to speak to him. I only want to see if I can find Matthew. He's likely around there somewhere."

Down the hall, a door opened and Annabelle motioned to Peggy, indicating the conversation was over. Peggy scrunched her face, but held her tongue. Satisfied, Annabelle strode past several doors marked with the room numbers. Peggy trailed along behind her like a petulant shadow.

A gentleman stepped out of the room marked 228. Dressed in a fine dark suit, he carried a silk top hat and had a light overcoat slung over his arm. Like most Northern gentlemen, he didn't seem to be aware that war had robbed half the nation of such finery.

Just as Annabelle came upon him, he turned his face to her. She drew a sharp intake of breath and stopped suddenly, her heart thudding in her chest.

No!

Peggy, unprepared for the halt, didn't stop in time. She tripped on the back of Annabelle's long dress and lost her balance. Both women yelped, and Annabelle stumbled forward from the sudden shove on her back.

The man reached out quickly and grabbed her elbow, steadying her before she could lose her dignity by sprawling face down on the rug. He cast an annoyed glance back at Peggy, but Annabelle's heart pounded too furiously for her to garner a defense. Peggy made a strange noise in her throat, but Annabelle's eyes remained locked on the man.

"I…um, thank you, sir…." Did he recognize her?

He offered a charming smile, one that no doubt had made him one of the most famous men in the country. "Certainly, miss. Good day."

Annabelle stood there like a swooning admirer for a moment before she could force her voice through her dry throat. "Good day."

He strode down the hall, leaving Annabelle staring breathlessly after him.

After several heartbeats, when the man finally began to descend the stairs, Peggy leaned in close to her. "What was that all about?"

Annabelle grabbed her skirts, remembering her wits. "Hurry! We need to follow him."

Peggy grabbed her arm, her own feet planted like a tree. "What're you talking about?"

Annabelle snatched her arm away. "That's Booth! The very man himself is staying on *our* floor!"

Peggy frowned. "That actor fellow?"

"Yes, now let's go!"

She hurried down the stairs, Peggy mumbling at her heels. Annabelle paid her no mind. They'd been staying in this hotel for days! Had he been here all along? Was it a mere coincidence? He didn't seem to have recognized her either time she'd seen him, but then, any actor of merit would be able to hide such a thing, wouldn't he?

She walked as briskly as she dared through the main lobby of the hotel and out the front doors. Outside, she paused to scan both sides of the street.

He'd disappeared.

"Do you need a carriage, miss?" A young man asked, appearing at her side.

"No." Annabelle waved him away. "Thank you."

The young man turned to an older couple stepping out into the mid-morning sun, not seeming bothered by Annabelle's rudeness.

Annabelle lifted her heavy skirts to avoid the dust and headed toward the Surratt house. As she suspected, Peggy refused to walk at her side and trailed silently along behind. She passed people going about their business, none of them aware of the plots that unfolded around them.

The mood of the city pulsed with joy and celebration as the people shed the heavy yoke of war. But not even the buoyant mood of the people and the warmth of a long-awaited spring could lift Annabelle's worry. Every moment she'd been forced to wait on others' dragging feet her anxiety had grown.

Eudora's lawman friend must not have taken her warning seriously. What about Mr. Clark, the driver? Wouldn't he have confirmed her story?

Annabelle clenched her teeth and walked faster, knowing she made Peggy struggle to keep pace. She needed to find out O'Malley's plans, if she had any hope of thwarting them again.

They passed several shops and the stables where they'd first found Lincoln's driver. The very fact that they'd entered the same stable, at the same time, was nothing short of a miracle. Had that been only a few weeks ago? She felt as though she'd already lived a decade in these past weeks. They passed by the White House and the eatery where they'd met with Mr. Crook, and finally approached the Surratt boarding house.

As soon as the building came into sight, Annabelle's heart hammered. She paused underneath the limbs of a struggling tree, pretending to need a moment's rest. Peggy stood silently by her side, watching. If she attempted to get closer, Peggy would undoubtedly protest, but for the moment they both seemed content simply to watch the house. She probably should have come up with some sort of plan before storming out here. But it felt good to be doing *something.*

Memories popped in her mind's eye. She reached into the pocket of her skirt. Her fingers brushed the cold metal of the little silver horse Matthew had given her on those very steps, the day of her twentieth birthday. An ache settled on her, but she pushed it away and removed her hand from the trinket.

Oh, please, Matthew, please be safe.

"What do you think staring at that house is gonna do?" Peggy asked, drawing Annabelle from her thoughts.

Annabelle lifted her chin, a motion which gained a scowl from Peggy. "Would you rather I go on over and see if I can have a chat with Mrs. Surratt instead?"

Peggy shivered. "I ain't ever cared for that woman."

Annabelle smirked. "I thought not." She chewed her lip, her momentary smugness evaporating. "I need to find out what they're doing, but I don't have the slightest idea how. I don't even know if they're still there."

"Foolish, I'd think, if they was."

Annabelle sighed. "You're probably right. Come on, let's just go and talk to the law. *Someone* in this city has got to take me seriously."

She'd not taken two steps before Peggy caught her arm.

Startled, Annabelle frowned. Peggy didn't usually grab her in public. "Peggy, what are you…?" The words died on her lips as she noticed Peggy's rounded eyes.

Annabelle followed her gaze back toward the front of the house. She gasped.

Matthew's unmistakable form strode down the stairs, in step with David O'Malley. The two men seemed to be talking amiably, both with smiles on their faces. Annabelle and Peggy stood dumbfounded as the two men walked down the sidewalk. O'Malley slapped Matthew on his shoulder, and the bigger man laughed as they turned a corner and disappeared from sight.

Panic rose in her chest, and they stood there for several moments as the horrible truth finally sank in.

Annabelle grabbed the silver horse and clutched it so tightly that the horse's metal ears dug into her palm and drew blood. Tears gathered in her eyes and burned with fury.

Here she'd been worrying herself nigh unto sickness over him, hardly eating, barely sleeping, her muscles so tight they felt as though they would snap, and for what?

Tears slid down her clenched jaw. Matthew had lied to her…*again.*

Twenty-Six

"For years I have devoted my time, my energies, and every dollar I possessed to the furtherance of an object. I have been baffled and disappointed. The hour has come when I must change my plan."
John Wilkes Booth

Washington, D.C.
April 14, 1865
9:00 a.m.

"I don't want to go to some silly play, Grandmother." Annabelle ignored the two dresses Eudora held out. She shifted in her dressing chair to shoot Peggy a look that said she'd better give Annabelle's hair a break. All the tugging on her tangles was giving her a headache.

Eudora scoffed. "You haven't even heard my reason."

"Reason?" Annabelle groaned. "You always have some reason or another to try to keep me preoccupied."

"You don't trust me, do you?" Eudora lowered her hands and let the two dresses skim the floor.

"I'd like to, truly, but can you really blame me?"

Eudora pressed her lips together so hard they nearly disappeared. "I only did what I thought best. I've already apologized for it."

Even so, didn't Annabelle have a right to mistrust her? Eudora's omissions, half-truths, and woven falsehoods caused trouble. Perhaps she'd meant well, but that didn't excuse her actions. People didn't just lie to the ones they cared about, no matter their—

The thought jerked to a halt. Her gaze darted to Peggy and her heart dropped into her stomach. She hung her head, the unspoken truth evident.

"You have. And I forgive you."

Peggy offered a gentle smile.

Eudora didn't seem to notice the exchange. "Good. Now, back to what I was saying. Which of these do you want to wear to the play? I think this Zouave set would be lovely on you with all this fine stitching along the jacket and skirt." She glanced at Peggy. "Wouldn't you agree?"

Peggy nodded. "Yes, ma'am."

"Very well." Annabelle gave a resigned shake of her head. "Whichever you like."

Eudora tossed it on the bed. "Oh, yes, and this blouse with the lace sleeves. It's perfect." She paused. "Don't be so petulant, dear. They *did* take you seriously on this abduction matter. You saw how Lincoln gave his speech. He didn't even leave the White House!"

Perhaps. The speech occurred just two days after their talk with Mr. Crook. "I suppose." She pulled her fingers through the loose ends of her hair, considering.

Eudora had finally received an actual response from Mr. Crook yesterday afternoon, just after Annabelle had seen

Matthew outside of the Surratt house with O'Malley. The note had said Lincoln would not go out alone, and that they were aware someone might try to abduct the president. Eudora insisted they'd done all they could. Annabelle disagreed.

She wrinkled her nose. "I still think it isn't enough."

"Yes, dear, that I can plainly see." Eudora looked down her nose. "You spent hours yesterday at the hotel, waiting to catch sight of Mr. Booth."

After seeing Matthew with O'Malley, Annabelle had put off going to the law and returned to the hotel, hoping to learn something from Booth. She hadn't seen him again. Had he been visiting someone rather than staying at their hotel?

"How did you know?" She cut her eyes at Peggy, but Peggy only shrugged.

"Don't be silly, child," Eudora said, returning to her perusal of Annabelle's clothing. "I don't need anyone to tell me something so obvious."

Annabelle rubbed her temples. There were more pressing questions on her mind. "Why must we go to this play?"

"Hmm?" Eudora fished out a long lace sash from Annabelle's trunk. "Oh, yes. You said Mr. Booth was in on this matter, didn't you?"

"Yes. And?"

A knock sounded at the door, and Peggy opened it to reveal George out in the hall. "You'll have to wait a bit, Mista Daniels," Peggy said. "Miss Belle ain't ready yet."

"Let him in, Peggy. I'm already dressed," she called loud enough for George to hear.

Peggy looked over her shoulder at Annabelle's hair hanging down around her shoulders and frowned. Annabelle waved it away. "We have important matters to discuss. Mr. Daniels is not affected by my loose hair."

Peggy looked to Eudora for confirmation. Annabelle stifled her annoyance. She merely sought an ally, not a mistress's permission.

Eudora hesitated, then waved her hand. "Let him in."

George strode into the room, but kept his eyes away from Annabelle. Peggy hurried over to her dressing chair and began ripping the comb through Annabelle's tangles hard enough that Annabelle had to bite her lip to keep from crying out.

"Mrs. Smith?" George cleared his throat. "You wished to speak to me?"

With a wave of her hand, Eudora brushed away his awkwardness. "It's time you took a part in this matter."

He lifted his brows. "How so?"

"My granddaughter says that Mr. Booth and Mr. O'Malley are at the center of this abduction scheme."

"They are," Annabelle said as Peggy's nimble fingers finished wrapping a braid around her head.

George kept his gaze on Eudora as though Annabelle hadn't spoken. "She did."

Eudora's eyes twinkled. "I say we turn the tide on them." She put a finger in George's chest. "Your brother's been sucked into their schemes again, if he was ever truly out of them."

"What are you saying?" Tight muscles in George's neck twitched with annoyance.

No sooner had Peggy placed the final pin than Annabelle was on her feet. "We agreed not to tell—"

George whirled around and glared at her, and suddenly he looked more like Matthew than ever. "You'll not keep secrets from me about my own brother."

Perhaps he had a point. She hated when people kept things from her, regardless of their good intentions. "You're right. We shouldn't have tried to keep it from you."

He remained stoic, a statue of indignation.

Eudora stepped between them and placed a hand on George's chest. "Easy there, young man. I know you're riled, but we didn't want to get your blood up if we didn't know for certain."

"Know what for certain?" George asked through his clenched teeth.

"We saw Matthew with David O'Malley, and they seemed to be in cahoots," Annabelle blurted.

George's nostrils flared.

She could understand his anger and hurried to explain. "Peggy and I saw them laughing and talking. I don't think it was because Matthew had convinced O'Malley to change his mind."

"You shouldn't assume what you don't know," he barked. "Have a little faith in him, Miss Ross. Perhaps he did that very thing."

Annabelle's heart constricted, but she could not bring herself to tell George he was wrong. He couldn't know that O'Malley would not be so easily swayed from his goal.

"Will everyone please stop bickering for a moment?" Eudora held up both hands like a mother trying to calm squabbling children. "I've been trying all morning to get someone to hear my plan!"

All eyes turned to Eudora, wide with surprise.

"Now." She clasped her hands at her waist and regained her composure. "I've purchased the three of us,"—she cast Peggy an apologetic look—"tickets to tonight's play at Ford's Theatre. My sources implied that the presidential couple might be in attendance."

Sources? Mr. Crook, no doubt. Understanding dawned. "And if Lincoln goes to Ford's, then likely so will Matthew and O'Malley." Annabelle paced as energy flicked through her. "It's brilliant. Booth wouldn't pass up an opportunity like this. He'll know the theatre and will be able to get O'Malley secret access. They could be making their abduction tonight!"

"As I suspected." Eudora's mouth tipped in a smug smile. "Mr. Crook will be on duty tonight. I've given him your description of Mr. O'Malley. If the man even comes near the president, Mr. Crook has promised to arrest him immediately."

"And my brother?" George asked, voicing Annabelle's own concerns.

Eudora looked at him thoughtfully for what seemed a long time. "Then let us pray it's as you say—that he has nothing to do with these plans." She stared hard at him. "But if he is involved, then it'll be up to you to see that *he* is the one stolen away."

Twenty-Seven

"For four years have I waited, hoped and prayed for the dark clouds to break and for a restoration of our former sunshine. To wait longer is a crime. My prayers have proved as idle as my hopes."
John Wilkes Booth

Washington, D.C.
April 14, 1865
10:15 a.m.

George stepped into the shadow of an alleyway and pulled his hat low. Despite the women's protests, he didn't think anyone in Washington would notice him. He doubted anyone looked for him. Even if they didn't think George had died in the river flood, the war was over. Who would haul him back to Elmira now?

He shifted his weight, his legs tired from standing in the same place for the last hour. He stared at the Surratt boarding house, hoping that what he'd said to Annabelle was true. Surely Matthew must have a plan. But why the secrets? Why hadn't Matthew come and told him before he left for Washington? George tried to push his doubts aside, but still they remained.

He'd just decided to go up to the house and pretend he needed a room when the front door opened and a short man with a fashionable suit and a black hat stepped outside. George narrowed his eyes. O'Malley? Perhaps he should've chosen a closer place to stand watch. He thought he recognized the soldier from his old unit, but he couldn't make out much more detail than stature and hair color from here.

The man paused on the steps and another gentleman followed behind him, this one dressed even finer than the first. George stepped out into the sunlight and walked casually down the street. The men paused at the bottom of the stairs. Judging by their tight countenances, they apparently were having a heated discussion. George watched them out of his peripheral vision as he drew closer.

The shorter man was indeed David O'Malley, and the taller was none other than the actor, John Wilkes Booth. O'Malley waved his hands in frustration, but George was still too far away to catch his words. Booth flung up both of his arms and began to stalk off, O'Malley on his heels. George quickened his pace, keeping up with them as best he could while staying far enough back so as not to be noticed.

He probably shouldn't have bothered. Neither man seemed the least concerned about anyone following them and continued to talk as George drew near. Too many people joined them on the street for George to pick out their words from the other voices around him. As they neared Ford's Theatre, his worst suspicions were confirmed.

The two men strode inside the building. George hesitated, knowing that he'd be discovered if he followed them inside. Instead, he approached a young boy standing near the theatre.

The boy waved pages at the passing crowd, flapping his arms to garner attention.

"Say, boy, what've you got there?" George kept himself turned so he could still see the door to the theatre house.

"*Our American Cousin* is playing tonight, sir. Still have tickets available if you're interested." He popped back his cap and beamed a salesman's smile.

"My companion mentioned she had tickets for tonight's show."

The boy's face fell at little. "Right good then, sir." He called out the play's name again and tried to get patrons to buy tickets.

"But I don't know anything about the play," George said, catching the boy's eye again.

The little fellow, who couldn't be more than eight or nine years old, gave him a friendly smile. "It's a good one. Right funny, you know."

"Ah, that's good. Comedy's a good thing these days."

"Right, mister. You'll like it, you'll see." He turned his attention back to the passing people again and George let him be. He wouldn't be able to keep up the excuse much longer, anyway. He stepped over to the corner of the theatre and kept to the shadows.

Presently, the two men exited from the building. George ducked his head to shield his features. Booth stuffed a stack of papers into the inner pocket of his jacket, and the two passed by without even a glance toward George. He let them go three steps before following.

"This is it!" O'Malley's excited voice carried over the crowded sidewalk.

Booth turned his head slightly to regard his companion, but

said nothing. The two men quickened their stride and George had to hurry to keep pace. O'Malley spoke again, but not loud enough for George to hear.

He followed the two all the way back to the Surratt house. They turned to go up the stairs, and George kept walking.

As he neared, O'Malley grabbed Booth's arm. "I can get the giant to aid us, you know. He's seen the error of his ways."

George stopped in his tracks. *Matthew.*

People continued around him, some casting him curious or annoyed glances. He ignored them. Whatever Booth said in reply, George couldn't hear.

The two men entered the house and closed the door. He clenched his teeth, not wanting to believe Annabelle may have been right.

Brother, if you've gotten yourself into another foolish scheme, so help me, I'm going to take it out on your hide.

George shoved his hands into his pockets and made his way back to the National Hotel, already dreading what he would have to tell the others.

Surratt Boarding House
April 14, 1865
11:30 a.m.

David's blood coursed through his veins with renewed vigor. *Finally! The end has come!* Four years of war and destruction, and now the tyrant would see his end. He rubbed his hands with glee. Oh, how he'd waited for this. He paced around the parlor again, his energy too high to sit in any of the womanly chairs.

Booth should be back any moment now to further discuss their plan. The man had begged to return to his room at the

National Hotel for a few moments after they'd made their discovery at the theatre, and then he'd come back here again to make arrangements for the coming night.

Fate had once again been on his side, and he had been in the entry when Booth had arrived this morning. He acted as though he'd come to speak to Mrs. Surratt, but of course David had known better. She was doing well enough running the middle for him, but it was time she stepped out of the way and let the men handle such important matters. She seemed reluctant to do so, however, and Booth was too caught up in his role as a gentleman to let on that she was no longer needed.

Booth might not have been ready for them to be seen together, but soon David's superior logic had won out. Booth had agreed that he needed to see the new routes David had mapped out, so he'd accompanied Booth to the theatre to pick up his mail, away from Mrs. Surratt's snooping.

David glanced at the clock on the mantle. The ticking hands trudged through molasses with each click of the gears. He turned and went to look out the window instead. Any moment now, things would begin and his place in history would be secured. His family would be avenged.

His heart clenched. Benjamin would have been three this fall, if he hadn't died with Liza in the tyrant's reign of destruction and fire. Where he'd once pushed those images aside, David now let them fester. They would stay ever in his mind, to remind himself that the man who'd brought such pain into David's life deserved no less than the torment he'd commanded upon others.

Just then, David spotted Booth coming up the front stairs to the boarding house. Not bothering to wait on the busybody, he hurried to the door and flung it open before Booth had a chance to knock.

"Ah, here you are, my good friend. Come, come." He gestured for Booth to enter. The other man gave a small frown, but otherwise said nothing. "Let's go on to the parlor."

"Where is Mrs. Surratt?" Booth glanced around the entry as he followed David to the parlor.

A pang of annoyance scratched at his veneer, but David kept it from showing. He waved his hand. "I don't know."

"Perhaps I'll go look for her." Booth turned back the way he'd come.

David grew tired of this ruse. He stepped between Booth and the door. "We haven't the time for these games. I know you've used her to keep our contacts a secret, and you were wise to do so. But the end is now upon us, and such precautions are no longer necessary."

Booth looked surprised for only an instant, then his features turned amused. "And her son John? Has he been about?"

David sputtered. What did that matter? Booth was here to meet with *him*. "He left a letter for me, but I haven't spoken to him." Then, remembering something in the letter, he added, "He says you went to New York."

"I did."

He waited for Booth to continue, but when he did not, David was forced to swallow the indignity of prodding him for more. "And? What were you doing there?"

Booth scoffed. "What business is that of yours?"

David's hands clenched at his sides, and he forced his fingers to flex. He applied his acting skills and let out a laugh, unsure if Booth was toying with him or if he was simply that dimwitted. He slapped Booth on the shoulder. "Anything to do with our goals is my business, of course."

Booth lifted his brows. "Is that so? And, may I ask, why did *you* have people in New York? Were you spying on me?" The bite in his tone snaked out and hooked its fangs in David's mask of humor, nearly pulling it free.

He struggled to keep his tone light. "Quite the opposite, actually. I sent Harry to keep an eye on Daniels. I wanted to be sure that he got his brother back and returned safely."

Booth stroked his mustache thoughtfully.

"But I suppose you know that already," David continued. "Since that's what you went to New York for, isn't it? To make sure I had not let any loose lips run free?" He placed his feet into a defensive stance and straightened his spine. "As you can see, I've handled it."

Booth tugged on the lapel of his jacket, his expression flat. "And how have you handled this…what did you say? Problem with Daniels's brother?"

David set his jaw. Surely he couldn't be serious. He acted as though he didn't remember *anything* about what David had told him. How could Booth have so easily forgotten how David had first conned the big man into his plan and had delivered Booth his prize? He forced a smile to turn up the corners of his mouth. "You remember, of course, that the giant wanted to see his brother released from prison with our leverage?"

Booth lifted his shoulders.

"Anyway, after our failure—"

Booth's face tightened. The word chewed at him as much as it did David. Good. That meant he wouldn't stand for failure again. This time, they *would* succeed in hauling the tyrant away, and then…oh, then they would make him pay for his crimes. In blood.

David grinned. "After the first attempt," he said again, "I let Daniels go to New York and see what he could do about his brother. While we've been waiting on the second opportunity, Daniels returned. He's eager to serve me."

"I don't need him."

Impossible. "Not intellectually of course. He isn't much value there, but when it comes time to do the grab you said you wanted—"

Booth shook his head. "I've changed my mind." He gave a dismissive wave. "I won't be taking Lincoln out of Washington."

Panic clawed at David, but he ignored it, painting on a mask of mild curiosity instead. "Oh? Then what's our plan?"

Booth's brow creased in thought for too long. Did he dare keep things from him? Finally, Booth leaned in close. "I have something very important that needs to be done, but I'm not sure who to ask. It needs to be someone who can be trusted, someone who can think quickly and make adjustments."

A thrill ran through him. *At last!* "What do you have in mind?"

Booth straightened. "There are two things really. Both are important, mind you."

David leaned against the mantle and plucked at a ragged fingernail, projecting nonchalance perfectly. As he suspected, Booth continued again in a moment.

"I'll need someone to go to the tavern in Surrattsville to retrieve the guns and ammunition hidden there."

Ha. Such an errand was beneath him. "And the other?"

Booth stroked his mustache. "The other requires a more delicate touch, you see."

David's fingers twitched. "And?"

Booth strode over to an armchair and took a seat, crossing one ankle over his knee. "Remember when Mr. Ford told us about the *special guests* arriving at the theatre tonight?"

Of course! The lanky woodsman would be there. Did he think David a complete fool? "Where are you going with this?"

He didn't seem concerned by the thinly veiled impatience in David's tone. "Not only them, but their guests as well."

"Grant," David spat. "Yeah, what of it?"

"What if instead of only chopping off the head, I also take out the enemy's hands and feet?"

David paced, his excitement boiling over. "Of course, take them both! We get the tyrant *and* the hand he used to defeat Lee."

Booth nodded. "More, even, but that will come later. Back to the important matter…I said needed someone who could be trusted."

David turned to him, his pulse racing. "I'm the one with the most merit, John. You know that."

The smile playing on Booth's lips seemed almost placating, but surely that was only because he also struggled to contain his excitement. He simply wasn't as skilled at it as David. "Of course," Booth said. "That's why I'm here, after all."

David breathed a sigh of relief. He knew looking for Mrs. Surratt had only been a cover.

"Someone needs to follow the Grants. We need to be certain they come to the play."

"Of course." David nodded eagerly. "I'll see it done."

"I'm sure you will." Booth checked his pocket watch. "We'll meet later this evening to discuss further details of my plan."

"I'll get right on it."

Booth pointed toward the door. He meant immediately. Certainly. David knew as much. He scrambled toward the foyer.

He almost made it to the door when Booth called out. "Oh!" He snapped his fingers. "I nearly forgot. Why don't you take that other man with you?"

David paused. "What man?"

"The big one. Daniels, right?"

"What for?"

Booth's eyes rounded in surprise. "I thought you said he was your dog, following along at your heels?"

David tilted his head. "He is. But he's not the brightest. More muscle than brain, you know. I don't see how he would be useful in gathering information."

"I wonder, though," Booth mused. "What if the Grants decide to switch plans and not attend the theatre?"

He grinned. "Then we'll need someone to snatch the murderous general before he has a chance to escape his sentence."

"See, there?" Booth beamed. "I knew you were a bright one. You'll see it done, now, won't you?"

David puffed his chest. "He will be at that play, or he'll be dead by the time we meet tonight."

Booth waved him away. "See to it, then. Not too quickly, mind you," he added. "Lest Lincoln find out and become suspicious."

David nodded vigorously and sauntered from the parlor with his chin held high. He snatched his hat from the peg and hurried toward the door. First, he'd have to grab his watchdog from the squalid inn Daniels couldn't even afford without David's help.

And then he'd partake in the feast of glory that fate had set out before him.

Twenty-Eight

"Heartsick and disappointed I turn from the path which I have been following into a bolder and more perilous one. Without malice I make the change. I have nothing in my heart except a sense of duty to my choice. If the South is to be aided it must be done quickly. It may already be too late."

John Wilkes Booth

April 14, 1865
12:00 p.m.

Matthew heard the footsteps on the stairs before the knock even came. He put down the newspaper he'd been trying to read and opened the door.

O'Malley looked up at him with excitement, his fist raised to knock. "Get your jacket. We need to go."

Matthew stared at him. "Go where?"

David sneered. "Who are you to ask questions? You said you wanted to redeem yourself. Now's your chance."

Matthew plucked his jacket off the back of a chair. Whatever O'Malley was up to, Matthew had better stay close. He'd nearly gone to the law this very morning, beginning to think that O'Malley would never give him any clues about his plans. He'd wanted to wait until he had something solid to bring to the law, so at least his sacrifice would bring results. He had no doubt the lawmen would arrest him, and he wanted to be sure that his detainment would be worth it.

With O'Malley holed up at Surratt's, he'd begun to think that some warning might have to be better than nothing. Thankfully, he'd decided to wait just one more day.

Matthew followed O'Malley down the narrow stairs and past the unsightly woman who ran the place before stepping out into the afternoon sun. The warm day made a jacket uncomfortable. He'd be more comfortable in just his linen shirt, gray woolen vest, and navy blue cravat.

O'Malley hurried down the street, not waiting to see if Matthew would follow. Grinding his teeth at being thought a hound brought to heel, he took three long strides and gained O'Malley's side. "What are we doing?"

"We're going to put my name on the lips of every person in this repulsive land. Come morning, I'll be written in glory for generations to come."

So, O'Malley was finally making his move. Matthew leaned down to be nearer to O'Malley's ear, feigning excitement. "We're going after Lincoln?"

At least now I'll have a chance to catch you in the act and then haul you off to the police.

"That comes later," O'Malley said, flush with excitement. "First, we cut off the hand that swings the ax for him." He quickened his pace, darting in and out of the people on the street.

Matthew struggled to stay at his side. "What do you mean?" He bumped into one gentleman and had to apologize. When

O'Malley didn't answer, Matthew added, "You know I'm not as clever as you."

He slowed. "I've been entrusted with something *very* important. Of course, it's obvious that I should be the one, wouldn't you say?"

"Of course, but in what way *exactly* are your talents being used?" Matthew twisted sideways to avoid a collision with an elderly man.

They turned a corner and came to a stop at the Willard Hotel. O'Malley grinned. "We're going to call on the Grants, my dear friend." He pushed through the doors before Matthew could reply.

They stepped inside a massive lobby. The tall ceiling balanced on huge columns that reminded him of the giant oaks flanking the drive into Westerly. Such opulence.

O'Malley sauntered up to the receiving desk and flashed the man there a charming smile.

"Good day, sir. I'm here to deliver a message to Mrs. Grant from Mrs. Lincoln."

Matthew glanced at him sharply. *Bold.* The man at the counter didn't seem the least bit suspicious about O'Malley's claim and gave them the location of General Grant's room.

When they reached the main staircase, Matthew whispered, "What are you going to do? Try to abduct the general here in the middle of the day? How will you get him out?"

O'Malley scoffed. "See, this is why you should've never been made a captain. Family wealth alone doesn't give a man the wits to lead."

What was this madman talking about? He shook his head and tried to focus on the task at hand. "Guess you're right. Still,

I'm not sure why I'm here."

They reached the second floor and O'Malley shot him an annoyed glance. "I thought bringing a bull along might be useful, should the need arise."

Refusing to say anything more on the matter, O'Malley strode down the hall until he came to the appointed door and gave a sound knock. A moment later, a dark-skinned woman opened the door.

"Yes, sir?"

O'Malley looked down his nose at her. "I've come to deliver a message to Mrs. Grant. Is she available?"

The maid shook her head. "She's still getting ready for her luncheon. I can pass along the message for you."

O'Malley plastered on a grin that wouldn't fool the dimmest drunk. How the man fancied himself pulling the wool over anyone's eyes, Matthew couldn't fathom.

"Pardon, but I must deliver the First Lady's message to Mrs. Grant personally. Surely you understand."

The woman's gaze narrowed, but she nodded. "One second, and I'll see if my mistress will see you." She closed the door on them, not even offering for them to wait inside.

Thrusting a finger into Matthew's chest, O'Malley sneered. "Don't go opening your mouth. You're not here to talk."

"I understand." Matthew clasped his hands behind his back. At least with him here, O'Malley wouldn't be able to do anything rash.

Presently, the door opened again and a woman with dark hair looked them over with slightly crossed eyes. Matthew wondered if she was just looking at O'Malley oddly or if it was a permanent condition.

"Yes?"

O'Malley gave a low bow. "I've come to deliver a message from Mrs. Lincoln. She wishes to inform you that the Lincolns will be here at precisely seven o'clock. She wishes for you and Mr. Grant to ride with them to the theatre."

Mrs. Grant shook her head. "My husband sent word that we're not attending the play tonight."

She eyed O'Malley for a moment, then slid her gaze over to Matthew. He opened his mouth to try to silently give her some sort of warning, but she didn't hold his gaze long enough. She tipped her chin and began to close the door. "Good day to you."

"One moment," O'Malley said, stepping forward.

Mrs. Grant paused, glancing behind her nervously. "Yes?"

"Might I inform the First Lady as to why you won't be in attendance this evening?"

"Oh, yes," Mrs. Grant said. "We will be visiting our children in Burlington, since my husband has been away so long. Please give Mrs. Lincoln our regrets."

"Yes, ma'am. I will."

Mrs. Grant gently closed the door, leaving the two of them in the hall. O'Malley's mask of composure shattered, and he snarled. "We'll have to follow them."

"What for?" Matthew followed O'Malley as the shorter man stalked away. O'Malley cast him a seething look, so Matthew snapped his mouth closed.

They returned to the lobby, where O'Malley chose a seat. From this vantage, they could still see the main staircase.

A few moments later, Mrs. Grant came down the stairs and greeted another woman, and the two of them turned toward the dining room. O'Malley rose and they followed, choosing a table as close to the women as they could.

O'Malley tried to watch her covertly the entire time she shared her luncheon with the other woman, but soon his glances turned to stares. The women placed their napkins on the table when Mrs. Grant finally glanced their way. O'Malley immediately turned his face from her, but Matthew tried to hold her gaze.

How could he warn her? He glanced at O'Malley, then back to Mrs. Grant and gave a small shake of his head. The woman's brows puckered slightly, but she dipped her chin and broke eye contact, ushering the other woman from the room.

The National Hotel
April 14, 1865
1:00 p.m.

"I'm sorry, Miss Ross. I understand your concern, but this is something I must do." George rubbed the muscles on the back of his neck, but the tension wouldn't ease.

"I, for one, agree entirely with Mr. Daniels," Mrs. Smith said from her perch on the dressing stool in George's room.

"Me, too." Miss Ross's maid crossed her arms and cast a determined look at her mistress.

George tried to keep his amusement at the woman's tone from turning up his lips. He'd grown accustomed to the strange relationship between Miss Ross and her servant, but the woman's audacity still caught him off guard at times.

Miss Ross shot the woman a withering gaze, but the maid didn't cower. Without the support of the other women, Miss Ross turned back to him. "I've been there before. I can simply ask Mrs. Surratt if she's seen him."

"That's too suspicious," Mrs. Smith said.

George agreed. "She's never seen me, so I can find a way to inquire about him without calling any attention to ourselves."

Miss Ross bit her lip. "Then what?"

"If my brother is there, I'll bring him back."

Miss Ross didn't look convinced, and he couldn't say that he blamed her. He had his own doubts. Matthew could be a mule, and no amount of whipping, cajoling, or tugging could move his feet once he'd set them. Miss Ross hung her head, but not before he saw the look in her eyes. No matter what she insisted, her affections for his brother were blatantly obvious.

"Please, make sure he doesn't do anything foolish." Her blue eyes bore into him.

George gave a curt nod and strode to the door, opening it so the women could return to their rooms to rest before dinner and the play that evening. "All will be well."

She mustered a half-hearted smile as she passed him, followed closely by her maid.

Mrs. Smith hesitated a moment and let the other two women continue down the hall. "I'd greatly prefer that you return in time to take us to the play. Regardless of what you find out."

"That's my sincere intention, ma'am. If he's there, I'll bring him back, and if not, then my best chance at finding him may be at the theatre."

Mrs. Smith seemed satisfied and returned to her room. George locked his door, pocketed the key, and left the hotel. He took a hired coach to the Surratt boarding house and, after tossing the driver one of Mrs. Smith's coins, stood at the bottom of the stairs where he'd seen O'Malley and Booth earlier that day.

Drawing a deep breath, George strode up the staircase and knocked firmly on the door. After a few moments, an older woman dressed in widow's blacks stood in the doorway.

"Good afternoon, sir. How might I help you?"

George tipped his hat. "Good afternoon. I'm calling on the lady of this house, a Mrs. Surratt, I believe?"

The woman inclined her head in acknowledgment. "I am she."

Successful so far. "I've come to inquire about taking a room, if any are available."

The woman gestured him inside. "Certainly, come in and we can discuss the terms."

"Thank you, ma'am. My brother mentioned your boundless hospitality, so when I came to Washington, I thought to come here first."

He followed her into a well-appointed parlor, spotless and filled with richly upholstered furniture.

Mrs. Surratt swished across the floor in a sweep of black silk and took a seat. "How kind of him." She gestured toward the chair across from her. "I currently have two rooms available for guests. The boarding fee also includes all your meals, should you choose to take them."

"Yes, as my brother said," George replied as he settled into his chair. "He stayed here not too long ago. I wonder if you might remember him?"

The lady smiled. "Most likely. What is his name?"

"Mr. Matthew Daniels."

A hard glint came into her eye, but her features remained pleasant. If George had not been looking for her reaction, he might never have noticed the shift in her features. She took a moment, as if thinking. "Oh, yes, I do remember. He was traveling with a young woman, I believe. They took rooms here a month or so ago."

George nodded. "That seems about right."

She didn't say more, so George decided to take the risk and push a bit harder. He propped his ankle on his knee and tried to sound casual. "I wanted to catch up with him again. In our last correspondence, he said he planned to return to Washington on business sometime soon. As luck would have it, business brought me here as well. Has he come back here looking for lodging?"

He watched the woman closely, but she gave no indication that her reply was not sincere.

"I haven't seen him." She glanced at a clock sitting on the mantle and then leapt to her feet. "I must be going. I have an important matter that cannot wait."

George frowned, and hesitantly rose from his seat.

Mrs. Surratt smiled again, though the hard lines couldn't be genuine. "Could you perhaps return tomorrow? I can set up lodging for you then, if that's acceptable."

Finding no other response, George dipped his chin in agreement. "Certainly, ma'am. I understand. I dropped by without an announcement. Shall I return at, let's say, nine tomorrow morning?"

She shook her head. "I won't be back by then. Two o'clock tomorrow afternoon should suffice, however." She gestured toward the door.

George obliged and walked past her. He plucked his hat from the peg by the door where he'd deposited it on the way in. "Thank you for your time." He turned to leave, and then, as though something just occurred to him, turned back just as he set one foot out the door. "Oh, if perchance my brother does come by, would you let him know that I was looking for him?"

The woman's nostril's flared slightly, but she offered a smile that didn't reach her eyes. "I'll leave word with the help."

"Thank you, ma'am."

As the door closed behind him, his stomach sank. Where could that fool brother of his be?

Willard Hotel
April 14, 1865
4:00 p.m.

David O'Malley straightened his collar and sat taller in the saddle. Any moment now the general would reemerge from the hotel with his plain wife in tow. The man had sauntered into the hotel a quarter hour earlier, and they'd leave for the train station soon.

The fact that the couple had decided not to go to the play wouldn't hinder his plans. He wouldn't let this amputation be foiled simply because some fool changed his fickle mind. No, the tyrant doing that very thing had cost them too much already. This time, David wouldn't let the whims of the weak-minded spoil his glory.

The giant sat astride a muddy brown gelding, and the poor beast seemed to sag under the weight. David studied the man from the side of his vision. Daniels appeared oblivious to the precipice over which they now hung. Not that David expected anything different. Daniels was nothing more than a pawn—a bit of muscle and sinew that served as a tool in the master's hand.

David, conversely, stood at the edge like an eagle, ready to take to flight and glory in all the heights he was about to achieve.

"That them?" Daniels asked, shifting on his horse and gesturing toward a couple across the street.

David squinted at them, the faces little more than a blur at this distance. No matter, the pompous way the man strutted and the scurrying movements of the little mouse at his side were all the indication David needed to know he'd found his prey.

He gave a curt nod, and in a moment the two of them moved their animals into the flow of Yanks. Witless sheep meandering about with no purpose. He cast annoyed glances at any who dared not dart quickly enough from his path.

One particularly annoying elderly man struggled along with a loaded cart, too old to complete the task with any efficiency. They were stuck behind him as the fool struggled to inch his load down a busy street he had no business blocking.

When David finally got his horse angled enough to squeeze up next to the bumbling fool, he reached out with his foot to give the man a nudge. The codger was probably too old to hear and too witless to realize he blocked most of the road with his load. Instead of looking up and realizing he impeded his betters, the old man stumbled and began to fall. As he did, he managed to take the cart with him. The rickety contraption turned sideways and spilled sacks of what appeared to be either sugar or flour all over the road.

David shook his head in annoyance and moved his prancing animal around the obstacle. He scanned the people walking, but had lost sight of the couple. David clenched his teeth and squeezed his legs. The horse bounded forward. There were shouts of shock, but David ignored them all, a lion stalking his prey. They would not escape him!

He cast a glance behind him to be sure his guard dog followed, and was appalled to see the big man had dismounted. Daniels's beefy hands righted the overturned cart. *Fool!* Didn't he see David had already made his way around?

He didn't have time to worry with the man's incompetence if he wished to keep up the chase. After furiously scanning the people on the crowded street, panic rose in his chest like bile.

No. David fought down the useless fear. He might've lost sight of them, but he could guess exactly where they were going. Just up ahead, nondescript black carriages pulled from a small stabling area. Likely, one of these hired rides would enclose the murderous general and his defective wife, bound for the train station.

His mount burst forward again and moved to intercept a carriage pulling out into the road. He drew near and peered into the window as the lumbering carriage swayed into the turn. Inside, two old hags stared at him with wide eyes.

Curse it! If not for that bumbling old codger and this endless press of sheep, he wouldn't have lost them.

He could *not* fail again. To fail now would rupture his very will to continue in this evil world. He suppressed a shudder, knowing the gnawing void that often called to him whenever he let his mind relax would become relentless, should he squander what fate had presented to him.

Perhaps he should embrace the darkness. Find peace as he passed from this life and found comfort in the arms of his lost family. It would be easy, really. Once he was gone, he wouldn't have to worry about the tyrant still choking this country and....

He shook his head violently to dislodge the thought. *No!* He must fight on. If only for Liza's sake. He couldn't return to her with her death gone unpunished. He ground his teeth and yanked hard on the reins, forcing the horse to spin on its hindquarters and face the opposite direction.

There! Another black carriage must have left only moments before the one containing the hags, and it was headed in the right direction. David spurred the horse, causing people to leap from his path, lest they find themselves underneath the pounding hooves.

He pushed the horse harder as the crowd on the road thinned and galloped up to the window of the carriage. Inside, he could see Grant's little mouse.

David strained his neck, but from this angle could not see if the person seated across from her was, indeed, her husband. If they had parted ways, causing David to lose the true prize, he couldn't return to Booth with such disgrace.

He lowered himself in the saddle and kicked the horse's side, pushing the animal to gallop faster. He darted past the front of the carriage and farther down the road, dust boiling up underneath the horse's churning hooves. When he thought he'd gained enough ground, David pulled up hard and spun the horse around.

The driver of the carriage seemed startled, but didn't pull up on the reins. Instead, he snapped them along the horses' backs and brought the animals into a brisk trot. David squeezed his calves and his horse surged into a canter. The driver of the carriage raised his arm to shake a fist at David, but he paid the man no mind.

Almost close enough…just a little more….There!

He passed by on the other side of the carriage and peered into the window. Jubilation lurched in his stomach as the bearded face came into view. The sword of the tyrant himself sat across from his wife, his dull mind occupied with the newspaper and oblivious to his nearing demise.

He'd done it! Now all he needed was the giant to snatch—

David pulled the horse to a stop and let out a frustrated growl as the carriage rolled away. When he actually needed Daniels, the man had failed him! *Of all the worthless….*

He'd put a bullet in that dimwit for costing him this victory! He glanced back at the carriage, which had slowed to a regular walk.

Just then, the sound of pounding hooves made him turn. Daniels approached at a canter. David pinned the man with a withering glare as he drew to a halt at his side.

"I'm sorry I lost you back there, I—"

"Enough!" David bared his teeth and held up his hand to cut off the excuse. "They're getting away!"

David spurred his horse forward after the carriage, and this time the lout followed obediently. He mentally flipped through the possible means of attack, finally settling on the most perfect of all of his brilliant ideas.

A smile bloomed on his face, and he urged the horse faster.

Twenty-Nine

"I cannot longer resist the inclination, to go and share the sufferings of my brave countrymen, holding an unequal strife (for every right human & divine) against the most ruthless enemy the world has ever known."
John Wilkes Booth

Washington Train Station
April 14, 1865
5:00 p.m.

A sickening feeling soured Matthew's stomach. O'Malley's eyes held a strange gleam as they followed the general and his wife, who waited just down the train platform. Thankfully, Matthew had been able to convince O'Malley not to attempt to snatch the general from his carriage. At first, O'Malley had berated Matthew for trying to think above his ability, but in the end, O'Malley's love for the dramatic had won out, and he'd agreed.

The day's warmth faded with the sun's final bow, coloring the sky deep purple. Dark clouds gathered overhead ushering evening in early.

Suddenly O'Malley turned wide eyes on Matthew. "We'll get

tickets…yes. Why bother trying to sneak aboard when we can present tickets?" Matthew couldn't be sure if the words were meant for him or not, so he said nothing. But then O'Malley fished money out of his vest pocket and thrust it at Matthew. "Here. Go get tickets."

He hesitated only an instant before plucking the money from the man's grasp. He walked toward the ticket counter, his boots pounding heavily on the wooden walk. He glanced around the platform. No uniformed policemen.

Matthew pushed the money O'Malley had given him through the window and purchased their tickets to Philadelphia. Then he put them in his pocket and turned away, taking his time as he returned to O'Malley's side. O'Malley hadn't shared his plans, but a dullard could fit the pieces together.

They'd board the train with the Grants, and somehow, during the trip, O'Malley intended to murder them. His pulse quickened with the thought. O'Malley's descent into madness now seemed complete, and Matthew feared the man he'd known in the army no longer existed.

Matthew approached O'Malley and assessed the man who'd not long ago been under his command. Somehow, he had to find a way to diffuse the situation and protect the general and his wife. With no lawmen around, he'd need to subdue O'Malley.

As though sensing Matthew's suspicions, O'Malley sidled out of Matthew's reach as he neared. Not wanting to chase him and risk losing him in the crowd, Matthew stopped short and plastered on a dumb look. "What's wrong? I got your tickets."

Frantic eyes darting about, O'Malley resembled a caged animal. Matthew pulled the tickets out of his pocket, tempting the man closer.

Just then, the conductor called for the passengers to board. O'Malley took advantage of the distraction and snatched the tickets from Matthew's fingers. He darted toward the train.

Alarmed, Matthew hurried after him. O'Malley nearly sprinted up to the train car the Grants had chosen, taking the doorway at the opposite end from the couple. Matthew looked at them, hoping to catch their eye, but neither of them noticed. He had no choice other than to stand in line behind two other passengers who'd reached the train car between him and O'Malley.

O'Malley handed a ticket to the man at the entry door and stepped out of sight. For a moment, Matthew feared he'd move in for the kill before he could catch him. But the Grants stood roughly in the same position in their line as Matthew stood in the other, and he could keep an eye on them.

He stepped up to the man collecting tickets and giving directions. "Ticket, please."

Matthew gestured into the car. "My companion should have already given my ticket. He's inside."

The man shook his head. "Sorry, sir. No one's presented two tickets. Step aside, please."

Matthew's heart raced. He glanced over to the other end of the car. Mrs. Grant stepped onto the stairs. "He must have forgotten when we were separated. I can wait here, if you prefer, while you ask him for my ticket."

Seeing the resolve on Matthew's face, the man sighed. "Which fellow?"

Matthew gave a brief description of O'Malley, and the ticket man stepped inside the train. The general boarded. Matthew's pulse marched double-time through his veins. Ticket or no, he couldn't let Grant and O'Malley out of his sight.

He leapt inside.

The Grants chose seats near the opposite door, and the general helped his wife settle into her seat. Matthew's eyes darted around the faces of the passengers crowding the aisle, but couldn't find O'Malley.

"Excuse me, sir!" A clear voice rang out.

The ticket man grabbed O'Malley's arm. Relief surged and Matthew let out a heavy breath. Behind him, people grumbled, but Matthew didn't spare them a glance.

The two men exchanged words, and after a moment, O'Malley frowned and reached into his coat pocket. He presented the second ticket and allowed the train man to guide him into a seat. His face turned an odd shade of red, glistening sweat visible even from here.

The man returned. "Got it." He looked at Matthew strangely. "Everything all right with your companion?"

"Thank you," Matthew said, thinking quickly. "He isn't feeling well." He leaned in close with a conspirator's whisper. "Between us, I think his mind's broken."

The man narrowed his eyes slightly, then, seeming satisfied, gave a nod. "I noticed something didn't seem right with him. Please make sure he doesn't cause any disturbances."

Matthew nodded. "He's in my charge until I can take him to his family in Philadelphia, and I assure you, I'll make certain he remains quietly in his seat."

"Very good." He stepped around Matthew to take his place at the door and address the grumbling passengers still waiting to be permitted inside.

Matthew hurried down the aisle and dropped next to O'Malley's side. "You forgot to give me my ticket," he said, putting equal amounts of confusion and petulance into his tone.

O'Malley glared at him. "This makes twice your slowness cost me my quarry."

Pretending a gesture of apology, Matthew placed his hand on O'Malley's shoulder. "You're right. I'm very sorry. But, of course, this hasn't changed your brilliant plan."

"It hasn't?"

Matthew shook his head. "You were going to wait until the train was under way, so that no one could alert the law until we reached the next station, right?"

O'Malley brightened. "Oh, yes. Of course. I'll have them finished and be back to the theatre in time."

Matthew cocked his head. "Theatre?"

O'Malley's eyes gleamed. "This isn't the end, you know." He chuckled, but the sound only sent a shiver down Matthew's spine. "Not only will I take the arm, but then the very head!"

Matthew fought to keep his composure, praying that O'Malley's pride would continue to loosen his tongue. O'Malley sat back against the plush seat and smiled wistfully. "It'll all be over soon. And then, peace. We take the arm now, and then it's back to Washington to kill the tyrant. Why let Booth whisk him away during the play?"

"No," Matthew agreed. "He's too weak. You're the only one with the fortitude to pull it off."

"See? Even a half-wit like you can see it. Oh, yes. Forget whatever abduction plans Booth has. While the tyrant laughs at that ridiculous play at Ford's, I'm going to put a bullet in his back," O'Malley whispered. His eyes danced with glee. "The waiting is done, my friend. The waiting is done."

Matthew rested his head on the cushion and willed his thudding heart to slow. When the last passengers boarded and the train let off a shrill whistle, Matthew formulated a plan. It stank of deception and cowardice, but he could see no other way. He couldn't risk being detained and not making it back to the theatre to stop the abduction.

The train moved forward and the heavy wheels ground beneath them as they rolled along the tracks.

Then, quick as a darting snake, Matthew's hand clutched the soft spot at the top of O'Malley's neck, just below the jaw. He began to squeeze.

The National Hotel
April 14, 1865
7:00 p.m.

Annabelle gathered her white skirt and stepped into the hired carriage. Eudora and George followed, and soon the three of them swayed onto the road to Ford's Theatre.

"What if they aren't there? Or we don't see them?" Annabelle asked.

"Then that's best, wouldn't you say?" Eudora lifted her brows.

Annabelle looked at her like she'd misplaced her wits. "How can that be a good thing?"

"Because it means maybe Mr. Daniels did, indeed, thwart this O'Malley." She smiled.

Annabelle glanced at George. "But what about Booth? He still has a part in this. I'm sure of it."

George nodded. "He was with O'Malley."

Eudora pursed her lips, still seeming unconvinced, despite all the evidence against the actor. "He was likely only brought into it because of his knowledge of the theatre."

Annabelle couldn't keep the bite from her tone. "No, Grandmother. I also saw him during their first attempt."

"Then we'll call upon Mrs. Lincoln tomorrow and let her know your suspicions."

Annabelle gaped. "You can do that?"

"Well," Eudora said, lifting her shoulders. "I can try."

Annabelle groaned and fell back against the cushions. They continued the remainder of the short journey in silence.

The carriage came to a stop and the footman opened the door, assisting the ladies out at the front of the theatre. George presented their tickets and they entered the playhouse. If not for the circumstances, Annabelle might have been excited to attend her first performance. Her insides gnawed with apprehension as she scanned every face, every detail of the theatre.

The seats on the floor curved around the stage, giving the audience nearly equal viewing. Above, lamplight danced gleefully from rows of sconces positioned along the edge of an upper balcony, sending a shimmering glow over the polished wood of the stage.

A man ushered them toward assigned seats near the rear of the viewing floor. Annabelle gathered her skirt and petticoat to slide between the rows and sat between Eudora and George.

"I'm sorry for the quality of the seats," Eudora said, "but I couldn't get anything in the boxes on short notice."

Annabelle followed her grandmother's gaze to the sets of private seats up above them. Presently, her gaze landed on a box nearly overhanging the stage, decorated in tassels and a Union flag. "Is that where he'll be?"

Eudora straightened herself to face the stage once more. "Of course."

Cupped mirrors decorated the edge of the stage, concentrating the lamplight on the performance space. The curtain glowed brightly. They'd have no trouble seeing the performance, even this late at night.

Below the stage, men with instruments began tuning, and a disjointed sound of mismatched notes flowed into the murmurs of the gathering crowd. Like many others around her, Annabelle's eyes kept turning up toward the presidential box.

When the curtain drew back and the box remained empty, her heart pounded. What if they'd already carried out their plan while she sat here like a fool watching a silly play?

The musicians played the opening notes. Something inside the box moved. Annabelle held her breath. A couple she didn't recognize entered and sat in two of the chairs. She strained to see. If he didn't come, she couldn't stand to sit here any longer.

There! Finally, the unmistakable height of the president stepped into the box, and Annabelle's racing heart slowed. She watched as he saw his wife seated, and then took his place next to her.

The others in the theatre must have noticed him as well, because a cheer arose. The actors on the stage paused, waiting as the president waved to an adoring crowd. Relief washed over her.

With Lincoln safely in his box and Mr. Crook watching for any sign of O'Malley, she could take a few moments to breathe easy. For now, they could simply enjoy the performance.

Philadelphia Train Station
April 14, 1865
7:00 p.m.

The train ground to a halt at the Philadelphia platform, and O'Malley was still unconscious. He breathed slowly, his face serene. To any observer, the man simply slept peacefully.

Matthew had hated to cut off the man's air, and his stomach had turned watching O'Malley struggle until his face had turned purple. Even so, Matthew had held on until he felt O'Malley's muscles go lax.

As soon as O'Malley stiffened, Matthew released his grip. Breath pulled back into his lungs and he slumped to the side, unconscious. He'd have a monstrous headache when he finally awoke, but he'd survive. It'd been the best solution Matthew could conjure.

Matthew waited until most of the other passengers, including the Grants, disembarked. As he pulled on his coat, he spotted the same ticket man who'd been at the door earlier. He waved the man over.

"How long before the next train back to Washington?"

The man looked past Matthew at O'Malley but dismissed the sleeping man. "One hour. Are you returning so soon?"

Matthew nodded. "My charge's family doesn't live far. They'll take him home. I want to be back in Washington to sleep in my own bed."

The man smiled. "Certainly, sir." He gestured to O'Malley. "Better wake him, if you hope to make it in time."

Matthew threw O'Malley's arm over his shoulder and pulled him from his seat. O'Malley groaned but didn't wake. Matthew tugged him from the seat and into the aisle, his feet barely skimming the floor. "Afraid I can't. Had to give him some sleeping draught to keep him calm, and it'll be awhile before it wears off."

The ticket man frowned and opened his mouth but then shook his head and walked away. Relieved, Matthew hauled O'Malley off the train and onto the darkened platform. If any of the busy passengers noticed them, they paid no mind.

Matthew set his jaw and dragged O'Malley along until he found what he needed. Ahead, sounds of laughter spilled onto the road. Music and the merriment of men deep into their ale directed him to the nearest pub as surely as the scent of pie brought hungry bellies to the kitchen.

Matthew nudged the door open with his foot and hauled O'Malley inside, but none of the Yanks celebrating their victory seemed to care about the unconscious man. He stood just inside the door, looking around until he spotted a man he hoped was the proprietor.

Men sat at several tables playing cards, their cigar smoke permeating the air and clinging to Matthew's clothing. He wove his way around the tables and past the jangling piano as the man sitting at the keys pounded out a vibrant tune. Instead of soothing, the buoyant song only further scraped at Matthew's already failing portrayal of calm.

Finally, he reached the serving bar and shifted O'Malley's weight. He might be a slight man, but carrying his full weight such a distance had still become taxing. The old wound in his calf began to ache, and he consciously had to keep a grimace from his face.

"Need something?" the man asked, handing a customer a mug of ale. He wiped his beefy hands on a towel.

Matthew gestured toward O'Malley. "My friend here needs a place to sleep off his drink."

The barkeep glanced at the drooping man and chuckled.

"Mighty early to be that bad off."

Matthew shrugged. "It's common enough for this one. He'll be a bear in the morning, though."

The large man, nearly as tall and broad as Matthew, gestured toward the stairs at the back of the crowded room. "I've got one room left, if you want it."

"Thank you. He just needs to sleep it off. I have business I must return to, so if I can just pay now…?"

The man shrugged. "Sure. Want me to let him know when he wakes?" Someone called for another drink and the big man shouted for him to wait a moment.

"You're busy. I'll leave him a message. I doubt he'll be up until morning."

The man seemed pleased with the answer and they decided on a price for one night and a hot breakfast. Matthew used O'Malley's funds to pay for the room, and then hauled him up the stairs.

He pushed open the door and dragged O'Malley to the single bed. It wasn't a fancy place, but it was dry, warm, and a good bit better than the alley where Matthew had briefly considered leaving him.

The unconscious man never stirred as Matthew removed his boots and covered him with a quilt. Matthew stepped back and looked at O'Malley, giving a small shake of his head. "I'm sorry, David," he whispered. "I just couldn't let you go through with it."

He turned and left the room, pulling the door closed behind him. He stuck in the key and turned the lock, and then he tucked it away and hurried back to the train station.

Thirty

"Many, I know—the vulgar herd—will blame me for what I am about to do, but posterity, I am sure, will justify me."
John Wilkes Booth

Ford's Theatre
April 14, 1865
10:20 p.m.

Annabelle found herself drawn into the play, giggling at another joke. She glanced up again as the room filled with the sounds of roaring laughter and could make out the president sitting in his box, leaning forward as his shoulders shook.

The man playing the cousin stood alone on the polished stage, strutting about like a deer in full antlers. Lamplight shone brightly on his wily expression. "Don't know the manners of good society, eh? Well, I guess I know enough to turn you inside out, old gal. You sockdologizing old man trap!"

The audience howled and the theatre filled with hysterical laughter. Even George, who'd seemed stoic throughout the first half of the performance, leaned over as he clutched his stomach and slapped at his knee.

A loud pop sounded from above. *What was that?* Annabelle's heart fluttered. *Gunfire?* She glanced back at the stage. The actors were still in the full swing of their performance.

Must be part of the play.

A scream tangled with the sounds of merriment. Startled, Annabelle's gaze immediately turned toward the president's box, still hoping she'd merely become paranoid.

In the darkness, two men struggled up in the box as one reached for the outer railing. O'Malley! How had Mr. Crook missed him? Words strangled in her throat as she pointed toward the box.

In an instant George leapt to his feet. He struggled out of the crowd, stepping across patrons who cried out as he climbed over them. The audience hadn't noticed the commotion in the box.

The man jumped up on the railing of the box and Annabelle wailed, springing to her feet. O'Malley had been caught in the act, but now he was trying to get away! Someone grabbed at the man's coat just as he prepared to jump, and O'Malley lost his balance.

As the conspirator leapt, his foot became entangled in the Union flag hanging off the railing. He landed hard on the stage. He hobbled across the stage, his leg obviously injured.

His plot had failed! He could not have abducted—

Her hope flickered out as the man came forward on the stage. There stood not David O'Malley but John Wilkes Booth. The crowd buzzed with confusion, unsure if the actor had performed the stunt as part of the show.

Then he lifted a bloody knife over his head, and chaos

broke out as the audience realized this was not part of the play. She'd expected Booth would help O'Malley to get the president captured, but not this!

Terrified, Annabelle looked back to the box, but the shadowed figures were hard to see. She squinted.

There. The president still seemed to be seated, but his head hung off to the side. His wife had her arms around him, screaming.

"Stop that man!" someone yelled from above.

Booth, seemingly undeterred, shouted something Annabelle thought to be Latin. Then as the truth of the matter finally took hold, the crowd surged forward. One man even made a mighty leap over the orchestra pit and scrambled up on the stage in pursuit. No way could Booth escape this many.

Annabelle struggled toward the end of the row, stumbling over Eudora in her haste and nearly falling. George pushed through scores of stunned people, heading for the stage. Eudora stood transfixed until Booth dropped the bloody knife and ran off the stage.

As though a spell broke, Eudora came to her senses and grabbed Annabelle's arm. "Come on!"

Annabelle watched George's progress for only an instant, then followed Eudora as they elbowed their way through the crowd, heading for the rear of the theatre. Pushing and shoving with all sense of manners forgotten, they made their way to the stairs leading to the private boxes.

When they reached the top, the hall stood empty. Annabelle stumbled to a halt, fear sending a shiver down her spine. No one guarded the private doors. Panic drummed in her chest. What had happened to them?

Eudora let out a wail, calling her friend's name, but Mr. Crook was nowhere to be seen. She picked up her skirts, and the two of them dashed toward the president's box undeterred.

They'd made it only a few paces down the carpet when footsteps sounded heavily behind them. Annabelle looked over her shoulder and saw a young man running their way, his mustached face set in hard lines.

"Excuse me!" he shouted as he passed them, nearly knocking Annabelle over as he darted around her.

The man grabbed the door of the president's box and gave it a hard yank just as Annabelle arrived, only steps behind him. Horrified, she lunged toward the stranger, grabbing his arm and trying to pull him away.

"Release me, woman. I'm a doctor!"

Stunned, Annabelle let go just as Eudora gained her side.

The man pounded on the door. "I'm Charles Leale, surgeon of the Union Army!"

No reply. The young man pulled on the door again, but it held firm. Finally, after several tries, a shout came from the other side of the door.

"Stand back!"

Scraping noises, and finally the door came open with a jerk. A man stood there, bleeding profusely from a deep gash in his chest that ran the length of his upper arm. He clutched the wound, his face pale.

Before anyone could say anything about his condition, the man gestured back toward the box. "I can wait. See to the president. He's been shot!"

The doctor's face became a storm cloud, and he hurried through a second door into the private box without hesitation.

Annabelle cried out, and the man who'd opened the door glared at her. She ignored him, her shock compelling her to move forward. She opened her mouth to tell the man she'd been a nurse's aide and could help, but before she could get the words out, he grabbed tight onto her arm.

"Please, miss. No one needs to be in here until the doctor can do his job."

Before she could reply, he turned away, leaving her staring dumbly after him as he once again closed the door.

Eudora clutched her arm and pulled her away from the door. "There is nothing we can do. Let the doctor work."

With blood pounding so heavily in her ears, she almost couldn't hear Eudora's words. Annabelle stumbled backward and slumped against the wall, her weak knees nearly giving out underneath her. She stood there transfixed, the scene around something from a nightmare.

Footsteps sounded down the hall, but Annabelle couldn't lift her eyes. Inside the box, a woman wailed, her frantic shouts echoing in Annabelle's mind and mingling with the clamor of her own jumbled thoughts.

Failed!

So much worse—

We should have been able to save—

Annabelle shook her head to dislodge the buzzing thoughts stinging her mind like wasps. She needed to pull herself together and think clearly. She steeled herself and raised her head to look at the door again. It stood open. The injured needed her help. She shakily took a step closer. Another cry came from within the box that brought a new chill to her veins.

"The president is assassinated!"

Her knees once again gave way, and she slumped against the wall. As the First Lady's cries of torment permeated the hall, Annabelle put her head in her hands and wept.

Washington Train Station
April 14, 1865
10:38 p.m.

Mist hung in the air as Matthew exited the train, and by the time he reached the end of the platform, the moisture clung to his skin. He flagged down one of the waiting coachmen and presented a stolen coin for the ride into the heart of Washington. He tried to assuage his guilt over the thievery by reminding himself he'd just saved two lives.

He instructed the driver to move with haste and swung up into the coach, ducking his head to make it inside. Matthew had barely pulled the door closed when the carriage began to sway.

The inside of the carriage was shrouded in shadows. Matthew took off his coat and brushed the water from his hat. Feeling better out of the damp clothing, he leaned back and closed his eyes. The more he'd thought about it on the train ride back, the more he worried over what O'Malley had said.

Would someone else seek to finish what O'Malley had started, or did the madman now work alone? He'd mentioned Booth, but he'd mumbled all kinds of things. Either way, he'd stop by the theatre, just to be sure. Then he'd go to the law and tell his story. Hopefully, when questioned, Mrs. Grant would recognize him and be able to affirm the tale. With any luck, they might even be able to get O'Malley from the pub before he could run off.

Presently, the carriage came to a stop. Shouts rang out on

the street. Curious, he pulled aside the curtain. An addled mob filled the street. His curiosity morphed into horror. Something was terribly wrong.

He pulled open the door and jumped out, not even bothering to grab his coat and hat. The driver shouted something at him as he bolted away, but he couldn't turn back. Just ahead, people flowed out of Ford's Theatre and gathered on the street, blocking the carriages. Women wailed and men shouted incoherently. Even in four years of war, Matthew had never seen such a chaotic scene.

He grabbed the shoulder of the nearest man. "What happened?"

The man looked at him with horrified eyes. "The president's been assassinated!"

O'Malley hadn't been the only one with murderous intent. "Where?"

The man nodded to the theatre. "They're saying he was shot during the play!"

Matthew thrust the man aside and pushed his way through the press of bodies. Men in uniforms of various sorts shouted and converged. Matthew reached out and snatched the arm of a passing policeman.

The startled man snatched his arm away. "What's the meaning of this?"

"I know who the assassin is!" Matthew blurted. "It's John Wilkes Booth!"

The man looked at him in disgust. "Everyone knows that, you fool. Join the search or be gone with you!"

Matthew stood there, too stunned to move. Everyone knew? Search? Matthew shook off his surprise and pushed farther into the crowd. Booth had gotten away? His mind raced. Surely he wouldn't be so foolish as to return to the Surratt house.

A thought slammed into him. During the abduction plot, Harry had gone to Mrs. Surratt's tavern in Surrattsville to deposit a stash of guns and ammunition. If he had to make a guess, Booth would head there. He searched for the policeman, but the man had already disappeared.

He started to walk toward another when a great wave of cries arose off to his left. A tight knot of men came out of the theatre, a man hoisted on their arms.

"Guards, clear passage!" one of the men shouted. Union soldiers thrust people out of the way and the group parted the crowd like the Red Sea.

When the crowd opened, Matthew got a glimpse of what he'd feared—the body of Lincoln, limp in their arms. Transfixed, he watched them somberly carry the body of their dead leader through the wailing crowd. Time slowed, each breath an eternity as the group waded through the river of tears and anguish poured out by the mourners on the streets.

As the fallen president passed, Matthew's eyes drifted back to the throng filling in behind the procession. There, at its head, trudged a small woman in a white dress, her sleeve smeared in so bright a red that even the dim light and misting rain couldn't hide its nature.

His senses snapped back to clarity, the fog of the moment giving way to the harsh light of reality. What was *she* doing here? He'd left her safe in New York!

He put his hands together like a plow and turned people aside, moving them from his path like stalks of wheat swaying in a desolate wind.

"Annabelle!"

"The president has been murdered!" someone shouted.

"Kill the murderer!" another screamed.

Annabelle struggled to keep her composure as she followed those carrying Lincoln out of the theatre.

Screams of fury mingled with the anguished moans of mourning as the people crashed down from their victory jubilation to the dark waters of loss below. In a matter of days, they'd tasted the sweetness of an ended war, reveled in the promises of a rebuilt nation, and now were doused in the bitter rains of hopelessness. The one who would see the nation restored and the reign of peace begin now walked the lonely road to eternity, leaving them behind to navigate uncharted territory alone.

Eudora latched onto Annabelle's arm, and they continued to follow the president's body across the street. Two doctors and several soldiers had passed by her and into that box, and all the while Mrs. Lincoln had sobbed so uncontrollably that Annabelle had known the president was dead.

But then she'd heard the young doctor say that he could hold a finger in the wound—that it might hold off the bleeding for a time. Not long after, they moved him, and Annabelle had trailed behind, praying that a miracle would see him restored to life.

As she walked, she continued to mumble prayers pleading

for God to have mercy. Somewhere off in the sea of chaos, she thought she heard someone call her name, but she didn't bother to look for the source. She could only cling to the fragile hope that Lincoln would make it through the night.

Eudora clutched tightly to her arm, a frightened cat digging her claws into the branch that swayed above the river. Annabelle forced her mind to remain calm lest she be caught up in the current. With plodding steps, they and many others followed the president inside a house opposite the theatre, and up the stairs to a small room.

Between shoulders and bobbing heads, she caught glimpses as they laid him across a bed. Someone shouted annoyance at those in attendance, and soon a Union soldier began pushing them all from the room.

Annabelle turned away, the tears on her cheeks rolling down to her chin. There were doctors with him now. And with the way her elder clutched to her arm, Annabelle wouldn't have been able to give assistance even if she'd been allowed.

With heavy steps the two women returned down the stairs and found a place by the wall near the front door. Eudora stood silently beside her, both of them too shocked to do much more than watch as people shouted for aid. Some were admitted into the house as others were turned away. Outside, the crowd called for answers.

None seemed to take notice of the two women, however, and Annabelle suspected that if she remained quiet and still, she might be allowed to remain. Men were sent out with telegrams and instructions to spread the news, and others hurried to take eyewitness statements.

Failed. Saving him from abduction that day on the road had gained nothing. She'd merely prolonged the inevitable. Tears welled again and slid down her cheeks, but she paid them no mind.

"Seward has been attacked as well," a man said as he passed, jarring Annabelle from her thoughts.

She glanced at Eudora, about to comment, but the older woman shook her head, tears running down her wrinkled face. They would learn more if they remained nothing more than a fixture on the wall, two bits of furniture easily dismissed.

As whispered words and bits of information drifted their way, Annabelle learned that there had been a series of coordinated attacks meant to take out key members of the government in a single blow.

There was a commotion upstairs, and a booming voice called out. "Take that woman out of here and do not let her in this room again!"

A soldier escorted Mary Lincoln down the stairs and into the parlor just off to the right of where they stood. The poor woman's body heaved with sobs and her wails tugged at Annabelle's already bruised heart.

Eudora's face melted with the compassion of one widow to another. In an instant, life could end. The ones you loved could be gone in a flash of pain.

Matthew's face filled her mind, and she choked on a sob. What would life have been if the war hadn't come—if she and Matthew had courted as their fathers had intended? Would she have had an unscarred heart, and he the easy laughter of a man not maimed by pain and desperation?

She bit her lip. There was little point in wondering what could have been. War had stolen those whispered promises and had trodden over them with thundering cannons. She couldn't undo what these last years had made her, and Matthew couldn't turn around and abandon the path he'd set himself upon.

Hot tears stung her eyes. Fool! She'd seen glimpses of the man he'd been and could be again. Why had he let his pride and bitterness steal it all away, just to be a part of a group so bent on their misplaced revenge that they destroyed everyone around them?

How could men who claimed to act in justice for wrongs done to the South commit the same atrocities they accused Lincoln of being responsible for? Blood to avenge blood served no one and brought only further heartache.

"Who here has borne witness?" A man shouted, jarring Annabelle back to her current surroundings. His gaze fell on them and she opened her mouth to respond. He pointed at them before she had the chance. "Get these women out of here! And no more people in here who don't have business!"

Someone took her arm. "Sorry, miss," he said gently. Annabelle didn't even look up at him as he guided her and Eudora out the door.

Outside, the damp air hit her face and jolted her system. They shuffled into the press of concerned citizens. Some pleaded for answers she couldn't give while others shouted incoherent venomous calls for revenge. Did they not see? Such things would only bring more pain, an endless watermill of blood that never found the final turn.

If only she had a bit of good news she could offer. Any words of peace and comfort that would sooth troubled brows and calm murderous lips.

Her gaze snagged on a figure in the crowd, standing tall

above the others, with a face wet from rain and eyes filled with worry. The very man she'd prayed hadn't been a part of this mess. She'd held on to a small seed of hope he'd abandoned O'Malley and Booth.

Matthew's worried gaze scanned the crowd. Searching.

Something within her snapped, and her precious little seed withered to nothing more than a shriveled husk.

Thirty-One

"So then, dearest Mother, forgive and pray for me. I feel that I am right in the justness of my cause, and that we shall, ere long, meet again."
John Wilkes Booth

Washington, D.C.
April 15, 1865
12:00 a.m.

Anger buzzed through Annabelle's veins like a swatted nest of hornets, and in a matter of moments, she pushed her way through the crowd, heedless of their protest.

"Annabelle! I was so worried." Matthew reached out to take her hands.

She glared up at him, and before she could stop herself, she wound back and released her fury as a slap across his face. Her palm stung and tears blurred her vision. She raised her hands to beat on the solid muscle of his chest in her blind rage, but he grabbed hold of both of her wrists and pulled her close to him instead.

"Please, my love, calm down. Tell me what happened."

She craned her neck upward to look at him, her breath

coming in rapid spurts. "You…you knew! You helped them!"

He shook his head, the pain in his eyes stopping her next words. "No! I thought I stopped him." He reached out and gently cupped her chin, the warmth of his hand bringing a balmy breeze that, despite her best efforts, thawed some of her resolve to despise him. "O'Malley planned to murder General Grant and his wife. I stopped him."

Annabelle stared at him with wide eyes, wanting to believe his words. He leaned his head low, looking at her with sincerity. "O'Malley said he'd planned on coming to this theatre to attack the president, so as soon as I knew the Grants were safe, I came here. I had nothing to do with this."

The Grants? She pulled her face from his hand. How many were intended to be murdered this night? Someone bumped into her, and she stumbled.

Matthew put a hand around her waist and pulled her close. She shivered, glad for the protection he offered even as her traitorous heart warred with her logic.

"I'll explain everything, but first we need to get out of here." Matthew gently tugged her away from the house where the president struggled to hold onto life.

She parted her lips, a protest ready to fly from her tongue.

"The tyrant got what he deserved!" someone shouted.

The crowd erupted. A pop of gunfire sliced through the cacophony. Annabelle screamed, her defiance forgotten. Lightning fast, Matthew lifted her off her feet and pushed through the crowd. Annabelle struggled to breathe as he pressed her against his side, her body jarring roughly with each of his pounding footfalls.

"Grandmother!" she finally managed to squeak, struggling

to expand her ribs with enough breath to make herself heard.

"What?" Matthew asked, his footsteps not slowing.

"Grandmother!" Annabelle yelled, struggling against his iron grasp.

Matthew jerked to a halt and released her.

Her feet dropped to the ground. She put her hand to her side, breathing hard. "Grandmother is back there!" In the mêlée of emotions, she'd left her grandmother alone!

Matthew grabbed her hand and pulled her toward a shop entrance, pressing her into an alcove and out of the throng of bodies. He hesitated. "Please. Wait here." He turned without waiting for her reply and pushed through people. Several stumbled out of his way.

Her heart pounded as she watched him trudge through the masses, his great height affording her the advantage of not losing sight of him. He neared the house where she'd stepped away from Eudora and bent down. After a moment, he turned back in her direction, wading through the mass of shouts and fury, tugging her grandmother along behind him.

When they finally reached the alcove and Eudora peered around Matthew's back to spot Annabelle, she pulled her hand from his grasp and ran forward. "You nearly scared the life from me!" She wrapped Annabelle in a crushing embrace.

Annabelle only briefly returned the squeeze, pulling away without apology. "Where's George?"

Matthew stiffened. "George? Did you *all* come?"

"Yes," Eudora snapped. "To try to save *you*."

Matthew scowled and opened his mouth to reply, but only shook his head instead. "Which way did George go?"

Annabelle shivered. "I don't know. He took off after Booth

in the theatre."

The muscles in Matthew's jaw worked, and the vein in his neck pulsed.

"We should get back to the hotel where it's safe," Eudora said, drawing Annabelle's attention away from the gathering storm on Matthew's face. "Surely he'll return there."

The thunderclouds on Matthew's face dissolved—replaced with worry and…something more?—as he looked back to Annabelle. "Let's move, then," he said gruffly. "I'll wait for him at the hotel, rather than risk missing him in this press of chaos."

His giant frame cleared the crowd as Annabelle and Eudora trailed behind. It took several minutes of walking as fast as they could before the streets finally cleared. Once they could move about freely, Eudora took the lead.

The mist gathered on Annabelle's clothing and made her dress damp. She reached up to brush it away, and noticed the bloodied fingerprints where the injured man in the box had grabbed her. Her stomach churned. She hoped the man's wounds wouldn't prove fatal.

They rushed into the hotel in a flurry of sodden fabric and left a trail of moisture on the polished floors.

No sooner had they barged inside than Eudora began waving her hands like a mad woman. "Oh, heavens. What a tragedy! The repercussions—" She shook her head and her eyes cleared. "I'm going up to my room to write a telegram to Lilly Rose." She scurried away, leaving them alone in the empty hotel lobby.

Annabelle turned to follow her, but Matthew caught her arm. "Please, wait."

Warring emotions threatened to pull her apart. "I know you lied to me." Her heart fissured and she had to bite back the threat of tears. "Nothing can repair what's already broken." His brows gathered, but she didn't give him the chance to come up with a response. "I saw you talking and laughing with O'Malley at the Surratt house. I wanted so much to believe that you'd told me the truth about coming back and telling the law." Her fists tightened at her side. "What a fool I am! I should have *known* as soon as you got rid of me and George was safe that you'd come back to finish—" Her voice cracked, and the tears spilled over.

Matthew suddenly snaked his arms around her waist and pulled her close to him. Before she could think to draw away, his lips fell on hers. She gasped against his mouth, and her eyes flew wide.

She told herself to pull away, but despite her best intentions, her lids lowered and her body melted into his. Everything else faded away as his soft lips pressed sweetly into hers, gently exploring. Forgetting her accusations, Annabelle returned the kiss, her lips automatically seeming to know what they'd never before experienced.

Sensing her response, he pressed in harder, deepening the kiss and sending an unfamiliar warmth tingling down her spine. She could spend forever here in his embrace.

Memories of all his lies suddenly surged and she thrust her hands up between them, roughly shoving him away.

He stepped back, hanging his head. "I'm sorry," he whispered.

Her fingers trembled. "You...you cannot just...kiss me like that and think it changes what you've done!"

Matthew placed his fingers under her chin and tilted her face up. "I'm so sorry that I've hurt you. Too many times. I don't expect you to forgive me for all I've put you through, but I beg you, please, at least let me explain."

She drew her bottom lip through her teeth, the feel of his

kiss still lingering. Unable to form words, she gave a simple nod.

"I went to confront O'Malley," he said, dropping his hand. "But he'd gone completely mad. I needed to know his plans. I was afraid if I went to the law too soon, my tale would only render me useless while I sat in detainment. I'd hoped to at least trade my freedom for solid evidence."

Remembering Mr. Crook and how difficult the same things had been for her, her shoulders relaxed.

Seeming to sense a least a morsel of her understanding, Matthew continued. "So I played along. Pretended I was a lout and begged to be back in his service. In his blinding pride, he agreed. I followed him, trying to learn what they would do. He came for me this morning, wanting me to help him find out if General Grant would be going to tonight's performance with the Lincolns. When that turned into murdering them instead, I had to find a way to stop him."

"He wanted to murder the Grants and then come back to the theater to kill the president?"

Matthew nodded. "I thought since I left him unconscious and locked in a rental room in Philadelphia that I'd stopped him on both counts." He hung his head. "But when I got to the theatre, they were carrying Lincoln across the road." His eyes bore into hers, begging her to believe him.

She wanted to. "And that's the entire truth?"

"Yes, dearest." He reached out and stroked her cheek. "From now on, I swear I'll never again keep secrets from you or lie to you. I give my solemn word that this is the complete and most earnest truth."

Annabelle studied the sincerity in his eyes, remembering the look Peggy had given her—stung by Annabelle's own deceptions. "I forgive you," she said with a tired sigh. "And I, too, ask for the same. Too many falsehoods have sprung from my own lips in the past."

Matthew watched her quietly for a moment. Emotions she didn't dare try to decipher played across his face. When he finally spoke again, it was with resolve. "There's another truth I must tell you now."

Her brows crinkled and she took a step back from him. How had she allowed him to kiss her, knowing full well what truth he now wished to confess? She laced her fingers in front of her and waited for the spoken truth to slam into her.

Matthew made a low noise in his throat, the sound carrying on the tomb-like silence of the hotel lobby. "All this time, I've lied to you."

Her jaw tightened despite her resolve to let this pain pass over her without showing him any signs of her true feelings.

"I told you that you'd be better off with George because he'd be able to provide for you." His voice rasped against her ears, filled with churning emotions. "But I was wrong, Annabelle."

Her heart quickened, pushing against her chest as though begging to break free.

"He can provide you with Westerly, a safe home, and the life a lady deserves." Matthew stepped closer. His hands rested on her shoulders. He leaned in, smelling of pine and rain. "But there's more to life than security. I may be a man of many faults, and I might not be able to provide you with all the things a lady should enjoy. But on my life, I swear I'll provide you with deepest love and boundless devotion."

She looked into his eyes, finding there all she'd longed to see and yet still feared to believe.

Matthew leaned closer still, so that all she could see was the intensity burning in his gaze. "I know I'm not worthy of you. I tried—how I tried—not to let you know I've loved you since before we even found George. I wanted you to be able to make your choice."

Annabelle tilted her head in confusion.

Matthew looked pained, then shook his head as if to clear his thoughts. "Forgive me, but the real truth of it is I wanted to see if you'd choose me even if I couldn't provide you wealth like my brother could."

"Oh, Matthew." She reached out and rubbed the stubble on his face, her heart pounding wildly. "I would've chosen you from the start."

His eyes searched hers. "More than one young woman saw only my father's money. Never has one preferred me for who I am alone."

In that moment Annabelle understood. She saw why he'd stood back, why he'd waited to see if her love for her home and her need for security would mark her only interest in him.

She gave a small cry and pushed up on her toes, wrapping her arms around his neck. "If we have nothing save the clothes we wear, I'll still always love you and no other."

His breath mingled with hers, and he pulled her closer. "Even if you lose your home, and I'm heir to nothing?"

She brushed her lips across his. "Even so. What is life without love? What are comforts when your heart's empty? Promise me you'll love me for always, and I swear my heart will forever be yours."

"I promise it, my love," he said against her lips.

She deepened the kiss and let her fingers wander over the back of his neck. He made a slight groan, then gently eased her away, resting his forehead on hers. "Perhaps it's best we take a moment."

Her rapidly beating heart agreed, and she dropped down to

the flat of her feet, looking up at him. "What happens now?" For all the glory of this moment, unanswered questions still abounded.

Matthew stroked her cheek, and she felt as though she might drift up off the floor.

"I don't know. The days ahead will likely be very difficult."

Annabelle nodded and pressed her cheek into his hand. "Whatever comes, as long as I have you, we can make it."

Matthew chuckled. "You don't know how much your words truly mean, my love," he said, his voice growing husky.

"Whatever happens now, promise you'll never again leave me."

Matthew's brows gathered and sadness pierced the joy in his eyes. "I cannot." He gently brushed his lips across hers once more. "But I do promise that if ever I have no choice but to go, I'll think of you every moment of my absence and pledge to return with the utmost urgency."

Annabelle gave an exaggerated sigh, the joy of his promise dampening the fear of his absence. Her lips curved. "I suppose that'll have to do."

He returned her smile and his fingers slipped up her neck to tangle in her hair. "Whatever tomorrow brings."

Annabelle pressed closer and ran her hand along his jaw. "Whatever tomorrow brings." Then she pushed up on her toes and found his lips once more.

The story concludes in *A Daring Pursuit*,
The Accidental Spy Series Book Three

To keep up with news and release dates, sign up for my newsletter at www.StepheniaMcGee.com

Dear reader,

I hope you are enjoying The Accidental Spy Series. If you would kindly leave a few words of review online and tell your friends about it, I would be so grateful! Word of mouth is the utmost recommendation an author can receive, and it helps me keep putting books in your hands!

Thank you!
Stephenia H. McGee

A Daring Pursuit

The Accidental Spy Series Book Three

One

"To sin by silence, when they should protest, makes cowards out of men."
Abraham Lincoln

Washington, D.C.
April 15, 1865
8:00 a.m.

Everything hurt. Annabelle's feet throbbed from walking, her raw eyes burned from crying, and her shoulders refused to relax after the harrowing night she'd endured. The physical discomfort brought a leaden weariness to her bones, but the exhaustion of feeling—the terror in the theatre, the momentary joy of Matthew's declaration, and then the crushing weight of despair at knowing the North would seek retribution for Lincoln's blood—made her truly ache.

She pinched the bridge of her nose and tried to remain calm. Surely they wouldn't make her wait much longer. Didn't they know she held information that could bring this all to an end?

Annabelle tapped her foot nervously underneath the table as she waited for the lawman to return. Her head pounded with the pulse of unanswered questions, lurking fears, and the lack of sleep. She closed her eyes and attempted to push aside her doubts. Soul weary or not, this had been the right thing to do.

Then she could finally return to Rosswood. If she had a home to return to.

She could hear the others, even this far down the hall—agitated voices and the hum of pent-up frustration and excitement. How many people were out there now? Fifty? A hundred? She suppressed a shiver and shifted her weight on the hard chair. Why were they detaining so many? It seemed as though every person in Ford's had either come—or been dragged—into the Washington police station.

The door opened with a bang and Annabelle jumped, her hand flying to her thudding heart. The officer, who'd introduced himself as Mr. Fitch, strode into the cramped office. He twitched his mustache as he flipped through a stack of papers in his hand. He looked even more displeased than when he'd first escorted her to this office. He circled around his plain desk and sat behind it, not meeting her eyes.

The exhausted man's oiled hair hung limp across his fore-head as he squinted at the pages in his hand, and he kept angrily flipping the locks away from his eyes. The more he did so, the more disheveled he appeared.

Finally, he leveled his deep brown eyes on her. "You say you have new information?"

"Yes, sir. Very important." She'd known O'Malley had plotted an abduction, but she hadn't known Mr. Booth sought murder. She glanced to the door, the noises of the people growing louder, and clasped her hands tightly.

He gave a sniff. "Already interviewed eight young ladies that were in the theatre last night. All claimed their particular story was important."

Had someone listened to her a week ago, perhaps neither of them would be regarding one another with thinly veiled distaste now. "I don't suppose any of *them* knows the identities of the conspirators nor foiled the original abduction plot on the road to the Soldier's Home a month past."

Surprise widened the officer's eyes, and she felt a momentary swell of satisfaction. A short-lived triumph, however, because now his face reddened. "How would you know about *that*?"

She ran her trembling fingers along the embroidered edge of her sleeve. "I warned Mr. Lincoln's driver about their plans." She met his assessing gaze. "Do you know how the president fares?"

He gave her a sour look. "He's dead. Passed about half an hour ago."

A single tear rolled down her cheek and she whisked it away. The tolls of the melancholy bells had long since told her what she'd not wished to know, and Mr. Fitch's clipped words only provided the confirmation she didn't truly need.

Mr. Fitch regarded her for a long time, and Annabelle held his gaze, unsure if she should speak further until he made his intentions clear. She flicked another nervous glance to the door.

Finally, Mr. Fitch pushed his chair away from his desk and the sudden movement made Annabelle startle. She offered a fabricated smile as he propped his ankle on his knee.

"Perhaps you should start from the beginning."

Her mind scurried back across the last weeks and her swirling tumult of emotions. Deciding succinct words might best appease the stern face across from her, Annabelle settled on firing out only the most pertinent details. "I first discovered the plot while here in Washington about a month ago. I overheard men talking in the boarding house parlor. They disclosed their intentions to abduct Mr. Lincoln later that afternoon and take him away to Richmond. They said they planned to ransom him for the release of Confederate soldiers."

Mr. Fitch nodded along, writing in his little book.

Remembering the disaster she'd almost caused when she'd told the major at Elmira prison that George was her brother, she'd decided to be forthcoming with everything she knew. "While looking for a hired coach to take me to my mother's family in New York, I happened upon a young man by the name of Thomas Clark, who claimed to be Mr. Lincoln's personal driver. I told him some men were planning on overrunning the carriage on the way to the Soldier's Home. It's my understanding that he warned Mr. Lincoln of this, and the president changed his plans, going to the National Hotel instead."

Mr. Fitch stroked the pointed beard on the tip of his chin. "And where were you when you learned of this plot?"

"At the Surratt Boarding House."

He scribbled quickly with a nub of pencil. "Which men had this discussion?"

"Mr. David O'Malley and Mr. Harry Thompson. There were other men involved, but the only one I recognized was John Wilkes Booth."

Forgive me, Father. I can't say Matthew's name. I cannot condemn him.

Mr. Fitch frowned at the remark and made another notation. "And you're certain you saw Booth?"

Annabelle ran her tongue over her lips, trying to get them moist again. "I followed the men—there were seven of them, I believe—to the road and watched the entire thing. I recognized Mr. Booth from a likeness I'd seen in town. A playbill, or some such, I believe."

"And you didn't think to inform the law?"

Annabelle offered an apologetic smile that Mr. Fitch didn't return. "I thought the matter settled, and since I had urgent business in New York, I left later that day."

"To see the family you mentioned."

Her heart thudded, but she'd promised herself to tell everything. "Yes, but not only that. I also went to Elmira prison."

"What for?"

"To find my…." *Friend's? Beau's?* "To find Mr. Daniels's brother. I'd learned from the Commissary General's Office here in Washington that he'd been imprisoned at Elmira."

"And this was your reason for being in Washington a month past?"

"Yes, sir." True enough. Finding George *had* been their reason to go to Washington. When she reached the part about Matthew finding George on the riverbank, she paused.

Mr. Fitch leaned forward in his chair.

"Matthew found George freezing and took him back to our room to warm him."

Mr. Fitch stared hard at her. "He helped a prisoner escape?"

"George would have died otherwise." She tugged on her pearl earring, but her hand shook so badly she quickly dropped her fingers to her lap. "It wasn't an escape. He'd already signed allegiance papers."

Mr. Fitch scribbled again. "Mr. George Daniels?"

"Yes, sir."

Heat crept up her neck. When George had come back to the hotel during the wee hours this morning, he'd found her and Matthew locked in an embrace.

"So why did you return to Washington after you took Mr. Daniels from Elmira?" Mr. Fitch asked without looking up from his writing.

"One of the men I mentioned, Harry, followed us. When Matthew questioned him, he found out that Mr. O'Malley was working on another abduction plot. He came straight to Washington to try to stop Mr. O'Malley."

"And when was this?"

Annabelle thought back. "I'm not sure exactly—but around the time when Richmond fell."

"And you came with him?"

She shook her head. "George, my grandmother, my maid, and I came separately."

He set his pencil aside. "And *none* of you thought to report this to the law?"

She straightened her shoulders, wishing she could rub the aching muscles. "Of course we did. My grandmother informed Mr. William Crook about the abduction plans. He said that the president received many such threats and that we shouldn't worry. They would see to his safety." Her tone held a touch of bitterness she couldn't contain.

Mr. Fitch scowled. "Indeed." He sat back in his chair and propped his ankle on his knee once more, regarding her. "And why, then, were you at the theatre last eve?"

"My grandmother purchased tickets. I knew that Mr. Booth had been on the road the day that O'Malley had first planned to abduct Mr. Lincoln. So when we learned Mr. Lincoln would be going to the theatre, we assumed Mr. Booth knew the building well and concluded it would be a good opportunity for the men to attempt another abduction." Her voice hitched. "But we never expected…." She squeezed her eyes shut.

"There, there, miss. It's all right." Mr. Fitch pulled a handkerchief out of his coat pocket, surprising her with a dose of sympathy. "We're all distraught over this tragedy."

She accepted the offered cloth and dabbed her eyes, then handed it back with a tired smile. "Thank you."

Mr. Fitch placed the handkerchief into a drawer in his desk. "Did you inform anyone of your suspicions about Mr. O'Malley and the possibility of an abduction at the theatre?"

"Mr. Crook knew. He promised Mr. O'Malley would be arrested immediately, should he be seen in the theatre."

Mr. Fitch's frown deepened, and he made another note in his little book before snapping it closed.

The policeman rose and rounded the desk, and Annabelle stood as he approached. Feeling relieved, she turned toward the door. "I do hope this information has helped you some, Mr. Fitch. I'll be in my room at the National Hotel, should you wish to ask me anything further."

Mr. Fitch's fingers clamped down on her elbow. His eyes looked sad, but hard lines firmed his mouth. "I'm sorry, Miss Ross, but I'm afraid you cannot leave our custody just yet."

"I…what?"

"I'm going to have to detain you until we can look deeper

into your claims."

Annabelle couldn't come up with a response as Mr. Fitch gently led her out the door.

Matthew paced the floor, his boots thudding against the wood in a steady rhythm. The holding area of the Metropolitan Police building overflowed with people of various degrees of unrest. Some seemed eager to be in the midst of the commotion while others fidgeted and paced nervously. Men, women, and even a few youths crammed into the small holding space and waited their turn at questioning. Had the policemen detained everyone on the street outside of Ford's?

He tightened his fists and tried to remind himself he hadn't been brought in for questioning. He'd come on his own volition to offer information. Flashes of the conditions at Elmira flitted through his mind, and he had to shake his head in a futile effort to dislodge them.

A strangled noise off to his left made him twist. His elbow clipped a disgruntled gentleman in a fine suit. The other opened his mouth to protest, then seemed to think better of it and ducked away. Matthew frowned at him, wondering what had sent the man scurrying like a mouse. People shifted and the space around him widened.

Heat swirled up from his chest and pulsed through the vein in his neck. He must look half-mad. Struggling to gain control of his emotions, Matthew forced his features to relax and lowered his eyes.

A door to his right opened and a young man of about eighteen or twenty years entered the lobby. He scanned the room with a determined gaze, his shoulders straight in his pressed suit. A policeman's polished silver badge shone brightly against his blue double-breasted jacket.

"Mr. Daniels?" the man called out over the hum of a dozen private conversations.

"Here!"

The younger man tilted his chin back to regard Matthew as he stepped near. "You're the brother of a Mr. George Daniels. Correct?"

"I am."

"This way, sir." The policeman gestured toward a hallway behind him.

Matthew tugged on the knot of his blue cravat in an attempt to keep the foul thing from choking him. George had been called back first, and it'd been hours since Matthew had last seen him. Then they'd taken Annabelle, and his composure had begun to slide as soon as her delicate fingers had slipped free of his grasp.

How long had he been waiting? At least what he'd shouted to a passing officer about the Surratt house seemed to gain their attention. As far as he knew, they'd since sent men to investigate. If they'd found anything, though, it hadn't made much difference. They still left Matthew waiting with the other people they'd collected off the streets without thought to who might know something important and who might be here only for a bit of the excitement.

He followed the young policeman down a hallway lined with closed doors. Where were George and Annabelle? When

George had returned to the hotel hours earlier, it had been to tell them he'd caught a glimpse of Booth galloping away but hadn't been able to stop him.

Matthew knew where Booth might be headed, but every person who'd been in the theatre or had joined the crowd outside in the streets thought they had something important to say.

Fools.

"Here we are, sir." The officer opened a heavy door at the end of the hall. Without waiting for a response, he turned and strode back toward the crowded waiting area.

Inside, a man with dark hair and a trimmed mustache stared at him expectantly. The man motioned toward a chair in front of his plain desk. "Take a seat, Mr. Daniels." He flipped open a small writing book.

Matthew pulled the door closed behind him and positioned himself in the chair without taking his eyes off the man across from him. Likely another officer, but he didn't sport a polished badge on his rumpled jacket.

The man rolled a short pencil between his fingers. "State your name please, sir."

"You already know my name."

The man looked up from his paper with a sniff. "I've been told your identity. I wish to hear it in your own words."

"Matthew Gregory Daniels of Westerly Plantation, Mississippi. Former captain, Mississippi Infantry, Confederate Army under the command of—"

The man held up his hand to slow Matthew's words and scribbled in his little book. "You served in the Rebel Army, is this correct?"

"I just said—"

"Brother to a George Daniels, also of Westerly Plantation, Mississippi?"

Matthew clamped the rounded edges of the armrests and refused to answer until the man lifted his eyes from his writing. "Who are you?"

"Mr. Fitch."

They regarded one another for some time before Fitch turned his attention back to his scribbling. "Are you brother to a George Daniels of West—"

"Yes," Matthew said, cutting the man's repetition short. "What does that have to do with Booth?"

The man's eyebrows dipped for only an instant before an indifferent look smoothed his forehead again. "You do understand, of course, that knowing the purpose and identity of everyone giving a statement is imperative to our search?"

"And you, *of course*, understand that you've already wasted valuable time and let your quarry escape. I told your men hours ago I knew where he was going. Not one seemed interested."

Fitch stroked his mustache. "How well do you know Mr. Booth?"

"Not well."

"On how many occasions have you met with him?"

"Only one."

"And this was…?"

Annabelle and George had both insisted that each of them give a full accounting. He'd even planned on coming here himself before O'Malley had followed the Grants. But now, sitting in this chair with a Yankee regarding him with thinly disguised suspicion, the words stuck in his mouth.

The man started writing again.

Matthew scowled. "What are you doing? I didn't say anything."

"Precisely."

Matthew made a low noise in his throat and Fitch looked up expectantly. "I met Booth on only one occasion, when he was introduced to me by David O'Malley. After that introduction I was in his presence only once more, on the day when they planned to abduct Lincoln and take him to Richmond."

"And you were a part of this ploy?"

"I was." The words felt like needles as they passed his tongue. They pierced and stung with the promise of painful repercussions.

"And were you aware that Mr. Booth planned an assassination of President Lincoln?"

"I was not."

"But you did tell one of my fellow officers—" he flipped through his pages, "—that you 'knew who the assassin was.'" He tapped his pencil on the page. "Is that correct?"

"It is." How much did this man already know? Judging by the look in his eyes, probably enough to decide Matthew's fate. Everything within him rebelled against this pretentious Yank and his foul little notebook, but he stretched his neck and tried to release some of the tension from his shoulders.

He'd promised Annabelle he'd give a truthful account.

Fitch looked at him curiously, then slowly closed his book and sat back. "Is there something you wish to disclose?"

Hoping he wasn't about to lose all he'd only so recently gained, Matthew nodded. "I was involved in a plot to abduct, but never to murder, your president. After the failed attempt to take his carriage, I left Washington. You can arrest me for that if you wish. But first, I can help you catch the men responsible."

Fitch snatched up his pen eagerly. "Men?"

"One was sent to kill General Grant. I can tell you everything you need to know about him. Booth would have gone to Surrattsville, where these same men stashed weapons and supplies at the tavern."

Fitch narrowed his eyes and stared at him for a moment, a myriad of emotions scurrying over his face. Finally, settling on determination, he gave a single nod. "Mr. Daniels, I have a proposition for you."

Continue reading in *A Daring Pursuit*, The Accidental Spy Series book three.

Historical Note

In the first chapter Matthew and Annabelle go to an observation tower overlooking Elmira prison. Surprising as it may seem, the platform with its refreshments and paid admission is recorded in history. Elmira prison was crowded well beyond its capacity, and the camping prisoners along the banks, as well as George's job as a coffin maker, are all true to the accounts. There was also a flood at Elmira, which occurred on March 16, 1865.

According to Mrs. Grant, some unknown men watched her at her luncheon and a man rode past her and General Grant's carriage twice, peering inside. She states that she was concerned about the men, but when nothing more happened on their train ride to Philadelphia, she dismissed it. History accounts say this may have been Booth himself, or perhaps Michael O'Laughlen. I decided to add my characters in instead and have Matthew be the reason they arrive unharmed.

The quotes at the top of each chapter are all taken from historical accounts. All words spoken by Lincoln are as they are recorded in history. In this story, I gave additional words to John Wilkes Booth. The places he went and the things he said on the day of the assassination are all accurate except for any dialogue with my characters. All of John Surratt's words (except in the letter to O'Malley) are quoted. All words spoken by Mary Surratt in the story were products of my imagination, as are those spoken by William Crook.

There are different accounts as to if Mr. Crook was supposed to be on duty that night, and if he was, why he wasn't standing guard at the box.

The timeline of the assassination plot, including Booth's trip to the theatre to get his mail, returning to the Surratt house, and having someone go after Grant, are all historically accurate. The doctors mentioned were recorded as being present, and except where they speak to Annabelle, all words spoken by additional historical figures are recorded quotes.

To the best of my ability, I tried to insert my characters into this turning point in history and show what it might have been like through their eyes.

Acknowledgments

Writing a book like this is an adventure. I'm thankful for the extensive online book selections at the Library of Congress.

A special thanks to everyone involved in the photo shoot and design of the cover. Melissa Harper for costume work and photography. I'd also like to thank the beautiful Katie Beth for her wonderful work as the cover model.

A special thanks to Colonel Walt and Miss Jean for allowing me to use their beautiful home as Annabelle's plantation.

Thank you to Rich Stevens, who helped me check facts in association with army movements and the proper details of a soldier's life. Any historical inaccuracies or misrepresentations are entirely my own. Thanks to Jessica, Momma, and my other early readers for helping me make this book possible.

Thank you to Kristen for your notes on the re-write from this book's original publication. And a *big* thank you, Linda, for your sharp eye with copyedits and for fact-checking my historical details.

To my dear husband, thank you for spending hours discussing my stories and helping me make them better. And to my two sweet little boys, who put up with Momma's strange work hours and wild imagination.

My dear readers, I love you so. Thank you for your enthusiasm about my books and for having fun with me on my Faithful Readers group on Facebook.

Finally, and most importantly, thank you Heavenly Father for the opportunity to tell stories and for everything You teach me along the way.

Books by Stephenia H. McGee

Ironwood Plantation

The Whistle Walk

Heir of Hope

Missing Mercy

**Ironwood Series Set*

*Get the entire series at a discounted price

The Accidental Spy Series

*Previously published as The Liberator Series

An Accidental Spy

A Dangerous Performance

A Daring Pursuit

**Accidental Spy Series Set*

*Get the entire series at a discounted price

Stand Alone Titles

In His Eyes

Eternity Between Us

Time Travel

Her Place in Time

(Stand alone, but ties to Rosswood from The Accidental Spy Series)

The Hope of Christmas Past

(Stand alone, but ties to Belmont from In His Eyes)

Novellas

The Heart of Home

The Hope of Christmas Past

www.StepheniaMcGee.com

Sign up for my newsletter to be the first to see new cover reveals and be notified of release dates

New newsletter subscribers receive a free book!

Get yours here

bookhip.com/QCZVKZ

About the Author

Award winning author of Christian historical novels, Stephenia H. McGee writes stories of faith, hope, and healing set in the Deep South. When she's not twirling around in hoop skirts, reading, or sipping sweet tea on the front porch, she's a homeschool mom of two boys, writer, dreamer, and husband spoiler. Visit her at www.StepheniaMcGee.com for books and updates.

Visit her website at www.StepheniaMcGee.com and be sure to sign up for the newsletter to get sneak peeks, behind the scenes fun, the occasional recipe, and special giveaways.
Facebook: Stephenia H. McGee, Christian Fiction Author
Twitter: @StepheniaHMcGee
Pinterest: Stephenia H. McGee

Made in the USA
Coppell, TX
14 December 2024